Needing Him

USA TODAY BESTSELLING AUTHOR

KENNEDY FOX

Hardcover edition
www.kennedyfoxbooks.com

NEEDING HIM
Bishop Brothers, #2

Cover Design by Outlined with Love Designs
Editor: Jenny Sims | Editing 4 Indies

All good boys go to heaven but bad boys bring heaven to you

"Heaven"
-Julia Michaels

BISHOP BROTHERS SUGGESTED READING ORDER

BISHOP BROTHERS SERIES

Taming Him

Needing Him

Chasing Him

Keeping Him

SPIN-OFF'S

Falling for the Cowboy

Roping the Cowboy

CIRCLE B RANCH SERIES

Bishop Second Generation

Hitching the Cowboy

Catching the Cowboy

Wrangling the Cowboy

Bossing the Cowboy

...and more

PROLOGUE

EMILY

FOUR MONTHS AGO

"Dr. Bell!" My eyelids snap open, and I blink the fog away before realizing I fell asleep sitting up on the couch in the lounge again. Olivia, one of the ER nurses, stands in front of me with a stack of charts. I give her a sheepish smile, then take the charts from her hands before heading to the ER.

I've wanted to become a doctor since I was five years old. Dressed in scrubs, I took my toy doctor kit to career day in kindergarten. My eighth-grade presentation was on healthy heart rates and blood pressure. In high school, I wrote a twenty-page paper for my senior final on why I wanted to become a doctor and how I was going to achieve my goals.

Being in this profession is in my blood especially since my dad's a top-ranked fertility doctor in Houston. Only the wealthy elite who want to get pregnant see Dr. Bell. He has the highest success rating in the country, and couples from all over book appointments months—sometimes years—in advance. I've idolized him for as long as I can remember, but that doesn't mean it's been easy living in his shadow.

My older sister, Annie, is an OB/GYN with an eighteen-month waitlist. She followed in our dad's footsteps, and they often share the same patients. My younger brother, Daniel, is in medical school but wants to become a plastic surgeon. He's already been accepted into a residency program once he graduates. However, as an adrenaline rush junkie, I wanted a more exciting specialty. After my residency, I got my license in emergency medicine and started my fellowship in Houston. I don't think anything could've quite prepared me for working in the emergency room other than diving in head first.

Saving a life is the biggest high I've ever felt. I experience it each time an unresponsive patient starts breathing, or their heart beats again. There's nothing in the world like it, and though doctors are constantly on their feet and are married more to their jobs than their significant others, I wouldn't change anything.

It's been twenty-eight hours since I started my shift. I'm on my sixth cup of coffee, and I'm ready to collapse. New Year's Eve always brings out the dumbasses who drink themselves stupid and think they can fly off the roofs of cars. Then there are the ones all cut and bruised from getting into bar fights and black out before they're even admitted.

"I'm taking twenty," I tell one of my interns, Georgia, so she'll cover me in the ER. I need to splash some water on my face and grab a drink. "Room fourteen needs discharge papers," I remind her before grabbing my phone from my pocket and walking toward the elevators.

Checking for new messages, I click on my boyfriend Justin's name and see he hasn't responded to the text I sent six hours ago. It's not uncommon for us to go days without speaking because he's a doctor, too. We both work eighty-hour weeks and spend our dates in the cafeteria catching up.

For most people, dating a doctor would be hard, but since we both understand the commitment and hours it takes, it works. We met during my first year of residency, and he was a second year OB/GYN resident under my older sister. They're both working their way up to become fertility specialists, so there's usually plenty to talk about during our rare family dinners. Justin and my father easily get wrapped up in conversations for hours. I love that about him. He looks up to my dad just as much as I do.

Once I've used the bathroom and grabbed a fresh bottle of water from my locker, I head toward the labor and delivery floor where I know Justin is on call tonight. I'll probably get less than five minutes with him, but it'll be the most I've seen him all week.

"Hey, Miranda!" I smile at one of the nurses sitting behind the counter at the nurses' station, and she smiles back. "Have you seen Dr. Hayes lately?"

The corner of her lips falls, and her eyes widen. "Um, no. Not for a while." She swallows before licking her bottom lip.

"Okay. I'll check his office; maybe he's napping between patients." I chuckle.

After finding his office empty, I decide to call him, but it goes straight to voicemail. As I walk down the hall toward the elevators, something in my gut tells me to look in the on-call room. We used to have quickies in there when we first started dating, but now we use our spare time to sleep instead.

I turn around and head toward the other hall. Noises come from behind the closed door, and as I step closer, I hear moaning and bodies slapping together. Figuring I don't want to interrupt, I spin to leave but freeze the moment I hear his name.

"Justin! Yes, yes!"

My eyes widen, and blood drains from my face.

That can't be right. I must be hearing things. I'm sleep deprived.

Yet I walk back and press my ear to the door.

"You greedy whore. You like that, don't you?" The voice is deep and familiar. Before she can respond, a loud smack echoes. The woman giggles as another smack rings in the air.

Now I know, without a doubt, Justin's in there. With another woman. He always spanks my ass when he's trying to hurry things up.

Most women would cry at a moment like this, but I've learned to push my emotions back for so long that I'm not even sad. I'm fucking pissed.

With my ear close to the door, hearing him fuck her, I figure I have two options right now. I can walk away and pretend I didn't hear a thing, living obliviously to the fact he's probably been cheating on me for a while, or I can barge in and catch the rat bastard in the act. Knowing Justin's love for my father, he'll tell me it meant nothing. Or that it'll never happen again. Or it was a one-time mistake. Whatever bullshit he tries to feed me, I won't be eating it.

I like to think of myself as a nice person. I'm caring and thoughtful, and sure, I have my moments, but right now, I'm sleep deprived, hungry, and PMSing. Not to mention, I haven't had sex in over a month, yet this asshole finds time with another woman in the same damn hospital we work in. I think "nice" Emily isn't the version Justin's about to see right now.

Twisting the knob the dumbass didn't even bother to lock, I push the door and watch as it opens. Justin is bare ass naked as he bends a girl over the bed. They're both moaning, not even realizing I'm standing in the doorway watching. My jaw clenches when I watch his fingers grip her hips as he slams harder inside. His eyes are closed, and I can tell he's close by the tight expression on his face.

Eyeing their clothes piled on the floor, I formulate a plan. Timing it just right, I wait for the perfect moment to make my presence known. His hands shift to her shoulders, pushing in deeper, which means he's seconds away from release.

"I hope you wore a condom," I blurt out. Both of their heads turn toward me as their bodies freeze. "I'd hate to see another STD breakout."

"Emily." Justin's voice is strained as he tries to catch his breath.

"Oh my God," the girl squeals, twisting her body so she's standing behind his tall frame.

I step into the room, invading the space. The smell of dirty sex fuels my anger even more.

He places his hands over his junk. "It's not what you're thinking." Yep. *Called it.*

"Oh really? Is having sex with patients a special form of fertility treatment? A new kind of sperm donation? Or an alternate payment plan?"

"It's not like that," he insists, taking a step backward as I move closer.

I purse my lips, nodding as if I actually believe his bullshit lies. The girl looks terrified, as she should be, but Justin looks like he's trying to put out a fire with alcohol. Absolutely clueless.

"Oh yeah? Why don't you tell me what it's like then?" I challenge, knowing he'll come up short.

"Just let Isabel go, and we can talk this out." I cringe when he says her name.

"Hmm…" I ponder, eyeing the distance from their pile of clothes to the door. "I don't think so. However…" I quickly bend down and scoop up their clothes, pressing them to my chest as I walk to the door. I feel his cell phone and pager in the pocket of his scrubs. "You two can spend all the time together you wish!" I smile as I back out into the hallway, knowing he can't chase me without being seen.

"Emily!" he shouts, rushing to the edge of the doorway. "Don't be ridiculous!"

"Oh, I'm ridiculous?" I muse. "Perhaps you should've thought about that before using your dick as her personal egg fertilizer." I flash a smug grin and walk away. He shouts my name as I round the corner and walk toward the elevator.

The moment I step back into the ER, I ditch their clothes into one of the soiled baskets and get back to work.

CHAPTER ONE

EVAN

"SHUT THE HELL UP," Jackson says, glancing down at me as he stands on the top step of the ladder.

"What happens if you fall off and break your neck right before the wedding?" I try to reason with him, but he's impossible. Though I'm holding the ladder steady with a death grip, it won't help a damn thing if he loses his balance and comes toppling backward.

"Then I guess I'll be glad you went to that fancy medical school so you can fix me right up."

I roll my eyes at his snide comment. "It's dangerous, and that's not how it works if you break bones. I can't just whip up a solution to fix you by Friday," I remind him. Being a doctor doesn't mean I can magically repair bones like some shit out of *Harry Potter*. It's much more complicated than that.

"Dangerous is my middle name." Jackson looks down at me, flashing a shit-eating grin in my direction as he continues to hang strings of lights in the tent with both feet on the top step. Our youngest brother Alex's wedding is in two days, and Jackson has a death wish today. If he makes it through this afternoon without hurting himself, I'll be surprised.

"You know there's a warning sticker for that right here. DO NOT

STAND ON TOP STEP. You're the only dumbass around here who gets on a twelve-foot ladder and stands on his tippy-toes."

Jackson shoos me away with one hand.

"Fine. Do whatever you want, but if you fall, I'm taking a step back. I'm not your damn landing cushion."

Jackson pretends to lose his balance, and I'm ready to climb up the ladder, drag him down to the ground by the collar of his shirt, then give him a good ole Southern ass whoopin'. I'd make sure not to punch him in the face, though; can't have two black eyes for the wedding. With a daring look in his eyes, he stares at me with a smile. Sometimes, I don't know how we're related.

"Go ahead. Fall then. Crack open your head. Might actually knock some sense into you," I say over his laughter just as he finishes hanging the last strand of lights.

"You're gonna hurt yourself," John says, carrying folding chairs across the tent as he looks at Jackson being an idiot.

"The both of ya need to live on the wild side every once in a while." Jackson finally climbs down the ladder and rolls his eyes at John. As they stand in front of one another, it's as if they're looking in a mirror, but personality wise, they're Dr. Jekyll and Mr. Hyde—complete opposites. Jackson is daring and reckless while John is reserved and responsible; it's the only way to tell my twin brothers apart.

"Are you three bickering in here?" Mama asks, tucking hair behind one ear as she carries a tray of sandwiches with her other hand. "There's barely been anything done in here other than a few chairs stacked and the lights hung. We're running out of time. Rehearsal is tomorrow," she reminds us, setting the food down on a table. The wedding day stress is making its rounds already.

"Yes ma'am," I say, giving my brothers a look, hoping they don't open their mouths and dig a hole for us because if they get Mama worked up, we're all dead. I've learned over the years that sometimes agreeing is the best response. Getting her annoyed when we only have days before the wedding isn't a good idea because if she can make our lives heaven, she can surely make them hell. Something none of us have time to deal with at the moment.

We go to the food like vultures and finish off the sandwich halves as

Mama walks around and gives us more shit to do. She was meant to be a lead foreman the way she barks orders left and right. Every day I realize how much of a saint my father really is.

"I expect all the tables and chairs to be set up before dark. The dance floor needs to be laid and speakers hung as well. Lanterns and lights placed in the oak tree. Chairs set up outside for the ceremony. Do I need to come out here and supervise you boys?" she asks with just enough attitude in her tone to instill the fear of God. "Please have it done before the sun sets."

"No ma'am," John responds, smiling. "We'll have it all taken care of, Mama."

Jackson bursts into laughter, and I nudge him hard with my elbow. Mama shakes her head and walks out of the tent, leaving us with a laundry list of tasks and a deadline.

"You're asking for it," I tell Jackson.

"I'm always asking for it," he admits. "Makes things more colorful."

"And this is why you'll be single forever. No woman's gonna take your shit for the rest of their lives," John adds, walking out of the tent toward the lowboy full of tables and chairs that need to be set up.

This time, I'm the one chuckling as Jackson's demeanor slightly shifts.

"You'll be single forever too!" Jackson finally yells, and I know John heard him because I can see him flying the bird high in the air. Just as I follow them outside, Alex pulls up and gets out of his truck with a big smile on his face. It's been there permanently since his engagement to River. At least one of us Bishop boys isn't doomed to the single life. After meeting in Key West last year, River and Alex have been inseparable since finding out they were expecting their little boy, Riley. She moved here from Wisconsin, and they've been a clichéd ending to a romance novel ever since.

"Finally!" John shouts over Jackson's bitching.

"You knew I'd be here to supervise," he taunts. "Just kiddin'. Couldn't let y'all do all the back-breaking work alone. Just had to make sure the animals were fed first," Alex tells us, grabbing as many chairs as he can carry.

Behind him stalks his best friend, Dylan, who's shaking his head. "I'm a ranch hand, not a damn party planner." He grunts.

"If Mama hears you say that, she'll slap you upside your head," Alex warns.

Jackson and I carry tables across the grass into the tent, then finish setting them up over spray-painted X's on the ground that Mama laid out for us. She takes her party planning to the next level. Once the tables and chairs are placed, it actually looks like a real reception area. I'm sure tomorrow we'll be responsible for setting tablecloths and centerpieces too. After we have electrical cords run from generators and the dance floor laid, the four of us walk inside and let Mama know our progress.

Flowers and lace, along with other decorations, are stacked and scattered around the house. It looks like a wedding threw up in here. As Mama reminds Jackson and John of what else she wants to be done, Alex and I stand by the door.

"How's River holding up?" I ask, knowing how much she's working and taking care of the baby all while planning their wedding. They live on the property, so Mama is around to help out with Riley a lot, but River still has to commute an hour to and from work.

"She's doing good but wearing herself out. Her parents and best friend are staying at the B&B, and she feels obligated to entertain them. Between that and Riley, she's overextending herself."

River and I work at the hospital together, and lately, she's been pulling double shifts. Even though she works on the pediatric floor and I work in the emergency room, we cross paths often because the hospital isn't very big. The last time we spoke, she swore that she'd relax the few days leading up to the wedding, but I knew that was a lie.

"So much for a mini vacation beforehand."

"Exactly. She's going to need to go back to work just to catch a break." He laughs.

Mama interrupts our conversation. "And you two boys can work on hanging more of those lanterns. The tree looks bare out there, and we're trying to set a mood."

After we've been given our reminder list of bitch work, Alex and I head out the door. Dylan follows, not paying too much attention because he's too caught up in his cell phone to care, probably texting Jessica, the girl he also met in Key West last year. Since she moved here from Ontario, it's become serious.

John and Jackson are busy stringing lights through dozens of extra lanterns Mama had. Before long, there are about one hundred of them on the ground with lights inside, and we stare with wide eyes. Mama wasn't kidding about wanting more lanterns, but this amount seems like it will light the whole damn town. Hell, the fire department might come out. Moving the ladder closer, I climb up and start hanging them on the hooks that Jackson and John are busy nailing to the bark. Alex and Dylan form an assembly line to hand them to me one by one.

"Are you nervous?" I ask Alex as I grab a lantern from his hand.

"I'm just ready to make it official and make River a Bishop. Something I've been looking forward to for a long time. Can't imagine her not being in my life now. It's crazy when you find the person you're meant to be with, and you just know she's your other half."

"Don't be getting all sappy on me, geez," I tease him with a smile just as I hear my sister yelling our names from the back porch.

"We're over here," Alex yells back.

In the distance, I can hear Jackson and John laughing with Courtney, and they're heading this way. As soon as Courtney sees Alex, she runs toward him and pulls him in for a big hug.

"So happy for you! So happy River will finally be my sister," she continues. "Now the rest of you need to go find a woman and have babies too. I need more sisters and nieces and nephews."

"Shut up. You're sounding like Mama more and more every day, which is scary as hell," I tell her, pulling her into a hug. "You look good, Court. Like you've been kicking Drew's ass for the past six months."

She chuckles. "I have. After carrying three babies, he deserves a good ass kicking."

For a moment, she stops and looks around at the tent and all the decorations and gets a little emotional. "Reminds me of my own wedding. Seems just like yesterday."

"And now look at ya; baby sister's all grown up being a mom and a wife," Jackson pipes in, and she stops him with a death glare before he can continue teasing her.

"Oh, I picked up all your tux rentals from the shop when we got Drew's. They're inside," Courtney adds. "Anyway. I should probably go check on Mama and Aunt Charlotte and make sure the babies are still doing okay."

"You're really going to make sure they haven't eaten Drew up and spit him out," Jackson adds.

Courtney flips him off and continues on her way.

Time flies, and I don't realize how late it is until it starts getting dark. We work on the rest of the tasks we were given until Mama yells from the back porch that it's dinnertime. Before we go inside, we plug in the lights to see our handiwork in action. The trees twinkle and glow with lights, and I get what Mama was saying about setting the perfect romantic mood—it's perfect.

"Wow. River is gonna love this," Alex says, standing back with his arms crossed over his chest.

Jackson pats him hard on the back. "Holy shit, dude. This party's gonna be the shit! Did you invite any single ladies?"

Alex shakes his head. "I have no idea who's showing up to this shindig. I think Mama invited three hundred people— basically the whole damn town."

"I'm calling dibs on the first hot one I see," Jackson claims while Alex laughs.

"You would." I roll my eyes.

As we walk toward the house, I can't help but think how Alex is really getting married to the woman he loves. He's grown up so much over the past year, I can hardly believe he's the same guy who went out and got pissed drunk the night River thought she was in labor. She called me hysterically because she couldn't find him, and I ended up driving over to help her through the Braxton Hicks contractions. None of us would've thought the youngest brother would be the first to get married, but I couldn't be happier for all three of them.

CHAPTER TWO

EMILY

"PLEASE?" Kiera bats her eyelashes, folding her hands in a begging hold. "Don't make me go alone."

Leave it to Kiera Young, my friend from my early college days, to master the sad puppy eyes, lower trembling pouty lip, and sweet, high-pitched baby voice to get what she wants.

"I'm not going to know anyone!" I protest for the fifth time since we've been FaceTiming.

"Which is perfect!" she exclaims. "This will be a chance to meet *new* people! The Bishop family is like *the* family, Em. They own a huge ranch on thousands of acres of land, passed down for generations, and they know everyone, which could be good for you."

I wrinkle my nose in disagreement. "How so?"

"Well, unless you want to be a nun for the rest of your life, it could help you branch out and network. It's important to know people in these small towns, Emily. You're not in Houston anymore," she reminds me, though she doesn't need to.

Moving from a large city high-rise to a one-bedroom condo hasn't been easy, to say the least. Not to mention I can't get Chinese delivery at midnight anymore or even my sugar-free Vanilla Latte from Starbucks that used to be a block away.

"So you're saying to crash this wedding to *network* and meet people?"

"You won't be crashing, because you'll be my plus one!" The smile on her face gets bigger when she realizes I'm starting to crack. "Also, there'll be lots of single men. The youngest brother is getting married, but that still leaves three single Bishops. Well, except Jackson."

I roll my eyes and smirk. "Trust me. I have no desire to invade your property."

She pinches her lips and scowls. "Anyway..." Clearing her throat, she continues, "So will you go with me or not? I don't want to show up alone like a big loser, especially if Jackson brings a date or something."

Her breathing always quickens when she talks about Jackson Bishop, her friend since she was in preschool—and I know that's because she wants to be much more than just that to him. She's had a crush on him for years, but as she explains it, Jackson doesn't settle down with anyone.

"You *should* bring a date, Kiera! He needs to see you're not just waiting around for him, and hell, maybe it'll even make him jealous, and he'll realize what's been right in front of him the whole damn time." I've told her this before, but I know she won't listen.

"It won't matter anyway. Jackson and Tanner were best friends in high school, and they're still friends, which means I'll always be off-limits to him." Tanner was her high school sweetheart and one of Jackson's best friends growing up. Even though that was close to ten years ago and shouldn't even matter anymore—another thing I've reminded her of—she refuses to listen. "That's even if he likes me that way," she continues. "Half the time, I can't even tell. He's like one of those fifty cent mood rings."

"Cheap and plastic." I snort.

She rolls her eyes and scowls. "No. Unpredictable and always changing."

I sigh, deciding not to add any more of my thoughts on the situation. Jackson has been the star in her sex dreams for as long as I can remember, but until they both get the sticks out of their asses and confess their true feelings, they'll continue this back and forth emotional roller coaster.

"Alright, fine. I'll go." I cave. Kiera's family and the Bishops are close, so I know she has to attend regardless, but at least this way I can keep an eye on her and make sure she doesn't drink herself stupid and do something else she'll regret.

"Yay! Oh my God, thank you!" She squeals so loud I have to cover my ears.

"On one condition…" I interrupt. "You dance with one guy at the wedding who isn't Jackson."

She twists her lips for a moment before nodding. "Okay."

"Who's under forty," I add, knowing my friend way too well. She'll dance with an old guy and say it counts.

Huffing, she relaxes her shoulders. "*Fine*."

I smile, victoriously.

"Same goes for you then. You have to dance with a guy under forty."

"But I don't know anyone," I remind her. "I'm not going to dance with a random guy so he can feel me up on the dance floor." Not to mention I have a strict no dating rule. Ever since my douchebag ex cheated on me, I have no desire to date. My only focus right now is on my new job and starting fresh.

"I'll pick a good one for you…promise." She grins before checking her watch. "Okay, I really have to go. We're supposed to get another trailer of horses in this afternoon, so I better get ready." Kiera's a horse trainer, one of the best in the state, which is why it's always hard for us to get together. Between both of our chaotic work schedules, we have to plan our chats in advance.

"Okay, see you soon!" I smile, excited I'll be hanging out with her again.

We hang up, and I click on my calendar app to write in the date. Crap. That's next weekend.

Kiera looks like she's dressed up for the Grammys instead of a country wedding. Can't say I'm really surprised though. She's already gorgeous with her strawberry-blonde hair updo and striking long legs, but she puts in extra effort knowing Jackson will be there.

"Are you going to a weddin' or a funeral?" Kiera frowns as soon as she sees my dress.

"Nice to see you too," I deadpan, opening my door wider for her to step inside.

She rolls her eyes and smiles, wrapping her arms around me for a quick hug. "You look beautiful, as always, but you can't wear black to a wedding."

My brows tighten. "Why not?"

"Because you just can't. You need a bright and colorful cocktail dress. Something that shows off your curves and chest."

"I'm not a show horse." My shoulders tense. "Plus, this dress is comfortable."

"Yeah, so is wearing a muumuu. Doesn't mean you wear it out in public." She grabs my hand and leads me down the hall to my bedroom. "I know you have some good stuff in here between all your scrubs." She goes through my closet like it's her life mission to find me the perfect dress. I've attended dozens of charity events for my dad, and each event meant a new dress because heaven forbid high society see me wearing the same thing twice. I don't mind getting dressed up, but between my work hours and lack of social life, I only wear them when I absolutely have to.

"This dress has gotten me plenty of free drinks, thank you very much," I tell her proudly as I reach around the back and unzip it.

"Probably because men feel sorry for your *loss*."

I snort, letting the fabric fall to my feet. "Fine. What do you suggest then?"

She pulls a few hangers and shows me the options. "Okay, these three have my approval. As long as you're okay with not wearing a bra." She shrugs.

"Great," I respond dryly.

After contemplating, I pick the dark blue dress with a sweetheart neckline and red belt. I pair it with my favorite red heels and a red clutch.

"Am I decent now?" I turn and ask Kiera who's watching me.

"Hell yeah. That's more like it." She grins, wagging her brows.

I roll my eyes at her and walk down the hall. "Let's go, Juliet."

She links her arm through mine. "Too bad Romeo is an idiot."

"Especially if he can deny you in that dress. Or at least I think it's a dress. The lack of fabric makes it questionable." I stuff my phone in my clutch and grab my keys before we head out the door.

"Testing his willpower is my favorite game." She smirks. "And him hooking up with random chicks is his."

"You two are so fucking weird." I open the door to her car and slide in. "How is it possible you two haven't drunk banged yet?"

"Considering Jackson likes to drink, it's a mystery to me too."

"Since I'll more than likely be sitting on the sidelines tonight, I'll be observing to see once and for all if he's into you or not. You two have danced around each other for so long, you've made the rest of us dizzy just watching."

"You're dizzy? How do you think I feel? One second, he's all protective and sweet, and the next, he's cold and distant. He's worse than a chick on her period."

"He's worse than a chick, period." I laugh. "Too bad he doesn't have an identical twin brother you could date instead. Oh, wait…" I tease, glancing over at her red cheeks.

"Identical in looks, opposite in personality," she retorts. "And John is like a big brother to me. There are no feelings like that at all."

We chat the entire forty-five-minute drive to Eldorado. She briefs me on the Bishop clan and tells me stories of growing up with the Bishop brothers and their sister, Courtney.

"You'll love Court. She's sassy and bold."

"Like you." I grin.

"Who do you think taught her?" She chuckles, turning into a gravel driveway with a huge sign that reads Circle B Ranch. "She and her husband have triplets, and Alex and River have a little boy." She continues filling my head with information that I'm probably going to forget later.

"So are you saying I'm going to end up at the kiddies' table?" I narrow my eyes at her suspiciously.

She bursts out laughing as she finds an open place to park. "Nah. I'll be by your side the entire time."

For some reason, I have a hard time believing her.

We walk down the path toward the huge oak tree where the outdoor ceremony will be held. White chairs are lined up and a beautiful arch decorated with flowers is at the front. There's a huge white tent on the other side, and people are crowding in everywhere.

"Wow…" I take in the view and how gorgeous everything looks.

"No one throws a party like the Bishops do," Kiera says matter-of-factly as we walk closer.

Since it's April and early spring in Texas, it's already warm out, but luckily, it'll cool down soon. It's almost five, and the sun will be setting in a few hours.

Kiera starts introducing me to some of the guests sitting near us. She acts like a tour guide, knowing everyone and their business. She whispers their secrets to me and tells me which guys are single.

The ceremony music begins, and everyone shuffles to their seats.

"That's Mama Bishop," she whispers. "John's escorting her down and behind them is Scott Bishop, the dad."

"How can you even tell them apart?"

She glances over at me and smirks. "John's much more serious. Jackson's hair is a little longer, too."

"He's pretty good lookin'," I whisper, admiring his chiseled and neatly trimmed jawline.

"If you dated John and I dated Jackson, that'd be perfect!" she whisper-shouts and gazes at me like the heart-eyes emoji. "We could have a double weddin' and get pregnant at the same time. Then our kids would grow up together and be best friends."

I furrow my brows, wondering how she went from zero to a hundred in less than three seconds. "Slow it down, Juliet. I'm not waiting for your Romeo to get his head out of his ass to get married. Although considering my luck with men, you two might actually beat me to it."

The woman in front of me glares back at us with a loud shushing noise, and Kiera giggles.

The girl has it *bad*. She needs to get laid and over Jackson Bishop ASAP. In fact, now that I'm single and starting fresh in a new town with a new job, I just might make it my mission to find Kiera a man. Someone who will actually give her the time of day and appreciate everything she has to offer.

We sit in silence as the wedding party continues to make their way down the aisle. I look up front and see all the men looking amazing in their black suits. They're all wearing black cowboy hats, except the groom is wearing a white one. Cowboys don't usually do it for me, which is ironic since I was born and raised in Texas, but I grew up in the suburbs of a big city. The guys I dated were from well-known families my father approved of, but they never lasted. However, these cowboys standing at the front of the aisle are looking pretty damn good right now.

Everything about the ceremony is beautiful. The weather is perfect, and the decorations are simple yet stunning. The bride and the entire wedding party are gorgeous. My little black heart even melts when they read their own vows, which causes everyone—including the wedding party—to wipe their eyes. When the bride and groom finally kiss, there's no doubt how much they care for each other. Everyone erupts in cheers, then it's over and time to party.

"Seeing Alex cry when he first saw River walking down the aisle made me tear up," Kiera says as we walk into the tent. The DJ is already playing music. "I don't think I've ever seen a Bishop boy cry."

"You could really see how much he loves her," I add, leading us to the bar for cocktail hour. "He looked at her like she was his whole world."

"They're sickly in love." She places a hand to her chest and sighs. "And their six-month-old son all dressed up in a tux with a little cowboy hat was the cutest thing ever!"

We grab a flute of champagne off the bar, and when we spot the appetizers, we walk toward them, eyeing the shrimp cocktail shooters. Just as I'm stuffing my face, people walk up to Kiera and hug her. We're greeted by her parents shortly after, whom I've met several times before, so at least I know them in case Kiera goes MIA later.

"Yee-haw!" I hear shouting in the background with lots of clapping. More people are filing into the tent, and I can't tell where the cheers are coming from.

"Oh lord," Kiera says, laughing. "That's Dylan. He's Alex's best friend."

I look around the crowd and recognize a man who was in the wedding party waving his arms over his head like he was roping cattle. He's hootin' and hollerin' as the rest of the party watch the bride and groom take pictures.

"He looks like he could be the fifth Bishop brother." I chuckle, watching his antics as I take another drink.

"Definitely. He's another Jackson, though," she states. "Parties and sleeps around."

"If I didn't know any better, I'd say cowboys are worse than the high-profile men I've dated."

She gives me a look that tells me I'm not far off.

When I look back at Dylan, I see he's wrapped his arm around a brunette woman. He pulls her into his side and presses his lips to hers. She adjusts his tie and smiles sweetly up at him.

Hmm. Looks like the Jacksons of the world might actually settle down after all.

We mingle and chat while music softly plays in the background. Kiera introduces me to as many people as she possibly can, and by the time the wedding party introductions start, my head is spinning from information overload.

The DJ gets everyone pumped and excited before announcing the bride and groom. They hold hands walking in, but after a few steps, he pauses and lifts her up in his arms. She squeals as she wraps her arms tightly around his neck and holds on as he walks them to the dance floor. The rest of the party is already waiting for them.

Once the music fades, the DJ announces the newlyweds' first dance as John Mayer's "Slow Dancing in a Burning Room" begins to play.

"I love this song," Kiera whispers to me as we take our seats and watch.

"It's not really a love song," I whisper back, curious as to why they'd pick this one as their wedding song.

"No, but apparently there's a special meaning behind it. Alex and River met in Florida a year and a half ago, and I remember something about this being the first song they ever danced to," Kiera tells me.

"Aw, that's kind of sweet." I beam, jealous of these two strangers' love.

Kiera's parents are seated by us, and I learn the other couple next to us are friends of the Bishops. We make small talk while we eat and drink. The bride and groom walk around to chat with their guests, and Kiera and her parents wait anxiously for them to approach our table.

"Alex!" Kiera squeals, wrapping her arms around him. "I can't believe you're married!"

He smiles and hugs her, holding River's hand who's holding their son on her hip.

"Congrats, you guys!" Kiera gives the bride a side hug and kisses the baby on the head. "You three are serious family goals."

Alex chuckles, and when his eyes lock with River's, the love soars between them. It's strong and fierce and everything I imagined I'd have one day.

"This is my friend—" She starts to introduce us, but we get interrupted by the baby. He starts to fuss, so they excuse themselves.

Once dinner is finished, I grab another drink, but this time, I order something much stronger. I'm going to need it if I want to get through this night of happy couples.

"Whiskey neat," I hear a deep voice next to me order as I reach for my glass. Out of the corner of my eye, I see he's wearing a tux and a scowl. His dirty blond hair is pulled back, and when his hand brushes through his locks, it looks perfectly messy. I turn slightly to assess him further, and that's when I recognize him from the wedding party. Checking his left hand, I see his ring finger is bare and wonder if he's one of the Bishop family members. I don't get the chance to find out because as soon as he grabs his glass, a woman approaches and hangs off his arm.

Go figure.

Taking my drink, I walk back to the table and see it's now empty. I look around for Kiera but don't see her anywhere before searching for Jackson. Knowing my friend, she's somewhere near him.

Emily: Where'd you go?

My text goes unanswered, so I send another one a few minutes later.

Emily: You better not be ditching me, or I swear to God I'm marching right up to Jackson and telling him you're secretly in love with him.

Emily: I mean it, Kiera…

Emily: I'll even tell him your new sex toy is named after him.

Kiera: OMG! You wouldn't.

Kiera: I'll be right back.

Emily: You better.

I end up back at the bar ten minutes later grabbing another drink. I can't believe she ditched me. When I see Jackson surrounded by other women, I speculate Kiera is in the huddle somewhere, but then I step closer and see she's nowhere near him.

What the hell?

Emily: Where are you exactly?

Emily: Are you okay? We can leave if you want.

I send her another round of messages. If she saw Jackson and his entourage, she could be crying in a corner somewhere.

Kiera: No! LOL! I'm fine, I promise.

I furrow my brows at the screen, wondering what she's doing. Or maybe, who she's doing? I chuckle to myself at that last thought. The alcohol burns through my veins, and I know I'm on my way to becoming tipsy.

Emily: Do you plan on coming back anytime soon?

Fifteen minutes later, I'm still drinking solo at my empty table with an empty plate of cake that I shamelessly demolished.

"I'll take that as a no..." I mutter to myself, checking my phone again and still no new messages. I'm going to kill her.

The DJ announces the bride is about to throw the bouquet and calls all the single women to the dance floor. Girls shuffle to the middle, throwing elbows and trying to find their perfect spot. I throw back the rest of my drink and scoff.

"C'mon ladies… last call to come out!" the DJ calls. I watch as Alex escorts River out to the dance floor and spins her around in circles. People chuckle as they watch the two of them play around.

"You're going to miss out…" the same deep voice from earlier says next to me. Blinking, I look over and see the same dirty blond hair and sleek black tux as before. He's holding a glass of amber liquid, and his lips are turned up in amusement as he studies me. He's even better looking now that I see his full profile.

"I doubt I'll miss much," I retort, wondering why he'd even care. His sky-blue eyes are hard to avoid as they burn into mine.

"Figured chicks lived for catching the bouquet," he states matter-of-factly, taking a seat next to me without an invite, and my heart races the closer his body is to mine.

"Not me." I shrug, gazing over at him. He's hard to read, yet his demeanor intrigues me to continue the conversation. "Are you going to go out there to catch the garter next?" I challenge.

He half-laughs, half-snorts.

"Why not?" I ask, smirking.

His eyes lock on mine, the question left unanswered. "I'll do it if you catch the bouquet." He nods his head to the dance floor where River is seconds away from throwing it, but then one of the bridesmaids tells them to hold on while she grabs a few of her friends.

I arch a brow and narrow my eyes. "A dare?"

He shrugs casually. "You've been sitting here by yourself for the past thirty minutes. What do you have to lose?"

The fact he just admitted to watching me doesn't go unnoticed. My cheeks heat, and I'm shocked my body is responding this way. The alcohol buzzes in my system, and if it wasn't for the last two drinks, there'd be no way I'd take him up on his offer.

Pinching my lips together, I bend down and slip off my shoes. "Okay, you got yourself a deal or rather a dare." Seeing this tall, brooding man fight for a garter will be entertaining at least.

He stands when I do, and that's when all the alcohol rushes to my head. I nearly stumble over my own feet, but I gracefully catch myself. He follows me through the maze of tables and chairs until I'm on the dance floor blending into the large crowd of overly excited women. I don't know anyone but him watching me fuels my adrenaline.

Once I secure my spot, I find him flashing me a sly grin. I don't know who this guy is, but he just turned my night around. Considering Kiera completely bailed on me, I'll take his company over sitting alone.

"It's time, ladies!" The DJ walks out onto the floor with a microphone. "You ready?" He tilts his head toward River, and when she nods, Alex grabs her shoulders and spins her around again. She closes her eyes and squeals when he spins her faster.

The moment she stops and raises her arms over her head, my vision clears, and I want nothing more than to fight for this bouquet. I couldn't care less about the meaning behind catching it, but for some strange reason, I want to prove to this guy that I'm a badass who follows through with dares. Normally I'd brush it off, considering he's a complete stranger, but the intense way he looks at me drives my actions.

When the bouquet flies into the air, everything seems like it's in slow motion. I've always been a logical person, so I tend to see things differently —even buzzed. She threw it high versus directly behind her, which means it's not going to launch very far to the back. Taking notice, I flee to the front of the group and eye it carefully as it descends toward the left side of the floor.

Something comes over me, and I push the girl next to me out of the way a second before the bouquet lands on my chest. I secure my arms around it and hold it tightly against my body. Two girls started running toward me as soon as they took notice it was aiming this way, and unable to slow themselves down, they smack directly into my side and knock me over.

I hear squealing and the DJ laughing into the microphone. Girls fall over each other, and we become a huge pile on the floor. A knee's in my gut, and someone's lying on my hair.

The weight finally lifts off me, and when I look up, I see the guy holding out his hand for me. I can tell he's trying hard to hold back his smile, and when I scowl up at him, he chuckles.

Taking his hand, I let him pull me to stand. I'm quick to adjust my dress so I don't moon the entire room and embarrass myself more.

"That was… *epic*." He smirks, leading me off the floor as his hand remains in mine. Some of the women are staring at me, giving me death glares, and I can only imagine what they're thinking right now.

"You mean... *humiliating*. I can't believe I let you talk me into that." I scoff, taking a seat and setting my destroyed bouquet down.

"It wasn't very hard to talk you into it, so you must've really wanted to do it." He winks as he takes the seat next to me at the empty table.

Shaking my head, I pinch my lips together and remember that he's up next. "Well, you're up." I nod my head to the dance floor where the DJ is setting up for the garter toss. "Hope you brought your A game." I cross my legs in anticipation.

"Oh, I always do." He shrugs off his jacket and winks. Once his jacket is secure on the back of the chair, he leans down to my ear. "What's your name, darlin'? I'd like to know who I'm winning this for."

The closeness of his lips steals my breath away. My entire body shivers, and I hate that this man has an effect on me. Though I have no idea who he is, he's already made me reconsider my *no men ban*. Dangerous—that's the only way I can describe him. I don't trust myself around him, and I most definitely don't trust *him*. After already making a fool of myself, I'm not about to tell him my real name so it can come back to bite me in the ass later. I'll never have to see him again after tonight, so I blurt out the first name that comes to mind.

"It's Stella."

CHAPTER THREE

EVAN

"STELLA." I let the word linger on my tongue for a moment. "That's a pretty name," I tell her, staring at her cherry-colored lips before I meet her eyes. She tugs on the corner of her lip with her perfectly straight teeth, and when I turn to walk away, she sighs. Realizing she's not following, I stop and cross my arms over my chest with an eyebrow raised. She gives me a huff and a cute smile, then I grab her hand as we snake our way through the crowd. The attraction between us is hot like fire, and it might actually burn us both.

Just as I get to the middle of the room with all the other bachelors, the DJ plays a sexy song that makes everyone laugh while Alex takes his time lifting River's skirt. He climbs up her body, placing his head under her dress, and when he pops back out, he has the garter in his teeth. Standing in the front, I crack my fingers, wanting—for the first time in my life—to catch the garter. Alex twirls it around his finger before he turns his back and flicks it toward the group of us. Most of the guys take a step back, trying to dodge it as the garter flies through the air, and I simply lift my hand and catch it. Alex walks over to me and gives me a big hug, and of course, the photographer has us stand together for a photo. River wraps her arms around me too, and I can hear Courtney in the background yelling over everyone.

"Get married and have some kids too!"

Laughter fills the room, and soon the DJ lowers the lights and turns on the slow music that's made just for dancing. I move across the room toward Stella who's wearing a smile.

"That's not fair. Hair extensions and nails get ripped off for the bouquet, and the guys basically gave the garter to you. Not a fair exchange."

I open my mouth to say something just as the photographer asks if she can take our picture together. Stella goes and grabs the bouquet that looks like it's been through a war. Wrapping my arm around her, we hold our treasures and pose for a photograph that I hope doesn't haunt me later on.

"I need another drink," Stella says, the sweetness of the wine she was drinking on her breath.

Before we make it to the bar, we're inundated by family as the slow song ends. I try to quickly introduce everyone before the guys flood me with questions. "This is Alex, John, and Drew. Then there's Dylan, Jacob, Mason, and William. That over there is Jackson. You're never going to remember any of this," I say with a laugh when I realize she's already lost.

"Howdy."

"Hey."

"Hello."

They all greet her, and I can tell they're dying to ask who she is. I'm not usually accompanied to family events, but after getting shit from everyone for not having a date to the wedding, I figured I'd take a page from my brother's book tonight and have a good time. It certainly helps that no one here knows who she is, so I won't be pressured into inviting her to have dinner with the family. It can't be anything more than what it is right now, but the guys are giving me side-eyes, and I just hope they keep their mouths shut for once.

"I'm Stella." She smiles sweetly at the crowd surrounding us.

"Now let's see if you can name us all." Dylan laughs, and Stella shakes her head.

"There's no way. I blame the alcohol."

"Speaking of." I place my hand on the small of her back and lead her over to the bar.

All the couples dance together, and Stella and I find seats at the bar and drink like we're anti-relationship, and in a roundabout way, maybe we are. We turn around to people watch, and we're laughing at nothing.

"So where are you from?" I ask her, knowing she's not from around here.

"East Texas. But honestly, I don't want to get all personal. Not trying to be an ass; I just don't want all that."

I clink my glass against hers. "Deal."

"Look at all the happy couples," she says, lifting her drink toward the dance floor.

"Fuck relationships," I tell her with a grin.

She tilts her body and sets her glass down. "Exactly. That's my motto at least. Relationships are overrated."

It feels amazing to let loose with someone who knows nothing about me or my past or anything. Right now, at this moment, I'm a man, and she's a beautiful woman, and that's it. Nothing personal. Nothing too deep. However, something about her makes me feel like I've known her for a lifetime.

I narrow my eyes at her as I finish off my whiskey and tonic. "You seem so familiar. I can't place it though."

She throws her head back and lets out a big laugh. "Maybe it's because we're both so goddamn cynical about relationships. Because honestly, most weddings make me want to vomit. Not this one though. But others. I usually try to wiggle my way out of them, but I didn't really have a choice today."

Tilting my head at her, I set my drink down next to hers. "Dance with me."

"No way. We'd just be giving in to the normalcy." Stella smiles.

I stand and hold out my hand. "Please?"

Shaking her head, she laughs. "I suck at dancing."

"You just haven't had a great teacher. That's all." I drop down to one knee and hold out my hand. "Please?" And just like that, I'm begging. Damn whiskey has turned against me.

She playfully rolls her eyes but stands and grabs my hand. Once we're on the dance floor, "Thinking Out Loud" by Ed Sheeran comes on. It's such a cliché wedding dance song, but I walk out to the middle of the floor, and she stops at the edge. I curl my finger, demanding she come to me, and after a moment, she hesitantly walks toward me. Placing one hand on the small of her back, I grab her hand with my other one and interlock our fingers together before pulling her close. Her breath hitches, and when I look into her eyes, it's only then I realize our faces are only inches apart.

"I knew you couldn't deny me," I tell her. She pretends as if she's going to walk away, and I pull her hand, making her spin toward me right before I dip her.

"Who the hell are you?" she whispers when I bring her back to her feet.

"Just another cynical human dancing with a beautiful woman."

I twirl her around again, and she can't stop smiling.

"You're not a bad dancer," I say against the crook of her neck.

"It's you. I swear I usually have two left feet." When Stella looks up at me with so much fire and passion in her eyes, I'm tempted to ask her a dozen personal questions, but I know I can't go there.

"Stella…"

"Yes?" she mutters.

"All we have is tonight. And that's it."

She runs her fingers through my hair. "I know."

"Come to my room with me."

Laughing, she pretends to have to think about it. "I have rules though."

Now *I* laugh. "I do too. Nothing personal. Just one night. The attraction is undeniable, and I know I don't want to wake up tomorrow with regret. Whaddaya say?"

"Me either," she tells me. "Just one night."

I cross my heart and tap her nose with my finger.

"Wait, did you just dare me?" she jokes because we both know this time I didn't.

"Uh," I hesitate, somewhat confused.

"I can never pass up a dare," she states confidently with a wink before licking her lips.

I run my fingers through her hair, and she leans into it. "Then hell yes, it was a dare."

"Can we go now?" she asks just as the song ends.

"Absolutely." I lead her outside where a few of the ranch hands are driving people to the B&B in the side by side utility vehicles.

"Seriously?" she says over the rumble of the engine. "Where are we going?"

"I'm staying up the road at the bed and breakfast. And don't you know, buzzed driving is drunk driving," I say seriously, witnessing many aftermath situations of drunk drivers. Charlie rolls his eyes but remains silent. It doesn't take any time at all before the front porch of the B&B comes into view. The warm glow of the lights on in the house beams like beacons in the night.

"Thanks, Charlie," I say, patting him on the back. Stella gives me a curious look, probably wondering how I know his name, and when I don't offer an explanation, she opens but quickly closes her mouth. *Nothing personal.* She doesn't need to know who I am or that this is my family's ranch. For tonight, I'm just a guy, and she's just a girl.

As we walk up the steps, I turn around and look at Charlie, placing my finger on my lips. He gives me a head nod and backs out of the driveway. Stella is my secret—one that I don't want to get around.

We left the wedding before everyone else, so I know the B&B will be empty minus a couple of workers. I decide I'm not going to worry about it, though because sneaking away with Stella has my adrenaline pumping with more desire than I've felt in a long time.

Opening the front door, I rest my palm on her back and ease her inside. It's eerily quiet, just as I'd hoped. She takes a moment to look around, but I quickly grab her hand and lead her upstairs to my room. I could've stayed at John and Jackson's house, which is within walking distance from here, but I know my brothers well enough to know the party wouldn't have ended when the reception was over.

"It's very rustic in here," she states as we make our way down the hallway.

"And floral," I add with a chuckle. I unlock the door and push it open. Before she can step inside, I grab her elbow and pull her back until my lips hover over her ear. "You sure about this?"

Her breath hitches before she exhales and turns her head to the side. "Are you backing out of the dare?"

I run my hand down her bare arm, my fingertips feeling the goose bumps forming over her skin. "I have no reason to, but I just want you to be certain. I know you've been drinking and maybe the thought of a one-night stand was exciting, and now that we're here, you're second-guessing yourself."

I don't know why the fuck I'm rambling, but I need to hear her say the words. I respect women too much to take advantage of the fact that she's had alcohol, and the last thing I need is a scandal with my entire family involved.

Instead of answering me, she steps farther into the room and turns around with her arms reaching behind her back. I slam the door shut behind me, and when I look at her, my cock presses against the fabric of my dress pants, begging to be released.

She's eye fucking me as she slowly and torturously undoes the belt that's nothing more than decoration around her waist, then unzips the dress that's hugged her body all night long.

Standing frozen with my legs parted and my arms crossed, I wait, anticipating her next move. When the fabric pools at her feet, I'm completely mesmerized by the sight of her. I shouldn't be shocked she's not wearing a bra, but her lacy black panties send a thrilling shock through my body.

"Does this answer your question?" she asks. The confidence radiating off her makes me hard as fuck.

I take two long strides before I'm standing in front of her, and when she lowers her eyes and sees the aching bulge, she bites down on her lower lip.

"Fuck, Stella. You're so goddamn beautiful." I lower my body, cupping her breast and wrapping my mouth around her nipple, swirling my tongue around the tall peak. A moan vibrates off her lips as she runs her fingers through my hair, and when she pulls roughly, it drives me fucking crazy.

After thoroughly sucking and alternating between her breasts, I straighten and watch as she tries to calm her breathing. I grasp the back of her neck, pulling her body flush against mine as I claim her mouth and sink my tongue between her full lips. She tastes sweet, and when she moans against my mouth, I don't know how much longer I can hold back. Her fingers tug harder in my hair as she angles her neck, so I take the opportunity to deepen the kiss.

Stepping back, I take a mental snapshot of how fucking gorgeous she is in red high heels and black panties. "I always heard a woman wore black panties because she wanted someone to see them." I take off my tux jacket and drop it to the floor.

"Then I guess tonight's your lucky night." She teases me by placing her thumbs in the waistband of her lace panties.

I smirk and watch as she slides out of them. Fuck, I want her so bad. "Any preferences, darlin'?" I ask, gripping her hips and inhaling the fresh scent of her shampoo.

She wraps a hand around my neck, pulling my head closer to hers, and then she says just above a whisper, "I want to be fucked so hard I feel you for days." Her words are meant to shock, but they don't. Instead, they flow directly to my cock.

With a popped eyebrow, I begin undoing the cuff links. "You have no idea what you just asked for, sweetheart," I warn her in a promising tone.

"I think I do," she quips, sinking her teeth into her bottom lip.

Goddamn, this woman just might be my undoing.

CHAPTER FOUR

EMILY

I DON'T KNOW what's come over me, but my entire body buzzes with anticipation. This man has my blood rushing, and I don't want it to stop anytime soon. My core throbs from his words—his *promise*.

Watching him undo his cuff links, I feel the heat pool right to my center. I've never wanted a man as much as I want him right now. Perhaps this undeniable desire is from the rapid shots of alcohol, or maybe it's because I've been sex deprived for way too long.

Whatever the reason, I want anything he's willing to give me. Just for tonight.

"Keep those heels on, sweetheart," he orders when I attempt to kick them off. "I have plans for you in those." He flashes a panty-dropping smirk, which reminds me I'm standing naked in front of him while he's still fully clothed.

"I will as long as you take off your clothes," I tease, desperate to see what's underneath them. It's obvious how built and muscular he is, but the moment he unbuttons his shirt and reveals his broad shoulders and chest, I nearly drop to my knees and thank baby Jesus for blessing me with this sinful view. Washboard abs that form into a delicious V have me moaning aloud.

"Like what you see?" His cocky grin only adds to his appeal.

Confidence is sexy in a man, no doubt, but this man brings confidence to a whole new level.

"I was just about to ask you the same thing," I retort, taking notice of his growing hard-on. "You're starting to look a little… constricted."

I yelp when he grabs my hand and pushes it against his erection straining through his slacks. Before I can stop myself, I'm moaning again when he rubs my palm along the length.

Pressing us close, he brings his lips to my ear. "How fast do you think I can make you come before I even take my dick out?"

I swallow—his words unexpected, but they drive a throbbing sensation right to my clit.

"Let's see, shall we?" His amused tone continues to turn me on when he slips one hand down my body and lands between my legs. "Are you wet for me, baby?"

"Mm-hmm," I hum, my head rolling back between my shoulders as he swipes a finger down my slit. He repeats the movement before inserting a finger inside. "Mmm yes."

"Fucking hell," he mutters, picking up his pace. "So wet and tight." He pulls out swiftly before thrusting two fingers and curling them deep inside my pussy. I release another hungry moan as I clench my muscles around him.

"More," I beg, wrapping my arms around his neck and pressing my lips to his. His free hand fists my hair as he holds my mouth to his with an urgency I've never felt before.

"What a gorgeous fucking sight," he praises against my lips, breaking our kiss. "You fucking my fingers and so goddamn greedy for it."

"Yes." I pant. "I am."

That makes him smile. His thumb reaches up and circles my clit with intense pressure as he continues twisting his thick fingers inside me. My eyes flutter closed as my head falls back, and I gasp when his mouth lands on my neck, sucking and kissing as my impending orgasm builds.

My knees go weak as he works me faster and manages to sink even deeper. I dig my nails into his biceps as I hold on and ride out the explosive orgasm that follows. He slows his pace, groaning in my ear as I come down from the high.

"That might be a new record." Blinking, I see his cocky grin again, and even though I just came all over his fingers, that grin does something to my insides. Oh God.

"Your turn," I say, reaching for his button and zipper. He lets me undo his slacks, and when he kicks his shoes off, I push them down till he's standing in only his briefs with an obvious hard-on. Sliding my hand inside, I'm greeted by the velvety smooth shaft, and when I pump him a couple of times, he groans in response.

"Fuck, you keep doing that and I won't be able to do all the things I've wanted to do since the moment I laid eyes on you," he growls as I pump faster. "Stella…" His warning tone has me smiling at the control I have over him right now.

"What do you want to do with me?" My tone is meant to taunt him, but his dark, hungry eyes let me know he doesn't appreciate being teased, which makes me want to do it that much more.

"So fucking much." His voice comes out strained as I continue to stroke him. My breasts are pressed against his chest, and when I feel him tense, he grinds his teeth. "Turn around." His order comes out rough and demanding.

Before I can obey his orders, he grabs my shoulders and spins me around. I feel his erection press against the small of my back as his hands slide down to my waist. "You see what you do to me? Aching so fucking bad for you, but I want to take my time with you."

I grin although he can't see my face. Sliding a hand up my stomach, he palms my breast and rolls my nipple between his fingers. My head falls back against his chest as he plucks it and harshly squeezes it.

"Ahh…" I groan at the pain that turns into pleasure within seconds. He does it again, harder this time. "Yes," I say on a moan. I love it.

Lowering his mouth, he whispers in my ear, "Bend over the bed so I can get a look at that pretty pussy of yours." His words send a thrill through me that I haven't felt in a long time. I can't remember the last time a guy has been so demanding, but I also *really* like it.

Moaning, I obey his order and bend down until my ass is sticking out. The height of my heels keeps our waists at the same level, and when he dips his head, I feel his lips trail down my spine. They send shivers along my skin, and when he grips my hips and stands back up, he kicks my legs open with his foot.

He kneels, slapping his palms against my ass cheeks and spreading them wide. His hungry growl is the only warning I get before his tongue sinks inside me. I yelp in surprise at how furious his mouth devours me and rest my elbows on the bed for support.

"Holy shit," I murmur, feeling his tongue massage over my clit before sliding along my slit and pressing deeper inside.

"Mmm, fuck yes." He slaps my ass, causing me to moan in pleasure. His firm hold on my thighs keeps his mouth planted on my pussy. He devours it like a man eating his last meal and doesn't stop until I crumple under him.

Before I can catch my breath, he lines himself up at my entrance and rubs the crown of his cock against my opening. I hadn't even realized he stripped out of his briefs and sheathed himself, but the moment he pushes through my barrier, everything goes dark.

He fills me, pushing deeper inch by inch, and once my body relaxes, I take all of him.

"Yes…" I whisper, loving the way he feels inside me. So full.

"Fuck, Stella," he groans, his hand sliding up my back until it twists in my hair, and he pulls my body up, so his chest is against my back. "You feel so goddamn good."

He continues his torturous pleasure, rocking into me and hitting every nerve ending possible. Pulling my head back, he exposes my throat, and his lips capture the flesh under my ear. His other hand rounds my stomach and circles my clit.

"Oh, God," I whimper as he increases his pace, working my clit so damn fast and hard.

"Yeah, baby. Tell me how much you love my cock fucking you," he growls in my ear, sending shivers through my entire body. Fuck, his gruff voice alone sets me off.

"Don't stop," I plead. "Harder."

"My fucking pleasure, sweetheart." Sinking his teeth into my shoulder, he kisses over the mark as he digs his fingertips into my hips and pounds into me with a ruthless pace.

"Please, *yesyesyes…*" My words scramble over another, my heart beating rapidly in my chest as he fulfills every fantasy I've ever had.

"What do you need, pretty girl? Tell me," he orders, his cock slamming into my pussy over and over again. "You need to come?"

"Mmm," I grit between my teeth, groaning in desperation.

Without responding, he flips me over, and I fall onto the bed. My legs are over his shoulders within seconds, and his mouth is back on my swollen clit. His tongue and fingers work me into oblivion until I'm crying out in ecstasy.

"Holy shit," I mutter, gasping for air. My throat is dry from the inaudible words that spewed out of my mouth, but I don't have much time to dwell on it because he hooks my ankles over his shoulders and leans over me until he's seated deep inside.

He cups my breast as he groans into my neck, chasing his own orgasm hard and fast. Digging my nails into his back, I encourage him, and he stills before jerking and releasing inside me.

"Fuck, Stella..." he groans in my ear before cupping my chin and pressing his lips to mine in a heated kiss filled with lust. Guilt surfaces for lying to him about my name but knowing this is only a one-night thing, I push the thought away because I doubt he'll even care.

"Mmm, buttercream." He licks his lips, getting a taste of the dessert I ate earlier. I see the corner of his lips tilt up as his eyes light up in amusement.

"Wedding cake," I confirm with a half smile, still trying to catch my breath.

"I like it. Suits you."

I narrow my eyes, pondering his words. "How so?"

After licking his lower lip, his grin turns into a wide, knowing smile. "Pretty on the outside, sweet and delicious on the inside." He winks before pushing his body off mine, and I admire his fine ass while he walks to the bathroom.

Lying on the bed, I try to sit up, but my legs feel like mush. He returns a minute later with a towel in his hand and offers it to me.

"Thanks." I take it and clean myself, unable to look at the man who just fucked my brains out. The alcohol hasn't worn off completely but knowing I can't even remember his name has me blushing with guilt.

"Where are you going?" He pulls my arm when I attempt to walk away. "I have plans for you, Buttercream. I'm not done with you yet."

"What kind of plans?" I tease, sucking in my lower lip as he sets me over his hips, so I'm straddling him.

"We only have one night, right?" He arches a brow, waiting for my confirmation, and when I nod, he continues. "Which means I'm going to make every minute count."

He cups the back of my neck and captures my mouth with his in a feverish kiss. Hands and lips cover my skin, playing and sucking until both of us have had our fill.

Which seems never-ending, considering he takes me three more times before the sun rises.

The obnoxious thumping in my head is the first thing I notice when I startle awake. Once I peel my eyes open, the sun rising and glaring through the barely there curtains is the second thing I notice.

I drank way too much last night, which I haven't done in a long-ass time. The last time I let loose like that was years ago when a bunch of my classmates and I went out to celebrate acing our exams. Between work and family engagements, I only drank a glass or two of wine at a time, so the fact that I'm not puking my guts out right now is a miracle.

It takes me a second to realize where I am. Blinking to clear my vision, I look around the room and remember he took me to his room at the B&B last night. Wait. Who is *he?* I know he told me his name, and I probably even screamed it a few times, but for the life of me, I'm drawing a blank.

Ethan? Nathan? Drew? *Fuck.*

It doesn't matter anyway since I don't plan on hanging around. I broke my own damn rule, and now I need to get the hell out before I'm face-to-face with him.

Slowly, I slide my body out of bed, grabbing the fallen sheet from the floor and wrapping it around my chest. I grab my clutch before tiptoeing to the bathroom and quietly shut the door behind me. Once I pee and fix the rat's nest on my head, I reach for my phone and see Kiera's already texted me.

Kiera: Please don't hate me.

Kiera: I can explain everything. I promise!

Kiera: Where did you end up?

Emily: I'll kick your ass later for ditching me, but right now I need a ride out of here!

Kiera: Where are you??

Emily: At the B&B.

Kiera: I can be there in a few! How'd you end up there anyway?

Emily: Well after you bailed on me, I met a guy and well… I woke up in bed with him.

Kiera: WHAT! OMG!

Emily: I know!! Now I need to get the hell out of here before he wakes up.

Kiera: What, why? Is he ugly?

I roll my eyes. Of course, she'd ask that.

Kiera: Wait. Who is it?

Emily: Uh, I don't remember his name exactly. I got really drunk. I think it's Drew? He was wearing a tux and in the wedding party.

Kiera: You need to get the hell out of there ASAP, Em. No joke. Do not let anyone see you!!

Emily: OMG you're freaking me out! Why?

Kiera: Drew is MARRIED! To Courtney!

Oh my God. My entire body starts to shake. Courtney is the Bishop sister.

Emily: That can't be right! He wasn't wearing a ring…

Kiera: It's easy to remove a ring, Em! If he got drunk and slept with you, everyone is going to FREAK OUT! Get the hell out of there!

Emily: I'm going to get dressed. Meet me in 5 minutes!

Kiera: I'll text you as soon as I'm there.

My heart is racing, and I don't know whether to cry or scream—or both. What the fuck? What kind of man cheats on his wife at the wedding of her brother? Where the hell was Courtney and the kids? I rack my brain to think of when I saw her last, but nothing comes to mind. Could she have left early to put the triplets to bed? I only met her briefly, but she and Drew were both in the wedding party, and I remember seeing her walk down the aisle with her long blonde hair and wide, giddy smile.

Oh my God, what have I done?

I tiptoe back out into the room and grab my dress and shoes. Once I've slipped my clothes on, I look around and see Drew's tux spread out on the floor. Anger fills my veins as I think about what my ex did to me and how shitty it felt to be cheated on. Why would this guy risk his whole life for a one-night stand? It was both of our ideas to keep things casual, but to cheat on your wife with her entire family nearby?

What a motherfucking douchebag. The thought brings up the moment I realized my ex was a cheating asshole, and that anger resurfaces, sending me into action.

Just because I'm bailing doesn't mean he should get away with this. Who knows how many other times he's cheated or plans to in the future.

I quickly gather up his clothes and shoes and walk out with whatever dignity I have left—which isn't much, considering the circumstances. I make sure to set his phone and wallet down on the nightstand, but let's see him talk his way out of this one. He won't be able to leave without telling people his one-night stand stole his clothes.

Take that, you cheating bastard.

I quickly go down the staircase and keep my head low, so no one stops me. I don't want anyone looking at me and wonder why I'm fleeing. Once I'm outside, I spot Kiera's car and run barefoot until I hit the door. Rushing inside, I slam it behind me and finally breathe.

"Go!" I tell her, not wanting to chat about this entire fucked-up situation.

My heart races as she speeds out of the parking lot, and I clench the tux and shoes to my chest. When we're finally a couple of miles down the road, I exhale.

"What are you holding?" Kiera finally notices my full arms.

I cringe, realization setting in to what I've done. "His tux."

Her eyes widen as she bursts out laughing. She's nearly rolling over and beside herself when she watches my deadpan expression.

"You fucking ran out with his clothes? The hell, Em?" She's still laughing as she scolds me.

"Well, I was pissed to find out he's married! He deserves it," I explain matter-of-factly. I throw them in her back seat as well as the shoes before slipping my heels on.

"Are you sure his name was Drew?" She narrows her eyes.

"No." I shake my head. "I just know that he was in the wedding party because he was wearing the same tux."

"Well, there were eight groomsmen. So let's figure this out. Process of elimination."

I nod. "Okay. Well, I know it wasn't Jackson or John." She gives me a side-eye glance that tells me it better not have been either of them. "I wasn't *that* drunk."

"Drunk enough to forget his name." She chuckles, and I frown. "Okay, sorry. That was mean."

"Continue…"

"That leaves his older brother, Evan, his brother-in-law, Drew—which I'm praying to God it wasn't—Alex's cousins, William and Mason, and his two friends, Dylan and Jake."

"None of those names ring a bell, to be honest," I admit.

"Process of elimination," she reminds me. "Let's start with Drew. Did he have a ton of tattoos on his arms and chest? He has dark brown hair and is really built."

I blink, picturing his naked body and trying to remember if I saw any ink on his body. "I don't think so, but I'm not positive." I close my eyes and think back to when he bit my shoulder, and my fingernails dug into his biceps as he fucked me hard. "Wait, no. His arms are bare."

"Are you sure?" There's a hopefulness in her tone.

Nodding, the image clearer in my mind now. "Yeah, I remember his arms now. Ink free."

She releases a long breath, and her shoulders relax. "Then it couldn't have been Drew. He has a tattoo sleeve on one of his arms."

"I would've remembered that much ink," I say.

"Thank God." She sighs. "I was going to have a stroke if it really was Drew."

"Yeah, I'm glad too." My entire body relaxes knowing I didn't help a married man cheat on his wife. "But then who the hell was it?"

"Five more to go through." She chuckles, finding my misery humorous when I glare at her. "The first time you slut around, and you can't even remember his name. I'm sorry…not sorry."

I roll my eyes, hating that I didn't have enough willpower to stick to my damn rules. "This is why I vowed for no more relationships or men. It always comes back to bite me in the ass."

"Not to mention you stole an innocent man's tux." She snorts. "You know that needs to be returned, right? Otherwise, there's like a five-hundred-dollar fee."

"I'm not returning it!" I squeal. "Am I just supposed to walk in and be like 'Oh hey, I took this but wanted to return it. Sorry.'"

"Well, none of the other groomsmen are married, so technically, you did steal it."

My head falls back on the seat as I groan and curse for getting myself into this situation. "Can't you do it for me? Just say that you found it or something."

"But that doesn't sound nearly as much fun as making you do it." She smirks.

"Kiera Georgina Young! I have bailed you out of so much shit, you owe me!" I point my finger at her. "Should I remind you of Billy Peterson our junior year and the two-hundred-dollar bra you left in his room that you *made* me sneak in and get back for you?"

"Ugh." She groans, curling her lip up in annoyance. "I hate when you use my middle name."

"You deserve it."

"Fine, but then I'm asking whose it is and figuring this mystery out once and for all."

"I don't even want to know," I say, wishing I could erase the memory of last night. Even though the parts I can remember were *really* hot. I turn and look at her. "Wait. You want to tell me where *you* were last night?"

Her cheeks redden, and it's all I need to know it's a juicy story.

"Spill it."

CHAPTER FIVE

EVAN

A HEADACHE that's about to split my head in two wakes me from a deep sleep. My inner doctor tells me I drank too much alcohol and should've had more water. I roll over, expecting to feel a body next to me as the memories from last night flood in. Peeling my eyes open, I place my hand on her empty side, which is cold but oddly still smells like her.

Looking around, I don't see her clothes on the floor, and that's all the confirmation I need to know she's gone, which is for the best considering I don't have time for anything serious. Stella was nothing more than a memory, a good one at that, but that's all she can be now. To think, if she would've still been here, I might've gone against everything I believe and asked her out again. There was something about her I liked, and I stretch and smile at the thought. Thankfully, she did leave, and now we can go on about our lives. I almost understand why Jackson does this often—*almost*.

I reach for my phone and realize it's close to nine in the morning. I can't remember the last time I slept in like this, but apparently, I needed the rest—especially after last night. Pushing off the blanket, I look around the room for my shoes, pants, and shirt and am slightly confused when I don't see any of my fucking clothes anywhere. They should be on the floor somewhere by the bed because I remember the exact moment when I took them off. Knowing this must be some sort of cruel joke, I stand, butt-ass naked and search around the room. After opening the drawers and looking in the bathroom and closet, I realize they're gone, just like Stella.

"Fuck!" I yell out in frustration, hoping no one heard me because the walls are thin. Remembering I left my overnight bag at home and didn't have time to go back and grab it, I have no other choice but to call for help.

In an angry rage, I pick up my cell phone that's conveniently next to my wallet on the nightstand and check my latest texts to see if there are any clues as to who this woman was. Nothing. Not one hint.

Stella and I kept things simple, leaving out all personal details, and not even twelve hours later, that decision has already come back and bit me in the ass. Not really knowing what else to do, I call Jackson in hopes he'll be awake and can bring me some clothes. I've bailed him out of shit plenty of times before, and at this point, he owes me. Of course, he doesn't answer, and I have to listen to his stupid voicemail where he does nothing but laugh before the beep.

"Jackson. What the fuck? You're supposed to answer when someone calls you. It's kind of important. Call me back." I end the call, then make my way down the list.

John's phone rings and rings, and he doesn't answer either. I listen to his overly professional voicemail, then leave him a message too. "Call me back." I hang up and sit on the edge of the bed, wondering if I can take the sheet from the bed, wrap it around my body, and make it to my truck without anyone noticing. Fat chance considering the B&B is full of family members and friends. My choices are limited, and I'm halfway tempted to call Alex, but it's such a dick move considering he's probably sleeping in after his big night.

Not knowing who else to call, I find Dylan's number. Just like the rest of them, he doesn't answer. Thank God this isn't some big emergency, or I don't need to be bailed out of jail or something.

The only other choice I have is to call Mama or Courtney, and I don't want either of them in my damn business. I'd hear question after question about what I did last night and why I need clothes brought to my room. As I glance around, hoping I missed them tucked in a corner, the realization of what my missing tux actually means hits me. Stella stole it, and if it's not returned, I'll be required to pay to replace it, which isn't cheap. The thought infuriates me. What the fuck was she actually thinking? More importantly—why?

"This is bullshit," I say under my breath and try to muster the courage to call Courtney.

I find her name in my favorites, and just as I'm about to press send, an incoming call from John flashes on the screen. At least I can count on someone to return my call.

"Hey, what's up?" John asks.

"I need a huge favor," I say.

He laughs. "Go on."

"Can you bring me some clothes and shoes? Please?" I sit on the edge of the bed naked and wait for his response.

"Why?" He lets out a small chuckle.

Rolling my eyes, I shake my head. "Can you just do what I ask?"

"Only if you tell me why."

I huff. "You're a real pain in my ass, you know that?"

"Considering I'm going to have to stop what I'm doing on my day off to bring you clothes at the B&B, I think it's the other way around. Waiting…"

Groaning, I explain how my clothes are gone, and I can't leave the room. He bursts into big hearty laughter, and the sound of it actually pisses me off.

"You do know that tux has to be returned Monday by ten, right?"

"Well aware," I mutter, trying to hold back my frustration.

"Alright. Give me twenty minutes, and I'll be there."

Though I want to question why it's going to take twenty damn minutes, I don't. Instead, I thank him before hanging up. Knowing I have a little time before he arrives, I take the opportunity to hop in the shower and wash Stella and the memory of her from my body. After I'm done, I dry off and wrap a towel around my waist. Just as I walk into the room, a knock is heard at the door.

I open it and see Jackson standing in front of me. Just by the shit-eating grin on his face paired with his pants tucked into his boots, I know immediately it's not John. The old switch and bait won't work on me. "Where's John? And you look like shit."

He rolls his eyes and hands me a plastic grocery bag with clothes inside along with a pair of old cowboy boots. "Rough night. But apparently not as rough as yours," he mutters, seeming amused.

I set the boots on the floor, then take the clothes from the bag and am shocked when I see a plaid, long-sleeve flannel shirt, a pair of white underwear, and blue jeans with rips in the knees.

"Are you kidding me?" I turn around and glare at him.

With his arms crossed over his chest, Jackson simply gives me a sly smile, and I know he's enjoying this way too much. "John said you needed clothes. Did you specify what you wanted?"

"Was a pair of boxer shorts, pants, and a T-shirt too hard to grab? Maybe some running shoes? Or something *normal*?" I ask, looking at the cliché cowboy suit lying on the bed. This outfit was picked out so he could get a good laugh today. I know him too well to think otherwise.

"Are these Dad's underwear? What the fuck is this?" I hold them up and look at him.

He tries to hold back laughter to the point where it looks painful. "Beggars can't be choosers; I think that's how the saying goes."

"You're a dick," I say, just as he bends over letting out a booming laugh. I push him out of the room and lock the door. *Asshole.* I'm seriously going to have a chat with John the next time I see him.

The towel falls to the floor, and I put on the clothes he brought me. My anger level rises as the pants hug my nuts like spandex. They're so fucking tight I can barely walk. Catching a glimpse of myself in the mirror, I see how absolutely ridiculous I look. I'm a walking Texas cowboy cliché with the flannel shirt, tight jeans that are cutting off the circulation of my dick, and the shit-kicking boots. All I need is a big ten-gallon cowboy hat and a fucking gold belt buckle the size of a plate.

Rolling my eyes, I find the keys to my truck on the other nightstand. At least she had the decency not to steal those too. After I open the door, I look up and down the hall to see if anyone is around. Considering the hallway is empty, I take that as my cue to hurry and try to make it out without running into a single person. Unfortunately, I'm not so lucky, because as soon as my foot hits the bottom step, I run into Jackson, Courtney, Mama, and John. Behind them, I see Drew and their kids, along with River's best friend, Natalie, and Natalie's husband. I totally forgot they were meeting for brunch this morning and can't get out of their presence fast enough.

"Evan, honey. What are you wearing?" Mama asks, confused by how I look. They all know I haven't worn clothes like this since I started dressing myself in third grade. Courtney bursts into laughter, which Jackson encourages.

"Holy shit," John says under his breath as he shakes his head, realizing Jackson set my ass up. He glares at Jackson, who does nothing but shrug.

"I've got to get the hell out of here," I say under my breath as all eyes bore into me.

"I don't even want to know." Courtney looks me up and down.

"You're not going to stay for brunch? Courtney, Drew, and the kids are heading back home soon." Mama asks as I head toward the door.

I lift my hand to stop the conversation and keep walking. I'm sure I'll have to apologize for my rudeness later, but right now, all I can think about is getting these pants out of my ass.

No matter how fast I walk, I can't get away from their laughter quick enough. I climb in the truck and roll up the flannel sleeves because it's hot as fuck outside and I'm already sweating. This is what I get for trying to be like my dumbass brothers and let loose. Honestly, I feel like I deserve this in some fucked-up way.

The drive home seems to take longer than usual, though there's no traffic and I drive over the speed limit, which is already seventy. Hugging curves, I haul ass, hoping to get out of these damn clothes as soon as possible. Jackson has it coming. The next time he calls me to cover for him because he's too trashed to hang out with family, I'll refuse. He made his bed, and I'll make sure he sleeps in it.

I let out a sigh of relief when my house comes into view. Considering I'm practically married to my job, I chose to buy a house that's closer to the hospital than the ranch. Mama wasn't happy, but this is the choice I made for myself, regardless if they supported it at first or not. Becoming a doctor was a dream, and all I ever wanted to do was help people. Not everyone is born with that characteristic, plus I'm good at what I do. By the time I park and get out of the car, it's nearly eighty degrees outside. Shaking my head, I walk inside, unbutton the shirt, and throw it to the ground, then force the boots off so I can peel the pants from my body.

I change into workout clothes, grab my keys, and head to the gym. There's too much built-up frustration, and I need to get rid of it so I can go to work with a clear head tomorrow. That goddamn tuxedo irritates the fuck out of me. After I'm at the gym, I warm up on the treadmill, then lift until my muscles can't handle any more. Just as I'm walking out, Alexis walks in, and I pull out my earbuds and smile. She's wearing shorts that barely cover her ass and a tank top.

"Hey, you, been a while," she says, lingering on my biceps a little too long before her eyes meet mine. Alexis is a doctor at the hospital who works on the cardiology floor. A year ago, she asked me out, and I refused for other reasons, but ever since, it's been awkward between us. Not to mention, I have a strict no-dating-doctors-or-nurses rule, or hell, anyone with a hospital badge. Mixing sexual relationships and work is like mixing oil and water; the two never go together and never will.

"Yeah, it has. How've things been going?" I ask.

She swallows hard. "Pretty good actually. Shorthanded as always, but that's life. I think I need a vacation."

"Yeah." I smile. "Vacation? What's that?"

People are trying to enter the gym, and I take that as my cue to go. "It was good seeing you, Alexis."

"You too. Take care of yourself, okay?"

I give her a head nod and walk out to the truck. My legs feel like gelatin as I open the door, climb in, and buckle. Sweat rolls down my cheek, and I wipe my face on my sleeve as I stare out at the clouds. A thought comes to me, and I'm pissed all over again when I think about last night. Aren't one-night stands supposed to be freeing? Aren't I supposed to wake up the next day completely okay with how things ended? It's exactly what I'd asked for, knowing one night was all I had to offer, but the repercussions aren't worth it. Honestly, I don't know how my brothers do it. It's not me and never will be. This empty feeling inside brings up more anguish than pleasure. Stella's venom is still streaming through my blood, poisoning my thoughts, and there's no anti-venom in sight. She was fucking deadly.

The morning comes early, and considering I've had the past few days off, I decide to go in extra early. No one's going to complain, and I already know I'll be here longer than usual today to try to catch up and get my head back in the game. Not being in the know is the only thing I hate about taking days off. I never know what sort of situation I'm going to walk into when I return.

Of course, as soon as I arrive, I'm filled in about each of the patients who are currently in rooms and look at their charts. One of the ER nurses, Brooklyn, falls into step with me, giving me the rundown as I sip my coffee. Four in the morning comes early but growing up on the ranch prepared me for the early hours and long days. One thing I'll always be thankful for.

"A few patients are waiting for rooms. There's an eight-year-old female who has a severe case of pneumonia and pleurisy. We have the room in respiratory isolation at the moment. Recently got the fever down, so if you sign off, we can move her to the pediatric intensive care unit but continue isolation."

"Which room?" I ask, setting my coffee down by the computer, not even wanting to sign on and finish reading the emails I didn't make it through last night.

"Seven. She's been here since midnight," she says.

Not waiting, I grab a face mask and read over the chart before walking into the room with Brooklyn behind me. Being as quiet as possible when we enter, I look at the current stats while trying to allow the little girl to continue to sleep soundly. Her mother shifts and blinks a few times before giving me a small smile. I give her a head nod and smile in return and continue to make notes, but I don't like the way she's wheezing.

Brooklyn follows me out of the room. "In a few hours, I'm okay with moving her to the PICU, but I want to start breathing treatments and chest physical therapy as soon as possible. She needs to stay on close watch. I don't want this progressing to bronchitis, especially with the pleurisy."

"Understood," she says.

Over the next couple of hours, I continue making rounds and checking on patients. Since a few other doctors are covering the emergency room, I go to the PICU to brief the doctor on duty about the eight-year-old girl we're sending up.

Just as I finish my conversation with the peds doctor, I see River stepping off the elevator with a shit-eating grin on her face. Fuck, she must know something. Of course, she does. My brothers have the biggest mouths in the south. My timing couldn't have been more horrible. I look down at the folders in my hand, hoping she didn't see me.

"So…how was your weekend?" She keeps a hint of sweetness in her tone, but I know better. River is the perfect match for my brother Alex—independent, but has just enough sass to scare any Bishop into place. I honestly don't want to talk about this weekend and was hoping to forget it.

"How do you think it was?" I try my best not to roll my eyes at her because she knows exactly how it was. Great then terrible, especially considering I'm going to have to pay five hundred dollars for that damn tux. Just when I get ready to walk away from her, Amelia, another nurse on the children's floor, walks up. That's when I really become a laughing joke for the two of them. At least someone's laughing, and it's not me, because nothing's funny about what happened.

I take a deep breath and try to release it slowly. River is family now, and I can't be a dick or Mama will have my head. Her rules, not mine. River continues to tell every detail, not letting one thing slide, especially not the clothes thing.

"Damn," Amelia says, her eyes wide. "Who does that?" She chuckles.

"Stella!" River laughs. "He would've been better off wrapping a sheet around his waist and making a run for it because they're never going to let him live it down," she tells Amelia. She got one thing right, that's for damn sure. I shouldn't have depended on my brothers to help me in my time of need. I try to tune her out and find my perfect opportunity to leave.

"Don't you think I've gotten enough shit from my brothers about this weekend? Just *had* to bring it to work too. Go ahead, laugh it up. I'm glad I could amuse you both." I groan, getting ready to walk away, but when the elevator doors slide open and I see her, my breath hitches.

"Who's that?" Amelia asks, looking back and forth between us.

"I'm pretty sure that's the new ER doctor they told us about last month. Dr. Emily Bell. She just finished her residency and has to work under Evan."

My body goes completely rigid, and Amelia and River glare at me, then turn and look at the woman who's walking off the elevator with a smile on her face. Her brown hair is pulled back into a ponytail, and she's wearing a black pencil skirt that's so tight it might actually rip when she bends over. Fucking hell. It doesn't help how her cream top is tucked into her skirt, accentuating her small waist that I had my arms tightly wrapped around when I fucked her senseless.

Of course, *this* would be my fate. My luck is comical, and it causes me to stifle a sarcastic laugh.

"Lighten up before you scare the poor girl away," River says and elbows me, but obviously she has no fucking clue who the hell this woman is. I overhear her asking for Dr. Bishop, and I shake my head.

"What's wrong with you?"

I glare at River with a tight jaw. "That's her. That's the woman who stole my goddamn clothes," I mutter, feeling my annoyance building. I run my hand over my jaw, trying to figure out why she lied about her name or why she stole my fucking clothes. A million questions run through my mind as River continues to question me. I'm pissed.

I cross my arms over my broad chest as she walks toward me with a smile on her face. Recognition flashes in her eyes, and the confidence she had when she stepped off that elevator slightly falters. This whole situation is bullshit. One-night stands with strangers are supposed to stay in the past. As she walks toward me, it becomes my present.

Just as she goes to open her mouth, I interrupt her, and I know she can feel my anger bleeding through. Hell, at this point, the whole hospital probably can.

"Emily? That's *real* cute." The sarcasm in my voice isn't lost on her. I don't regret many things in life, but hooking up with Stella or Emily, or whatever the fuck her name is, is at the top of my list. I should've known better than to have a random hookup, and now I'll pay for it every fucking day I come to work. The truth is, she's going to pay for what she did too. And the look on her face says she knows as much.

CHAPTER SIX

EMILY

I WAKE up with a smile on my face, letting everything over the weekend escape my mind. Today's a new day and the first day of my new job.

When I did my residency in Houston, my father and sister had already made a name for themselves. I was constantly compared to them and lived in their shadows, but not anymore.

New town. New job. New me.

At least that's what I'm telling myself. I know I'm good at my job, but people treated me like I was fragile. Being Dr. Jason Bell's daughter meant my father knew about everything I did—good and bad. I couldn't slip up without it getting back to him even though I worked in a different department and on a different floor.

Though I consider myself knowledgeable in my field, everyone being in my business, knowing my failures and successes, made me want to branch out and be on my own. Work in a hospital where no one knows my family or history. I want to be treated just like everyone else—no favoritism or special treatment. I want to prove to him, and more importantly, myself, that I'm capable of living up to the expectations all on my own.

When I caught my ex cheating four months ago, it was the last push I needed to make the change. I'd been thinking about it ever since I finished my residency, but because my father waved around his magic wand and got me a permanent job at the hospital, I felt guilty for wanting to leave and pursue another job. But I wasn't letting fear keep me there anymore. My dad heard the rumors before I could even tell him about my ex, and once I told him I needed a fresh start, he gave me his blessing, and I applied to San Angelo General Hospital the next day.

Moving from a large, busy city to a small town is an adjustment, to say the least, but I think it'll grow on me. I've already slipped up and had a random one-night stand, so I'm more determined than ever to focus solely on my career and find new roots here. The weekend is still a blur, and I'm ready to forget it ever happened.

Kiera: Good luck today! You're gonna kill it! :)

Kiera: Whoops, sorry. No pun intended.

I chuckle and shake my head at Kiera's messages. After Saturday morning's escapades of waking up in a stranger's room and stealing his clothes, Kiera spent the rest of the weekend with me. Mostly because she wanted to help me figure out who the mystery man was, but it'd be our last weekend to hang out for quite a while. Spring and summer are a busy time of year for her horse training business, and my hours at the hospital will be unreliable.

Emily: Thanks! I'll text you and let you know how it's going when I can! Cross your fingers for me that all the doctors are old and ugly. I don't need any more distractions.

Kiera: No way! Hot doctors all the way! I need to live vicariously through you, so I expect a briefing after every shift!

Emily: Highly unlikely! My life is mostly boring, so I should be the one living vicariously through you… and the vet :-)

Once my adrenaline slowed down and we were back at my place, I finally got the scoop from Kiera about where she ended up the night before. Dr. Trent Laken is an equine vet who specializes in horses and has been Kiera's family vet for years. On top of training horses, they have a ranch for showing horses and trail riding. He's also the Bishop's vet, which explains why he was at the wedding. They ran into each other and had some drinks before Trent whisked her away. According to Kiera, though I'm not sure I completely believe her, they only talked all night long, and she ended up falling asleep in the bed of his truck.

I couldn't even be mad at her for ditching me because any chance of her getting over Jackson and finding a decent man has my approval. I don't know Jackson well enough to form a real opinion about him, but I've seen how crazy he's made Kiera over the years, and if he hasn't made a move on her yet, he's never going to. I'd rather she find someone who makes her happy so she can get over him once and for all.

Kiera: He called me this morning. We're meeting up for lunch! Squee!

Emily: Yay! That gives me something to look forward to later. I want all the juicy details! Gotta go! Talk later! Mwah!

Dropping my phone on my bed, I walk to my full-length mirror and look over my outfit again. Cream blouse, black pencil skirt, and red heels to match my bold lipstick. My hair is pulled back into a sleek ponytail, and I forgo my contacts and wear my black-rimmed glasses instead. Normally I'd be wearing scrubs with my lab coat, but I have orientation with the director this morning before I meet up with the department supervisor.

I packed my bag last night, so all I need is my purse before heading out. It's barely eight o'clock in the morning, and I have a thirty-minute commute to get to the hospital. Grabbing my to-go cup of coffee, I swing my bag and purse over my shoulder and lock up before walking to my car.

My father calls me while I'm driving and wishes me luck on my first day. I tell him thanks, and I thank him again for everything he's done and taught me. He still wishes I would've stayed but understands why it was time for me to do this.

The hospital is much smaller than the one I'd been working at. I knew this beforehand but seeing it now in person makes it real. This hospital specializes in trauma, which makes sense considering it's the only medical facility for miles. Every trauma or patient flown by Flight for Life gets brought here. It's one of the reasons I specifically applied here.

I make my way to the help desk, and the receptionist directs me to where I need to go. My nerves escalate, and my palms sweat as I make my way up the staircase.

Dr. Abbott greets me with a smile and ushers me into his office. He goes over my contract and all the specific details about the hospital and my position. He's the only one who knows who my father is and where I came from—information I don't plan on sharing with anyone else here.

"Here are your new lab coats." He hands me a stack of folded coats in plastic. They have the hospital name and logo on one side with *Dr. Bell* embroidered on the other side. Smiling, I thank him and press the stack to my chest while I try to hold on to everything else. "Dr. Umbridge is the department supervisor, and he should be here to go through protocols and specifics with you. I'm sure we do things a bit different here than in Houston." He flashes me a wink, and I know he's probably right. Though I'm well practiced in medicine, each hospital has their own procedures and protocols, which is one thing I'm actually nervous about. Over the years, I've only had to learn things one specific way because I was hired at the hospital where I completed my residency, so breaking the rules that were ingrained into me won't be easy.

"Thank you again," I tell him, shaking his hand. "I look forward to working here."

"You'll fit right in, dear. We're always understaffed and even more so since Dr. Lockhart retired." He winks again, and I take that as my cue to leave before things get weird.

I make my way out of his office and downstairs, then head to the ER unit. It's actually quite large, considering the size of the hospital, which both terrifies and excites me.

Once I step inside, I ask one of the nurses for the supervisor, and she directs me to a tall man who's reading through charts. I excuse myself and let him know who I am, and by the wide smile on his face, I can tell he's been expecting me.

"Nice to meet you, Dr. Bell." He shakes my hand and smiles while his eyes lazily roam over my body. I shiver, second-guessing my outfit. I wanted to look professional, but now I'm wondering if I should've gone the muumuu route instead.

"You, too, Dr. Umbridge. I'm excited to be here." I pull my hand away and slide it down my skirt.

"I'll show you to the lockers where you can place your belongings, then you'll be training with Dr. Bishop till you're familiar with our procedures."

"Oh, I won't be working with you?" I ask, puzzled.

"No, I'm leaving for vacation tomorrow, so Dr. Bishop will be in charge till my return."

"Oh, got it." I follow him into a room and choose an empty locker bin for my bags. I rip open one of the lab coat bags and slide it over, relieved that it fits nicely. I brought my dark blue scrubs with me just in case, but I'm not exactly sure what I'll be doing today, so I don't change into them just yet.

"Dr. Bishop is on the fourth floor checking on a patient. You can head up there and let him know you're here. He should be expecting you."

He leads me to the elevators and asks if I have any questions before I step in. I have so many, starting with who Dr. Bishop is and if he's from the same Bishop family I just met over the weekend. It'd be nice to know someone or at least recognize a familiar face, though I probably wouldn't remember anyway. Not after the number of drinks I had.

I thank Dr. Umbridge again before the doors slide closed, and I inhale a deep breath. I can do this. *New beginnings,* I remind myself.

The elevator doors slide open to the pediatrics unit. It's quiet with only a handful of employees standing near the nurses' station.

"Excuse me," I say softly to the woman sitting behind the desk. She looks up at me and smiles. "Could you tell me where Dr. Bishop is by chance? I was told he's up here." She narrows her eyes at me suspiciously, obviously not recognizing or knowing who I am. "I'm the new ER doctor, and he's supposed to be showing me around," I explain to ease her concern.

"Oh! Welcome!" Her mood changes instantly. "Dr. Bishop is actually right over there. The tall one with blond hair." She nods to the right, pointing him out with her finger, and when I follow her eyes, my heart drops.

No fucking way.

"The dreamy one," she mutters under her breath with a sigh, though I'm sure she didn't mean for me to hear that last part.

I swallow, blinking, and do my best to hold my composure. Just because my one-night stand also happens to be Dr. Bishop doesn't mean things have to get weird.

Oh, who the hell am I kidding?

The second I glance at him, I immediately recognize him. All the questions that swirled in my mind since Saturday morning were now answered. It wasn't the other random groomsmen I hooked up with; it was Alex's oldest brother, Evan Bishop.

Fucking hell.

I smile, pushing back all my emotions as I walk toward him. He's standing with a few nurses in light blue scrubs, and the moment his eyes meet mine, he crosses his arms over his broad chest. Fuck. He recognizes me too. And he's *pissed.*

Regret sets in on the way I handled things the morning after, but maybe with any hope, we can get past it and move on.

"Emily? That's *real* cute."

Guess not.

His deep voice makes his words sound like a scolding, and that's when I remember I gave him a fake name. He has every right to hate me, especially for stealing his clothes, but I'm not going to let him treat me like shit for walking out on him after a hookup. I don't owe him anything except his tux, which I already gave to Kiera to take back to the shop.

I suck in a deep breath and release it slowly. "And you're Dr. Bishop, aren't you?" I've mastered the fake smile over the years of dealing with people, but I won't let him get under my skin, and I most definitely won't let him know he has the opportunity to with his attitude.

We battle in a stare down, neither of us speaking and the tension in the air getting thicker.

"Hi," one of the women standing next to him blurts out, holding out her hand for me to shake it. "I'm River Bishop. Evan's sister-in-law."

I take her hand and smile. "Yes, I remember. I was at your wedding actually." Our hands fall apart, and I wonder why the heck she'd be at work already, but I don't get the chance to ask before she speaks up again.

"Wow, that makes a lot more sense." She chuckles. "I was just giving Evan shit for his mystery girl."

My brows shoot up. "His what now?"

"Don't you have a job to do?" Evan's deep voice booms, and his reaction tells me exactly what she's talking about. *Me.*

"Come on, Amelia." River smirks at the other woman standing by them, and together they walk off.

"Evan, I'm so—"

"You will address me by Dr. Bishop, Dr. Bell." His scowl is permanently etched on his face, and his cold tone sends shivers down my spine.

"Right. Dr. Bishop, I'm so sorry for—"

He grabs my elbow before I can finish and leads me back to the elevator.

"Hey!" I jerk my arm out of his grip. "You can't just manhandle me."

"You want the entire floor to be in our business?" He perks a brow, and his mouth is in a firm line.

"Well, no."

We step into the elevator, and Evan waits till the door closes before speaking again.

"Then watch what you say because everyone here is in everyone's business. Small town, big mouths."

"Oh, right." I shake my head and close my eyes, needing to get my bearings back. "I'm sorry," I blurt out. "I can explain if you give me a chance." Maybe he'll find it humorous once he realizes it was an innocent mistake? Doubtful.

Seconds pass, which feels like an eternity, and when the doors slide open, we're back to the ER floor.

"No explanation needed, Dr. Bell." He pinches his lips together before stepping out. "Let's go."

"Dr. Bishop…" A nurse approaches him with a medical computer cart. The name tag on her top pocket says Veronica, which I make a mental note of so I don't forget. The sooner I learn everyone's name, the sooner they won't treat me like the newbie. "Four-year-old male came in with complaints of a stomachache, and his mother said she thinks he swallowed something, so we did X-rays."

Evan stops walking to look at the films on the screen. "How long has he had a stomachache?" he asks, examining them.

"Three days," Veronica answers.

"Looks like he's swallowed multiple things. They should've worked their way through his digestive tract by now."

I tilt my head and zoom in on the marble-shaped objects in his abdomen near his rib cage. There has to be at least ten of them.

"Does he have any allergies?" I ask without thinking. Evan stiffens next to me, obviously not happy with my interruption.

"Not that his mother knew," Veronica responds even though she looks skeptical because of Evan's body language.

"He needs an esophagoscopy. After two days, foreign objects can start to cause internal damage or an infection may set in if the body can't pass them through the digestive tract or worse the longer they stay inside."

"Thank you, Dr. Bell," Evan clips, handing the screens back to the nurse. "But this is my patient. Prep him for a balloon catheter," he directs to Veronica who nods at his demand.

"That's too risky on a child," I interrupt.

"Boundaries," he growls. "Perhaps that needs to be your first lesson."

I roll my eyes before he walks away. Struggling to keep up with him in heels, I yank his arm and am hardly able to pull him back. "Look, I know this is an awkward situation, but I'm not an idiot. I was at the top of my class and have worked with hundreds of kids during my residency. A four-year-old won't be able to lie still during that procedure, especially if he's already in pain and scared. If he moves, you could puncture his esophagus or something else."

"You don't know me well enough to underestimate my skills, and you'll need to learn to respect my decisions, Dr. Bell. I won't suggest putting a child under anesthesia if I don't have to since that can lead to more complications. So if you'll allow me to do *my job*, you can stand and watch how we do things here, or you can walk yourself out the front doors. Either way, I'm doing things my way, which will be the safest option for him."

I swallow, his tone firm and harsh. His eyes narrow as he talks down to me. "We're colleagues," I argue, stupidly. "Aren't we supposed to discuss the best options for patients without letting our caveman tendencies get in the way?" I challenge, propping my hands on my hips.

He brings a hand to his chin and rubs his palm over his five o'clock shadow, studying me with a crooked grin. "Let's get this out of the way now, sweetheart. I'm your boss until Dr. Umbridge returns, and even then, we aren't on equal playing fields. I've busted my ass for years to get here, and I won't let you undermine my decisions. Are we clear?"

I swallow, my eyes narrowing at his condescending attitude. If this is how he wants to play this, then fine. I'll suit up.

"Crystal clear, *boss*."

CHAPTER SEVEN

EVAN

After the procedure goes off without a single complication, Emily stands somewhat smug in the corner of the room. There was a moment when she tried to interject her suggestions once again, but after a single look, she shut the hell up. Considering I've dealt with children swallowing toys more than a handful of times, I understand what works and what doesn't. It takes experience to know these things—experience I'm not sure she actually has. I would never do anything to put my patients at risk for a complication, especially a child, and for her to make insinuations pisses me off. We're not off to a good start.

Once I fully explain aftercare to the child's mother and answer a few questions, Emily and I walk into the hall, then I turn to look at her. "It's as if you wanted me to be wrong."

She opens her mouth, then closes it as she tries to stay in step with my fast pace. "I would never. I was just concerned."

"I don't need your concern. I know you're new, but I'm one of the best doctors in this hospital—which I've *earned*."

"I'm not *new*. I was an intern with one of the strictest attending doctors in one of the largest cities in the US. I've done my dues. I've worked my ass off to be here. The last thing I need is you treating me like I'm lesser than."

I laugh. "And I don't need you acting like you know everything."

The silence is so sharp it cuts through the moment like a knife.

"Are you ever going to allow me to explain this weekend, or are you going to keep treating me like the biggest inconvenience of your life?"

I finally make eye contact with her. "That's a great way to put it."

She shakes her head and walks past me. "You're impossible."

"So are you. Take your lunch. I'll see you back here in thirty minutes, *Dr. Bell.*" I don't wait for her to reply before I turn and make my way toward the cafeteria.

Memories from Friday night come in flashes. Her body pressed against mine, and how her lips felt as they slid across my skin. As I stand in line for a grilled chicken salad, I try to shake the thoughts away, but they keep coming, which is goddamn frustrating. Thankfully, the day is going by much faster than I anticipated but still not quick enough. Sitting at a table close to the windows, I pull out my phone and read the missed texts from Jackson as I eat.

Jackson: Fair warning, your ass just got signed up to be in the bachelor auction fundraiser.

Jackson: Actually, we all did. Even Alex.

Jackson: Great. I'm going to have to go on another horrible fucking date that doesn't come with a happy ending.

Jackson: FUCK! Just avoid Mama. She's signing us up for EVERYTHING.

Evan: Thanks for the warning.

Dammit. I thought I'd get out of participating this year because she hadn't said a thing about it. I'm sure Mama already made sure I had off too, considering she basically knows everyone in a one-hundred-mile radius. I've tried to use the excuse that I had to work more than once, and to this day, it's never worked. Just as I close out of my texts and open my email, a body plops in the chair in front of me. I'm actually relieved when I look up and see River.

"How's it going so far?" River smirks as she pours ranch on her salad.

With a single look, she knows the answer.

"It's already been a hell of a day, and I'm ready for it to be over," I tell her truthfully.

River smiles. "It can't be that bad. And only a few more hours left."

I actually let out a laugh. "You mean *five* more hours. That's a lot more than a few."

"You sure know how to ruin a good time." She leans forward. "And I'm sure there's a handful of people here that'd agree with me."

"You better be glad you're family. That's all I have to say." There are times when I'm known for being too serious, and River likes to rub it in any chance she gets. None of the other Bishops have seen both aspects of my life except for River. She understands the medical field and might be the only one who gets me on that level, which is nice. Unfortunately, though, it doesn't excuse me from getting extra shit from her on a daily basis—at work and on the ranch.

Sometimes when River starts talking, it's almost impossible to get a word in edgewise, but I'm relieved for the much-needed distraction. She goes on about traveling for the honeymoon, the baby, and work drama. Once we've finished eating, I head back to the ER. My pager goes off, and a nurse walks up, speaking in a rushed tone to fill me in on the situation. At least there's never a dull moment.

"We have a patient who went into cardiac arrest as soon as he was admitted for chest pains. Dr. Bell is in there now."

"What the hell?" I pick up my pace and enter the room, which is in complete chaos. A nurse is holding a barrier mask on the patient's face while a defibrillator is used to try to resuscitate the patient.

"Charge it to three hundred," Emily orders, rubbing the gel and paddles together before pressing them to the patient's chest. The heart rate stays flat, and she asks for another charge, then another. Eventually, the heart begins beating slowly before moving to a normal rhythm. Oxygen is placed on the patient's face, and nurses scatter around the room.

"Blood pressure is rising," Veronica says. I look over at Emily who is as calm as can be. She gives orders, and the nurses in the room follow her instructions. Moments later, the patient is stabilized, and the cardiologist enters the room. I stand back and watch as Emily speaks with him, giving a full detail of what happened. After the patient is conscious and is told he'll be moving to cardiology, I exit the room with Emily on my heels.

"Dr. Bell." I turn around, but before I can get another word out, she unleashes her wrath.

"I'm not a fucking intern so quit treating me and watching me like I'm one. And if I ever have to choose between saving someone's life and pissing you off, well… you're gonna have to be pissed."

Not sure I really deserved that response, but I chalk it up to being in the heat of the moment. Since that man flatlined and could've died on her watch, I get it.

"You've been here for exactly one day, and you have a lot to prove. Sorry, sweetheart, but you're not in Houston anymore, and as far as I'm concerned, you might as well be a damn intern. You're fresh out of residency."

"What does Houston have to do with this?" she asks, glaring at me.

"Considering who your father is, I think it has a lot to do with things. Bottom line is if you want respect, you're going to have to earn it, Dr. Bell. Simple as that. No one here gives two shits who your daddy is, and you're not going to get any favors because of it. And I refuse to kiss your ass like all the other guppies who knew your father. I'm well aware how all this works."

If looks could kill, I'd be dead, but luckily, I'm already standing in the ER, so hopefully, someone would quickly resuscitate me. I'm sure, by the way she's glaring at me, she'd let me flatline. Her jaw tightens, and she balls her hands into tight fists before storming off. It's obvious I struck a nerve.

Good.

In medical school, I had to work hard, and it didn't get any easier during my internship. There were no favors handed to me because my father was a reputable doctor. Every opportunity I was given was earned. I refuse to allow someone with a silver spoon in her mouth to come in and act as if she's running something. With every chance I get, I'll knock her down a few pegs. It's the least I can do for her sweltering ego.

Before Emily was hired, I was given a rundown of her history, how she graduated from the top of her class, received her residency at one of the busiest hospitals in Houston, and how she just happens to be the daughter of the famous Dr. Jason Bell. She's more than qualified for the position here, but I've learned over the years that being tough teaches people to be better. It's the number one reason I've been successful.

The silent treatment continues for hours, and when she's forced to speak, it's short and to the point. If we're able to keep this up, I might actually be able to work with her without any issues. She's so quiet as we check on patients it's as if she's not even there, which I like. Maybe she'll actually learn her place in this hospital after all.

As we're standing at the nurses' station, Dr. Creevey stops me with a smile. She's older and knows the family, but she works up in the Dialysis Unit, so I hardly see her. She was one of the first people Mama called when I announced I was going to medical school. If it weren't for her talking my parents off the ledge, I don't know if they would've been so supportive of me moving away.

"Evan. It's been so long since we've crossed paths. How're things going?" she asks, then politely says hello to Emily.

"Great. Still the same ole stuff. Work, ranch life, more work."

"You're still helping at the ranch on your days off? How's your mama? I need to give her a call one of these days."

"Yes, ma'am. Dad needs all the extra hands he can get. Plus, it shows them I still care. Mama's doing really good. Getting ready for the big fundraiser for the food bank."

"Oh yeah, you'll be there?" she asks, already knowing the answer to that question. I don't think I could even pay my way out of participating at this point.

Before we can finish our conversation, we're interrupted by a nurse. We quickly say our goodbyes, and once Dr. Creevey is out of sight, I glance over at Emily and watch the scowl return on her face.

She's so pissed at me that I have to hold back laughter. I've somehow already lodged myself under her skin. She's been under mine since the moment I woke up without clothes or a clue to what the fuck happened. Considering I'm going to have to pay hundreds of dollars for that tuxedo, which, by the way, I want to fucking know about.

Before the shift is over, I make it my goal to find out regardless if she's giving me the silent treatment. As we're finishing paperwork at the nurses' station, I notice we're alone, which creates the perfect time to mention it.

"Question." I glance over at her. "Where the fuck is my tuxedo?"

"Oh, now you want to talk?" She rolls her eyes.

"Not really but considering my credit card is going to be charged for a tux and shoes that I'm currently unable to return because a crazy person stole them, I'd like to know where the hell they are."

Emily finally looks up from a chart she's been studying for way too long to avoid me and gives me a death stare. "Wouldn't you like to know."

She looks directly into my eyes, and the air between us stills. I can't deny the attraction between us, but I push it back to the depths of hell where it belongs. If I would've known who she really was, this would've never happened. Maybe if we were two different people who didn't work together, things could be different between us, but the reality is, we aren't, and there's no avoiding her. Considering our night together was based on lies, I'm not even sure being friends is in our future. Sure, she's tried to explain herself, but nothing she could say would excuse the fact she lied or stole my fucking clothes.

"Actually, I would like to know," I finally say, breaking the silence.

"That's just too damn bad, isn't it?" There's venom in her tone, and I know she's still pissed from earlier. She walks away, shaking her head, and with that, she single-handedly started World War III.

If she thought today was bad, well I have news for her: it's going to get a lot worse.

CHAPTER EIGHT

EMILY

I'M ready to get this day over and soak in the tub for an hour. I'm used to being on my feet, but that's not the issue. A certain Dr. Asshole has been fueling my agitation all damn day.

When I return to my locker, I finally check my phone for the first time in hours and see I have a few from Kiera.

Kiera: I returned the tux this morning and did a little digging to find out who the mystery man was...

Kiera: God, I hope you see this in time. The tux was Evan's... Alex's oldest brother. Single, not married, DOCTOR.

Kiera: He works at the same hospital as you...so just beware.

I groan, wishing I had looked at my phone earlier to see her messages. However, it probably wouldn't have helped much, considering Evan loathes my very existence and plans to make my life a living hell.

I hang up my lab coat and grab my bag before heading out. Avoiding Evan at all costs, I double-check the hallway before leaving. Swinging my purse over my shoulder, I focus on my phone, and just as I'm about to text Kiera back, I walk straight into a wall.

"Shit," I mutter as soon as strong hands land on my shoulders, and by the way his nails dig into my arms and the musky scent that fills my senses, I know who it is before I even look.

"I know you're eager to get out of here and all, but you should still watch where you're going so you don't end up being the patient, and I'm forced to admit you." I hear the amusement in his tone, but when I look up, his expression is stone.

"Yeah, well, that won't be necessary, Dr. Bishop." His hands are still on my shoulders, and when he notices my eyes glancing over at the contact, he removes them.

Without a response, he shifts out of the way and starts walking away. I finally exhale, trying to get my bearings together when I hear him call out my name.

"Dr. Bell."

Turning around, I study him for a moment as he speaks over his shoulder. "See you tomorrow."

Licking my lips, remembering how his mouth felt on me, I push those thoughts back and stand straighter.

"Goodnight, Dr. Bishop." I walk away before I can say or do anything stupid. The man infuriates me, but that doesn't mean the attraction to him isn't there. *Which I fucking hate.*

Once I'm in my car, I pull up Kiera's number and call her.

"Oh, for fuck's sake, I've been waitin' all day." Her voice is breathy when she answers. "So I'm guessing you didn't get my messages in time?"

"Nope." I sigh. "Was a real nice surprise on my first day."

"God. I'm sorry, Em. Had I thought Evan was really a possibility, I would've warned ya sooner, but honestly, I never suspected him to be the hook up kind."

"Well, I'm not either," I remind her. "We were drunk and stupid. I'm sure he's thinking the same thing, or rather… I'm certain that's what he's thinking."

"So I take it things didn't go well?" I can hear the cringing in her tone, and I replay moments of our day together.

"You could say that. He was pissed, to say the least, wouldn't let me explain, and basically treated me like I had the Ebola virus. And what's worse is that River was there, too, and witnessed the whole thing."

"Oh fuck. I forgot she works there now too."

I roll my eyes. "Yeah. She heard all about it too. She called me his 'mystery woman' and then laughed when Evan gave her the stink eye."

Kiera releases a small chuckle of her own, and I groan again. "I'm sorry, Em. I know it's not funny, but considering the circumstances of how it all went down, and then him being the same doctor you work with, it's a little comical."

"He's my boss until the supervisor returns," I inform her with bitterness to my tone. "And he's training me on all their protocols, so I'm literally stuck with him until they think I'm fine on my own."

"Seriously? This just keeps getting better and better." She's full-on laughing now, and I want to reach through the phone and smack her.

"You're the worst best friend ever," I deadpan. "How am I supposed to prove myself in a brand-new town and job while my one-night stand works at the same hospital as me?"

"Well I'd say small town perks, but…"

I roll my eyes again, hating that I got myself into this mess.

"Maybe it's not as bad as you're thinking. Once the shock has worn off, you can both work together like nothing happened. Or… you could just take advantage of the situation and make out in the on-call rooms instead." Her voice is light, but I know she's serious right now.

"He hates me," I explain. "He's not going to forget that I stole his clothes anytime soon or that I lied about my name."

"You lied about your name?" she asks, remembering I forgot to tell her that part.

"Of course, I did! I didn't know who he was and wasn't planning on letting him know much about me."

"Except your body." She chuckles. "Evan is a hardass most days, but I'm sure he'll warm up to you in no time. He's probably just pissed about the tux and that he was embarrassed in front of his brothers, but I'm sure he'll get over it sooner than later." I know she's trying to reassure me, but I'm still not so sure.

"His brothers gave him shit, huh?" I should've suspected.

"Oh yeah." She laughs. "Apparently, he called John for some clothes, but Jackson's the one who delivered them, which were all ranch work clothes he would never wear, then when he tried to leave, the entire family was downstairs of the B&B."

"Oh my God." My cheeks redden. Now I feel worse than before. "No wonder he fucking hates me!" I groan, trying to inhale a deep breath.

"I texted Jackson this morning once I figured out it was Evan, and he told me the story. He was cracking up the whole time, and by the sound of it, I'm pretty sure Evan wanted to put him in his place for it."

"That's it. I'm going to make him hear me out, so I can at least apologize and tell him it was a misunderstanding. It's the only way he'll stop treating me like shit." Even though he asked me about it before I left, I was too busy being upset with him to say anything.

"Just explain what happened with Justin and why you took his clothes when you thought he was a cheating bastard."

"I am not telling him about my ex or anything personal."

"Why not? You're going to be working with him almost every day. It's not like personal things aren't going to come up."

I scoff. "They won't if we don't talk."

"There are lots of things you guys can do that don't require talking."

I try to hold in my laughter but fail miserably. "Damn you."

She chuckles, and the sound brings a smile to my face.

"Evan isn't an easy egg to crack, but he's a good guy. He works long hours at the hospital, volunteers for charity and helps host fundraisers, and on his rare days off, he's at the ranch helping anywhere he can. Probably why he doesn't have much of a social life, but I'm willing to bet there's a deeper side to him. He's witnessed a lot of shit in that ER I'm sure. Mama Bishop has told me some here and there, but I have a feeling it's just the tip of the iceberg of what he's been through."

"Well maybe if he wasn't such an ass, I'd want to get to know him, but right now, he's dead set on pissing me off and being a jerk."

"Sounds like sexual tension to me," she teases.

"Okay, I'm done talking to you now."

Laughing, she ignores me. "You're the one who has to work with him every day, so you might as well make the most of it."

"I would if he wouldn't treat me like I'm an idiot."

"Guess you'll just have to show him instead."

"He knows about my father," I murmur sadly. "I didn't want anyone to know, or at least not right away, so they wouldn't assume I only got to where I am because of him."

"They'd be stupid to think that because you're brilliant." Her kind words make me smile for a moment.

"Evan had no problem rubbing it in my face the first chance he got. Said he got where he is because of working his ass off and not because of someone else's hard work. That really struck a nerve." I grind my teeth just thinking about it.

"Oh my God!" she shrieks, taking me off guard. "That's a dick move. Wow."

"Told you! He hates me." I groan.

"Well, fuck him then."

I chuckle at her change of heart.

"Oh wait, you already did that!" She laughs so loud I have to pull the phone away from my ear.

"I'm seriously done with you," I retort dryly.

"No, you're not."

"Wait. You gotta tell me about your lunch date with Trent," I say, remembering her text from early this morning.

"Oohhh…" She releases a dreamy sigh, and I take that as a good sign. "I think I'm in love."

"Really?" My brow arches surprised to hear her talk about another guy like that. "That's all it took to get over the infamous Jackson Bishop?" I tease.

She groans in response. "Shut up. Trent is so sweet. And hot. We have a lot in common, too, which makes for easy conversation. We talked all through lunch, and he made me laugh and smile the whole time."

"That's awesome, Kiera." I smile wide.

"Then he started texting me, and we've been texting all afternoon and night."

"Wow, sounds like things are moving fast then."

"Well, we're just getting to know each other on a more personal level. He's been our vet for a while, but I never gave him a second thought until he asked me to have a drink with him at the wedding. Then it was like sparks just flew."

"I'm so happy for you, babe. Truly. You deserve it."

She releases a short sigh. "I just hope it's not one-sided, ya know? I've been on that side for way too long, and it's no fun." She's talking about Jackson, and it makes me sad to think about how she's been waiting for him to open his damn eyes and see what's been right in front of him this whole time.

"Well, I can't say for sure, but from the sound of what you're telling me, it absolutely isn't one-sided. Most guys don't want to text for hours with chicks they aren't into."

"That's true. Jackson sucks at texting."

"Well, Jackson is an idiot." I chuckle.

"Don't I know it? Ha!"

"Okay, well I'm pulling into my driveway now. Text me tomorrow?"

"I will! I want updates."

"Yeah, we'll see." I snort, thinking of how I plan to kick ass tomorrow.

After hanging up, I enter my condo and immediately get into the bath. The hot water soaks my sore muscles from wearing heels all day, but I'll be in scrubs tomorrow and plan to show Evan Bishop just who he's messing with.

"Good morning." Veronica greets me with a warm smile as soon as I walk in. She's a nurse I'd guess to be in her mid-thirties. Her blonde hair is pulled back into a French braid, and her green eyes sparkle in the light.

"Morning." I smile back sweetly. "How are things?"

"They're crazy as always." She shrugs, holding a cluster of charts in her arm. "Dr. Bishop wanted me to tell you to meet him in trauma room two."

The corner of my lips tilts up in amusement. "Well you can tell Dr. Bishop I'll be at my locker, and he can come find me when he's ready."

"Oh, um, okay." She looks flustered, and I feel bad for putting her in this position, but I will not let Evan boss me around and relay messages to me from a nurse. If he wants me to meet him somewhere, he should've paged me and told me himself.

Once I'm at my locker, I change my shoes and adjust my hair. I unpack the items in my duffel and start shoving them all inside. I grab my bag of black licorice and tear it open, taking a piece before I set the rest on top.

"Dr. Bell." I hear Evan's clipped voice behind me. His tone is deep and unfriendly. I decide I can handle him in two ways: give attitude right back so he has a taste of his own medicine or I can be super sweet and pretend his brooding demeanor doesn't faze me.

I go for the latter, and if that doesn't work, I'll try plan B.

"Well, good morning, Dr. Bishop. It's a lovely day, isn't it?" I turn around and flash a bright smile at him as I wrap my stethoscope around my neck. When his expression softens, I can tell he's taken aback by my kindness. When he realizes he broke character and showed some real emotion, Evan purses his lips and continues toward me in long strides.

"Another day in paradise," he grunts, looking down at me and my bag of licorice. "What the fuck are you eating?"

I hold up the bag and offer it to him. "Black licorice. Want one?"

The face he gives me makes me burst out laughing. "I'll take that as a no."

"You should know that shit is no good for you. Not to mention it smells and looks awful."

"Well, not everything we put in our mouths is good for us, yet many people do anyway." I flash him a smug grin, and when he groans, I know he gets exactly what I'm talking about.

He clears his throat and shoves his hands in the pocket of his lab coat. "You were supposed to meet me this morning."

"Yet here you are."

He releases a frustrated breath. "You need to learn to follow the rules, Dr. Bell. When I tell you to meet me somewhere, I expect your ass to be there."

"Relaying a message to me through a nurse is not the same as telling me. You can page or text me yourself if you need me to meet you somewhere. I'm not going to relay messages to you through someone else. This isn't first grade."

"No, but I am your superior, so you will listen to my orders," he barks.

"So give me your phone then." I hold my palm out, and when he eyes it like it's going to bite him, I continue. "So I can give you my number. That way there's no more miscommunication." I give him a reassuring grin, knowing I have him backed into a corner to give it to me.

"Fine." He hands it over, and I add my contact information, then text myself, so I have his.

"There." I hand it back. "That wasn't so hard, now was it?" I smirk, lowering my eyes to his crotch before gazing back up at him with a shit-eating grin.

"Now hurry up so we can get this day over with." He turns around and walks away before I can respond to his snide comment.

What an ass.

Now I don't even feel bad for texting myself "I love cock" from his phone number.

I take my sweet time, finishing another piece of licorice and rinsing my mouth with mouthwash before I make my way out of the locker room.

"We have a lot to do today, so it'd be in your best interest to pay attention," he tells me without looking in my direction. I walk next to him, and he's walking faster than necessary, which seems to be a common occurrence. He's much taller than I am, which means I have to walk twice as fast just to keep up.

"Can you let me explain about last weekend, please?" I push, needing to get it out in the open, so we can move past it and be civilized since we have to work together.

"We aren't discussing this, Dr. Bell. I already told you that. Perhaps you need a hearing aid since you lack listening skills."

Gah! I want to throat punch him. He's making it real hard to take the high road and be nice to him. *Really* hard.

"For your information, I just had a full physical before my transfer, and my hearing is impeccable. My tolerance for assholes, on the other hand, is low."

He grunts in response, avoiding eye contact at every opportunity.

"A trauma hospital is different than the ER you're used to working in." And, apparently, we've moved on to the next topic. "We get paged when a trauma is coming in—usually from an accident—and then everyone gets prepped and ready, so we aren't wasting any time once they arrive. We're the closest trauma hospital in a fifty-mile radius, which means we often get helicopters and ambulances rushing in at the same time. That means when you're given a position, you stick with it and do your job."

He walks us into one of the trauma rooms that I'd already familiarized myself with yesterday. "Everything we need is in each of these trauma rooms, and it's important they stay stocked. We're fully staffed with trauma surgeons, respiratory specialists, radiologists, and technicians, so we don't ever have to wait for someone to get here. That means the room fills up quick, and it's our job to make sure everything runs smoothly."

"So you're the one in charge, I take it?" Flashes of our night together and how he took charge plagues me, and before I can push the thoughts out of my head, I become flushed.

He quirks a brow at my reaction but doesn't mention it.

"For now, yes. When Dr. Umbridge is here, he's the lead point person and will be the one to direct the scene."

"Sounds straightforward."

"It gets crazy usually, so our job is to stabilize the patient and prep them for surgery if it's needed. Stop any bleeding or administer any pain medications."

"Yes, I went to med school too." I snort, annoyed he's treating me like an intern who has never practiced medicine before.

"This isn't an easy job, Dr. Bell, so I'll need you to be on your A game at all times."

"Well give me the chance to show you before you criticize me then."

I start to walk out, tired of hearing his bullshit, but I don't get far before he yanks my arm and pulls me back. "This hospital is my whole life, and I don't do well with change."

Looking up at him, I notice his pained expression. "Well, that almost sounded like an apology."

Before he can respond, our pagers go off. We both look down and reach for them.

"Trauma coming in. Showtime."

He walks out, and I follow him into the triage where a bunch of nurses are already running around to get beds ready.

"What's the ETA?" Evan asks.

"Six minutes," Veronica answers.

"What's the situation?" I ask.

"Four-car collision with five people being brought in. Three are stable as of right now, but two are unconscious," she explains as she reads her notes. "One is a child."

My heart sinks every time I hear about a child being in an accident, and this time is no different.

"Okay, Claire and Landen, you'll take the first unconscious patient to trauma room one with Dr. Moody. Veronica and Heather, you're with me in trauma room two. Grant, Brooklyn, and Fiona—you'll take the other three and assess their injuries first, then give Dr. Bell or me an update if you need a consult." Evan gives instructions flawlessly and without missing a beat. He directs the nurses to their stations, and they scramble to prepare.

Evan and I suit up in our surgical gowns, gloves, and masks, but before I can ask for help to tie me up, he's behind me, knotting the ties around my neck and waist.

"Thanks."

He only nods in response without making eye contact. I see Veronica is already tying him up, and that's when I get the impression she's his right-hand man. She always has his files ready for him, relays his messages, and I'm pretty sure she handed him a coffee yesterday afternoon.

She's his work wife.

I giggle a little to myself at the term I've heard my dad use about one of his assistants. When you work in the hospital as much as we do, you're married to the people you work with more than the actual people you're married to.

"Something funny?" He shoots daggers at me.

"Are you seriously going to scold me for laughing to myself?"

"This isn't a laughing matter. We have a job to do."

I roll my eyes, but he walks off before he can see me. You'd think the guy didn't just get laid last weekend or something by his bad attitude.

The paramedics rush in just moments later, and the whole scene unfolds. Three stretchers are brought in with patients with minor injuries, and Evan directs them to the three nurses to assess them. An unconscious patient is brought into trauma room one, and when the last patient is rolled in, I follow Evan into trauma room two.

"Transfer on three," Evan orders before counting, and the nurses and I help him move the patient off the stretcher and onto the hospital bed.

"Patient is a twenty-nine-year-old female and was the passenger when she got T-boned on her side. The driver said she smacked her head and couldn't get her to wake up. BP was at ninety over seventy," one of the paramedics tells us. Veronica is already hooking her up to the blood pressure cuff and heart rate tracker.

"That blood pressure is too low," Evan mutters, unwrapping his stethoscope from his neck and listening to her heart. "Her heartbeat is slow, and her breathing is unsteady. Bag her."

Moments later, Veronica hands me the equipment to manually ventilate her, and Evan watches as I push the tube down her throat and into her lungs. I've done this hundreds of times, but with his piercing eyes on me, I get nervous.

"Dr. Bell…" His warning tone has my nerves on fire.

"I've got it," I say, attaching the bag to the mask and pumping.

Once he checks for himself, I roll my eyes when his expression doesn't change. He orders Veronica to check the head wound where blood is pooling, and Heather places an IV in the woman's arm so she can administer medication.

"She has a deep incision near her right temple. Going to clean it up and will probably need some stitches," she tells Evan.

"She might have some internal bleeding, so let's get radiology in here to do some scans while her breathing is stable."

Evan gets radiology within minutes since they're in the next room. Once the X-rays are done and processed, we see she has a bleed in her spleen.

"Ruptured spleen," Evan confirms what I already knew.

"Her abdomen must've been hit pretty hard," I say, handing off the ventilator bag to Heather so I can look closer at the X-rays.

"Or she wasn't wearing a seat belt." Evan's body tenses, and his eyes go dark. His mood shifts, and I wonder what the hell just happened. "Veronica, she needs to be prepped for surgery. Page me when she's in recovery," he orders before facing me. "Stay with Veronica and help her prep the patient, then find me."

He walks off before I can respond.

I do as he says and help Veronica while the trauma surgeon comes in all ready to go. We roll her down to the OR, and once she's securely inside, Veronica and I walk out.

"Good job, Dr. Bell," she praises me, which takes me off guard a bit. I don't even feel like I did that much, but I smile at her compliment.

"Thanks. You too. You're the superhero of nurses." I smile.

She blushes, a small smile gracing her lips. "Thanks, I love my job. Dr. Bishop makes it easy to do my job well."

My stomach twists at her words, wondering if that means what I'm thinking. Does Veronica have a thing for Evan? I mean, I wouldn't blame her in the least, but this is only my second shift, so who the hell knows.

"It's obvious you two make a great team. I envy that."

"We do. It's nice." She smiles wide, and that's all the confirmation I need that she definitely has feelings for him.

Once we're back to the ER, I find Evan and wait for his next order. The other three patients are in beds and all stabilized with minor injuries. The other unconscious patient is a child, and I rush in to help once Evan calls for my assistance.

"She's crashing," one of the nurses shouts, announcing the code.

Evan grabs the crash cart, and I add the gel to the paddles before I charge it to three hundred, and he shouts, "Clear!"

He shocks her chest, and her heart begins beating again. She's so little; I'm relieved that we don't have to do it again.

"Bag her," Dr. Moody orders.

Veronica hands me the tube and supplies, but the tube is too big. "Her throat is too swollen."

"Here," she says, handing me a smaller sized one.

I'm quick to grab it and attempt it once again with no luck.

"Veronica, take over for Dr. Bell." Evan's tone is cold and harsh.

"I can do it," I bite out, trying again, but the way he's scolding me with his eyes has my nerves all over the place. I can do this in my sleep, so my frustration grows the longer it takes.

"Veronica, now."

"I said I got it!" I shout, but it doesn't matter because Veronica grabs the tube from me and pushes me out of her way. She manages to ease the tube down her throat and quickly attaches everything together.

"Compress the bag." Evan directs his order at me, keeping his eyes down as he assesses her other injuries that have already been checked. Veronica steps aside so I can take over ventilating. My blood is boiling, but I know I need to remain calm and indifferent right now.

Six hours later, the ER is calm again, but that doesn't mean my annoyance has died down. Evan continues his bossy demeanor, and I'm so irritated with myself that I let him get to me. I've done that procedure so many times in my career and have never had issues, but him watching me and shouting caused my nerves to get the best of me.

I'm sitting in front of my locker, taking angry bites of my licorice when I hear the door behind me open. I immediately know it's him when the hair on the back of my neck stands up, and I prepare myself for an ass chewing.

"That's a gross habit," he starts, walking to his locker that I realize is next to mine.

I snort at his first choice of words. "Eating?"

He scoffs, digging around his bag. "That isn't eating. It's high in sodium and carbs and filled with corn syrup."

"Well, I could be a smoker. Or drinker." I smirk. "Or I could—"

"Or you could eat food that'll help sustain your energy levels instead of falling asleep on the job."

"I did not fall asleep on the job!" I stand, appalled at his accusations.

"Could've fooled me."

"Your screaming and shouting at me while I'm trying to do something isn't how I work!"

"You want to be an ER doctor at a trauma hospital?" he taunts, stepping right into my space. "Then act like it. There's no time for emotions or your feelings to get hurt. You focus on the patient, and you get your shit done. Bagging is med school 101, so forgive me if I have my doubts about you, Dr. Bell."

We're both breathing hard, and my heart races at an intense speed. Knowing what he looks like under those scrubs has my brain malfunctioning on a witty response. I want to grab his face and kiss the attitude right out of him, but I won't let him win.

"Though considering your last name, I expected more from you."

His words sting, and I know he said them to get under my skin, but I won't give him the satisfaction that it hurt. I ignore him and pretend it doesn't faze me at all.

"Goodnight, Dr. Bishop. Hope you sleep well," I say smugly, widening my smile before taking another bite of my licorice.

I see the corner of his lips twitch, and the thought of driving him crazy the same way he does me makes me do a little victory dance in my head.

"Sweet dreams, Dr. Bell." He reaches for his bag, and before he turns, he grabs the half-eaten piece of licorice out of my hand and walks out.

Bastard.

CHAPTER NINE

EVAN

Blood is everywhere.
On my hands.
On my scrubs.
On my skin.

It's all I can see. The deep red, almost black hue is warm.

I try to wipe it away, but the blood stays. It always does.

The painful, semi-unconscious moans from the woman on the gurney fill my ears. Her body is completely broken, and I try my damnedest to save her. She can't die. Not yet. Not now. The swelling has already taken over, and the light purple bruises cover her body. The cuts on her arms, legs, and face are so deep that all I want to do is kill the motherfucker who did this to her. She tried to avoid the head-on collision, but it was too late. The man who chose to fucking drink and drive should be the one lying here, fighting to breathe, fighting to live. Instead, he's belligerent in another room, cursing and accusing someone of crashing into him. From the corner of my eye, I see the police standing outside the door. I hope the bastard rots in hell for this.

When I look down at her, she's almost unrecognizable. Blood mats her hair, and all she does is moan out in pain. The sound is deafening, one that'll haunt me for years to come. This woman is someone's daughter, sister, friend, and as I study her, I can't help but question why bad things happen to good people.

As her life dangles from a fragile thread, all I know is I have to do something. I have to try. She needs more blood; she's losing it too quickly, and I know deep down she's too far gone. Regardless, I refuse to give up hope that I can save her. Medical miracles have happened. One can happen now.

I try to speak and move, but I can't, even though time is of the essence. Her chances are slim and dwindling, but we have to try to save her because that's what we do. I open my mouth to speak, to scream, but nothing comes out. I try to move, but it's as if I'm standing in glue, stuck to the eggshell colored floor of the hospital, and everything is silent. For the first time in the emergency room, I feel helpless.

I WAKE UP IN A PANIC, and it takes me a minute to realize I'm in the hospital and had fallen asleep again. The day has been slow, so I snuck off and found an empty, quiet room where I could close my eyes. Mistake number one. The fucking nightmares always come back. No matter how much I've tried to push it away, some things can't be unseen. Stress and sleep deprivation encourage the horrors I've witnessed over the years to haunt me in my sleep. I scrub my hands over my face, trying to get a grip on reality while trying to think of something else.

Being an emergency room doctor at a trauma hospital isn't easy. If it were, there'd be more people signing up for this profession. It takes a certain type of person to choose this life, and the things I've seen would make a grown man cry. Hell, I have. I became a doctor to save lives and to make a difference even though it's impossible to save everyone who comes in. It's a hard pill to swallow.

I stand and stretch, then walk down the hall until I'm in the break room. Though my shift ends in fifteen minutes, I need coffee before I drive home. Of course, the coffeepot is empty, so I make some. Leaning against the counter, I watch the fresh coffee brew and hope to God the caffeine works quickly because I need it. After working seven days straight and staying later than I wanted a few days this week, I'm exhausted and worn out.

As soon as the coffee finishes dripping, Emily enters, but her face is glued to her phone. As soon as she notices me, she shoves it into her pocket.

"Dr. Bishop." The rudeness in her tone isn't lost on me. Before I can grab the handle of the pot, she beats me to it. She gets a cup, fills it full, then adds a shit ton of sugar and cream.

"Want some coffee with that?" I ask, looking at her light brown liquid.

After I pour myself a cup, I let it steam for a minute, then take my time drinking it black. When I was an intern, there wasn't much time for all the froufrou sugar and creamer shit. Coffee was a necessity and time was limited, so we got in and out of the break room in less than a minute. I almost felt like I was in hyperdrive with how fast everything happened after med school.

She smiles then takes a sip, overexaggerating how good it tastes. "You're always so judgy."

Just as I'm about to say something, Emily's cell rings. She pulls it from her pocket with a huge smile, and she answers it. Her face lights up, and I'm curious as to who she's talking to. I almost wonder if she has someone back in Houston, a boyfriend she failed to mention. It has me questioning our night together, and why she lied about her name. Then again, I've had way too much fun shutting her down each time she tries to explain herself. I'd like to think she's not the cheating, one-night stand type. Some things are better left unknown.

I drink my coffee slowly, watching her, listening to her chuckle and speak softly.

"I can't wait to see you too," she says, tucking loose strands of her chestnut colored hair behind her ears. "I'm sorry. I love you too. Okay, sure. Yes, I promise. Bye."

Love? That's a strong word to use, but I keep my thoughts to myself.

"What?" she says, picking her coffee up from the counter and raising it in the air as if to give cheer about her sugar water. She lets out a soft throaty moan as she swallows it down, and that sound reminds me of our night together. I try my damnedest to push the thoughts away and forget it ever happened, but it's nearly impossible with her standing so close to me. The sweet smell of her soap and the hint of her perfume fills the room, and it's so fucking intoxicating that I swear she does it on purpose. I can't help but look at her lips before we make eye contact, and I hate the fact that my body even responds to her. She feels it too. I know she does by the way she's fighting with the bottom corner of her lab coat. The magnetic pull is forcing us together, and the chemistry we have is electrifying and undeniable—it's what drew us together in the first place. Emily Bell is dangerous because she tries to push my fucking buttons and tease me with her presence every chance she gets.

"That's what I thought," she finally says, breaking the awkward silence that so easily filled the room. A part of me wants to kiss that sarcastic smirk off her damn face, and the other part of me wants to be a dick and say something I shouldn't. Instead, I choose the high road and try to make my exit. What happened between us before can never happen again. Ever.

"Whatever you say, Dr. Bell. Goodnight," I tell her after I finish my coffee and walk out of the break room. When I clear the doorway, I hear her groan, which makes me smile. I'm getting to her, breaking her down little by little. I bet she's wondering which one of us will snap first. It sure as hell won't be me. Since the moment I saw her step off that elevator, I've tried to push her away. I've tried to make her hate me, but this woman is impossible. Just the thought of her pisses me off and excites me at the same time. I'm pretty sure it's the exhaustion taking over.

After I change out of my scrubs, I try to leave without seeing Emily again, and I'm successful. As I walk across the parking lot to my car, my phone is going off like crazy in my pocket. Ignoring it crosses my mind, but I don't because I always think about the what-ifs. It's the doctor in me who assumes every call is an emergency. It's the first place my mind always goes, and it's not an easy thing to live with or habit to break. As I open the truck door and buckle, my phone rings again, and this time I answer it.

"What the fuck?" Jackson asks. "I know what time you get off work."

"You and I both know my scheduled hours don't mean shit. What's up?"

"Tonight. Me and you. Drinks at Duke's," he states matter-of-factly.

I immediately start shaking my head. "No thanks. I'm exhausted."

"You owe me one. Remember that time I brought you clothes when you were butt-ass naked?"

"And remember the type of clothes you brought me knowing I had no other choice but to wear them?" I remind him.

He lets out a chuckle, which doesn't help his case. "You're right. But I really need to get away. John refuses to go with me, and Alex is too busy being a dad. I'd ask Dylan, but they were worked ragged today."

"And you think I wasn't?" I question him, starting the truck and pulling out of the parking lot.

"Did anyone die?" he asks.

"Not today." Which is true, thankfully.

"Then you weren't worked ragged. Just one drink, that's all I need. I swear." He practically begs, and I know he wants to talk. Jackson is all fun and games ninety-nine percent of the time, but there's always that one percent when he's not. By the tone of his voice, it seems like today falls in the latter.

"One drink, then I'm leaving. I'm not kidding. I will leave your ass to be hit on by all the cougars who want you in their beds," I warn.

"The thought of that is almost appealing." He laughs. "See you there in fifteen minutes."

I head toward Duke's, a restaurant located between my house and the ranch. It's our small town version of a sports bar that serves drinks and food, and during football season, it's packed with people rooting for the Cowboys. It takes me longer than usual to get across town because of all the damn lights, and by the time I arrive, Jackson's standing by the door waiting for me.

"You look like shit," I tell him.

"You smell like it," he says with a wide smile as we walk inside and find a place at the bar.

In no way am I a regular here, but the bartender knows Jackson by name and uses it as she takes our order. I give him a side-eye, and all he does is shrug.

"What's so important?" I ask as I look over the menu. If I order dinner now, then I can go home, shower, and go straight to bed. At this point, I need about twenty hours of solid rest, considering I haven't been able to catch more than a few hours each day. The past few nights I've found myself waking up and not being able to fall back to sleep. It's a vicious cycle. I've been hoping it would work itself out, but this week, I'm not sure it will.

"Are you going to fill me in on what happened with Stella after the wedding?" Jackson asks.

"Long story short, she stole my clothes. That's where you enter with a fuckton of clothes I wouldn't be caught dead in." I groan before adding, "But it gets better." Jackson is a gossip and is at full attention as I give him the details, which up to this point, no one knows other than River. I'm actually surprised she hasn't told Alex, and it hasn't made its way back to Jackson and John.

"On Monday morning, guess who the fuck walks in?" I glare at him.

His eyes light up as realization hits. "No!" He smacks a hand on top of the bar, chuckling.

"Yep. Stella who is actually Dr. Emily Bell. She gave me and everyone else at the wedding a fake name. Emily just so happens to be the new ER doctor that I have to fucking train for the next month."

"I almost feel sorry for her because I know you're being a huge bastard especially considering the situation, but with what she did, she probably deserves it anyway."

Shrugging, I don't deny it. The bartender sets our drinks down, and we order our food. I try to finish the conversation we were having when I notice Jackson is in a trance as he stares across the room. At first, he looks confused, then realization flashes across his face.

"What?" I try to see what he's looking at and when my eyes land on Kiera, laughing, having a good time, I know exactly why he's acting this way. She's not alone. I can't make out who she's with, but it's clear she's on a date.

"Great," he mumbles under his breath, and his entire demeanor changes. Jackson has had a thing for her since they were kids, but he'll deny that shit until he's blue in the face. Everyone knows too; everyone except the two of them. I wish they'd just date and get it over with, but they're both too damn stubborn.

"She looks happy." I state the obvious, and he offers me nothing but a grunt.

"Who the fuck is she with?" He stands and tries to look around the people on the other side of the bar. Then, without warning, he ducks.

"What the hell are you doing?" I look down at him.

"I think she saw me," he admits.

"Why does it matter?"

Knowing I'm right, he slowly stands. When he finally sits on the barstool, he keeps his hat and head down, and I find it way too amusing.

"That should be you over there laughing with her having a good time. You know that? Maybe you should try to get over your bullshit bro code and ask her out. You've only had a thing for her since you were five, and all you're wasting is time," I tell him; something I've told him a handful of times before.

"Well hello pot, meet kettle." He rolls his eyes. "You're not really the person to be giving anyone relationship advice," Jackson says, lifting the beer to his mouth and drinking half of it.

"You're right. But if you wait around, you could miss out on a good thing. I know I did," I admit, thinking about Alicia. She's been on my mind a lot lately, and the anniversary of her death is approaching, which doesn't help either. The entire mood of our conversation shifts, and I can't help but think about the what-ifs.

Every morning before work, I'd stop by The Grind Cafe to pick up a cup of dark roast coffee. It had quickly become my routine after I was hired at the hospital. Alicia was a barista, and we'd make small talk until we eventually formed a friendship. She'd greet me with a warm hello, and soon I found myself going in there just to see her. Perfect smile, beautiful personality, intelligent—Alicia was the full package. I stare at my drink and think back to the moment I decided to ask her on a date—one that never happened. The might-have-beens almost destroyed me.

"Sorry, man. I didn't mean to..." Jackson trails off. He knew how much the tragedy of losing her affected me. I wasn't the same for a long time.

Before I can tell him it's fine, he jumps off his seat and ducks behind the bar again.

I glance over at him. "You're a fucking weirdo."

"Is she coming? Is she walking over here?" he asks.

I look up, and I see Kiera walking this way. She smiles and waves.

"Nah, you're good." I grin because things are about to get interesting.

"Okay," he says, letting out a relieved breath.

Kiera makes her way around the bar and sees Jackson squatting. He doesn't notice her until she's practically standing in front of him.

"What the hell are you doing?" she asks.

Jackson darts his eyes toward me as he stands. "I dropped my, uh, contact."

"You don't wear contacts." Kiera shakes her head while glaring at him.

"How do you know?" he asks her, positioning himself back on the stool.

"Because I've been your friend since you used to pick your nose, Jackson Bishop. I know everything about you. You can return to your shitting in the woods position if you'd like, I have to pee. It was good seeing you." She gives him a sweet smile, and he gives her a head nod before she walks away.

"What the fuck? You could've at least warned me," he finally says, punching me in the arm.

"Remember the flannel shirt and nut cruncher pants you brought me? Now we're even," I tell him. I almost feeling like an ass but not really. When Kiera exits the bathroom, she takes an alternate way around the bar to avoid us. But I don't blame her. Jackson was being weird as fuck. He watches her settle into the booth across the room, then changes the subject to something else. After he finishes his drink, he doesn't order another one and actually sticks to his promise, which, after seeing Kiera, shocks the shit out of me. Usually, he's drinking to forget her, though he'd never admit that.

Once our food arrives, I finally cut to the chase.

"So what did you want to talk about?" I ask.

"It's probably stupid, but have you ever felt like you're just living the same day over and over again?" The tone of his voice tells me he's sincere. Not many of my brothers feel as if they can have real conversations with me, but Jackson always has even though we're complete opposites. I guess that's why we get along so well even though I think he's an asshole most of the time, but then again, he most likely has the same opinion about me. All of my brothers do. I'm the hardass. What can I say?

"Truthfully?" I take a sip of my beer. "Yes. That's why I went to med school. I love being here because it's home. But I knew I needed something more fulfilling in life, something that wasn't the same shit day after day. That's why I enjoy being in the ER. Every day is different, and I never know what's going to happen."

Jackson stalls, holding his beer as he finds his words. "I love working with horses. Breaking them. Teaching them. But I feel like I'm missing something. I can't help but see how happy Alex is with River and the baby and wonder if I'll ever have that."

"This isn't classic fuck boy talk," I tell him with a laugh.

"Yeah, you're right." He chuckles. "Maybe I just need a little more excitement in my life to break the monotony of it all. I'm not trying to get married anytime soon, trust me on that," he admits.

"Go to Key West for two weeks. Apparently, that's where all the babes are," I joke, and Jackson rolls his eyes. After Alex got back from vacation and met River, it was all we heard about for three fucking months. Now that they're happily married, we're glad we don't have to hear about it anymore.

We chat about the ranch and the bachelor auction while we eat, and an hour passes so quickly that I don't even notice. The bartender smiles and gives Jackson another beer, but I'm ready for my check.

"I didn't order this, Shay," he says in a flirty tone, using her name for the first time tonight. I'm starting to think he's not just a regular at the bar.

"It's on me," she tells him with a wink.

"You know what else should be on you?" His question causes her to giggle, and my suspicions are confirmed, but maybe not. Jackson is so bold when it comes to women that it's hard to tell if he's already slept with them or just wants to. When I listen to the cheesy pickup lines, it makes me happy I'm not pursuing anyone and have to play these stupid games. As they continue, I look across the room and see Kiera and her date stand to leave. I still have no clue who she's with, but he places his hand on the small of her back as they walk toward the exit. Jackson notices, too, and he doubles down when he looks back at Shay.

"What time do you get off tonight?" Jackson asks her as she mixes a drink for another customer.

"In about an hour, actually. I'm not closing." She walks to the computer, and Jackson's eyes are dialed in on her ass. While she's cute, I don't think she's his forever woman, but what do I know?

"This is perfect," Jackson says loud enough for only me to hear, but I can't help but wonder if he's talking about Shay or the fact that Kiera is leaving with someone else.

Once Shay's finished serving drinks to other customers, she comes back, leans over the bar, causing him to lean in, and whispers something in Jackson's ear. His eyebrows perk up, and by the look on his face, I can only imagine what she said.

"Can I get my check?" I interrupt their rendezvous planning because I'm tired.

"Sure, babe," she says, not taking her eyes off Jackson.

I hand her my card, then I look at him as she moves to the other side of the bar.

"Wear protection. I'm not helping you with herpes," I tell him before she returns.

All he does is laugh. "I'm always packing."

"I'm pretty sure Alex said those exact words before going to Key West, and now he's married with a baby. So unless you're ready for that, don't be stupid. Also, your ass better be on time for work tomorrow."

"Don't jinx me, you bastard," Jackson says under his breath.

When Shay returns, he smiles wide at her, and I shake my head. The fuck plan is already set in motion—that much is obvious. As I'm leaving, I give him a pat on the back and tell him to be careful getting home, though I have a feeling he'll be at Shay's for the rest of the night.

CHAPTER TEN

EMILY

After ten days of working nonstop, I finally have a day off.

Thank God.

Working side by side with a man who makes me loathe his very existence has made for very long days. I'm still technically training with him, and though I don't need to be watched, he's still treating me like I'm about to light the place on fire.

But it doesn't matter because I have the day off, and I plan to soak in the tub, catch up on my DVR, and drink wine until I pass out.

Evan is also off since I'm working on his rotation schedule, but I highly doubt he'll have as much fun as me.

Sleeping in till ten has me feeling like I'm on cloud nine. You know you've crossed the line from adolescence to adulthood when six straight hours of sleep feels like winning the lottery. Step one on my day off is calling my dad back finally and giving him the update he's been begging for.

"How's my girl?" he asks, sounding more tired than usual. The older he gets, the more I worry about him because he works long hours and doesn't take vacations.

Yawning, I stretch in my king-size bed. "Enjoying the day off," I say with a smile. "It's been a rough couple of weeks," I admit,

"How do you like it?"

"Trauma ER is definitely different, but I love the thrill. It's an adrenaline rush like no other." The excitement in my tone is obvious, and he laughs.

"You know you could've just taken on extreme sports or something instead of moving away," he teases, though I hear the sincerity in his tone. He was sad to see me leave but knew it was something I needed to do for myself.

"I miss you, too, Dad," I say, my words soft with emotion. "How are Annie and Daniel?"

"They're both fine. Busy like the rest of us."

I hear his pager go off in the background. "Okay, well I'll let you go. Give Mom my best." At the mention of my mother, I tense, waiting to hear if he's going to give me a lecture on not calling her.

"Will do, baby girl. Talk soon."

I exhale, relieved when he doesn't bring her up. "Love you."

Once the call ends, I roll over in bed and grin. I could stay in here all day and not feel an ounce of guilt.

Reaching for the remote, I click on the TV and start scrolling through my long list of recordings. While trying to decide what show to start, my phone goes off with a text.

Kiera: You better not be spending your day off moping in bed.

I roll my eyes at her message.

Emily: For your information, I'm not moping because there's nothing for me to mope about but celebrating my day off is another story.

Kiera: Let me guess…you're flipping through the TV and contemplating on even moving from the bed all damn day.

Damn. She's good.

Emily: So? I need some old-fashioned R&R. Leave me alone.

Kiera: Nope. Get your ass in the shower and meet me at the ranch in an hour.

I furrow my brows, groaning.

Emily: And why would I want to do that?

Kiera: Because I have a horse to run out today, and Trent will be there, so if you want to meet him, this will be your chance.

Damn her again.

Emily: That's not fair. You play to my weaknesses.

She knows I've been dying to meet him, but with my work schedule, it was starting to look like it wasn't going to happen anytime soon.

Kiera: See you in an hour! :)

Reluctantly, I get out of bed and take a shower. Knowing I'll be at the ranch and running errands with her, I search through my closet for something appropriate but end up coming up short. I rarely wear jeans since it's always hot, and I wear scrubs ninety percent of the time. Five percent is yoga pants and leggings, and the other five is dressy clothes for fancy occasions.

After some intense digging, I finally find a pair of jean shorts that are way too short, but with no other option, I slide them on. They're ripped in random places, and the inside of the front pockets hangs lower than the actual jean fabric. God. I look like a desperate housewife. Fuck it. I'm going with it and make a mental note to go clothes shopping at some point this decade.

Once that's settled, I grab an old college T-shirt. It's a tad snug, but I make it work anyway. After blow-drying my hair, I throw it up into a high ponytail and brush a light layer of foundation over my face. I'm presentable at the bare minimum, but it'll have to do because knowing her, she'll put my ass to work.

Slipping on my worn cowboy boots, I grab my purse and keys and head out. I blare my music and am excited about spending the afternoon with Kiera. It's been a while since I've been to her ranch, and it'll be a nice change of pace.

Slowing down to turtle speed, I drive under a large sign that reads WHISPERING TRAILS RANCH and head down the gravel road to her parents' massive farmhouse. Kiera moved back home after we graduated, which makes sense considering she eats, sleeps, and breathes the ranch. I smile knowing how much she loved growing up here. Such a different lifestyle than the city, but regardless of our differences, I knew we'd be friends for life when we first met.

"It's about damn time!" Kiera squeals when I step out of my car. I barely have time to register her presence before she's full-on running toward me.

"Jesus, Kiera." I laugh as she collides into me. "We saw each other two weeks ago," I remind her. Two weeks ago, on the night I met he who shall not be named.

"Hot damn. Look at you." Her eyes bug out of her head when she takes in my appearance. "You come to help or work the pole?"

"You're such a bitch," I mutter, laughing. "My closet isn't filled with Levi's and tank tops."

"Well, that's an easy fix." She winks. "Come on," she says, grabbing my hand and pulling me with her. "I'm loading up the horse now, and then we can get going and hopefully see Trent."

I can practically hear the lust oozing from her voice. She's been texting me updates every time they meet for lunch or dinner, and last weekend he even took her out for their first official date. It's been nice seeing her this happy, even if it seems to be happening quickly. No one deserves it more than her.

"I can't wait to meet the infamous Trent Laken," I mock.

"He's perfect, Em. So sweet and charming with a good head on his shoulders. Runs his own vet business and is just everything I could ever imagine wanting."

"Damn." I fan my face when I see the dreamy look in her eyes. "Does he have a brother?"

"As a matter of fact, he does, but he's forty and married to his high school sweetheart."

"Of course." I snort. My damned luck.

"How old is Trent?"

"Thirty-six," she replies shyly as if him being that much older is something to be embarrassed about. "But he honestly doesn't look it. He's so damn sexy."

"He's older and established," I say. "Nothing wrong with that."

"You're right. And it's only five years, so it's not that big of a deal."

I follow her to the barn and watch her round up the horse we're dropping off at another ranch. Before leading him out of the stall, she sneaks him a carrot. I have to stifle a laugh when she tells him not to tell the other horses.

Kiera is one of the best horse trainers in the area and has made a career doing it. She was passionate about training and had clients as a teen, and the only reason she stopped was to go to college for ranch management to learn the ins and outs of running a business. She's been mentored by her parents since she was a kid, but she wanted a degree and to prove she could do it. She was the first in three generations of Youngs to go to college and actually graduate.

"Come on, Spirit. Stop being a stubborn ass." She finally gets him loaded in the trailer and locks it up. "That's my boy. You'll be back home before ya know it."

I sit in the passenger seat as we make our way down the gravel driveway.

"So what else should I know about this Trent guy?"

"Well, he's a really good kisser."

"I didn't need to know that, but either way, I'm glad to hear it. For your sake, at least." I chuckle, watching her cheeks flush. "Is he one of those bossy types or a real gentleman?"

"He's a sweetheart down to a T. Finds any reason to touch me even if it's just my hand or arm, but I love that about him. It really cements his feelings for me are mutual, and there's no second-guessing."

"And the sex?" I arch a brow, wondering. "Lots of chemistry and heat, I'd imagine?"

"We've been on one date, Em!" Her cheeks flame brighter.

"Okay, sorry." I chuckle. "I just assumed with all this swoony goodness, there was some action happening between the sheets."

"We're waiting, okay? Taking things slow while getting to know each other, but every time I see him, it gets harder and harder to resist ripping his clothes off." She groans as if it physically pains her to think about waiting.

"Fuck. You've got it bad."

"Shut up."

I chuckle as she makes a turn and another gravel driveway comes into view. Recognition overwhelms me when I realize this is the same ranch where the wedding was held. Then I notice the big sign that reads CIRCLE B BED & BREAKFAST, and I know for sure this is the Bishop ranch.

"Why the hell are we here?" I ask in a panic, looking around the pastures.

"I told you. I have a horse to drop off, and I wanted to see Trent. What's wrong?"

"What do you mean, what's wrong? How could you not tell me this was the ranch you were going to?"

"Em, stop worrying. Evan only works here on his days off."

"Today *is* his day off!" I shriek, my voice growing louder.

"It is?" she asks, and when I turn to face her, I see the corner of her lips tilt up into a devilish smile.

"You sneaky asshole," I mutter. "I should've known." I cross my arms over my chest and pout like a child. "He hates me and will be even more pissed that he has to see me on his day off." Not to mention I don't want to see his moody face on *my* day off.

"Nah. We're on the north side, and he's probably working in the pasture across the property already." She tries to comfort me, but I know better. I don't get the chance to respond because as soon as she pulls up to the barn, she sees Trent and squeals. Barely putting the truck into park, she jumps out and runs toward him.

Scanning the area to make sure it's safe to come out, I open the door and walk toward Kiera who's giggling at something Trent said.

"Em, come here!" She waves her hand eagerly. "Trent, this is my best friend, Emily."

"Howdy, ma'am." He tips his hat toward me with a charming smile.

"I've heard a lot about you. It's nice to finally meet you." His arm is wrapped around Kiera's waist as she stands flush against his side. She's eyeing him like he's the best thing since chocolate cake.

"I've heard *a lot* about you too." I chuckle, making Kiera blush.

"It's probably all lies," he teases, looking down at her as if she's the reason the sun rose this morning. Fuck. After two weeks and not even sleeping together yet, you can feel the attraction between these two. It's thick and evident, and I feel like I'm intruding on their intimate moment just by standing here.

"Mostly good things; don't worry." I wink, flashing a teasing smile.

"Want help with Spirit?" he asks when Kiera walks toward the trailer.

"Sure, that'd be great!"

I continue looking around, making sure a specific Bishop doesn't pop out, and when I make my way around the trailer, I see a very irritated Jackson walking up.

"Don't touch my horse, Laken." His tone is harsh and unnecessary, but it barely fazes Kiera.

"Jackson," Kiera warns, putting a hand on his chest. "What's your deal?"

There's rage in his eyes as he sends a silent threat to Trent. My guess is he had no idea the two were seeing each other, and it's evident he's not happy about it.

"Nothing," he finally says between gritted teeth. "I'll get him out. Trent has work to do." Without another look, he unhooks the trailer door and rips it open.

"I can help," I blurt out, wanting to defuse the situation. Jackson's face jerks toward me, his eyes widening when he watches me walk toward them.

"And who are you?" His brows rise, the corner of his lips tilting up. *Great.*

"This is Emily," Kiera introduces. "She came with me to the wedding..."

Please don't say it, please don't say it. I chant in my mind as Kiera speaks.

"She's Evan's mystery girl from the other weekend."

I'm going to murder her.

"No shit!" Jackson releases a low belly laugh, and I want to die of shame. "Well fuck. I can see why he's been more of an asshole than usual."

What's that supposed to mean?

"Nice to meet you, Mystery Girl." Jackson holds out his hand for me.

"You too. It's Emily for short." I wink, taking his hand and getting another smile out of him.

Whew. Situation defused, even if it was at my expense.

"So does my brother know you're here?" he asks with an amused grin, which worries me he's up to something.

"No, and he doesn't need to, Jackson Bishop!" Kiera responds for me in a low warning tone. "Just help me get Spirit out, and we'll be on our way."

Trent holds the trailer door open as Kiera and Jackson step inside and coax Spirit out. I hear Jackson mumbling to Kiera, and she gives him an eye roll in response. By the way he's shooting daggers at Trent, I can only assume it's some snarky comment about him.

"That's my good boy," Kiera praises Spirit, rubbing her palm down his nose as Jackson holds the rope. "You be on your best behavior now, ya hear me?"

He lets out a huff and nibbles along Kiera's shoulder. She laughs, and when I look up at Jackson, I catch him watching her with admiration in his eyes. His jaw is tight, and he swallows hard when Kiera kisses the top of Spirit's nose. It's so obvious he has feelings for her, but he chooses to be an idiot and not do anything about it. Instead, he pushes Kiera away until another guy comes along and realizes what a catch she truly is.

Go figure. He's not happy about it either.

"He'll be good. Won't cha, boy?" Jackson tugs on the rope and starts leading him into the barn. Trent helps Kiera shut the trailer door, and once it's locked, he wraps his arm around her waist and presses a sweet kiss to her smiling lips.

I grin as I watch the two of them and am really happy she's found someone like Trent who worships the ground she walks on. I've known Kiera for most of my childhood, and she's like a little sister to me, so if Jackson's going to be a moron and let her get away, then he deserves to feel the anguish.

Jackson returns moments later, his strides long and his expression hard as stone. His eyes flicker to Trent's hand that has slid down to Kiera's ass, and he looks like he might murder him. Before he loses his temper, I step in and walk straight into Jackson's path.

"Any chance you'd show me around the barn? I haven't been on a ranch in a really long time, and I'd love a tour."

His jaw tightens, and when he looks at me, his face finally softens. "Sure."

I follow him back into the barn, and when we walk down the path of stalls, he's listing off all their names. I hear Kiera and Trent walk in moments later and brace for an altercation.

"Laken, can you finish your job, so I can put Shadow back out into the pasture?" He doesn't look over his shoulder as he shouts the question.

"I'll call you later, babe." I hear Trent say to Kiera before he kisses her.

"Okay, we'll let you guys get back to work." She pops up on her tiptoes and presses a chaste kiss to Trent's cheek. "Bye, Jackson," she says and flicks her head toward me, telling me it's time to go.

He grunts in response, waving a hand over his shoulder.

"Nice meeting you both," I call out before we walk back down the path and out to Kiera's truck.

"Well, that was brutal." I snort the moment we shut our doors. "I thought Jackson was going to rip Trent's head off."

"I'm goin' to junk punch him for that," she hisses, her body tense as she puts the truck into drive. "I swear, he's bipolar. One minute he's completely normal and everything's fine. Then all of a sudden, he's this overbearing, protective asshole."

"You know why that is, right?"

"Because he's a guy." She pauses before continuing. "A stupid one."

I chuckle, shaking my head at her. "He's protective because he doesn't like seeing you with someone else. Now meeting the infamous Jackson Bishop, my suspicions are confirmed. He wants you the same way you've always wanted him."

She inhales a sharp breath and chokes when I finish my sentence. "You really can't see it?" I ask. "He has feelings for you but keeps you in the friend zone and doesn't want anyone else to have you. Seeing you with another guy makes him realize what he doesn't have—which is you."

Slowly, she turns her head and furrows her brows at me, and the intense look in her eyes tells me she thinks I've gone crazy.

"I'm serious!" I throw my arms up. "After hearing all the stories you've told me and witnessing his behavior back there, there's no doubt in my mind he's jealous as fuck."

"If he's so jealous, then why the hell hasn't he done anythin' about it all these years?" The aggravation spews from her tone. "It's not like I haven't given him hints. I've basically thrown myself at him only to be rejected. So what the hell?"

"Maybe he thinks he's not good enough for you. Or that you'd reject him? Or he doesn't want to ruin your friendship by taking things to the next level and worries he'll lose you for good if it doesn't work out."

"Geez, how long have you been thinking about this?"

"Sadly, too much. I have no life." I shrug. "You've been talking about Jackson since the day we met, and after all these years, I feel like I know him personally and now officially meeting him has sealed the deal."

"I've dated before, and he's never really liked them, which I just figured was because they ended up being idiots, but the way he acted with Trent is something I've never seen him do before. Considering he knows him and knows that he's a decent guy, there's no reason he wouldn't like him."

"It's because he wants you, Kiera," I state the obvious.

"Well, too fucking bad. He's too late then. I really like Trent, and I'm not going to let Jackson ruin this. Trent's the first guy in a really long time who's made me feel this way, and Jackson's just gonna have to learn to be my friend and suck it up." She nods her head in affirmation. The serious look on her face makes me giggle.

"Where are we going?" I ask when she turns onto another gravel driveway toward a large farmhouse.

"I want to go see Mama Bishop quick and say hello. Is that okay?"

"Sure, if you think it's safe for me."

Now she's the one chuckling. "Don't worry. The men are all out working."

She better be right.

Once she parks, I take in the view and admire how gorgeous the house looks with the land surrounding it. It goes on for miles and is completely breathtaking.

"What a gorgeous sight," I say as we walk toward the house.

"It sure is."

Kiera doesn't even bother knocking and walks right in. I follow her and take in the beautiful, rustic detail of the house decor. "Mama Bishop?" she calls out.

"Who is that gorgeous woman coming to visit me?" Mrs. Bishop asks as soon as she sees us come through the kitchen. "Kiera Young! It's about time you came to visit me!"

Mrs. Bishop is wearing an apron, and her blonde hair is pinned up. She was stunning at the wedding, but even in the kitchen working and baking, she looks exquisite.

"It's only been a couple of weeks," Kiera reminds her with a laugh, hugging her back. "I hope you don't mind, but I brought my friend, Emily. She was helping me with Spirit."

"Oh heavens no." Mrs. Bishop turns toward me, enveloping me in her arms. "Lovely to meet you, dear."

"You too." I reluctantly hug her back, feeling how awkward this could get if she only knew about her son and me.

"So what are you baking? Is that apple crisp I smell?" Kiera inhales deeply.

"You know me so well. It just came out of the oven thirty minutes ago."

"Smells delicious," I agree.

"Stay, and I'll get you ladies some. The boys should be in any minute for a food break."

Oh shit no.

Kiera senses my panic and gives me a small pity smile. "Would you mind if we took it to go? I have a ton of work to do back home and Emily—"

"What the fuck are you doing here?"

All the hair on the back of my neck stands up as I hear his deep, tortured growl. I don't even need to turn around to know Evan just walked in. Fuck.

CHAPTER ELEVEN

EVAN

"Evan Tyler Bishop! You watch your mouth," Mama scolds, but I barely hear her words as I zoom in on the ass with hardly any fabric covering it. I only got a glimpse of her profile, but then I heard her voice and knew. Fucking hell, why is she in my parents' house?

"Evan!" Kiera squeals, walking toward me with a fake smile plastered on her face. Once she's in front of me, she balls her hand into a fist and punches me in the shoulder. "How ya been?"

I don't even flinch at her pathetic attempt to hit me.

"What is she doing here?" I grind the words out, my eyes shooting daggers in her direction.

"Calm down, Hulk. She was just helpin' me unload a horse."

I snort, trying to imagine her doing any kind of hard labor.

"Evan, quit being rude. You're never too old for me to bend you over my knee and smack you with a wooden spoon."

I grunt. "Sorry, Mama."

"You apologize to Miss Emily. She's a guest, and we don't treat guests that way," Mama orders.

My jaw clenches, and my body tightens when Emily turns around and finally faces me. She crosses her arms over her chest, pushing her breasts up and making it nearly impossible to keep my eyes off them. A smug smile pulls at her lips, and she knows I'm pushed into a corner with Mama watching me.

I adjust my ball cap and scrub my hand over my face, breaking the tension of her intense stare. "Sorry. I wasn't expecting to see you is all." It's a pathetic apology, but I don't care. She's not supposed to be here.

"Trust me, it was a surprise to me too." She grins overenthusiastically.

"I was just servin' up some of my famous apple crisp. Take a seat, and I'll get y'all some." Mama doesn't wait for a response before cutting into her dish.

Moments later, Jackson and Alex come barging in, laughing and talking shit before they even notice the awkward scene unfolding in the kitchen.

"Hot damn," Jackson hoots. "I missed the reunion." They both chuckle as if they'd just been talking about her.

"It's a pleasure to meet you," Alex says to Emily in an overly sweet tone. He cups his hat and places it against his chest.

"We met at the wedding actually, but it was kind of a crazy night." Emily takes his hand and shakes it.

"Ah yes, the wedding. I do remember you, but didn't you say your name was—"

"Don't you have work to do?" I blurt, grabbing Alex's attention, so he shuts the fuck up. I don't need Mama knowing the details of my personal life.

"I'm takin' a break, asshole."

"Boys," Mama warns, pointing down at the table for all of us to sit as she cuts the apple crisp and hands us heaping plates of it. "Jackson, hat," she reminds him. I remove my ball cap as well, brushing a hand through my hair that's sticking to my skin with sweat.

"Where's your father?" Mama asks, and Jackson mumbles something about him finishing up in the barn still.

"Mama Bishop, this is delicious." Kiera begins moaning, drawing our attention to her. I glance over at Jackson who looks tense as fuck. He's barely looked at her since he walked in, which tells me something else is going on.

"Kiera, you keep moaning like that, and Jackson's gonna come in his pants," I say just loud enough for the five of us to hear.

Emily chokes on her food as soon as the words come out of my mouth, but luckily Alex is quick to pat her on the back. "You okay?" he asks. The bastard is lucky he's married, or I'd rip his arm off for touching her. The smug grin on his face tells me he knows about Emily, our night together, and her working at the hospital with me. Fucking Jackson. I need to stop telling him shit. Or maybe it was River. It was probably both of them.

Jackson kicks me under the table as a blush tints over Kiera's cheeks. Those two have been playing tug-of-war for as long as I can remember. Shit's getting old.

"I'm fine. Just went down wrong," Emily insists, her face reddening from the unwanted attention.

"From what I've heard, choking is your specialty." The moment Jackson spews his words, I slide my chair back and jump out of my seat.

"You motherfucker!" I fist his shirt in my hands and push him up against the fridge.

"Evan!" Mama shrieks but knows better than to get in the middle of a fight.

"Dude, chill the fuck out," Jackson spits out, wrapping his fingers around my wrists. "You started it with that last comment of yours, so back the fuck off me." He pushes against my chest, and I release him.

"What the hell is all this ruckus about?" Dad asks in a low, deep tone as he walks in and watches the entire scene unfold. "Haven't I told you boys to take your shenanigans outside?"

"Just Evan and Jackson doing the same shit they always do," Alex groans.

"Boys! That's enough. I'm going to wash all your damn mouths out with soap if y'all keep up that language." Mama is pissed and breathing hard. We know not to bring her to that level. I glare at Jackson, and he gives me a smug ass look before we sit back down.

Mama eyes us all as she serves Dad a plate. The room grows silent as we finish our dessert, and just before I stand to clear my dish, Mama speaks up.

"Kiera, did the boys tell you about the bachelor auction this weekend?"

"Oh, is that coming up already? I almost forgot!"

Mama's annual fundraiser always forces everyone to get involved, even when I argue that I can't. I'm proud of her for spearheading the event, but I hate that she makes me participate.

"Yes, and Emily, you should come too. There's going to be a dinner, silent auction, and bachelor auction. If you're single, you could find a new date." She flashes her a wink, and my stomach sinks.

"A bachelor auction? What is that?" she asks.

"You bid on the guys, and the highest bidder wins a date with the bachelor!" Mama announces so casually. This is the worst fucking day of my life.

"Oh wow… that sounds intense."

"It's a blast," Kiera chimes in. "Everyone gets all dressed up in fancy dresses and tuxedos, and then once dinner is over, the auction starts, and all the women lose their damn minds! Jackson always causes a crowd of madness because he's a big flirt and gets the highest bid of the night."

"Of course he does." Emily chuckles.

"You know it, baby." He winks at her, and my hands ball into fists.

"So who gets auctioned off?"

"All my boys, of course. Then some others around town and friends of the family. Usually get fifteen to twenty," Mama explains. "Trent and some of the ranch hands, too."

Jackson grunts under his breath, but no one pays him any attention. No telling why he's pissed, but my gut tells me it has something to do with Kiera.

"River isn't gonna want me to auction off my goods, Ma," Alex interjects, but Mama waves him off.

"Then she'll have to bid on you."

He sighs, giving up the fight.

"Who're you?" Dad finally glances at Emily and realizes she's a new face.

"That's Emily. Kiera's friend," Mama answers. "She also works at the hospital with Evan."

Fucking hell. She knows, too.

"You're a doctor?" Dad asks.

"Yes, sir. ER doctor."

"Just like Evan," he states with a distaste in his mouth. No matter how many lives I save or how hard I worked to get here, he's still bitter that I didn't choose to work on the ranch full-time. I wish he'd understand that the ranch life wasn't in my blood like his or my brothers. I loved growing up here, but I didn't want that to be my life forever. I needed more—needed something that made me feel like I was making a bigger difference—and until my dad can see that, he'll never respect my decision.

"Well, I'm smarter and better than Evan but don't tell him that." Emily flashes a wink in his direction, making his face soften just slightly. Damn. She's going to turn my entire family against me.

Jackson and Alex chuckle at my expense, and I groan as I roll my eyes.

"It's time to get back to work," I remind them. "Let's go."

They slide their chairs out and give Mama a quick wave before handing her their empty plates.

"Hope to see you again soon, Emily." Jackson flashes a smirk at her, and she winks in return. He's fucking dead.

"Maybe at the bachelor auction," Emily teases. "I don't know that my wallet is big enough for you though. I may have to bid on someone else."

"No hard feelings, darlin'. Just say the word, and I'll take you out for a real good time."

Kiera chuckles, knowing exactly what Jackson is doing. He's pushing my buttons and eating it all up while Emily plays into his hands.

"Let's go, asshole." I place a hand on Jackson's shoulder and give him an encouraging push toward the door.

"Bye, Jackson!" Emily calls out after us.

"Bye, darlin'! See you real soon!"

Alex shakes his head as he follows Jackson out, and I fall in line behind them both.

"She's a hot piece of fine tail, Evan. No wonder you've been moodier than usual. I would be, too, if I had to look at that every day and not be able to tap it," Jackson taunts as we walk back to the truck.

Grunting, I probe. "Who says I'm not?"

Alex chuckles while giving me a look. He knows better, but he doesn't say anything.

"Yeah, right. She's too good for you," Jackson mocks as we slide into the truck. I'm going to teach him a lesson with my fist about pushing me to my limits if he doesn't stop his shit.

Alex drives us back out to the pasture where we continue to clean up overgrowth and trees from around the fence line. We talk shit and work our asses off for another four hours until we're finished with at least one section. Mama always insists on making a big meal every time I'm here, so I know I won't be able to leave until after dinner.

"John wants us to come pick him up at the B&B before we head to Mama's," Jackson announces as Alex drives us down the road. John fully manages the bed and breakfast, which means he gets shit for being in the air conditioner most of the time.

"What the fuck?" I growl when we pull up, and I see Emily standing on a stool bending over a horse. Her shorts are being eaten by her ass since they're barely covering it, and all my brothers are gaping at it.

"Hot fucking damn!" Jackson whistles, gawking out the window.

I pull a hand back and smack him upside the head. "Eyes off, jackass."

"Why? You haven't claimed her since that one night so—"

"Don't push me," I warn.

"Or what?" he taunts. "You'll grow some balls to tap that again?"

"You're an idiot," I mutter.

"You're both idiots," Alex adds, putting the truck in park. "Tell John we're here."

"Don't need to. He's the one working Emily." Jackson chokes out a cough. "I mean, helping Emily."

I grit my teeth and shake my head, forcing my hands to stay down, so I don't smack him again.

Following Jackson out of the truck, I walk straight for Emily and wrap my hands around her hips and pick her up off the stool. She yelps in surprise and then smacks my chest when she realizes it's me.

"What the hell are you doing?" she hisses when I drop her to her feet. "You can't just manhandle me!"

"Why are you still here?" I ask, ignoring her question.

"What's it matter to you? John offered to show me around, and Kiera said it was okay if I stayed."

Glancing around, I don't see Kiera anywhere.

"Where is Kiera?"

"She had work to finish at the ranch and said she'd pick me up later. What's the big deal?"

I grab Emily's arm and lead us away from my eavesdropping brothers. She squeals at me again, but I don't release her until we have some privacy behind a shed.

"The big deal is that you're here, and you're at work, and you're always around. You're flaunting your ass around my brothers and getting chummy with my family. It was bad enough that you bailed on me the morning after, but then you had to show up at work on Monday and ruin my life."

"Ruin your life?"

I roll my eyes at her hard stance. "You know what I mean. It's impossible to forget a one-night stand when that person is always around."

"Maybe if you let me explain why I left that morning in the first place, you wouldn't hate me so much, and the thought of seeing me all the damn time wouldn't turn you into a damn caveman!"

"Fine." My jaw tightens, narrowing my eyes at her. "Explain it to me then. Explain to me why we fucked all night long, and then I woke up to an empty bed and had no clothes." I cross my arms over my chest, challenging her.

"I drank a lot the night before, and when I woke up, I couldn't remember your name and worried how you were going to react to seeing me. I called Kiera from the bathroom because she was my ride home, and when I told her the situation, she tried to help me figure out who you were. I told her I thought your name was Drew, and you were one of the groomsmen."

"Drew?" My brows raise.

"Yeah, I don't know why. I must've gotten the names mixed up when I met a bunch of them at the bar or something. It was the first name that popped into my head, and when Kiera told me Drew was married to Courtney, I freaked out. I knew I couldn't be seen walking out, and I most definitely wasn't going to wake you and confront you about it, especially if I was the mistress."

"Okay that explains you leaving, but what about my clothes?"

"Well I didn't want to be the one to break the news to anyone. I didn't see a bag or any personal items in the room, so I figured if you didn't have any clothes, you'd get busted and wouldn't get away with cheating on your wife. You'd have to call someone for help and explain why you were there."

"So let me get this straight. You thought I was Drew who's actually married to my sister and to get even at me for 'cheating,' you took my clothes with the hope I'd get busted?"

She thinks about it for a minute before nodding. "Precisely, yes."

I pull my hands back behind my head and exhale a deep breath. "Jesus Christ."

"I'm sorry, I didn't know! I had no idea who you were, and by the time I realized you weren't Drew, it was too late. Kiera told me he has tattoos and dark hair, which is why I had her return the tux Monday morning. Then, of course, she found out it was actually you, but it was too damn late because I was already at work."

"She couldn't have told you those details earlier?" I groan.

"I know, trust me, I know. I should've asked her to describe him to me, or I should've described you to her, but I was freaking out, okay? I don't do one-night stands, so—"

"Then why the hell did you agree to it?" I growl, pinning my eyes to her as I step into her space. She's seriously testing my willpower with those cutoff shorts and her delectable lips.

Her breath hitches as I cage her in with my arms against the shed. Her back presses against the cool metal as her eyes stare into mine.

"I don't know… I guess I was looking for a good time. Kiera had ditched me, I was drinking, and you were so…"

"So what?" I ask, my voice lowers as my face inches toward hers.

"So… fun and charming. You looked so good in your tux, and you were seducing me with your eyes all evening long. I couldn't help but fantasize about what you'd feel like on top of me, pinning me down with your weight, kissing me, touching me. You were flirting with me, and it was the first time in months a guy had paid any attention to me who didn't make me want to junk punch them."

The last shred of my willpower breaks as she talks about that night, and I press my mouth to hers, capturing her in a desperate and heated kiss. My hand cups her cheek, and as I hold her in place, I press my tongue between her lips, seeking permission. Her body relaxes, and she moans against my lips, giving me all the permission I need. It's a kiss filled with want and desire, and the heat shoots straight to my dick the moment she grabs my shirt and pulls my body against hers.

With her body still against the cool metal, she falls into my chest, greedily taking everything I'm giving her. I suck on her lower lip and groan when she brushes her hand under my ball cap and threads her fingers into my hair.

I'm lost in the moment, and as soon as I hear my brothers laugh in the distance, I quickly remember where we are and release her.

Her breathing is rapid, and as she tries to catch it, I smooth a hand down my shirt to adjust myself. That definitely got out of hand way too quickly. Fuck. I didn't mean for that to happen, though I can't say I haven't thought about kissing the sass out of her a couple of times at work.

"I imagine guys being all over you all the time," I say, breaking the silence and returning to our previous conversation before I lost all self-control. "Fuck, look at the way my brothers have been acting. They're like dogs in heat."

She chuckles softly; the sweet sound makes me grow harder.

"I caught my ex cheating four months ago, and when I walked in on him and the other woman together, I grabbed his scrubs and pager and ran. It was in the hospital we both worked at, so he was basically stranded in one of the on-call rooms."

My brows shoot up to my hairline, shocked at her honesty, and the fact that any guy would be stupid enough to cheat on her.

"You took his clothes and left him in the on-call room?" I chuckle, shaking my head at her admission.

She bites down on her lower lip. "Yeah, I was completely blindsided by it and hadn't really recovered from it, which is why when we met I wasn't looking for anything serious. So when you propositioned me for one night, I couldn't say no." She lowers her eyes as if she's embarrassed to admit it.

Pressing my fingers to her chin, I tilt her head up until her eyes lock back on mine. "Your ex is a fucking idiot for cheating on you and an even bigger idiot for doing it at the same place you worked. He obviously didn't appreciate what he had." The words effortlessly flow out of me, yet I hadn't meant to say them aloud to her.

"Well I found out afterward that he got herpes, so it soothes the burn a little." Her lips tilt up, cracking a smile.

"How'd he end up getting out of the room anyway?" I ask, curiously.

"He took the sheet from one of the beds and wrapped it around himself, so he could walk to his locker, but it was three floors away." Her laughter becomes contagious, and soon I'm laughing too.

"I really am sorry," she says, wrapping a hand around my arm. "I heard what happened with Jackson bringing you clothes and your entire family being downstairs when you were trying to leave."

I cringe, hating that she knows the story. Why can't anyone keep their damn mouths shut around here?

"Don't worry about it. I plan to get even with you." I wink, though I'm only half-joking.

"Evan!" She squeals, bringing a hand up to swat me in the chest, but I see it coming and catch her wrist. I pull her body closer and wrap my other arm around her waist until there's no space left between us. When I run my nose along her cheek and bring my lips to her ear, her breath hitches.

"From now on, you wear clothes that actually cover your ass and tits, understand? I don't need my brothers gaping at you and giving me shit over it nonstop."

"What's it matter what I'm wearing? It's my day off," she reminds me.

I lower my eyes, getting the perfect view of her gorgeous tits. "Because, *Dr. Bell,* seeing you in those things you call shorts and wearing cowboy boots gives them ideas. Ideas of what your tits would look like bouncing on top of them and ideas of your boot-covered legs wrapped around their necks as they bury their faces between your legs." I feel her body shiver. "Like I said. Bad, *bad* ideas."

She swallows, her chest rising and falling as she takes in my words. I don't miss the way she cringes when I don't call her by her first name. It doesn't matter that we slept together; the reality is that I'm still her boss and we still work together.

"Are you sure you're not the one with those ideas, *Dr. Bishop*?"

I smirk, the corner of my lips tilting up slowly. "I don't need to have ideas. I already know."

CHAPTER TWELVE

EMILY

AFTER YESTERDAY'S EVENTS, I'm actually nervous about work this morning. Things got intense at the ranch really quick, and I'm not sure I'm ready to face him after all of that. During my commute, I think about Evan—about what he said and how his lips felt pressed against mine. My heart rate quickens every time the thought of him consumes my mind, which doesn't surprise me. He's sexy, smart, and the way he says my name in that deep, silky smooth Southern drawl makes my traitorous body react. And if I'm truthful, I hate him for it.

I had two rules when I moved here, and I'm pissed at myself that I broke them within the first week. No random hookups and no dating a co-worker—it should've been a simple plan.

After finding a parking spot, I grab my duffel bag, then get out of the car and walk toward the employee entrance of the hospital. Once I've changed into my scrubs, I realize I left my phone in the passenger seat. Damn. Oh well. I'll go out and grab it on my break because while I don't use it during work hours, I somewhat feel lost without it.

As I'm walking down the hall that leads to the nurses' station, I see Evan chatting with Veronica. When he looks over at me, he slowly lifts one eyebrow, and the ghost of a smile lingers on his lips. The memories of yesterday cause heat to course through my body, and I try to push them away, but they're running on repeat in my head.

Fuck, I'm doomed, I really am, and all it took was one look.

I grab my pager, clip it onto my lab coat pocket, and smile at Veronica. Evan's expression hardens, and he's instantly back to his cold, hardass self, but he's not fooling me anymore. Yesterday I found the chink in his armor, and it's cowboy boots and cutoff shorts.

"Dr. Bell. Nice of you to join us this morning." He glances down at his watch.

"I'm not late," I defend, knowing I left home with plenty of time to spare.

Veronica pinches her lips together and looks at Evan and me.

"Ten minutes early is being on time. If you arrive when your shift starts, you're late. And if you're late again, you're fired. Please make sure you're taking this seriously, Dr. Bell. You're not an intern anymore, right? We have a job to do, so it's important you're punctual."

I let out a frustrated huff because he's a bigger dick than usual. I didn't imagine yesterday, right? Pretty sure I was kissed like I was his lifeline and now today… *this*. I roll my eyes at him. "Whatever you say, *Dr. Bishop*."

"Now back to what I was saying," Veronica interrupts before we can continue. Over the last week, she's become immune to our constant bickering and has found ways to veer the conversation away from the jabs we instinctively throw at each other. When we're wearing our lab coats, it's as if there's no history between us. The secret moments we shared are just that.

I don't expect him to hold my hand at work or announce to the whole world what we've done behind closed doors, but damn, a little respect would be appreciated. The tone he set for the day puts me in an irritable mood. I don't know what I expected, honestly, but I hoped it wouldn't be a repeat of last week. Unfortunately, I don't think I'm going to be so lucky.

The morning seems to go by so fucking slow. It gives plenty of opportunity for Evan to ride my ass on every little thing, and by the time I take my break, I'm so annoyed that I need to walk away. Remembering my phone in the car, I walk outside to grab it and see if I have any messages from Kiera. It's one of the only things I look forward to lately. I might as well adopt five cats and learn to knit because I'm so single that becoming a cat lady is in my future. The weekly engagements and pregnancy announcements on my friend's list drive that fact home.

Before I open the door to my car, I see a bouquet of colorful tulips lying on the hood. A smile hits my lips, and I look for a card or something that says who they're from, but I don't find anything. I hurry and unlock my car then grab my phone and take a picture. Of course, Kiera had already sent me at least ten text messages telling me all about her lunch date with Trent and how much she likes him. I send the photo to her and instantly see her text bubble pop up.

Kiera: Ooh! Who are they from?

Emily: Not sure? No note or anything.

Kiera: My money's on Evan :)

I actually laugh out loud at that one.

Emily: LOL... doubtful. He's been a bigger ass today than usual.

Kiera: Probably why he wants to make it up to you ;)

I'm five seconds away from telling her to stop sending me smiling and winking face emojis, but then I contemplate the thought of these actually being from Evan.

Emily: Is he a flowers kind of guy? He seems like a giant confusing asshole kind of guy to me.

I don't need to go into detail for Kiera to know about the magnitude of his mood swings, and after telling her all about our encounter at the ranch yesterday, she's just as confused about him as I am. Men say women should come with a manual. Pfft. Men are the ones who can turn off their emotional radar and go from hot to cold in point five seconds.

Kiera: I don't know. I can't remember the last time I heard he was

dating someone, so I'm no help there, but considering the moment you two shared yesterday, I wouldn't cross him off as a potential sender.

Hmm. The thought of Evan not dating in a while pleases me, but I wouldn't admit something like that to him.

Kiera: And maybe it's a peace offering for having to pretend nothing's happening between you two when he's your boss. Like a secret he has to keep, and the only way he can separate that is by overcompensating his asshole ways at work.

Maybe she's right. It makes sense now that I'm thinking it over. And if she is, I probably shouldn't bring these flowers back to the ER, but I do anyway because I want to see the look on his face and gauge his reaction. He'll either pretend they don't exist or he'll ask about them, and then I'll have my answer.

I lock my car and head back inside, then grab my sandwich and bag of black licorice from my locker. As I'm on my way to the break room, I pass Evan with the flowers in my hand and a smug smile on my face. Of course, he turns around, and I feel him walking behind me.

Showtime.

I sit at a small table and take my sandwich out of the Ziploc bag, remaining silent. He stands next to me, looks at the flowers, then back at me. His lips in a firm line as he places his hands on his hips and glares. "Who the fuck are those from?"

I actually laugh out loud again. "None of your damn business," I say around a bite of my sandwich, pretending I'm already bored with this conversation.

Tilting his head, he searches my face before lowering his palms to the table and drops his voice low enough for only me to hear. "Emily." His tone is a warning, but I'm not taking the bait.

"It's Dr. Bell," I say, amused by his irritation.

He grunts. "Don't push me."

Rolling my eyes, I grab a piece of licorice and take a bite. "Quit playing, Evan. I know they're from you."

He narrows his eyes, studying me, and stands up straight with his arms crossed over his chest. "Those aren't from me."

I swallow hard and can tell he's serious. My mind goes down the list of everyone who could possibly send me flowers, and I come up with nothing. If it were my skeezy ass ex, he'd send a stupid note with something he plagiarized from the internet and would make sure they were delivered where an audience could see what he had done. Egotistical asshole. If it were my parents, they'd leave a note and have it delivered to the hospital too. The fact they were just left on my car is strange, but I try to blow it off for now. Perhaps someone put them on my car by accident, thinking it was someone else's, but I don't say that aloud. He doesn't need to know that's probably the best-case scenario since my life revolves around working and very little social interaction outside the hospital and Kiera.

"I guess I have a secret admirer then. I wonder who it could be?" I tease, knowing it's eating at him by the way his jaw clenches. "Maybe Matthew, the surgical assistant?" I smile, taking another obnoxious bite of licorice. With each ticking second, his stare becomes lethal. All these damn Bishop boys are exactly the same. Yesterday, Jackson acted the same way—possessive and pissed off—but the difference is he and Kiera actually have some sort of friendship and history. What Evan and I have is…honestly, I don't know what it is. Complicated?

I notice he's staring at me, so I continue taunting him. "Maybe it's Jeffery. The cardiologist. He was really flirty the other day," I add in my best serious tone, glancing back at him.

"He's fucking married," Evan says between gritted teeth. His eyes darken, and I know he's seconds away from snapping.

Damn.

"Oh. Hmm." I tap my finger on my lips and think of all the people who've been overly nice since I've arrived. Shrugging, I go back to eating my lunch as if it's no concern. Evan groans, looking like he might actually implode, then walks out of the break room shaking his head. This reaction makes me want to order myself flowers once a week just so I can get under his skin, but I'm not an asshole. The thought makes me laugh though.

As I'm finishing my sandwich, I look back at the flowers. The sweet smell of them fills the small room, and when I inhale deeply, the scent brings up a moment in my life I haven't thought about in over a year.

It was raining hard as I drove to the funeral home. I'll never forget how much water was on the road as I traveled across town to pay my respects to my deceased patient, Susan, and her family. I should've let it go. I shouldn't have shown up, because there's a fine line I should walk as a professional, but this felt different. It felt *personal*. When I walked inside, the room was filled with tulips, and the scent, to this day, has always reminded me of her.

If I could go back to that day and change what happened, I would go in a heartbeat. It all boiled down to miscommunication from the doctor on the previous shift, but since she didn't die on his watch, he wiped his hands clean of it. I was told her diagnosis was nothing more than flu-like symptoms with a rash, and her condition wasn't life-threatening at the moment. She wasn't a top priority since we had a room full of patients waiting to be seen.

I was instructed to monitor Susan's fever due to it being too high, and she wasn't to be discharged until it went down, and she was stable. She was given fluids to keep her hydrated and medication to help with her symptoms. The flu was spreading like wildfire, and we'd had a record number of patients come to the ER with it. After I did my rounds, the day transformed into a complete clusterfuck due to a seven-car pileup. Sixteen people were admitted, which kept us busier than usual.

Richard, the patient's husband, was determined that something else was wrong with his wife. Her rash had spread, but I was told by the previous doctor that he had done a full exam on her along with collecting all of her medical history. She had no known reason to have a bacterial infection, so I had nothing else to go on. Richard insisted we do more tests, and though I tried to explain this strain of the flu was one of the worst we'd seen in years, he was adamant we do more. The signs were clear, or so I thought, that it was just a bad virus. My supervisor denied any further testing, considering we were already tackling extra patients and were short staffed due to other doctors and nurses having the flu.

Susan's husband became irate, but nothing more could be done. My hands were tied, and we couldn't do anything except monitor her stats. The virus had to work its way out, and she needed a few days to recover. I made sure she was comfortable before checking on my other patients, and by the time I made it back to her room, she was weak and noticeably worse. Her fever had risen, and her stats had all fallen. By the time I realized what was happening, that she was showing symptoms of toxic shock syndrome, her blood pressure had dropped so low that she went into cardiac arrest. I immediately hit the code and lowered the head of her bed. A nurse brought in the crash cart, and I attempted to resuscitate her four times… but it was too late.

Richard became hysterical. Nurses had to remove him from the room as we called her time of death. He started spewing threats at me and fighting the nurses who tried to block him from me. I sympathized with him, realizing his grief, but I never expected the levels he'd take it.

Knowing he'd just lost his wife, I understood his anger but was completely taken off guard when he made a huge scene at the funeral home. He blamed me; he still blames me. Things got out of hand quickly, and he threatened me every chance he could. It got to the point where I had to get a restraining order on him, so if he went the hospital or near my home, I could call the police, and he'd be arrested. Since the day he got served with the paperwork, he's left me alone, thank God. But that doesn't help the memories of losing Susan go away. I was angry, too, hurt, and confused. The doctor who admitted her had lied about doing a full exam and had I known she had symptoms for the past seventy-two hours and a preexisting skin infection, I would've ordered more tests to check for bacteria in the blood. But it was never in her chart when he passed it on to me.

I think back to that day and wished I would've asked more questions. I should've asked more questions and not rushed to conclusions, but I trusted that doctor. I blindly trusted all of the staff and ended up learning a very hard lesson.

I close my eyes tightly and try to push the thoughts away and actually become repulsed by the smell of the tulips lying on the table because it brings too many bad memories to the surface. Just as I stand to throw them in the trash, my pager goes off, and my head is instantly back in the game. I run down the hallway and see all the triage nurses getting into position. Finding Evan, he gives me a quick rundown of the situation.

"House fire. The entire family is badly burned, but the father is the worst. Possible smoke inhalation. Two adults and three children," he says, before quickly turning to one of the triage nurses.

"I need scrub techs, plastics, anesthesiologists, and I need a burn care nurse down here immediately. Everyone needs to be lined up because time will be limited once they arrive."

Evan stays calm, and every move he makes is calculated. Within minutes, two ambulances pull up, and I make eye contact with one of the paramedics as she speaks with Missy, one of the triage nurses. By the look on her face, I know this isn't good. As they're unloaded, it takes Missy less than thirty seconds before she's calling red tags for each family member, which means they can't survive without immediate assistance. Gurneys are swiftly pushed through the hallway, and Evan is directing nurses and interns to trauma rooms. The ER is in calm chaos, running like a fine-tuned machine, but I can't deny the worry I feel when I take one look at the father. I've barely dealt with burn victims. We had a renowned burn center in Houston where patients with severe burns went. I'm so out of my element that I start to internally panic as I understand the severity of their condition.

"We're going to need advanced life support; he's having trouble breathing. Massive swelling. Intubation is needed, or his airway will close," Evan demands as the gurney is wheeled into a trauma room. The nurses move in place, taking his direction. I open my mouth and close it, not able to find my words after witnessing how charred and melted the man's skin is. Sure, I did case studies on burn victims in med school but never witnessed anything of this magnitude. His legs are covered in blood, soaking the fabric of what's left of his jeans. The sounds that rip from his throat are ear-piercing. I'm sure it hurts him more than anything, but that's the body's natural response.

"Dr. Bell. Get your head out of your ass! You need to move," he snaps, and I pick up my pace and follow closely behind him.

Once inside the room, one nurse hooks up an IV to give massive amounts of fluids to help save his kidneys. Pain medication is administered to keep him comfortable. Seconds later, Evan is standing over the patient and gently places the tube down his throat. The ventilator kicks on and helps him breathe. Oxygen levels rise almost immediately.

Nurses move around Evan and begin measuring the percentage of burns on the body. I stand to the side, not wanting to interrupt their flow, but I feel so useless.

"Dr. Bell, get over here," Evan demands. It feels like all hell is breaking loose around me, and I have to remind my feet to move.

I walk closer, really getting a look at the skin and how bad the burns are. As I look down his body, I see the lower half of his leg's severed. The heat of the fire burned right through his skin.

"There's nasal singeing," Veronica adds. "Sixty-five percent burns, lower half of the body is the worst. Epidermis and dermis are badly damaged. Severe blistering. We actually have both second and third degree."

"Page Dr. Dursley and get trauma surgery down here," Evan tells another nurse. Everything happens so fast, yet it all feels like we're moving in slow motion. The patient is sedated, but his legs worry me the most. The way they're bleeding and exposed places him at a higher risk of infection and amputation.

"You should page the orthopedic surgeon," I suggest, looking up at Evan's hard stare. The patient's leg is in bad shape, and without a doubt, he'll need surgery.

"I need sterile sheets, saline bottles, and blankets NOW!" Evan yells, ignoring my words completely. Within minutes, all the items he requested are being handed over.

"He's going into shock. Blood pressure is dropping," Evan explains in a rushed tone.

"Hypovolemic shock?" I question. He just rolls his eyes at me and continues giving orders. "We have to get started on a transfusion right away. He's lost too much already. I need O negative blood stat!"

Claire rushes out of the room to retrieve the blood.

After he's finished giving instructions, I add my suggestion. "We need a dopamine drip." This time, he nods in agreement, and Fiona rushes around to grab the supplies just as Claire returns. Another line is started for the blood transfusion, and once that's inserted, Fiona begins administering the medicine while Dr. Dursley, the burn victim specialist, enters and starts assessing his burns. Dr. Vance, the trauma surgeon, enters next to help. The burns are extensive, and once all the supplies are in place, they begin debriding the burnt skin tissue. I swallow hard as I watch him peel layers off his body like shaved meat. I've never seen anything like it, but I swallow down the bile that threatens to surface and try to get my head back in the game.

The patient's heartrate begins to increase steadily and so does his blood pressure. I consider it a small win, but there's so much more that still needs to be done for his recovery.

Lines and tubes are all over the place. The man is hanging on by a thread, but at least he's more stable now.

"His right foot is ghost white," Dr. Dursley says softly to Evan, but since I'm standing next to him, I hear the sadness in his tone.

"No blood flow," Evan confirms, shaking his head. "Shit."

"I'm concerned about his exposure to infection if we don't get the blood flowing. The longer his foot goes without it, the higher the chance an infection will get into his blood," Dr. Vance adds.

"He might already have an infection," Evan states. "Still waiting on the blood test results."

"My guess you could be right. After assessing how bad his burns are and how much skin is gone, I wouldn't be surprised if he'd need an amputation of this leg. The damage is so extensive. Even if we could repair it, he'd have lifelong pain. The nerves are all shot, and he'd continue to struggle to walk. At least with an amputation, he could wear a prosthesis and learn to walk again with therapy," Dr. Vance says.

"I'd recommend an above-the-knee amputation to avoid further complications of needing skin grafts, but I'll let the orthopedic surgeon make the final call," Dr. Dursley adds.

My heart sinks, and I release a loud gasp without meaning to.

"You have something to add, Dr. Bell?" Evan asks, but not in his normal condescending tone. "I'd love to hear about your expertise on the matter."

Oh, there it is. Asshole.

CHAPTER THIRTEEN

EVAN

"An above-the-knee amputation makes it harder to walk with a prosthesis since there's no knee to stabilize the prosthetic and hip," Emily says.

"That's correct," Dr. Dursley clips.

Emily is testing my patience, and with all the commotion, I'm not sure I have much left before I snap at her insubordination.

"Dr. Bell." I shoot her a warning glare, but she barely flinches, which pisses me off even more. She's wasting our time arguing about this when I know Dr. Dursley is highly proficient in burn cases.

"He's a father and only thirty-five. At least consider a below-the-knee amputation, so he has a better chance of walking again and playing with his kids," she continues.

I glare and give her a silent warning to stop arguing, but of course, she ignores me.

"He can get a skin graft from his butt to cover the burn once it heals, and then he can at least work toward getting a prosthesis if he has his knee." Emily's bottom lip is trembling, which makes me think she's running on pure adrenaline and needs to calm the hell down before she makes a scene.

"Dr. Bell," I warn, my voice growing louder.

"Ultimately, it's up to Dr. Wood, the ortho surgeon. I'll give him my notes, and he'll examine Mr. Brauer before making any decisions," Dr. Dursley explains.

"But you can encourage him to at least do a BKA instead," Emily insists.

"A below-the-knee amputation won't be as successful since he has a lot of burns below his knee," I interrupt, needing to end this back and forth bickering. "Going above the knee gives him the best chance at healing."

"At least consider it, Dr. Dursley. I've done a lot of work with amputations in my residency," Emily continues, dismissing my words completely.

"Is that so?" He arches a brow but continues to debride the patient's wounds.

Emily visibly swallows at the tension filling the room. Veronica and Fiona are still in the room, and by the way they're acting, I know they can feel the uneasiness brewing. I'm tempted to haul Emily over my shoulder and carry her ass out of here.

"That hardly makes you an expert," I snap, turning to Dr. Dursley. "I apologize. She's new and still learning her place." I narrow my eyes to her, hoping she understands my final warning.

"Learn my place?" Her voice goes up an octave. "Just because I didn't train in a trauma hospital doesn't mean I'm a clueless twit. If you'd asked about my work history *at all* instead of making assumptions, you'd know that I've worked side by side with some of the top-rated orthopedic surgeons in the country. I've seen predicted amputations of every limb that were deemed damaged and unrepairable end up getting saved. I've witnessed a man's severed ankle hanging on, *literally* by a thread of a blood vessel. The surgeon reattached it after sixteen hours of surgery, and the man ran a 5k a year later. A motorcycle crash victim almost seven feet tall was hit at fifty miles an hour, and when his leg got tangled in the wheel tire of the other driver's truck, the surgeon did everything he could to only amputate halfway up his calf and saved his knee. His long legs made it nearly impossible since the nerves were shot from the knee down, but he made it possible and salvaged everything he possibly could. The man has his knee and walks flawlessly with a prosthetic, so he can work and play with his three young children. So with all due respect, doctors, I think you should consider leaving this man's knee, so he doesn't have to depend on a wheelchair before he even hits middle age." Her breathing is rapid, and her face is turning red at the long-winded speech she just spewed. She swallows, her chest rising and falling as she awaits a response.

"You make some great points, Dr. Bell." Dr. Dursley finally speaks but doesn't get to continue before I interrupt.

"Every doctor has to evaluate their risk tolerance and if that risk is worth the potential of losing the patient or not. Mr. Bauer isn't old, but he's not young and athletic either. His body has taken its toll from working construction the past twenty years. His blood pressure is naturally high, which is why his doctor has him on medication. His medical history states heart disease runs in his family. These are all factors in deciding his care. As a physician, you have to look at the whole story, not just what's happening on one page." My words come out fast and harsh, but I don't care.

"I understand that, Dr. Bishop," she says my name with exaggerated expression. "But the facts also attest that people with amputations or become wheelchair bound are more susceptible to mental health diseases and sometimes even become suicidal."

I stand with my arms crossed over my chest, slowly shaking my head at her. She's brought me to an unnecessary level of anger. "Those factors can occur in any form of illness, Dr. Bell, whether or not the patient can walk. A man who once ran his own company and supervised hundreds of employees has a stroke one day and is now dependent on being fed by his wife. His life changed in a second and oftentimes that brings depression, anxiety, and even suicidal thoughts."

Veronica clears her throat, dismissing the heated argument that's unfolding in front of everyone. "Dr. Wood is on his way," Veronica announces.

"Please Dr. Dursley," she starts begging. "He needs his knee."

"I appreciate you voicing your concern, truly," Dr. Dursley begins, but Emily's face drops when she realizes she's not going to get her way.

"I've learned lots of things in my life, a lot of life lessons and a lot of lessons passed down to me from my father. Something he's always told me is that when I'm passionate about something, I do everything in my power to voice that. Regardless of titles or years served, I won't allow anyone to make me feel inferior because I truly believe this is the right thing to do, especially in this instance," she states matter-of-factly. "Mr. Brauer is stable for now, and he might not make it through surgery, but he also might survive all of this and continue to live another forty years. Doesn't he deserve to live the best possible life? If down the road the leg causes problems, he can have revision surgery and then go above the knee, so why not try to give him the best possible outcome first?"

I'm grinding my teeth so hard, the pain is shooting through my head.

"Dr. Wood," I hear Fiona greet. The silence grows between us when he walks up to Mr. Brauer.

"Hello." He gives a small smile. "Someone want to brief me?"

"Dr. Dursley will," I blurt out before anyone else can speak up. "Excuse us." I grab Emily's arm and turn us toward the door. "We'll be right back."

"What are you doing?" she asks between gritted teeth the moment we're out of the room.

"What the fuck do you think you're doing? You cannot undermine me," I whisper-hiss, my anger about to boil over.

"Let me go," she scoffs, trying to jerk her arm away, but I hold her firmly as I lead us down the hall to the on-call rooms. "What the hell is your problem?"

Checking for an open room, I shove her inside before closing and locking the door behind me. "You have pushed me far enough, Emily." I get in her face. "You do not call the shots on *my* patients. You might've gotten away with that at your other job, but here we have boundaries, and I'm getting really pissed off that you keep crossing them."

"I was voicing other options!" she shouts in my face, her cheeks burning red. We're both still running on the adrenaline from the scene that unfolded today. "Boundaries or not, a patient's quality of life will always come first in my book."

"You will listen to your superior's instructions, or you'll end up killing a patient! What don't you understand about that? We have protocols for a reason, but you need to fucking follow them, or everything goes to shit." She backs up, and I step right into her space.

"Not when your protocols aren't the only way to do things!" She pushes a finger into my chest for emphasis. "I'm sick of your macho bullshit and never taking my suggestions because God forbid mine actually might be better than yours!" She shouts louder this time, and I know the nurses down the hall can probably hear her. The last thing I need is them in our business, considering our history.

"Keep your voice down, Dr. Bell," I hiss between my teeth.

"Oh screw off," she shouts, her neck pulsing with anger. She's red in the face, and I can tell she's past the point of pissed. This discussion needs to end so I can get back to my fucking job.

"You do what you're told, and you do your job. You don't argue with specialists who have years of experience on you and know the right procedures. Do you understand?"

"I *am* doing my damn job. Hell, I'm the only one doing *anything* out there while you stand around and bark out orders. Then when I actually give an alternate option and speak up for a patient who can't speak for himself, you get your caveman panties in a bundle because it wasn't *your* way!"

"I told you to keep your fucking voice down," I warn. I don't let anyone get away with talking to me like this, especially at work where I'm a respected doctor, and people are expected to take orders from me.

"Fuck you, Evan," she spits out loudly. "I'm so sick of—"

Cupping her face, I push her until her back hits the wall then cover her mouth with mine and immediately silence her. She won't lower her voice, which leaves me no damn option. She's hesitant for only a second before sinking into it as we battle for control. Her arms wrap around my waist and pull me closer as I slip my tongue between her lips and seek out her taste.

"You want to defy me, Emily?" I whisper against her lips as she pants. "You do it outside of work. Do you hear me?" I kiss along her jawline and neck until my mouth is over her ear. "Do we have an understanding?" Sliding my hand around her body, I cup her ass in my palm and squeeze.

"You can't use kissing to distract me, Dr. Bishop," she states boldly, making me smile against her skin.

"Are you sure about that?" I push my groin against her stomach, so she can feel how hard I am.

"I think you like it when I defy you," she taunts, wrapping her fingers around my shaft through my scrubs. "In fact, I think you like it a lot. I think it makes you hard as fuck."

Fucking hell.

"Emily…" I warn, nipping her bottom lip between my teeth. "You're playing with fire."

"What? Afraid to put your money where your mouth is?" She lifts up her head, and I catch her mouth with mine. Goddamn, she tastes so fucking good.

"I hope you know what you're doing." I release a frustrated moan when she starts stroking me faster. "I'm not going to play these games with you."

"Who says I'm playing?" she whispers against my lips. "I'm so fucking wet right now."

I release a deep growl, and I shut my eyes trying to regain control, but it's fucking useless.

"See for yourself, Dr. Bishop," she taunts in a low, seductive tone.

Taking my hand, she slides it into her panties where I feel how soaked her aching pussy is. "Jesus Christ," I mutter, pressing my forehead to hers as I slide the pad of my finger along her slit, and her wetness coats my skin. "Shit."

I'm battling with walking away—knowing how bad this is for our professional relationship—and taking what she's offering. She gets me so goddamn worked up, I can't even think straight.

"Fuck it," I mutter, going against my better judgment. Hungrily, I take her mouth and kiss the fuck out of her. Hands and lips roam each other as heavy breathing fills the small room. I cup her breast and eagerly untie her bottoms. Once her shoes and scrubs are removed, her fingers fly to my pants, and she releases my throbbing cock in her palm. I reach a hand behind my neck and pull my shirts off, tossing them to the floor.

She kneels, pulling my scrubs down with her as she wraps her luscious lips around the crown of my cock. My head falls back as she licks from the base all the way to the tip and sucks it urgently into her mouth.

"Fuck, Emily," I hiss, bringing my eyes down to watch her masterfully suck me off. I fist a hand in her hair and control her pace, knowing she'll probably give me shit later for taking charge. "Stand up," I order, releasing her head and helping her to her feet. "Turn around, baby."

Spinning around to where the bed frame is, I lower my eyes and admire her ass. She's probably caught me on more than one occasion staring at it, but for a damn good reason. It's a fucking fine ass.

Unable to hold back, I slap a hand across her ass cheek, and her surprised gasp turns me on. "Let me be real clear, Dr. Bell." I align my cock at her entrance as I whisper the words over her ear. My free hand wraps around her throat as the other fists my cock and pushes an inch inside her. "I'm the one in control here." I push in another inch. "At work…" Another inch. "And inside you." Another inch. "You undermine my orders again…" Another inch. I release her throat and bring my hand down her stomach and circle her clit. "And I'll work your pussy so good until you're begging for release, but—" I push my cock the rest of the way inside her tight cunt, and she moans at the way her pussy stretches around me. "I'll stop." My finger rubs her clit faster as I start thrusting in and out of her. "I'll bring you right to the edge; you'll be pleading for me to make you come, but until you learn to stop pushing my goddamn buttons, I'll torture this sweet pussy instead."

I slide out of her as my fingers increase their pace on her clit, and she's nearly gasping for air. Reaching behind her, she grasps my cock and strokes it. "Do we have a deal?"

Her head falls back on my chest as she shakes it. "No?" I ask, amused.

She arches her back and slides my cock back inside her. I give in, letting her take control but only for a moment. Gripping the plastic bed frame, she pushes her ass against my pelvis, and I squeeze her hips to increase the pace.

"Is this what you needed?" I bend my body over hers until my lips are pressed against her ear. "My cock need to remind you who's in control here?" I thrust deeper, earning a throaty moan in response.

"Fuck off," she hisses.

"Tsk tsk," I tease, pounding harder against her. She nearly falls onto the bed, but I wrap my arm around her waist and catch her. "I'm going to fuck that sassy attitude right out of you because I've had enough of your defiant mouth."

"I'm not a puppet you can control, Evan. I'm allowed to have my own opinions and suggestions, and they won't always match yours. So fucking deal with it," she says, clearly out of breath, but she doesn't let that stop her from telling me off. Ironically, I find it fucking hot.

"You can have your own opinions, but when I'm the one in charge, you will listen to my orders. That's not up for discussion."

"We'll see."

She has me so fucking riled up, I can't take her defiance anymore. "You're going to make me lose my goddamn mind, Emily."

Before she can respond, I kneel between her legs and spread her ass cheeks then move my mouth to her swollen pussy. Her knees buckle, and I hold her up as I sink my tongue deep inside her.

"Oh my God…" she says, her legs shaking.

I can't take her like I want to, knowing the longer we're in here, the more suspicious everyone will be, but I wasn't about to let her go without tasting her again. I know she's close when her pussy tightens against my tongue, but I don't give her what she needs. Not yet.

Standing back up, I cover her mouth with mine again, so she can taste how fucking good we are together. She releases a moan when I slide back into her and lift her leg, thrusting deep and hard.

"Evan, please," she begs as her arms wrap around my neck.

"What do you need, baby?"

"I need to come. Please."

"Then you know what I need to hear," I taunt, not feeling the least bit guilty keeping it from her.

"That's not fair," she hisses, arching her hips and seeking relief.

"Never said it was," I remind her, pressing my lips to her neck and sucking. "How bad do you need it?"

"Fuck you," she seethes.

I smile. "Better keep that pretty mouth of yours quiet, or we're going to draw in an unwanted audience," I caution, raising her leg up even higher so I can fill her deeper. Her pussy is aching for it, I can feel it, which means I'm closer to getting what I want.

"*Please, please, please,*" she whimpers, and I love hearing her desperate moans. God, she's so gorgeous when she's like this—vulnerable and eager for release.

"Say it, Emily," I demand roughly, running a hand down to her clit and softly brushing the pad of my thumb against it, just enough to drive her wild. "I'm about to come, baby, so if you want me to send you over the edge, you better—"

"Fine!" She groans, tossing her head back as she seeks out her pleasure.

"Fine, what?" I growl, my patience growing thin because I'm not sure how much longer I can hold off. I'm about to fucking burst.

"When you're in charge…" I increase my pace, hitting her deeper.

"Keep going," I encourage, knowing she's getting close because her walls tighten around me.

Grinding her teeth, she fights to hold back her moans and bites down on her bottom lip. I know she's almost there, so I make an abrupt stop, and her eyelids fly open in shock.

"I'm about to come all over your perky tits if you don't finish your sentence," I say, palming my cock in my hand and pumping. "I'm so goddamn close, Emily." I'm provoking her, and I know it, but I'm a man of my word. If I don't show her who's in charge now, she'll never take me seriously in or out of work.

I can almost see the steam blowing out of her ears when she realizes I'm not going to finish her off until she says what I need to hear.

"I hate you," she mutters, shooting daggers at me through narrowed eyes. "I can finish myself off anyway."

"Good," I reply immediately. I slowly pump my cock as I step into her space, pinning her eyes to mine as she backs up to the wall. "But you and I both know it won't be as good as coming from me."

Her lips tremble as our eyes remain locked. She's contemplating her words carefully, but nothing she says will push me away. I know she needs the release as badly as I do, and I'm not leaving this room until she admits it.

I place my palm flat against the wall next to her ear and dip my head until our lips are nearly touching. She's breathing heavily as she anticipates my next move, waiting. Arching my hips up, I brush the tip of my cock against her pussy and smack it against her clit over and over. When she releases a moan, I press my mouth to hers and capture it. She digs her nails into my arms and wraps a leg around my waist, desperate for her release.

Sliding my cock down to her entrance, I push in just slightly, and she groans angrily when I don't go all the way in. I nip at her ear, grazing my teeth along her neck as I tease her pussy.

"When I'm in charge, you listen to my orders. Got it?" I ask, my tone deep and deliberate. This is her last chance to answer my question, and she knows it.

"Yes," she finally responds, arching her hips and seeking my cock.

"That's my girl." I smile victoriously against her lips. It was a dick move, I know, but I never said I played by the rules anyway.

"Now," she begs her voice soft and pleading. "Please, Evan."

"Hang on, baby." She tightens her hold around my neck as I plunge fast and deep inside her. Gripping her hips, I increase the pace and fuck her with everything I have. She struggles to stay silent, so I press my mouth to hers and inhale every one of her throaty moans as she comes hard and long on my cock. "Fuck," I curse, feeling her pussy tighten around me like a vise grip. I'm only seconds behind her, so I quickly pull out and come on her stomach.

All that can be heard is our heavy breathing, and now that we've both come down from our highs, I notice the hesitation in her eyes as we stand naked and sated. When I pulled her aside, I had no intention of this happening, but I can't say I regret it either. Emily gets under my skin like no other, and until we can learn to respectively work together, we'll have to fuck each other out of our systems first. That's the only solution I can think of right now, especially since all the blood has rushed out of my brain.

Emily's the first to move as she scrambles around the room for her clothes. My undershirt is near my feet, and I hand it to her, so she can clean up. I pull my scrub bottoms up and throw my top on as quickly as I can. We can't walk out of here at the same time, looking guilty like we just did some seriously hot fucking. She's standing in her bra when I look down and see the thin lace panties she was wearing. Instead of handing them over, I scoop them up and shove them into my pocket.

"I'm going to walk out first, so it doesn't look—"

"Yeah, good idea," she interrupts without looking up at me.

I decide it's best to leave before things get awkward. We still have a few hours left of our shift, and I won't let what just happened affect my work or my team.

"Toss the shirt when you're done," I say since I definitely don't want to carry that around. Taking a quick glance at her before leaving, I open the door and walk out, her panties securely tucked in my pocket. I smile, knowing she's going to be freaking out any second—the same way I did the morning she left me with no fucking clothes.

CHAPTER FOURTEEN

EMILY

My shoulders relax, and I exhale as soon as the door closes behind Evan. Oh my God, what just happened? Better yet, what did I just do?

I caved.

Fuck me. I caved, and now he thinks he's in control and God's gift to the world.

Fucking great.

I won't let him manipulate me with sex. He must not be that smart if he thinks that's actually going to work. I said those things in the heat of the moment and because I really needed to fucking come, but that doesn't mean I meant it. Hell, I would've told him the sky was purple if that meant he'd give me what I needed.

Regardless, that was really damn hot. The way I yelled at him, and he yelled back, and then we just attacked each other. Every moment of our first night together has replayed in my head since it happened, but now… angry Evan is the one who will haunt me in my dreams. Angry Evan is hot and demanding and knows just how to tease the fuck out of me. I almost hate him for it. Except I could never hate a man who knows how to worship my body like he does.

But God, does he really have to be such a controlling asshole?

I scoop my scrubs and shoes off the floor and adjust my just-fucked hair. Once my top is on, I search for my panties. When I don't find them on the floor, I shake out my scrub bottoms, but they aren't there either. *What the fuck?*

Panic starts to surface at the realization that I lost my damn panties. Shit, shit, shit.

My pager beeps, and it's painfully obvious I'm going to have to put my pants on without them. Quickly, I finish getting dressed and push my shoes on before grabbing my lab coat and the soiled shirt and flying out the door.

I throw Evan's shirt in the trash before anyone can see me and ask questions.

Rushing to the nurses' station for an update, I look around but don't see any commotion or people scrambling like normal. "What's going on? You paged me?" I ask, trying to catch my breath.

Fiona looks at me like I've gone crazy. She swallows and lowers her eyes before bringing them back up to look at me. She witnessed the heated argument back in the trauma room, and now she looks uncomfortable as hell. "Dr. Bishop asked me to page you. He wanted me to tell you that your break is over and to get back to work." I can tell she's uneasy delivering the news, but that doesn't stop the anger from brewing inside me.

The vein in my forehead is about to burst, but I remind myself to play it cool. For all they knew, Evan sent me on the break to calm down, and now I'm the one looking like a slacker.

"Okay. Thanks." I pinch my lips together to prevent any further words from spewing out of me. No one can know that Evan and I are…whatever the hell we are. Considering I came to this hospital to make a name for myself all on my own, the last thing I need is people thinking I sleep my way to the top.

Crap.

"Dr. Bell," Evan barks from the other side of the room. He's holding a pile of charts in his hands that are no doubt from the huge fire incident that just unfolded.

Taking a deep breath, I put my lab coat on and dig my stethoscope from the pocket and wrap it around my neck. We have to act impartially to each other publicly, but hell, I didn't realize how hard it'd be now that we're together.

"Yes, Dr. Bishop?"

He doesn't even look up at me when I approach him, and I hate that it irritates me.

"I need you on beds seven through fifteen until the next shift rotation, then finish these charts before you leave." His head tilts up, his lips in a firm line as he piles the stack in my arms. "I also need an update on the Brauer kids once an hour."

Swallowing, I adjust the charts in my arms to prevent them from falling. I won't let my pride get in the way of doing my job, and if charts are what I need to do right now, then I won't make a scene. At least not in front of everyone. However, once we're alone, I'm going to give him a piece of my mind for treating me like a damn intern again.

"Absolutely. Anything else, *sir*?" My tone is laced with fake sweetness, and he doesn't flinch a beat at it.

"Yes, actually." He takes a step forward and dips his head until his mouth hovers over my ear. "Make sure those charts are done *correctly* before you leave. I'll be looking through them extensively."

"Of course." I grind my teeth, wishing I could give him a piece of my mind right now.

"And since I know you're going commando, I won't ask you to perform any oral procedures." He winks before walking away, making my blood boil.

That asshole stole my panties!

By the time my shift ends, my annoyance with Evan has only grown. Charting is an easy job compared to some of the grunt work I could be doing but recalling the argument we had about Mr. Bauer with the other two doctors and how this is my punishment for that causes my rage to resurface. I may not have worked in a trauma hospital for the past five-plus years like Evan, but the jerk wouldn't even consider my suggestion even after giving thorough reasons why they should.

After I change and walk to the parking lot, I get in my car. I keep replaying the roller coaster of a day over in my head as I head home. I'm cursing and muttering to myself while driving when I realize the car behind me has made the same turns I have since leaving the hospital parking lot. Normally I wouldn't think much of it, but since finding those tulips on my windshield this morning, I'm more on edge about what they could mean.

Deciding to call Kiera, I reach for my phone, and she answers almost immediately after hitting her name.

"Are you sure?" she asks after I tell her I think Richard is following me. I explain the flowers and how the car is continuing to switch lanes every time I do. I'm trying to not be paranoid, but my racing heart has me mildly freaking out.

"I can't see the face because the visor is down, but I'm almost positive it's him. It can't just be a coincidence," I tell her, eyeing my mirror and squinting. "He's driving just far enough away that I can't read his plates, but close enough for me to notice I've been followed the past fifteen minutes."

"You need to call the cops, Em. He's violating the restraining order." I hear the concern in her voice and wonder if she's right.

"As soon as he sees the lights, he'll bail."

"Isn't that the point?"

"Well yes, but I also want to know what he wants."

"That's dangerous, Em. He's dangerous," she reminds me, though she doesn't need to because I remember the events clear as day.

"If I scare him off with the cops, he'll know I know it's him, and what if that just pisses him off even more? Who knows what he'll do next."

"And if there's no paper trail of him harassing you again, he gets away with it."

Ugh. I chew my lower lip, keeping an eye on his car as I contemplate what to do.

"You aren't driving home, are you?"

"Well, yeah. That was my plan, but shit, I can't now."

"He's probably following you, so he can find out where you live." Her rushed tone sends a panic wave through me.

"Fuck. I didn't think about that. How did he even find out where I work now?"

"Because he's a psycho!"

"He suffers from PTSD," I explain, although that's no excuse for his actions. "And grief."

"Call it what you want but do not go home. Can you park somewhere public and see if he drives away?"

"I'm already on the country road. It's only two lanes, and the shoulders aren't very wide. There isn't anywhere for me to go. It looks like the *Texas Chainsaw Massacre* out here." I start to panic, wondering what the hell I'm going to do now that the city lights are behind me. It's already dark, which means I won't be able to see my surroundings as well.

"What about Evan?" she asks.

"What about him?"

"Did he get off work the same time as you?"

"Yeah, I think he was leaving shortly after me."

"He lives about thirty minutes from the hospital and can tell you where to drive to until he can meet you."

"Fuck." I release a deep breath.

"If you call him now, he can give you directions to his house or a gas station or something." Even though I've been out here for a few weeks, I don't know any of the backroads or the surrounding small towns. Kiera drove us to the wedding, so I didn't pay attention to our surroundings, and I only drive to work and back.

"Okay, let me see if he even picks up my call." I roll my eyes, hating that I'm about to ask him for help.

"If he doesn't, call the cops and tell them where you are so they can scare him off at least."

"I will."

The car lights get closer, and I know he's gaining speed now that we're out of the city. Shit, shit, shit.

Quickly, I pull up Evan's contact info and call him.

"Dr. Bell," he answers in a flat tone.

"Evan, I need your help." I get right to the point because the closer the car gets behind me, the harder my heart pounds in my chest.

"Emily, what is it?" he asks in a panic, rushed voice.

I quickly give him a rundown of my patient's husband and how he came after me because he blames me for Susan's death. I explain how someone's been following me since I left work, and I'm almost positive it's him. He asks a few questions about what took place, and when I tell him all the crazy things Richard did, his breath hitches.

"Call the cops, and whatever you do, don't stop the car. I'm already on my way home and should only be about ten minutes behind you, but I'm picking up speed as soon as I can."

"Then he'll know I know it's him." I explain the same thing I said to Kiera. "I'd rather just lose him, so I don't give him another reason to come after me."

"He should know you know, Emily!" he barks. "He should know he can't get away with this, and that you aren't going to tolerate it."

Fuck, he's right. I have no idea what Richard's gone through over the past year or if he's even more dangerous than before. He'd threaten me with his words and say my boyfriend or father should die because "an eye for an eye." At first, his threats were just empty words, but then he'd show up at my job, and I'd catch him walking outside my condo building. I notified the police of his stalking and verbal threats, but the most I could do was get a restraining order. Only if he violated it could they take him into custody. However, he stopped or got smarter. Either way, he's back, and I know he's out for blood this time. He wouldn't have tracked me down after all this time if he wasn't seeking revenge.

"Okay, I'll call them right now," I tell him.

"Call me back as soon as you can."

"I will."

"And just keep driving on that road. Don't stop or pull over or slow down."

"Okay." My lips tremble.

"Emily." He says my name in a low, gravelly voice, making my body shiver.

"Yes?"

"Everything's going to be okay. I'll be behind you in just a few minutes."

After hanging up, I call the cops and explain everything to the operator. I give her my license plate number and a description of Richard's car along with the mile marker, so they can find me. She reassures me an officer will be on their way within fifteen minutes, which doesn't give me a lot of comfort, considering how long he's already been following me.

Looking up in the mirror again, I see another set of headlights as they start to pass the car behind me. When I see it's a big truck, I know it's Evan. Relief washes over me knowing I'm not alone.

"Emily," he says when I call him back.

"An officer is on the way," I tell him.

"Good. This asshole isn't letting me pass."

I look and see he's riding my ass even closer. "Shit. What should I do? Should I speed up, so you can pass him and get behind me?"

"No, I'm going to speed up until I can pass both of you. Then once I'm in front, I'm going to slow down so you can pass me. Once you're ahead of me, I'm going to close the gap between us, so if he tries to pass, he won't be able to. He'll have to pass both of us or stay behind me."

Sucking in a breath, I agree to his plan. "Then what?" I ask.

"Then we wait for the cop to show up. He'll either drive away or get pulled over. Then we stop and speak with the officer, and you can file a report against him for breaching his restraining order."

"Okay."

"Stay on the phone with me," he orders. "I'm about to pass you."

Evan revs his engine loud and hard as he speeds around Richard's car. When I look over, he gains more speed and drives ahead of me. Once he gets back in the lane, he slows down just enough for me to pass him.

"Be careful," he tells me.

"You be careful," I tease.

"I meant be careful and don't hit my truck. It's my baby."

I release a small chuckle at the sound of him calling his truck that. "Of course, you'd have feelings for your precious truck." I'm tempted to say something about him being capable of having feelings for an object but not women, but I clamp my mouth shut. Now isn't the time.

"She has a name," he informs me, but I hear the smile in his voice.

"Probably after a porn star." I snort, pulling my car around his and gaining speed.

"How you going to give me shit when I'm the one helping you?" he muses, but his teasing tone isn't lost on me. This is what we do. Neither of us can be serious with each other for too long. "You going to pass me or what?"

"I am!" I defend, pressing my foot down harder on the gas. When I look in the rearview mirror, I see Richard following close behind me, trying to keep up with me as I pass. I knew he wasn't going to let me go that easy. Considering this is a two-lane road with dangerous curves, I push on the gas harder, picking up my speed.

"This asshole thinks I'm letting him in?" Evan growls, noticing Richard is trying to pass too. "This will show him." Evan swerves into Richard's lane, which causes him to brake hard.

"Oh my God, Evan." This is all escalating way too quickly.

"I think I confused the fuck out of him."

I know Richard is thrown off because he jerks his car behind Evan's truck. Looking in my mirror, I watch as Evan stays inches from my bumper and successfully blocks Richard. Relief floods through me for a moment, and I feel safer than I did before. "There."

"Okay. Now slow down, and I'll stay on your ass."

Unable to control myself, I laugh at his choice of words.

"Get your head out of the gutter, Dr. Bell."

"I didn't say a word. However, you're the one who lives in the gutter, so maybe you should be telling yourself that."

"Well—" he starts but cuts his words off. "Motherfucker," he mutters, and I know something's wrong.

"What?" I ask, panicked.

"He's trying to pass again."

"What the hell?" I groan, confused by what this guy thinks he's going to accomplish by doing this.

"Just stay put. I'm keeping up with your speed, so he can't wedge in, and the only option he has is to pass us both and be ahead of you."

"Okay." I look in my side mirror and see Richard's headlights approaching. I brace myself to see his face as he passes me, but he remains in the left lane. "What the hell is he doing?" I whisper, though I know he can't hear me. If another car comes in the other lane, he'll hit them head-on. There are too many curves. This is too dangerous. Panic coats me like a warm blanket, and I just pray an innocent person doesn't get hurt because this asshole is driving in the wrong lane.

"He's waiting for me to let him in. Not gonna happen, dickwad," Evan mutters, revving his engine.

"What does he think—" my words are cut off when I feel a small bump on the side of my car. "Oh my God did he just—"

"Fuck!" Evan's words echo in my ear as Richard continues to drive beside me.

"He hit my car!" I shriek. "Evan, what do I do?" I grip the steering wheel tightly and take a deep breath, trying to remain calm.

Before Evan can respond, the line goes dead. Just when I'm about to hit redial, I look over and see Richard veering into my lane at a much faster rate. Before I can do anything, he crashes into the side of me again, this time causing my head to hit the side window. The wheels of my car straddle the shoulder and gravel, and by some miracle, I'm able to recover control. Headlights appear in the opposite lane, heading straight toward us, and to avoid a head-on collision, Evan is forced to make room. Risking someone else's life isn't worth it. Having no choice but to move, Richard quickly jerks his car behind me, but overcorrects and slightly loses control. We're right back to square one.

"Shit!" Not knowing what else to do, I drive faster and try to keep watch in my mirrors. Just as I'm about to call Evan back, Richard flashes his brights and practically blinds me. I flick the rearview mirror to save my eyes and lose my train of thought when I'm slammed into from behind at a high speed. "Fuck," I curse. My head jolts backward from the impact and smacks against the headrest. My adrenaline rushes, and I put all my focus on the road as I slightly weave from pavement to gravel to pavement again. I'm almost in shock. I didn't expect him to do that.

Evan's loud truck comes barreling down the left lane with his window rolled down and points for me to pull over. With Richard right on my ass, I don't know how I'm going to do that without him slamming into my car more aggressively than before. My heart pounds in my chest, and I halfway wonder if I'm going to make it out of this alive. As I round the bend, I jerk the car onto the shoulder, and Evan is somehow able to cut him off again as I begin to slow. I brace myself for a side impact, but Richard speeds past me as if nothing happened. My car comes to a stop once I hit gravel, and I put it into park and try to catch my breath. Police lights flash behind me, and then I hear sirens. No wonder Richard kept going. Chicken shit.

I step out of the car because I need air and my chest feels tight. Everything from my past floods in fast and almost knocks me over. How can this all be happening again? My entire world is caving in around me, and the effort to come out on top is going to bury me alive.

Once my feet touch the ground, I walk a few steps and lose my footing. No matter what I do, nothing can stop me from falling. I try to brace myself, but it doesn't help. I land the exact wrong way and close my eyes tight right before my forehead crashes into the sharp edge of a large rock that's protruding from the ground. Maybe if I lie there, all of this will go away, and I'll wake up and realize it was a bad dream. Though I feel weak, I try to the find the strength to push myself up. I hear Evan's truck pull up, then feet running on gravel toward me. With strong arms, he lifts me to my feet and holds me steady.

"Emily!" I hear him shouting, but it sounds distant. My heart thumps in my ears as my eyes struggle to stay open. "Emily, are you okay?" Evan keeps a tight grip on me as he searches my face. "Shit, you have a cut on your head."

I groan, trying to catch my breath and slow my heart rate down. Lifting my hand, I finally feel the warmth of the blood. When I look down at it on my fingertips, it's still hard for me to register.

"Say something," he demands. "Keep your eyes open."

"I can't," I barely mutter the words out. "My chest is tight, and my head is pounding. I'm a little dizzy." And I might throw up, but I keep that to myself.

"Jesus." He guides me to his truck as he waves the cop down.

"Stay with me, Emily. Sounds like you're having a panic attack. Take slow, even breaths."

I've had panic attacks before, but nothing to this extent. Everything closes in around me, sucking the air right out of my lungs. My eyelids are heavy, and my palms are sweaty against my skin. My body is already starting to feel stiff from the impact.

This can't be happening. Not here. Not now.

"Is she hurt? Does she need medical attention?" the officer asks before speaking into his radio.

Evan tells him he's taking me to the hospital and that we'll give our statements there.

"Follow me," the officer tells him. Evan puts me in his truck and shuts the door. He jumps into the driver's side, and soon, we're taking off.

"What about my car?" I mumble, trying like hell to stay focused, so I don't pass out.

"I'll call a tow truck. That asshole broke a taillight and did some damage to your bumper."

Ugh. Motherfucker.

The lights from the city reflect inside the truck, and I know we're close now. I'm dreading walking into the same ER where we work, knowing it's going to raise questions especially since Evan is with me. Hopefully, he'll tell them all to mind their business, but like I keep hearing: small town, big mouths.

"Evan," I say as he pulls into the parking lot.

"What?"

"Thank you."

He doesn't respond, but within minutes, he's back at my side, pulling me out of the truck.

"I can walk." I try to stand, but he tightens his hold in response.

"I've got you."

Wrapping my arms around his neck, I rest my head on his chest and focus on the rapid beating of my heart. Except now I don't know if it's from the panic attack or the fact that Evan Bishop is holding me as if his life depends on it.

CHAPTER FIFTEEN

EVAN

VERONICA NOTICES me the second I walk in carrying Emily. She rushes to my side, and I immediately ask her which beds are open. I'm staying strong for Emily's sake, but I'm boiling with anger inside as the realization of what happened hits me hard in my gut. Richard could've driven her right off the road, her car could've rolled over, and her condition could be much worse right now.

"Put her in bed thirteen," she tells me, leading the way. "What happened?"

I give her a brief rundown as the officer stands nearby. Emily is pale, and the cut on her forehead is bleeding. She might have a concussion from whiplash or the fall, depending on how hard she hit her head, but I need to lay her down first and make sure her heart doesn't burst out of her chest.

Dr. Moody walks in with Fiona as I'm putting pressure on Emily's bleed. Veronica hands me supplies so I can clean her and examine it to see if she needs stitches. I ask her the same questions she's asked patients many times.

"You shouldn't be doing that," Dr. Moody barks. "You're off the clock. Let me look at her."

"I've got it," I clip. "She smacked her head and might have whiplash.

There's a cut on her head that needs to be cleaned. She was also having trouble breathing."

"It's just a panic attack," Emily mutters, glancing over at the police officer standing in the hallway.

"Veronica, give her fluids and an order for alprazolam."

"Do you have these often?" Dr. Moody asks Emily. I'm relieved when she shakes her head.

"I've had a few over the past year, but nothing regular," she admits.

"Do you want a psych evaluation?" he asks, resting his palm on top of her wrist, and it takes everything inside me not to rip off his hand. "It might help if you target the triggers leading to them and lower the severity."

I turn my head and roll my eyes. Emily isn't just a regular patient; she's a goddamn doctor. She knows this shit.

"Her trigger is getting hit in her car and nearly getting run off the road," I blurt out, bringing everyone's attention to me. I give them a quick rundown on Richard—who he is, and why he's after Emily.

"Evan's right." Emily speaks up, breaking the awkward silence once they learn of the situation. "I'm okay." Her chest is rising and falling rapidly, and I know she's trying to be brave in front of everyone.

"Can Dr. Bell get some privacy?" I snap. "It's not helping her to have an audience right now."

"He's right," Veronica chimes in. "I'll finish her IV and give her the Xanax as soon as the order is filled."

Dr. Moody gives me a pointed look, and I know he's not happy with me, but I don't give a shit. Emily and I may bump heads ninety-nine percent of the time, but I'd never want her to get hurt.

"Here's my number," the officer says, entering the room and handing me his business card. "Call when she's feeling up to it, and we'll get her statement for the police report."

"Thank you," Emily and I both say.

"It'll be within the next day or two," I tell him. That asshole isn't getting away with this.

The room clears after Veronica hands her the pills, and then it's just Emily and me alone. She tilts her head and looks at me as I take another look at her cut.

"It's gonna bruise," I say softly, getting my tools ready to stitch it up. "But fortunately, you'll live." I smirk.

"Thanks to you," she says with a grin. "However, if I *had* died tonight, I would've been really pissed I had no underwear on, and the coroner would've seen an eyeful."

I burst out laughing, completely forgetting I'd put them in my pocket. "Guess that'll teach you to always have a spare pair on you."

"You're relentless, you know that?" she quips.

"We should talk about today," I say in all seriousness. "But later."

"No, we don't have to." Her eyes lower as I bring my hands up to her forehead and start the sutures.

"It's a deep cut, but it shouldn't scar," I tell her once I'm finished, needing to fill the silence.

"Dang. No sexy battle wound?" she mocks, lifting a finger to her head. Looks like the Xanax is kicking in.

"Do you have a headache or feel any neck pain? I want to make sure you don't have a concussion."

"No, Dr. Bishop. Just a little sore," she tells me with a lifted eyebrow.

"Let's get you discharged then," I say, fighting to hold back a smirk at the goofy smile on her face. Grabbing her hand, I help her move to the edge of the bed. "I'm going to drive you home tonight and call for your car in the morning, okay?"

"That's not necessary. I'll just call Kiera."

Studying her face, I realize it's probably for the best if I don't drive her home tonight because then I'll be tempted to stay and watch over her. "I'll call her," I say, reaching for my phone.

Emily's discharge papers arrive, and Veronica checks her stats one more time before taking out the IV. Thankfully, her heartbeat has steadied to normal, and her dizzy spells aren't as bad. She looks so vulnerable sitting on the hospital bed, and I feel an urge to hold her in my arms right now. Tonight was tense as hell, but I'm so relieved she's okay. If I ever come face-to-face with that Richard guy, there's no telling what I might do. The bastard is lucky he drove off when he did.

"You ready?" Kiera asks once the papers are signed, and Emily is free to leave. Emily agrees to stay at Kiera's house for the night and is told to take tomorrow off. She wasn't happy about the last request, but I don't give her the option to argue.

"Evan." Emily grabs my attention once Kiera is out of hearing distance.

I raise my brows, waiting to hear what she has to say.

"Don't think because you saved my life tonight that I'm not going to get back at you for stealing my underwear," she states, a smirk playing on her lips.

The corners of my mouth tilt up, enjoying this side of her even when she drives me crazy more times than not. "Don't worry, Dr. Bell. This changes nothing." I wink, knowing the bachelor auction is this weekend, and if I've learned anything from Emily thus far, it's not to underestimate her abilities.

It's been a few days since Emily's injury, and thankfully, she's feeling just fine but still a bit on edge. She took a couple of days off, and I was glad when she came back and looked a hell of a lot better. We worked side by side as we normally do, but I could tell some of her light had dimmed, though she reassured me she was still planning to come to the bachelor auction today to taunt me.

Mama insists we wear slacks and a tie to this thing as if we're not capable of dressing ourselves. Then I remember Jackson, and well damn, he can't be trusted, so I somewhat understand. I choose navy slacks, a white button-up dress shirt rolled to the elbow because it's hot as fuck outside, then a navy tie for good measure. I run my fingers through my hair, then head to the venue. The sun is barely setting over the horizon, and I hope the night goes by quickly because, while I love supporting the event, I'd almost rather write a check in lieu of being up for auction. I wonder if bidding on myself is against the rules. I laugh at the thought and know Mama would kick my ass if I even attempted it.

As soon as I walk in, I'm amazed at what Mama was able to do with the old bank building. Lanterns and soft lights are strung around the high ceilings of the brick building, creating the perfect ambience. A stage with black velvet curtains and colored lights is the main attraction. Music lightly plays in the background, setting the mood that this party is fancy as fuck. Round tables with chairs line the outer edges of the room, and waitresses walk around with cocktails. Mama knows if you want people to spend money, the best thing to do is serve booze to loosen the hold on their wallets.

As I look for Mama to get the rundown of the itinerary for tonight, I feel a hand on my shoulder.

"Almost didn't recognize you without a scowl on your face," Jackson says, trying to make a joke but failing miserably.

"Shut the hell up," I tell him, grabbing a shot from the waitress.

He adjusts himself. "I hate these clothes. I feel like an idiot."

"You look like one too," I say just as John walks up.

He's pissed, and when I look over at Jackson, I realize it's because they're wearing the same thing, to a T.

"How're the ladies going to tell you two apart?" I joke, trying to contain my laughter.

"Considering Jackson doesn't know how to keep his damn mouth shut, I doubt it'll be too hard." John says with a smile.

Alex and River walk through the entrance. River is smiling wide at the whole display, but Alex doesn't look pleased to be here. Not even being married could get us out of this "bachelor" auction.

"I hate this shit," Alex says, walking up to us. "Ridiculous I even have to participate."

"It's for a good cause," River reminds him. "Be a good sport; I am."

Alex rolls his eyes, then pulls her into his arms. "You better bid high. All the ladies want this," he says semi-seriously, but all she does is laugh.

"I think you going on a date with one of the older ladies from church would be cute. And Mama already told me Jackson brings in the most money out of all of you, so stop exaggerating." River looks at Jackson who is obviously proud of his big accomplishment.

"Reigning champion, five years in a row. We're gonna make it six tonight." He's already trying to make it a competition, but none of us are taking the bait. We're not that stupid.

"It's only because you have no standards and sleep with whoever wins," I remind him. "They all know it. And the divorced cougars are desperate."

"And they're sixty and up," John adds, and we all laugh at Jackson's expense as he flips us off with both hands.

"They'll be here soon," Jackson leans in and whispers. I furrow my brows and look over at him. He shoots me a wink as if I'm supposed to know what that even means.

The place is filling up quickly, and Mama is busying herself with greeting everyone and giving orders to the other volunteers. I find myself glancing at the door more times than I'd like to admit, and just as we're about to head to our table, Kiera and Emily enter the building.

My eyes widen as I take her in. Jackson slaps me on the shoulder, grinning. "Told ya. Looking fine as fuck too. Have fun." He snickers before walking away.

I clear my throat to throw a comment back at him, but my mouth goes dry. Emily's wearing a long, glittery dark blue dress. The straps wrap around her neck, showing off way too much cleavage—not that I'd typically mind, but I hate the idea of anyone else looking. Her hair is half pinned up with curls at the ends, and she's wearing long, dangly earrings. She's fucking stunning. Seeing her all dressed up brings back memories of meeting her at the wedding and everything we did that night. The taste of her lips, the smell of her hair, the smoothness of her skin pressed against me. Shit. I'm so fucked.

Her eyes finally meet me, and a red-stained smile appears on her face. Kiera walks toward the table where Mama is standing with the boys and River while Emily comes right for me.

My breath hitches the closer she gets. Something hits me right in the gut, and it's a feeling I've never had before, but seeing her brings all kinds of new ones to the surface.

"You look gorgeous," I tell her, unable to take my eyes off her. "Way too gorgeous."

She smiles, brushing a piece of hair off her face, and I'm almost certain I see a faint blush on her cheeks. "You clean up nice," she replies. "Blue is definitely your color."

"Yeah, it's why I made the hospital switch to navy blue scrubs. I had to make sure I looked good at all times."

She chuckles, and the sound goes straight to my dick. Goddammit. "I'm sure you made a very convincing case."

"Oh I did. I'm pretty sure I was a lawyer in another life. I'm good at arguing to get my way." I flash her a wink, and she responds with an eye roll.

"Now *that* I don't doubt for a second."

"So you ready to spend some of your hard-earned money?" I taunt as we walk to the table.

"Oh definitely. From all the rumors, Jackson's a sure thing, so I plan to bid as high as it takes to get a piece of the action."

Jackson overhears her comment and whistles. "Well, don't you look stunning?" He stands up and takes her hand, pressing a kiss to her knuckles. I'm two seconds away from ripping his hands off her when Kiera interrupts.

"Jackson is always a sure thing so don't bother wasting your money. Just wear a cowbell around your neck, and he'll come running."

"That's a mildly disturbing image." Emily snorts, pulling her hand back.

As Mama taps on the microphone from the stage, we take our seats. Dad finds his chair and sits next to River who's holding Alex as if he's her lifeline. Poor River. I know she'll claw any woman's eyes out who tries to outbid her.

"Welcome everyone! Thank y'all for coming to the sixth annual food drive fundraiser! We're so glad y'all are here, and tonight we expect to beat our goal from last year, so we hope you brought your wallets with you." Mama continues talking about the charity, and everyone applauds. The servers bring the food out, and we chat casually as we eat. There's a silent auction where you can bid on basket items until the end of the event.

"Where's Trent?" I hear Emily asking Kiera.

"He's sitting with his folks since we haven't exactly made it official, but after tonight, I plan to make it known to everyone in town that Trent Laken is *mine*." She smirks while Emily giggles. Looking over at Jackson, I see his jaw is about to snap in half.

Stupid bastard.

I shake my head, grinning at his expense.

"So how are you liking the hospital?" River asks Emily. "Too bad I don't get to see you guys more. We've been jam-packed for weeks."

"Yeah the ER is basically nonstop, but I'm really enjoying it." Then she turns her head toward me. "Mostly."

"So you guys are working well together then?" Alex chuckles.

"Why wouldn't they?" Dad asks, and I almost forgot he was sitting here with us because he's so quiet.

"It's fine," Emily blurts out. "He's just an egotistical bastard most days."

That gets a smirk out of Dad, which surprises me. "Sounds like my son."

"Sounds like all of your sons," Kiera adds.

"Hey, I'm a married family man, thank you," Alex protests.

"Yeah, but what about your first twenty-five years?" Kiera teases.

Alex looks into River's eyes and grins. "Was just waiting for the right one to come along; that's all." He wraps his arm around her shoulders and kisses her cheek.

"Oh for fuck's sake, some of us are trying to eat here." Jackson grunts.

"I think it's sweet," Emily says, smiling at Alex and River.

"It is sweet," River confirms. "Plus, how hot is he as a dad? I mean, seriously."

Everyone groans at their sickly-sweet moment, and I thank the stars when Mama comes back to the mic. She announces the bachelor auction will be starting in ten minutes and then tells the women to get all their money out.

"Evan Bishop!" I hear my name being screamed, and the voice makes all the hair on the back of my neck stand. It's one I recognize, and unfortunately for me, not one you really want to hear screaming your name in the first place. "Evan, oh my God! I was hoping I'd see ya here!" April comes barreling through, and when I turn to see how far away she is and whether I have time to run away, she stumbles when someone suddenly pulls their chair out and falls right into my lap.

"Well, that's one way to say hello." She giggles, and it's the most annoying sound I've ever heard.

"You okay?" I ask before pushing her off my lap.

"I plan to bid on you tonight. You're not getting away from me this year." She bops me on the nose as if I'm a child. She giggles again, though no one else is laughing.

Emily sees how uncomfortable I am and fortunately takes mercy on me by interrupting.

"Hi, I'm Emily." She puts her hand out, and April reluctantly shakes it, giving her a look as if she's the competition.

"I'm April. Evan and I go way back." *Way back to misery.*

"Oh how nice. What a great friend for bidding on him, too." I hear the condescending tone in Emily's voice and fight back a smile, but April misses it completely.

"Well he got away from me last time, but I've been saving for a year and plan to finally get a date with Mr. Undateable over here."

Oh God. Kill me now.

"Mr. Undateable?" Emily inquires with a mischievous smirk. "Hadn't realized he penned a nickname."

"Uh yeah. He doesn't date, and anytime I've asked, he always tells me how busy he is with work, which yeah, I get, but you'd think he'd get one day off eventually, right?" April's rambling on and on, and I pray my ears burn off because I can't take another minute of this.

"I think it suits him," Emily agrees. "Well, I hope you win and get your date." She winks, causing an overly excited squeal from April to erupt.

"C'mon, it's time to head back," Alex says, breaking this whole awkward situation.

"Alright, April. Well, I better get going."

"See you soon!" she calls as she skips off.

I inhale a deep breath, wondering if I can fake a stroke or something to get out of this, but then Mama walks over and tells us we need to get lined up.

I stand while Dad and the ladies stay at the table. The guys are all pouting, rightfully so, but before I walk off, I stop behind Emily's chair.

"Emily…" I whisper in her ear. "I will do anything if you bid on me. And I do mean *anything*."

I see her cheeks heat as she contemplates my words.

"Hmm, I don't know. I kinda enjoy watching you sweat."

"C'mon, you can't hate me that much. Plus you kind of owe me for saving your life and all." It's a low blow, I know, but I'm desperate at this point. I can't go on a date with April Devin. She'll attach to me like a guppy fish as she claws her nails into me.

She turns her head slightly and clenches her jaw. "I worked half my shift with no panties on," she reminds me. "Hate is an understatement."

I groan, getting ready to beg before Jackson grabs my arm and pulls me away.

"Good luck," Emily shouts with a cocky smile, flashing me a one-finger salute.

Fuck my life.

CHAPTER SIXTEEN

EMILY

WATCHING Evan sweat was worth the three hours it took to get ready tonight. Between curling my hair, doing my nails, makeup, and getting dressed—it nearly took a village. Most days when I go to work, I throw my hair into a ponytail or low bun with minimal face coverage. I'll put on some lipstick and mascara, then call it a day. Maybe if I can't find my contacts, I'll put my glasses on and rush out the door. Getting dressed up is fun every once in a while, though Kiera was more than happy to "sex me up" for tonight—her words, not mine.

"Trent looks good in a suit," I tell Kiera as I watch him walk on stage.

"He looks fucking fuckable," she blurts out with a wide grin.

"Tonight's first eligible bachelor is Trent Laken. He's a thirty-six-year-old veterinarian who enjoys grilling and watching football in his downtime. Six-foot-one with brown hair and brown eyes—the epitome of tall, dark, and handsome," the young MC reads from her notecards.

"Who's the MC?" I ask Kiera because she looks oddly familiar for some reason. "I think I saw her at the wedding."

"Yeah, that's Jessica. Dylan's lady."

I vaguely remember meeting him at the wedding, and she must've been the girl Dylan was there with that night.

"So ladies, what do we think?" Jessica gets the crowd of women excited. "Starting the opening bid at fifty dollars."

Kiera immediately speaks up. "One hundred dollars!"

Trent looks in our direction and flashes her a secret wink.

"Do we have one-fifty?" Jessica asks.

"Two hundred!" someone across the room shouts, making Kiera glare.

"Three hundred!" Kiera shouts before Jessica can say anything.

"Three hundred, ladies! Do I hear three-fifty?"

Kiera stands up, glaring at anyone who dares to outbid her. I chuckle at her death stare and wonder if Trent already has something planned for their special date.

"Going once, twice, sold to Kiera Young for three-hundred dollars!"

Kiera does a little happy dance and walks toward the stage to greet Trent. He jumps down and immediately wraps his arms around her before giving her a kiss.

"Well damn, if I'd realized kissing was involved, I would've put my own bid in," Jessica teases. "Just kidding, honey!" she calls out to Dylan who's backstage with the rest of the guys. Trent sits at our table with Kiera sitting on his lap.

"Next up, we have a Bishop. Y'all know about these Bishop boys, don't ya?" Jessica gets the crowd to laugh. "Come on out."

John appears uncomfortable as he walks down the stage.

"Next up, we have John Bishop. He might be the quiet and reserved twin, but ya know what they say about the quiet ones. Amiright, ladies?" Jessica taunts, getting the attention of everyone in the room. "He's six-foot-three with light blue eyes, and rumor has it abs of steel and a few tattoos in some very *personal* areas."

Laughter echoes in the room as Jessica starts the bidding. John goes for five-hundred to a girl who Kiera tells me is a woman who teaches at the high school. I cringe, but then shake off the image.

"Alex Bishop," Jessica announces as he struts down the stage in a suit, cowboy boots, and a hat. "He's a hunk of a cowboy with his signature grin and icy-blue eyes. Just his flirty grin will melt your panties right off, so if you want a night of platonic romance—unless you're his wife—let's start the bidding, shall we?"

River immediately bids at two hundred dollars, and no one else dares to compete with her, which makes them both happy. Alex jumps off the stage and immediately engulfs her in a hug and kiss.

The anticipation of Evan's turn is making my insides flutter. I want to play hard to get, in a way, and wait until the very last second to bid on him. He doesn't know that I planned to bid on him the whole time, but it's his turn to suffer for a bit.

"Dr. Evan Bishop. Ladies…you ready for this one?" Jessica calls him out, and he reluctantly walks down the stage, looking fucking edible in his dress shirt and slacks. The way his sleeves are rolled up to his elbows gives me really bad thoughts. "Evan Bishop is six-foot-three, sky-blue eyes, and messy blond hair that's perfect for roaming your fingers through." Evan looks back at her, and Jessica flashes him a taunting wink. He shakes his head and continues walking up the stage.

"Five hundred and sixty-nine dollars!" April shouts from the front table, standing and waving her arms around as if she's a contestant on *The Price is Right*. Good lord.

Jessica chuckles. "Alright, do I hear six hundred?"

"Seven hundred!" another girl calls from the back. *Son of a bitch.*

I look over at April who's digging more money out of her purse. "Eight hundred!"

"Nine hundred," the other girl yells.

"Damn, ladies." Jessica whistles. "Current bid is at nine hundred. Do I hear a thousand?"

"One thousand, forty-two dollars!" April shouts, and I can tell she's at her max bid.

The girl in the back remains silent, and I know this is it. April wants this date so damn bad that I almost feel terrible for what I'm about to do. Then again, if I do this, then Evan will owe me, and that thought alone makes me shiver with excitement.

"Do I hear one thousand two hundred?" Jessica asks. "Going once…"

Kiera narrows her eyes at me, waiting to see if I'm going to bid or not. I look over at April, and she looks so damn hopeful. Then I look up at Evan whose lips are in a firm line with a tortured expression that cracks me up, but I hold back the smile, so he doesn't think he's going to win.

"Going twice…"

I swallow, jerking my hand up. "Fifteen hundred!" I shout louder than I meant to, and all eyes turn toward me.

"Sold for fifteen hundred dollars!" Jessica announces.

April gives me a look that says she might murder me, and I give her a shrug with a grin. Healthy competition is good for her, but before I can say anything to her, she grabs her bag and storms out.

"You seriously had me worried up there," Evan says from behind me, taking me by surprise when I feel his hot breath against my cheek. "Thought you were going to leave me hanging high and dry." Goose bumps form over my skin the closer his body gets to mine.

"I almost did," I tease, turning my head, which is a bad idea because our lips are now only inches apart. "You owe me a fifteen hundred dollar date now."

"Don't worry, baby. I'll make sure you get your money's worth." He winks, before taking the seat next to mine.

"Dylan Hart. You're up next, baby." Jessica's voice pulls me out of my daze, and I watch as Dylan struts up the stage in a fitted suit. He's tall and lean, wearing a cowboy hat and boots. "If any of you ladies are brave enough to bid on my man, you better be fifty and older."

The crowd chuckles.

"Dylan's a hardworking rancher with a six-pack that makes you want to lick honey right off him. His dark hair and chiseled jawline will make you swoon in two seconds flat. And don't even get me started on his strong, large hands, ladies. All that muscle you see is earned from hard labor, and his calluses feel amazing roaming down your bare back."

"Jessica!" Dylan scolds, walking over and spanking her right on the ass.

"What? I'm just stating facts." She giggles.

"Baby, my grandma is here," he tells her, and the crowd laughs because neither realizes we can hear them on the mic.

"Okay, anyway. Let's start the bidding." Jessica positions Dylan in the center of the stage. "I know what he's worth, ladies, but what are y'all willing to pay for a date with my man? Let's start at one hundred dollars!"

The room is painfully silent as no one dares to cross Jessica. It's almost comical, but I feel bad, considering men and their egos.

"One hundred!" a woman finally calls out, and everyone's head turns.

"Thanks, Aunt Katie." Dylan groans, blushing, making the rest of us laugh at his expense. The bidding only goes a few rounds, and his mom ends up winning at three hundred and fifty dollars.

A couple of ranch hands are auctioned off before Jessica announces the final bachelor. I already know it's Jackson by the flock of women rushing to the front of the room.

"Geez," I say, looking at them all.

Kiera rolls her eyes, shaking her head.

"This is where the real moneymaker is," Jessica says. "Ladies, get ready for Jackson Bishop."

They hoot and holler as if this is a male strip joint, which isn't too far off, considering how many women are standing at the stage waving their arms around. Jackson walks down the stage with a shit-eating grin, wearing a nice suit that fits him in all the right places. You can tell he doesn't dress up often, but he sure as hell knows how to fill it out.

"Six feet, three inches of solid perfection, Jackson's a horse trainer who works hard and plays even harder. He's wild in and out of the bedroom, and if you're looking for a good time, Jackson's the mayor of Wham-Bam-Thank-you-Ma'am, so don't say I didn't warn ya," Jessica quips.

Chuckling at her MC humor, I lean toward Kiera. "I feel like Jessica and I would be great friends," I tell her, and she nods her head in agreement.

"I don't know her really well, but from what I've heard, she's really good for Dylan."

"Persistent," Evan adds himself to our conversation. When I turn and look at him, he continues, "Basically mauled Dylan the first time they met and hooked her claws into him."

I shrug. "Sometimes that's what it takes."

"We're going to start the bidding at four hundred; otherwise, we're going to be here all night. Do I hear four hundred?"

A parade of women yell, and I know for sure they weren't kidding about him. The bidding goes back and forth for what feels like forever when finally it ends at two thousand five hundred.

"Sweet Jesus," I mutter when it's finally over. "I was waiting for clothes to start coming off soon."

Kiera snorts. "Give it a few minutes."

Mrs. Bishop comes back to the mic and thanks Jessica while everyone applauds. She announces the total amount raised from the event and how it's more this year than the previous one, which makes the room erupt into applause.

"Six years, baby!" Jackson comes out shouting, holding his arm up in victory as if he's holding up a trophy. I shake my head at his antics and wonder how the hell he and John can be twins. They're so different, it's comical at times.

"I'm going to say goodnight to Trent, then we can go," Kiera says as I stand and push my chair in.

Nodding, I dig into my wallet for my checkbook and write out my donation. Evan watches me with a smirk and an amused look.

"Yes?" I arch a brow.

"Just thinking."

"About what?" I ask, tilting my head down to sign my name.

"What panties you'll be wearing on our date. I think I'll start a collection."

I look up at him and scowl. "The only panties you're going to add to that collection are ones you go and buy yourself."

I rip the check out and hand it over to the volunteer who's collecting the winning bids.

"We'll see." He winks.

"You're so full of yourself," I say with a laugh, unable to stay mad at him when he gives me that cocky grin of his.

"It's called confidence, sweetheart. But, if I recall, you were full of me not that long ago, so don't say it like it's a bad thing." His crass words make me want to smack that smug smirk right off his face.

Such an ass.

The next morning on my way to work, I stop at The Grind Café and pick up two coffees. I normally bring a travel mug from home for my commute, but I woke up and realized I was all out of coffee beans, causing me to spew a variety of curse words.

Knowing how Evan likes his coffee, I order one for him, too, and decide to play nice today since our date is coming up. However, if he decides to be an asshole, I can threaten to throw it at his groin instead.

Though I wouldn't because it's a sin to waste gourmet coffee.

"Good morning." Veronica greets me the moment she sees me. I swear that woman never sleeps. I'd almost bet she's here more than I am, which is saying a lot since we work on rotation for ten to fourteen days straight.

"It *is* a good morning, isn't it?" I smile wide, bringing the coffee to my lips, then taking a sip. I notice her eyes widen as she looks at my cup. "Something wrong?" I ask her curiously.

"Oh um, no. Sorry." She waves it off and plasters on a smile.

Okay, that was odd.

I can sense Evan before I see him, and when he walks up behind me, I feel his hand on the small of my back. "Since you brought me coffee, I won't even yell at you for being late."

Turning my head to face him, I roll my eyes. "Pretty presumptuous in thinking it's for you." I pick up the cup and hand it over to him. He flashes me a wink before tilting it up to his lips.

"Black," he confirms with a knowing grin. He takes another sip, and his brows pull together as if something's wrong. "This tastes like…" He doesn't finish his sentence before shifting the cup and reading the logo. His eyes widen just like Veronica's did, and now I know I'm missing something.

"What's wrong?" I feel like I'm in the twilight zone with Veronica and Evan's reactions. "Is it a bad coffee shop or something? Are the owners republican or puppy murderers or something?" When Veronica lowers her eyes, I know it's deeper than that.

"Nothing," Evan clips, swallowing hard. "Thanks." He sets the coffee cup down and walks off before I can say another word.

"Veronica," I whisper her name in a plea. "Can you please explain what I missed?"

"It's not my story to tell," she says, pursing her lips together, and I'm worried she's not going to give me anything until she leans forward and continues. "But a woman named Alicia worked there, and he went there every morning before work. They grew close from what I understand, and one morning, she was brought in from a car accident."

"Oh my gosh." I inhale sharply, feeling remorseful that I basically just handed him a reminder of those events.

"He'd been running late that morning and skipped grabbing his coffee. A couple of hours later, she arrived and was in really bad shape. Long story short, Evan went above and beyond to save her life, but it was too late."

"She died," I say, my voice flat and sad. "Wow." Is that why Evan shuts people out and has a brooding nature to anyone who tries to get close to him? Perhaps. But as doctors, losing patients is part of the job. Unless there's a connection that makes it more than just personal.

"And not that he ever came out and said it, but I'm pretty sure he liked her. Evan's always been all work and no play, but every morning, he'd come in with his cup of coffee, smilin' like a fool, and it set the tone for the entire day. After she died, he stopped going in there completely, and his whole demeanor changed. He blamed himself for a long time, and I think a part of him still does."

CHAPTER SEVENTEEN

EVAN

I STEP out of the shower, quickly dry off, then wrap a towel around my waist. As I walk to my bedroom, drips of water fall from my hair and run down my chest. Standing in front of the clothes I laid out across the bed, I wonder if I'm overthinking this.

It's been years since I've been on a real date, but it feels like decades. Medical school and focusing on my residency took most of my time, and when I finally found the courage to ask a girl out, the opportunity passed me by. I deserve the title Mr. Undateable. I think about Alicia for a moment, and sadness rushes over me. It's hard to know when it's our time to go, but I know for a damn fact her life was cut way too short.

The day after the bachelor auction when Emily brought me that cup of coffee, I froze. Tasting that coffee and seeing the logo on that cup dug up old, painful memories. I've avoided that place for years, and I'd done a pretty good job until then. I shouldn't have reacted that way, but I'm human. Sometimes it's difficult to be emotionless when a wound has been partially reopened. Fortunately, she let it go and didn't ask questions. I know I owe her some kind of explanation, but I'm not ready to go down that road yet.

It's almost been two weeks since the bachelor auction since we had to wait until our next day off. I pulled some strings so we both have a later shift tomorrow. Instead of going in bright ass early, we'll start midmorning instead. Seeing Emily every day at work and knowing this night was approaching had us both anxious. With private glances and stolen kisses, she'd tease me and work me up, push me into the supply closet and kiss the hell out of me, then walk out, leaving me to suffer from a major case of blue balls.

I haven't told her what I have planned for tonight other than I'm picking her up around seven, which is in forty-five minutes.

To say I'm rusty when it comes to dating is the understatement of the century. We're technically doing this because of a fundraiser, but it feels much more than that. It's personal at this point. Considering I owe her a massive favor for bidding on me in the first place and saving me from my number one crazed fan, I'm sure Emily's loving every minute of this. Though she'll never admit it, I think she intended to bid on me anyway.

The past few auctions, I've gone out with women who were twice my age. We'd have an early dinner, conversation that always revolved around church and their grandkids, and then it was over. This, on the other hand, is much different and directly conflicts with our unspoken agreement that what we have stays private and between us only.

After Emily won, it encouraged Mama to pry, which complicates things. As a joke, I asked if I could double the bid that Emily made and go on a date with myself. Mama slapped me upside the head for even insinuating I didn't want to fulfill my end of the bargain. She's called and asked a handful of questions about us working together, and I politely asked her to stop. If Mama's already acting this way before the date, it won't be long until the whole town's talking about Emily and me. It's exactly how the rumor mills start around here. Considering we were seen at the wedding together and then she eagerly and so easily outbid April, they probably already have.

After I tuck my button-up shirt into my slacks and snap my belt closed, I put on my shoes. I'm even wearing Oxfords for her. The realization that I actually care about this date hits me pretty hard. Emily Bell is going to ruin me and everything I've tried so hard to avoid. She just came barreling into my life so easily, and now she's inescapable. She's at work, outside of work, and in my fantasies—the woman is dangerous.

I finish drying my hair with the towel, put on my watch, and check my phone. My brothers have done nothing but antagonize me all day about this. Baiting and taunting me about my Mystery Girl and if I'd be able to seal the deal like last time. I'm getting ready to send them all a middle finger emoji and call it a day. Though for me to pull this date off, considering I've worked all week, I had to get their help because the truth is, I'm not going to half ass this. Even made them swear and cross their damn hearts they wouldn't tell Mama or Kiera. Instead of being a dick, I don't respond with a finger salute and instead shove my phone back in my pocket, grab my keys, then head to my truck.

As soon as I step outside, I realize how damn hot and humid it is and roll my sleeves to my elbows as I walk to the driver's side door. I back out of the garage feeling both excited and slightly nervous. Before I pick her up, I stop at a flower shop on the way and grab a fresh bouquet of roses.

"Gettin' your mama some flowers?" the owner, Mary, asks. Occasionally on my days off, I'd bring Mama fresh flowers because I know how much she loves them, but not today.

"No, ma'am." I smile.

"Oh, for a special lady then?" With a smirk, she wraps them in white tissue paper and hands them over.

"Something like that." I shoot her a wink and pay my bill.

Fifteen minutes later, I pull up to Emily's condo and see her rental car. My heart rate increases as I grab the flowers and walk toward her door. I swallow hard, then knock. After a moment, Emily opens the door, and she's so fucking beautiful it takes my breath away. Being the prowess she is, Emily looks down, causing her dark hair to fall into her eyes. It takes everything I have not to kiss the fuck out of her right then. The black dress hangs off her shoulders but hugs her tightly around her waist. My eyes gaze down her body and long, sleek legs until they land on her black fuck-me heels. I'm tempted to run my lips across her skin and skip dinner completely. If how she's dressed is any indication of how much she plans to tease me, then I'm already fucked.

"Hey," she finally says, looking at me from head to toe with a smirk on her face. "You look really nice."

"Hi." I step forward, pressing a kiss to her cheek, then handing her the flowers. "For me? It's almost like a real date," she teases, but I can tell she's genuinely happy about them. She steps aside and allows me to walk inside.

"Well, I have to make sure you get your money's worth and all. Otherwise, my mama will kick my ass. Plus, I kinda owe you."

She laughs, but I'm not joking about Mama.

Instantly, we fall back into our typical routine of teasing each other, and my nerves melt away. I watch her as she walks through the living room and into the kitchen to grab a vase. Images of me ripping her dress off assault my mind before I shake them away. This is more than just one night, and I'm not going to jeopardize it by not being able to control myself around her. Though that tight little number is making things really *hard*.

I watch as she fills the vase with water and places the roses inside. "Thank you for these. They're really beautiful."

"Beautiful flowers for a beautiful woman," I tell her with a smile, and I'm not remotely joking. "But before we leave, you might want to pack a change of clothes and a jacket or something," I add.

She tilts her head and steps from behind the island. "You don't like my dress?"

"I fucking love it and have already fantasized about a dozen different ways I'll peel it off your body, but for what I have planned later, you might not be too comfortable."

Shaking her head, she smiles. "Do I even want to know what you're up to?"

"I wouldn't tell you even if you asked." I wink.

"Fine." Emily playfully rolls her eyes and heads to her bedroom. As she walks past me, I can't keep my eyes off her. When she disappears, I look around her place, and the photographs on a decorative table catch my eyes. There are photos of her on vacation, a picture of her and an older man, probably her father, then a photo of whom I assume are her with her brother and sister dressed up for Halloween in matching *Three Musketeer* costumes. They all look exactly the same; there's no doubt they're related. There's one photo when Emily is a child with her parents, but it looks over twenty years old. Other than what I've read on paper, I barely know anything about her personal life, and I'm determined to change that tonight. I'm surprised when I don't see her mother in any of the recent family photos. I'm so focused on her pictures that I don't notice her return until I feel her body standing next to mine.

"This is my dad," she says, picking up the first photo I saw and looks at it for a moment. "The only man who I'm trying to prove anything to." She sets the picture down and smiles.

Her words become a little too real, and at that moment, I understand so much more about her than before. She's grown up watching her father, knowing he's one of the best in the country, and has siblings who have followed in his footsteps as well. I'm sure it always feels like a competition —always something to prove while standing in the shadows.

I feel regret remembering the words I said to her about her father that first day at the hospital. I insinuated she hadn't worked for her accomplishments, and I know that's not true. Emily's one of the hardest working doctors I've ever met, but not only that, she's also compassionate and driven. She's trying to prove to her father the same way I'm trying to prove to mine that being a doctor isn't just a career, it's a life calling. That's something we'll always have in common.

"I'm sure he's very proud of you."

"Yeah." She looks up at me, and I tuck loose hair behind her ear. Tonight will be a lot harder than I thought, but I promised myself this wouldn't end in sex. However, when she's standing in front of me, looking too fucking irresistible, I'm not so sure I'll be able to keep that promise.

"We should get going. We've got reservations." I look at my watch, then back at her.

"And I know how punctual you are." She smirks and grabs her duffel bag before we head toward the door.

After she locks up, we turn, and I place my hand on the small of her back as we walk to my truck. Opening her door, she glances up at me, and our eyes meet. It feels as if the air stills around us before she gets inside. "Thank you."

I shut the door behind her and get ahold of myself before walking around the truck and climb in. We drive across town, and the awkwardness returns. What the hell do we talk about? Work?

"So," she says at the same time as I do, the nervous tension filling the truck. We both laugh.

"Are you going to tell me where we're going and what we're doing tonight?" she asks.

"No, ma'am. No can do," I tell her and she glares. "Don't you like surprises?"

"Not particularly. Too much of a control freak," she admits.

I chuckle. "Well, you don't get to be in control tonight. But remember, darlin', you ultimately chose this." We drive through Old Town San Angelo and park in front of Da Nonna, an old Italian restaurant that's been around for as long as I can remember, but it also requires a reservation.

"Da Nonna? What kind of name is that?" Emily asks.

"It means Grandma's Place in Italian, apparently. It's the best we've got in this little town, but I'm willing to bet it's better than any fancy schmancy place in Houston."

She snorts. "Houston doesn't have it all. I can't say I've actually been to an authentic Italian restaurant unless you count Olive Garden."

I playfully roll my eyes before I get out of the truck and open the door for her. She loops her arm in mine as we walk inside. The lights are already lowered in the restaurant and candles flicker on each table.

"It smells amazing," she whispers, as I tell the host the name for the reservation.

"Dr. Bishop." The woman smiles. "So good to see you again." The woman comes around to give me a side hug.

"How's everything going?" I ask. A few months ago, she was admitted for pneumonia and had it pretty bad.

"Better, thanks to you." She winks, studying me from head to toe.

"Glad to hear it." I give her a smile, and she glances at Emily, then looks back at me. "Guess I should get you two seated."

We follow her across the restaurant to a secluded corner of the room and take our seats. We're handed menus shortly before the waiter arrives and tells us the food and wine specials for the day. I order a bottle of Merlot. When he walks away, Emily chuckles.

"What?" I ask.

"The hostess wants you so bad," she tells me over the menu.

"Okay, sure she does." The sarcasm isn't lost on her.

"She *does*. Are you always this oblivious when it comes to women?"

She sets the menu down and closes it. The smirk on her face may be permanent.

"I don't know what you're talking about." The waiter thankfully walks up with the bottle of wine and pours it into our glasses. After we give our order, Emily sips her wine and continues the conversation.

"I know a lot about you, Evan Bishop. Probably things you wished I didn't know."

"Oh yeah? Kiera must be getting the scoop from Jackson then." I narrow my eyes at her, then laugh. "I'm not dumb, you know. I know where you're getting your info, and honestly, I wouldn't trust anything he says. Unless it's good things, of course." I throw a wink at her, and she tries to hold back a smile but fails miserably.

"Well, I know that no one in your family wanted you to go to med school or become a doctor. That ranching is in your blood, but you were the only one to break away from it. When you aren't working your ass off at the hospital, you work at the ranch because you still give a shit about your family and their business. You're known as a hardass to everyone who knows you, but you have a soft side when it comes to children or animals or helping others. You also put up a front to scare people away, but that's not who you really are. Also…" She leans in. "You should know you don't intimidate me. At all."

"Damn. Hit the nail on the head. Sounds like I have a stalker," I tease, lifting an eyebrow at her. "But it doesn't take a rocket scientist to figure those things out. Where're the deep, dark secrets? The juicy stuff that no one ever wants anyone else to know?"

She looks at me, and I see the color in her face slightly drain, and it confuses me. I furrow my brows. "What?"

"Nothing," she says. "Just forget about it."

"No seriously, what is it?" The mood shifts, and my curiosity has the best of me.

"We can talk about it later." She smiles. I decide to drop it, especially if she doesn't want to talk about it, whatever *it* is.

We chat about work and med school, and I find myself noticing the little things about her again. The way she smiles, laughs, and randomly licks her bottom lip or nibbles on the corner. She's gorgeous, but she's also so much more—intelligent, funny, and easy to talk to. Had our circumstances been different from the start, I would've asked for her number the morning after our one-night stand and taken her out on a proper date.

Before long, our plates of pasta are being placed in front of us. Emily eats with proper etiquette, and I almost laugh.

"What?" she questions as she cuts her pasta, rolls it with her fork on her spoon before placing the small bites in her mouth.

"I've never in my life seen someone eat pasta the proper way," I admit.

"You remember who my father is, right? My childhood wasn't normal between the nannies and housekeepers raising us. I'm actually jealous of you in that regard. I'm sure you just got to be a normal kid living on the ranch."

I nod. "I did, but I worked my ass off too. I learned there was no play without work at a real early age, shoveling horseshit and doing yard work in scorching temps. I did a lot of stupid chores until I was old enough to really help on the ranch. Then once my brothers got older, I made them do all the stupid shit for me instead." I laugh, remembering when I finally had my license and would dump their asses out into the pastures and drive away. "But I had fun and loved what I did. I think that's why everyone was so shocked when I chose this path."

"I envy you. I really do. I went to private school for as long as I can remember. The nanny was more of my mother than my own. At age five, I had to learn proper etiquette so I could impress my father's social class in public situations such as charity events and fundraisers. Sure, I traveled around the world when I was a teen for medical conferences, but my views were from a hotel window. I may have gotten luxury cars and expensive things, but it just proved to me that money doesn't buy love, and I started to resent it all. I didn't get to choose my friends or boyfriends until I went to college, and even then, I didn't feel like I had complete control of my life. But I was able to discover who I was without being my parents' perfect little puppet 24/7. Being *medical royalty,* as they all called me in medical school, fucking sucked. Everyone either expects greatness or wants to be chummy to get on my father's good side. As sick as it makes me to admit, I'm pretty sure every guy I dated was more in love with my dad than me, and my friends just wanted to be in my family's social circle. That's why I really like living here, and why Kiera and I have stayed such good friends. She never gave a shit about any of that, and it's been freeing. For the first time in a while, I feel like my true self."

"I had no idea." I try to process it all. I can't imagine living that life. The more she tells me about herself, the more I want to know.

She chuckles. "It's just not as great as it seems. But it has some perks. I could've gone to any medical school I wanted, and I had people begging me to work for them. But after my residency, I put my foot down and chose to do what I wanted for once. But the stigma of being Dr. Bell's daughter doesn't go away regardless of where I work, apparently. You even proved that one."

"I'm sorry for that," I tell her. "Really. You're nothing like I thought you'd be."

"In a good way, I hope." She lifts an eyebrow and takes a sip of wine.

"In the best way possible."

We continue eating, and the way she moans as she takes small bites makes me think she might actually be having a foodgasm.

My voice drops low enough for only her to hear as I lean across the table. "If you don't stop moaning like that, we'll be leaving this restaurant and going straight back to your condo."

"It's just so good. You were right; this is the best I've ever had." After she takes another sip of wine, she sucks on her bottom lip, and it drives me fucking crazy.

"Fuck," I whisper as I watch her, and she lifts an eyebrow, knowing exactly what she's doing to me. Before I can say another word, the waiter returns and hands me the check. She hurries and grabs it.

"No, ma'am. You're not paying for this," I tell her with my hand out.

"Yes, I am. The only reason you're here is because I paid for you to be, so the least I can do is treat you," she says with a smirk. The waiter walks away with a smile as we continue to argue about it.

"You're being stubborn." I give her a pointed look.

"*Dr. Bishop*, you should already know stubborn is my middle name." She pulls out a credit card from her clutch.

"Emily Stubborn Bell. It does have a ring to it," I joke, before standing and taking the ticket from her hand and sitting back down.

She rolls her eyes at me. "Not fair. I wasn't expecting you to do that."

"A true gentleman never allows a woman to pay for a meal."

Smiling, she places her hand over her heart. "I guess I'll oblige, sir."

"Shut the hell up," I say with a laugh as I hand the waiter my card and the check. After I sign the receipt, I stand, and we walk to the door. As she walks in front of me, shaking her ass in the short dress, I lean over and whisper in her ear. "You keep teasing me like that, and you *will* be paying tonight."

She looks over her shoulder at me and licks her lips. "You know how I love a good dare."

Of course, that'd be her response.

CHAPTER EIGHTEEN

EMILY

As Evan leads us out of the restaurant, his words repeat in my head. *You keep teasing me like that, and you will be paying tonight.* Teasing him? He hasn't seen anything yet.

While we walk to his truck, our arms brush, and it causes goose bumps. My heart flips, and I can't recall the last time I've felt this way. Having any sort of emotion toward him only complicates things because he's my co-worker, and I swore I'd never do that again. Plus, he acts like an asshole toward me any chance he gets. But tonight he's pulled out all the stops—roses, a great restaurant, dressing up for me. His shirt and pants hug him in all the right places, and he smells so damn good. I don't know what I expected tonight, but it certainly wasn't this. Although he's only here because he's obligated to fulfill his commitment, it feels all too real.

While we head to wherever the hell we're going, I decide that for the rest of the night, I'm going to pretend we're just two regular people on a date. By the way he looks at me before he buckles his seat belt, I don't think he minds too much.

The sun has already set, and the city lights flood the streets. We drive across town until everything is behind us. "So where are we going?" I look over at him.

He just laughs. "You'll see."

Thirty minutes later, we're pulling up to the ranch, and my mouth falls open.

"Remember when I told you to grab that extra pair of clothes? This is why." He smiles and continues down the rocky road that leads directly to the B&B. All the feelings I had the first time I saw this place come flooding back in, and I can't stop thinking about the first night we spent together as Evan parks his truck. The bliss of that night then the panic of the next morning—it was a whirlwind.

"Ready?" He smiles, reaching into the back seat, grabs a backpack, then hands me my duffel bag.

"As ready as I'll ever be," I tell him, taking the bag. I get out of the truck, and we walk inside. The lights are low, and I suspect most of the guests are already in their rooms for the night. As I glance around, I see John tidying up around the main room, and when he looks up and sees us, he flashes a knowing smile.

"There's a bathroom right over there to change." Evan points at a door on the other side and goes to meet his brother.

My heart flutters as he watches me walk away. It's as if he can see me, the real me, the me that not many people know. Being in this part of Texas, away from the hustle and bustle of Houston and my family, actually thrills me. This part of Texas is a little sliver of heaven on earth. I slip out of my dress and put on a pair of jeans, a T-shirt, and tennis shoes. When I walk back out, I see Evan's changed into a pair of boots instead of his fancy Oxfords. That must've been what was in the backpack. "It's gonna get cold out there, so don't forget your jacket."

I glance over at John. "Do you know what he's up to?" I ask, digging for my fleece jacket and pulling it over my head.

"No, ma'am. And I don't ask." He chuckles. "You'll have a good time, though, guaranteed."

I look at Evan. "If I don't, I'm asking for a refund," I quip, zipping my bag. John holds his hand out for the bag, and I gladly let him take it for me.

"I already told you what will happen to me if Mama finds out you're not fully satisfied," Evan says, grabbing my hand and pulling me toward the back door with his bag in his other hand. I laugh at his eagerness. As I cross the threshold, I stumble, and he catches me. I fall into his chest, and when I look up at him, the air stills around us.

"I've got you," he whispers, and my breath hitches. I'm at a loss for words as I stare up into his bright blue eyes.

We're lost in a trance until John opens the door and pulls us back to reality. He hands Evan his cell phone. "Almost forgot this. Left it on the table while you were changing shoes."

Evan clears his throat and releases me. "Thanks."

John gives us a sly look and smiles before turning and shutting the door behind him.

"Let's get going." He holds out his hand. Without hesitation, I take it as he guides me down the steps. It's so dark outside that I can barely see in front of us.

"I can't see anything," I admit, holding him tighter hoping I don't stumble again.

"Do you trust me?" he asks as we continue walking.

"No," I deadpan, but a laugh slips through my lips. "Yes, of course I do," I answer truthfully. Evan has a no-bullshit attitude and a what-you-see-is-what-you-get kind of demeanor. It'd be impossible not to trust a guy like him.

"In a few minutes, your eyes will adjust to the darkness, and you'll be able to see better." His grip tightens as he guides me past the barn and down a trail. The crickets are so loud out here. I can't recall ever hearing them in the city. After a few minutes, just as he promised, my eyes begin to adjust, and I can make out the path in front of me. Eventually, the trail ends and opens onto a large, open field. As a light breeze brushes across my face, I almost close my eyes to take it all in. I can't even hold back a smile at his thoughtfulness for this date. He really put in the effort to do this for me, which gives me butterflies just thinking about it.

Evan stops and unzips the backpack, then pulls out a pair of binoculars and a blanket. I look up at the sky for the first time tonight, and my mouth falls open. There are so many stars visible, and they shine like bright diamonds.

"Oh my God," I whisper, trying to take a mental snapshot of what I'm seeing.

"It's beautiful, isn't it?"

"Yes," I say, completely amazed.

He guides me over to a spot on the ground that's cleared and lays out the blanket. Sitting, he taps the place next to him, and I follow.

"Lie back," he says, and I do, and the sky is all that I can see. Evan lies down next to me, our arms brushing one another's, and my heart is racing so fast I feel like it may burst straight out of my chest.

"Do you see the backward question mark?" His voice is low and silky smooth as he points up at the sky.

"Yes. How cool. I've never seen the stars like this before," I say, glancing over at him. We're face to face, and I need him so fucking bad, but I refuse to make the first move tonight. He's going to have to cross that line if he wants it as badly as I do.

"That's the constellation Leo. The brightest star at the very bottom of Leo is named Regulus, and it's also known as the Lion's Heart. I kinda figured you've never seen the sky like this. There's so much light pollution in cities that it's hard to believe this even exists. So many people take this for granted, but when I get the chance, I try to come out here and appreciate the night sky. If I wouldn't have become a doctor, I like to think I would've become an astrophysicist."

I chuckle. "You'd make a sexy astrophysicist." I look back up at the stars and smile because I've only ever seen the sky like this in pictures. I'm practically speechless.

Evan places the binoculars to his eyes, then hands them to me. "Look in this area of the sky. Scan it until you see a V shape. It's a loose association of bright stars, and they're amazing to look at with these. It's the Beehive Cluster, or if we're really nerding it up, Messier 44. It was one of the first objects Galileo studied with his telescope."

I scoot my body around and lean my head against his stomach, then place the binoculars to my eyes and do exactly what he says. It takes me a minute, and right when I'm ready to give up, I see them. "Holy shit!" I can't believe what I'm seeing.

"Take your time to really look at the star fields. The first time is the best." He chuckles, causing my head to bop up and down on his stomach. I take the binoculars from my eyes and look over at him.

"Show me something else," I tell him, sitting up.

He smirks and scoots close to me, then points at the horizon. "Do you see that star right there? Try to put it in your view, and when you see four other stars in a line very close, you'll see it."

I point the binoculars in that direction and search the sky exactly like he says. I place my elbows on my knees to help steady the binoculars. It takes me a few minutes, but when the stars come into view, it's obvious. When I gasp, he knows I've found them.

"That's Jupiter and its moons," he continues. I could listen to him talk about this all night long. My interest is piqued, and seeing how excited he is makes me interested in learning more.

"Seeing Jupiter like this is unbelievable. I guess this is where I make a corny joke about how you're out of this world, right?" I turn and look at him.

"Sweetheart, we both already know that." He winks.

Evan moves closer to me, his head close to mine so he can see where I'm looking as I scan the sky with the binoculars. Each time we touch, a jolt of electricity soars through me, and I know he feels it too. His voice is just above a whisper as he directs me where to look in the sky to see more star clusters and constellations. I don't want this night to end. I've never experienced anything like this, especially not on a first date.

As I'm completely entranced by this view, he grabs his backpack, digs inside, then pulls something out.

"I got you a surprise," he says, handing me a small gift bag.

I grab it and place my hand inside and laugh as soon as I feel what it is. "Black licorice. Really?" I pull out a piece and happily take a bite. "You know the way straight to a girl's heart."

"Sweetheart, if that's all it took, I would've knocked on your door earlier with a bag of black licorice and called it a night."

I playfully smack him. "Yeah, right. You only knocked on my door because I paid for you."

Evan's smile softens, and he tucks my hair behind my ear. He leans in close, his mouth just inches from mine. "If you wouldn't have snuck out and left me butt-ass naked, I'd probably have asked you out that morning."

I swallow hard and am shocked by the truth in his words. "Evan. I was…"

It's the only words I can get out before his lips crash violently into mine. Tonight, I don't think either of us will survive as we lose ourselves in each other. The stars, the crickets, everything around us disappears as his tongue swirls with mine. He pulls my bottom lip into his mouth and tugs. The sparks ignite between us, causing a fire to blaze deep inside my core. The tips of his fingers brush across my cheek, and I feel as if I'm falling into a dark abyss with him as he deepens the kiss. I can't seem to catch my breath, but I can't get enough of him. My heart is ready to rip straight through my chest as I take my time memorizing his mouth, the way his hair feels entwined in my fingers, and the taste of him. I need his kisses, his touch searing my skin, his heart beating rapidly against mine. I need him in ways I've never needed or wanted him nor anyone before.

I lightly tug at his hair, and he lets out a deep, throaty moan.

"You're going to be the end of my resolve." He smiles against my mouth, painting my lips with his.

I can't hold back my smile either. "And to think it all started with a dare."

He places a quick smack on my lips before pulling away and lying back on the blanket with his arms open. "Come on," he tells me as I scoot my body close to his and lay my head on his arm and look up at the vastness and shining stars.

"Oh," I say, pointing up as I watch a star shoot across the sky leaving a glittering trail behind. I turn and look at Evan, and the way he looks with messy, wild hair and that sexy smile is enough to bring a woman to her knees. I can't help but think how lucky I am to be right here, right now, out of all the places I could be in the world. I will never forget this night for the rest of my life.

His voice pulls me from my thoughts. "The Lyrid meteor shower was a week ago, so watch this area of the sky. If we see more, they'll be around there. And tonight's your lucky night because it's clear and the transparency is great."

Evan holds me tightly against his body, and all I can hear is our staggered breathing and the faint sounds of the crickets. Another star zips across the sky, and I would've missed it had I blinked. His fingers brush against my arm, and as he leans over, he whispers in my ear. "Make a wish on your star."

I smile. "I already have."

Lying there for a little while longer, it's obvious that neither of us wants the night to end, regardless of the yawns coming in quicker succession. It's late, considering we have to be back at work tomorrow. I sit up and stretch, and so does Evan.

"Guess it's about that time, isn't it?" he asks, looking at his watch.

I nod. "Guess it is. Maybe we can do this again sometime?"

Evan stands and holds out his hand for me. I take it, and he pulls me up and into his arms. "I'd like that."

My eyes flutter closed when Evan kisses me softly and sweetly, and I can't help but think that tomorrow all of this will be a distant memory. Things will go back to how they were, and we'll pretend that nothing ever happened—as always. It's these precious moments when he's completely vulnerable that allow me to see who he really is. He hands me the licorice and shakes the blanket out before folding it and shoving it back into the backpack.

I take a piece out and tear off a bite.

"You're such a savage with that stuff." He laughs. "They say that shit causes cancer."

I shrug. "Yeah, I hear coffee can too apparently," I mock. Pushing the bag in his direction, I offer him a piece. "You should try one."

"No fuckin' way. I tried black licorice jelly beans as a kid and almost puked. You must have zero taste buds to think it's delicious. Reminds me of NyQuil."

Now, I'm laughing. "I've been trying to give it up, especially because it's filled with sugar, but I just can't shake it. I haven't found the willpower."

"Well, if you need any help, I'd be glad to assist you in a three-step program for kicking the habit," he muses.

"How gentlemanly of you to offer." I snicker, looping my arm in his as we walk down the trail leading to the B&B.

"I'm always a gentleman." He winks.

"So I've heard." I laugh, though I'm joking. We walk in silence for a few moments before his expression turns somber and he rubs his fingers along his jaw.

"I've been meaning to ask you something," he begins. "I know there's gotta be some kind of backstory as to why you were so adamant about Mr.

Brauer and his leg. I couldn't see it before, which is why I was such an asshole, but Emily, I can see it now. It was written all over your face. You looked so defeated when Dr. Dursley couldn't assure you it could be saved," Evan continues, wrapping his arm around my shoulders.

I let out a long sigh, wondering if I want to go into this right now because the night has been so perfect. Since he's my colleague and "more than just a friend," I trust him, and he deserves to know the truth. I don't have anything to hide, at least not from him, but it's still a painful part of my past I don't willingly share.

"Well, when I was fifteen, I was driving with a learner's permit, and my mother and I were having a heated argument. It was important for me to practice my driving skills, and usually, she was the only one around who could accompany me. Unfortunately, we typically spent those times fighting about me participating in extracurricular activities that would look good on my college applications. I enjoyed science more than sports, and she was constantly on me for not being diverse enough. Anyway, one thing led to another, and the bickering went on, distracting me from double-checking my surroundings. We were at a stoplight, and as soon as the light turned green, I drove into the intersection, and we were T-boned by a truck who ran the red light. I should've looked in both directions before going because I always did, especially as a brand-new driver, but I just wanted to get back home and away from her constant nagging. The truck plowed into my little BMW on my mother's side, and there was nothing I could do. She was trapped between the door and the middle console from the impact. The pressure stopped the blood flow to her leg, and by the time they sawed her out and got her to the hospital, it was too late. Her foot was white, and they couldn't find a pulse. The skin was mangled from her ankle all the way to her thigh." I pause, inhaling a deep breath as I recall the events that changed our lives forever. "Anyway, she ended up needing surgery, and her leg was amputated to prevent infection since there was no blood flow. The surgeon did an above-the-knee amputation, and since then, I've seen firsthand what it can do to someone. It took a huge toll on her and on the family, and my father started working even more to avoid her, which left me at home to help and take the emotional abuse my mother dished out. At first, she was too proud to allow my father to hire someone, so she relied on us kids most of the time. I didn't mind helping her, but I saw the way it destroyed her life. She gave up easily, became depressed, bitter, and basically a shell of who she once was."

"Emily, I had no idea. I'm really sorry," he quietly says, the sorrow evident in his tone. Most people don't know how to respond to a story like that, and I know it's a heavy thing to hear.

"Needless to say, I know what it was like for her, watching her struggle to do everyday tasks. It wasn't easy considering she was so independent beforehand and was left to rely on other people for almost everything. It took away her pride and affected her mental health. And still, to this day, I can't help but wonder how different her life would be if the doctors would've tried to take her leg below the knee, so a prosthetic could've been a real possibility. I truly believe our relationship and her life would've been different. She tried to wear one, but it was too painful, and you know as well as I do, without a knee, it's doable but almost impossible. My father had the money to buy whatever she needed, but the pain was unbearable, and it made her not want to try anymore. Being unable to walk put a strain on our relationship because I felt as if it were my fault. She stopped being a mother, and we've lost years together because of it. Now, it's something she'll have to live with for the rest of her life, and so will I."

"So that's why you worked with ortho surgeons during your residency?" he asks as we walk into the B&B, and I grab my duffel bag that I left with John. After being in the dark for hours, it seems bright inside, though the lights are turned down low. The girl working the night shift sits at the desk, and between a yawn, she greets us. We both say hi at the same time.

Once we get out of earshot and walk toward the front door, I continue our conversation. "Yes, it became a passion of mine to learn everything about orthopedics that I could, hoping that one day I could help other people avoid what my mother went through. I wanted to be their voice when they didn't have one. It was more than just helping patients; it became personal. I know as doctors we're supposed to cut all that off, but seeing Mr. Brauer brought it all back."

"I can understand that. I would've reacted the same way." Evan smiles and opens the door for me to walk out first.

Before he unlocks the truck, he grabs my hand, then pulls me into his arms and holds me.

"I'm always here if you want to talk about anything," he tells me. "Going forward, if this happens again, pull me to the side. Tell me to quit being an asshole. Sometimes when I'm in the moment, it's complete tunnel vision, but you were right. You were completely right, and I'm sorry again."

He smiles, then softly places a kiss on my forehead. This is a whole new side to Evan I could definitely get used to; however, I won't keep my hopes up, knowing that as doctors we pride ourselves on being professional. He's letting his guard down with me tonight, but I know as soon as things get too real, his walls will go right back up. Either way, I'll take him any way I can get him, and if he wants to be sweet and supportive Evan outside of work, I definitely won't stop him.

"I forgive you this time, but don't let it happen again," I joke.

"Don't push your luck, Bell." He smacks me on the ass as I step up to get into the truck.

On the way back to my condo, we talk about the stars and the Milky Way, and Evan explains that if we'd've stayed out a few more hours, we would've seen it rise. I make him promise to show me one day, and he tells me with certainty that he will. As he pulls into my driveway, I know the night is coming to an end. Like a perfect gentleman, he walks me to my door, places my cheek in his hand, and kisses me so sweetly that I almost melt.

I unlock the door, and he watches me step inside.

"Goodnight, Emily," he says before turning to walk away.

"Evan." I muster up the courage to allow my heart to speak, throwing all logic out the fucking window. I know I shouldn't, but right now, I don't care. "Wait…"

He turns and looks back at me, and when our eyes meet, I know I can't let our night be over.

"Please stay."

CHAPTER NINETEEN

EVAN

I STARE into Emily's pleading eyes and see the hopeful way she's looking at me. Her chest rises and falls, waiting anxiously for my response. We haven't hooked up since that last time in the on-call room, but I've thought about ripping her clothes off every fucking day since then. There's something about her that drives me wild and makes me walk toward her to give her exactly what she's asking for.

"I want more than one night with you, Emily," I tell her, brushing my lips against hers. "For the first time in a long time, I want… *more*."

My thumb traces along her jawline, feeling the cool softness of her skin. Texas gets chilly at night, and her cheeks are tinted a nice rosy hue. She nods her head just the slightest bit, so I take a small step back to double-check her response.

"Yes," she confirms.

"Yes what, baby? I need to hear you say it."

She sucks in her lower lip before breaking out in the sweetest smile. "I'm all in."

I tilt my head back and exhale. "Thank fuck."

Grabbing her face in my hands, I plant my mouth on hers and kiss her deeply. She moans against me, clasping her hands around my waist and bringing us together. The urgency to get each other naked so I can bury myself deep inside her takes over. I push us farther inside and kick the door shut with my foot. Her condo is pitch black, and as I follow her steps down the hall, we run into things and knock them over as we stumble our way through.

"Hope that wasn't important," I mumble against her lips when I hear something else fall. When her knees hit the end of the bed, I know we're in her bedroom.

"It's just an artificial plant my ex-boyfriend gave me."

I growl against her smirking mouth. "It's going in the trash first thing tomorrow."

"Why? The plant didn't do anything. It's innocent." Her fingers fidget with the buttons on my shirt.

"It's an accessory to a crime. If you really want a plant, I'll buy you one."

She smiles, bringing a hand up to my cheek. "I kind of like this possessive side of you when you aren't barking orders and pissing me off."

"Oh, I still plan to order you around." I wink, and she rolls her eyes in response. "But you know we'll still have to be professional at work, or we'll never hear the end of it."

"I'm pretty certain Veronica has been onto us since day one anyway."

"Probably. She knows everything." I shrug, not really concerned if she does know because I trust her enough to keep her mouth shut.

"She's the Gretchen Weiners of the hospital."

"Her hair is full of everyone's secrets," I add, smiling at the way she slowly unrolls my sleeves.

"Surprised you're a *Mean Girls* fan." She chuckles.

"Not by a long shot. Don't get cocky, Dr. Bell."

"You know…when you call me Dr. Bell in the bedroom, it makes me think of my father so—"

"Fuck," I mutter, shaking the image out of my head. "You could've warned me sooner."

"I'm warning you now," she says, pushing off my shirt.

I step forward, closing the gap between us and brushing my lips against her ear. "Alright, baby. Your turn." I bring my hand down to the bottom of her jacket and toss it over her head. I pull her shirt off next and quickly undo her bra before throwing that too. Unbuttoning her jeans, I have just enough room for my hand to slide inside. "Are you not wearing panties?" I lean back, watching her expression.

"Nope. After the last time, I didn't trust you." She laughs, then stills when I slip a finger inside her.

"Fuck, sweetheart." I groan, pressing my forehead against hers. "You're so wet."

"I've been waiting eagerly for you to touch me again," she admits, arching her hips. "I've even contemplated on how to piss you off so you'd punish me at work like last time."

Her confession has my cock throbbing against the fabric of my boxers. "You like it when I punish you?" I push a second finger inside, going deeper.

"God, yes." She moans, her head falling back between her shoulders.

"It's amazing what a little spanking and coming will do for your attitude," I tease, thrusting harder.

"Yes…all of that."

"Goddamn, Emily." I release her, kneeling between her legs. I take off her shoes, then her jeans. Once everything is moved out of my way, I sink my tongue inside. Her fingers tightly grip my hair as I work her body, bringing her closer and closer to the edge.

"Evan…please." Her hips arch against my mouth, eager for her release.

Repositioning our bodies, I lift her slightly until she's flat on the bed and bend her legs back, so I can devour her the way she deserves. "Hang tight, sweetheart." I bring two fingers up to her mouth and watch as she sucks them before I sink them back into her pussy. My tongue finds her swollen clit, and I work her simultaneously as she moans and begs for more. She squirms underneath me and tries to cage my face between her thighs.

I pin her leg down with my free hand and drive my fingers as deep as I can, increasing the pace as I lick up her slit and wrap my tongue around her sensitive bud. She's close, but I'm not anywhere near done tasting her.

Her hips arch, her legs shake, and her nails dig into my arms as she rides out her orgasm. Licking my lips, I press a soft kiss to the inside of her leg before leaning back and looking at her. "You look so beautiful."

"That was intense." Her chest rises and falls quickly as she tries to catch her breath.

Standing up, I remove my shoes and pants and boxers. "I'm just gettin' started, baby."

Completely naked, I hover over her body and press a soft kiss to her lips. "I could hibernate between your legs all winter."

"Is that right?"

"It's warm and soft. Tastes like Christmas. Can't think of a better place to hide out for months at a time." This earns a loud, hearty laugh as she wraps her legs around my waist and pushes her hips against my cock.

"And what does Christmas taste like?" she asks.

I cover her mouth, tangling my tongue with hers and letting her taste for herself. She releases an earth-shattering moan that has my cock pressing against her entrance.

"Fuck, baby. When you moan like that, it does shit to me."

Without warning, she reaches down and wraps her hand around my shaft. She strokes it a few times then arches her hips up until my cock slides inside her.

"Yes." Her head falls back slightly as I grab her leg and hook it over my shoulder, driving deeper inside. As she wraps her arms around my neck, I pull out and thrust back in again.

I fuck her hard and fast, building her back up, and when her pussy squeezes my dick, I know she's close. Quickly repositioning our bodies, I put her other leg on top of my shoulder and lean over her body until I'm so deep inside her she completely unravels around me again.

"Oh my God," she screams, palming her breasts as she rides out her release. Once her body relaxes, I know she's thoroughly sated, but I'm not done with her. Not by a mile.

Releasing both of her legs until they fall onto the bed, I press my mouth against her neck. I suck and kiss down her jaw, collarbone, then between her breasts on my way to her belly button. Knowing her body needs a break, I don't go any lower. Kissing back up her stomach, I wrap my tongue around her nipple and suck hard, then switch to her other breast and suck the other. I fucking love her tits, especially how hard her nipples get.

Grabbing her hand, I pull her up as I stand. I bring my mouth to hers, wrapping my arms around her and cupping her ass cheeks. "Your ass is amazing," I mutter against her lips.

"Oh yeah?"

"It fucking taunts me all damn day."

"You can't even see it with my lab coat." She laughs.

"Maybe not, but I'm still picturing it, remembering what it looks like and imagining it under those scrubs of yours."

"How do you make scrubs sound so damn sexy?"

"They're only sexy when they're in a pile on the floor."

She laughs, nodding her head in agreement.

"With the exception of them on you. They hug all your curves, and every damn time I look at you, my cock salutes the gods."

"Oh, you poor baby. Guess that means you've been walking around with blue balls all this time." Her taunting words drive all the blood down to my groin.

I groan. "You have *no* idea, Emily. I think I've jerked off more in the past two weeks than I did when I was a teenager and hoarded nudie magazines."

"Well then the least I could do is take care of that for you." She kneels, wrapping her hand around my erection. I watch her tongue slide up my shaft, and when she moans, my cock jerks in her palm.

"You better be careful," I warn her. "I'm not coming in that pretty mouth."

She sucks on her lower lip, looking like a sex prowess on a mission. Wrapping her lips around the tip, she strokes my shaft and creates a rhythm that has my hips bucking wild. Her hot mouth works me as the sight of her in front of me drives me insane. This woman is my undoing, and I never knew it'd be possible to feel this way again. I stopped believing in that notion years ago, but Emily's awakened something inside me, and I'll do anything to keep it this time.

"Fuck," I groan, my head falling back as she continues to tease the crown of my cock, and I know if I don't stop her, I'm going to explode. "Baby, stop." I tilt my head down, tangling my fingers in her hair to pull her away, but she's persistent and keeps her mouth on me. Reaching down, I grab under her arms and pull her body up. "Why must you defy me?"

She licks her lips and smirks. "Because I enjoy watching that vein in your forehead twitch."

"You sure have a mouth on you," I taunt, pressing my lips to her neck.

"What are you going to do about it, doctor?" Her teasing tone urges me to show her exactly what I'm going to do about it.

I spin her body around, palming her breast with one hand and sliding my hand between her legs with the other. Her head falls back on my chest as I work her clit and pinch her nipple.

"Your defiant attitude is starting to grow on me; however, you still need to learn who's in charge around here."

Her body shakes under my touch as I work her clit, then slide my fingers back inside her. As I feel her tighten around me, I lean my body over hers until she falls against the bed.

"Evan!" she squeals, bracing herself. Holding my weight up with my elbows, I dip my head and kiss the soft spot behind her ear before making a trail down her neck and shoulder.

"You have me so goddamn worked up, sweetheart," I growl when she arches her back and presses her ass against my cock.

"Then fuck me," she whimpers, pushing her body harder into mine. Reaching down, I grasp my shaft and position it against her until I effortlessly slide back inside her. She moans and pants as I thrust in and out.

"Your cunt is so tight. Fuck," I growl into her neck. "Keep your ass up, baby." Reaching above her head, I wrap a fist around her headboard and increase our speed. As I thrust deeper and harder, our bodies move up the bed from the forceful rhythm. The sound of skin slapping against skin echoes throughout the room, and when she cries out, I give her ass a quick slap. Her pussy grips my dick, and she comes undone—moaning and screaming. I thrust twice more before I'm losing myself along with her.

Our bodies collapse on the bed, and I pull her into my arms. Our rapid breathing is all that can be heard, and I can feel the beating of my racing heart. The fact that I think about her way too much, always want to be around her, and try to find any reason to touch or be near her tells me I'm already in way over my head when it comes to Emily Bell.

She's absolutely beautiful, witty, smart, and makes my dick hard at first glance. She's everything I've tried to stay away from, but I can't anymore. I won't miss my chance this time.

Waking up with Emily in my arms is definitely new for me, but I don't mind it one bit. Her warm body presses against mine, and when she purposely wiggles her ass, my cock stirs and pushes against her lower back.

I move her messy, dark hair to the side and expose her neck. "I'd stop doing that if I were you," I growl in her ear, wrapping an arm around her waist and sliding a hand up to cup her breast. "Otherwise, we're going to be about three hours late for work."

She reaches back between us and wraps her fist around my shaft, stroking it roughly. I bring my hand down between her legs and feel how wet she already is for me.

"Fucking hell," I mutter against her neck. "You're a bad influence."

"I doubt it's that bad if it means you're getting laid," she teases.

"Okay, I can't argue with that." I chuckle, working my fingers inside her. She grinds down on my hand, and I feel the pressure build. Needing to feel her again, I lift and bend her leg until she's exposed and I can slide into her tight pussy. Thrusting in and out, I dig my fingers into her hips and increase the pace, driving deep and hard into her. "Fuck, baby. You feel so goddamn good."

"Right there," she purrs. "Don't stop."

She brings an arm back and wraps it around my neck as I hold her tighter and fuck her like my life depends on it. She hangs on tightly as I bring us both over the edge, and soon, our quick breathing is all that can be heard.

"C'mon," I say, slapping her ass. "Let's take a shower, you dirty girl."

"But you like it dirty," she teases, letting me lead her to the bathroom.

Once we're showered and changed, I head to her kitchen to make some coffee. Luckily, I have extra scrubs in my locker at work, so I don't have to stop home on my way. However, if Emily and I will be spending more time together outside of the hospital, I have a feeling I better have extra clothes in my truck just to be on the safe side.

"Hey, did you move my pictures?" Emily shouts from the living room.

"What pictures?" I respond, walking over to where she's standing.

"The ones of my family that we were looking at yesterday. I walked in here, and they were all face down."

"Uh, no. The only time I was in here was with you before our date. Do you think they fell over when we were stumbling in last night?"

"Yeah, perhaps." She releases a relaxed breath. "It's just weird that all of them fell down face forward. You'd think they would've fallen down the other way."

"Well, all I know is that you mauled me like a tiger in heat, so it's possible we shook the entire place."

"Oh my God," she says, laughing. "You mauled me first."

I spin her, so we're face to face and wrap my arms around her. "Maybe, but if our co-workers find out, I'm telling them you came onto me. I don't need a sexual harassment complaint in my file."

"Yeah, that'd be very believable." She rolls her eyes. "If I'm going down, though, you're going down with me." She reaches around and smacks my ass. "We better get moving if we're going to keep you punctual, or they'll all know something's up. Especially since Dr. Umbridge is back."

CHAPTER TWENTY

EMILY

"BEFORE I FORGET," Evan stops me before I can get into my car. I finally got it back after getting it fixed. That asshole cost me fifteen hundred dollars.

"Yes?"

He cages me against the door with his hands on both sides of me. "My sister, Courtney, and her husband are coming down next weekend for the triplets' first birthday, and we're throwing a party. They're bringing all their friends, and their kids and my entire family will be there."

"So you want me to scram, is that what you're saying?"

He tickles my side, making me wiggle closer to him. "No, I want you to come with me. Introduce you to everyone."

"I've already met most of your family," I remind him.

"Yeah, but now I want to introduce you as my girlfriend."

My eyes widen as my smile spreads, threatening to split my face in two. "Girlfriend, really?"

"I mean, girlfriend sounds so juvenile, but I don't think I can get away with kissing you and calling you my *friend* around my family. If I don't set boundaries from the start, they'll start planning our wedding and future kids' names."

"Well, if that isn't enough to induce an anxiety attack," I tease because I already adore his family. They're so different from mine that I don't even mind their antics.

"Plus, I'd love for you to meet Courtney. She has her hands full with the triplets most of the time, but they'll be captured by Mama and the family once they're here, so we can actually sit and chat with my sister."

"Okay, sounds fun. I'll have to brush up on my interview skills, but I think I can handle it."

He laughs and kisses my forehead. "She'll love you; don't worry. They all will."

Evan opens my door for me and waits for me to get in and settled before shutting it. We're driving separately to the hospital to continuing playing the part. I reminded him in the shower that he can't act differently at work, but even I know that's going to be hard. Pretending to bicker back and forth will have to be something I remind myself or perhaps I'll just give him something to get angry about so neither of us cracks.

The thought makes me laugh as I follow him down the road. Irritated and annoyed Evan is actually really hot, so I usually don't mind when he gets that way. Needing to purge my brain, I call Kiera so I can tell her everything.

"It's about time! I've been pacing anxiously to hear about your date!" she says as soon as she picks up the phone. "So tell me everything."

"Everything everything?" I tease.

"Oh God, yes please."

"You're such a freak." I laugh. "It was an amazing date," I start, ready to gush about it all. I tell her about dinner and his surprise outing under the stars. I explain all about the constellations and planets he showed me and how gorgeous it was.

"Damn, who knew Evan Bishop had a romantic bone in his body? Damn!" she whistles, pretending to pant. "So did you do it under the stars then?"

I chuckle, rolling my eyes at her ability to have no boundaries whatsoever. "No, but he did stay the night."

"Ooohhhh…"

"And you'll be happy to know we're…*together*. I guess."

"Together?" she asks with a hint of amusement.

"Yes, like together-together."

She releases a breath. "Well, it's about fucking time."

I groan at her tone. "Yeah, yeah. Well, anyway, it was perfect. The perfect night with dinner, stargazing, and lots of mind-blowing sex."

"I'll make sure the MC adds that to Evan's bachelor auction card next year." She laughs.

"I better bring extra cash just in case April returns with a vengence." I chuckle. Sorry, April. Evan's *mine*.

We chat the entire drive to the hospital. When I look in my rearview mirror, I notice the same car has been behind me almost since I left my house. Feeling more paranoid than normal, I try to relax, so I don't have another panic attack.

"What is it?" Kiera notices my sudden mood change.

"A car's been following me, but I was so distracted I didn't really realize it at first, but now I remember it's been behind me for a long time now."

"Do you think it's Richard?"

"It's not the same car, but that doesn't mean anything. He could've rented one after smashing into mine."

"Keep me on the phone until you're in the hospital."

"Evan's driving in front of me, so I'll park next to him."

"Okay, good."

"I'm pulling into the parking lot now." I look up and see the car turning. Squinting, I get a better look at the driver. Exhaling, I release a relieved breath. "It's a woman," I tell her. "False alarm."

"Thank goodness."

"Okay, well, I'm at work now, so I'll text you later when I get a break." We say goodbye, and I hang up just as Evan appears at my door.

"You can't be opening my door for me and being all sweet. People are going to get suspicious before we even walk inside." He takes my hand and helps me stand.

"I said I'd be careful *at* work. I didn't say anything about the parking lot." He winks, leaning in to kiss me, but I put a finger against his lips and stop him.

"Technicalities, Dr. Bishop." He narrows his eyes in disapproval. "Someone could still see us out here, so unless you're okay with everyone and their mamas knowing about us, I suggest you control yourself."

He grunts, lowering a hand to his groin to adjust himself. I chuckle at the pained look on his face before grabbing my bag and locking my car.

"That's more like it," I tease, licking my lips. "Remember to act annoyed and moody. Shouldn't be too hard, though." I wink, looking down at the bulge below his waist, then pat him on the cheek.

"You're playing with fire, woman," he warns, his voice low and gravelly, the very combination that soaks my panties anytime he speaks like that. He smacks my ass before walking toward the employee entrance.

"Guess I better stock up on burn cream," I mock, walking ahead of him, so we don't walk in together.

Once I'm at my locker, I grab a couple of pieces of licorice out of my bag and stuff the rest of my things inside. Evan went to report to Dr. Umbridge and get a briefing on what's been happening since we had yesterday off. Butterflies swarm in my stomach as I think about how the past twenty-four hours have been, how things have changed, and where things between Evan and I are heading. Admittedly, I'm nervous, considering the last time I dated a co-worker and how that ended, but I know deep down that Evan is different. He's not dating me to get to my father or to advance his own career. He's only ever been interested in me and only me.

As soon as I walk to the nurses' station and see Evan standing with Dr. Umbridge, I slap on my game face. He probably won't notice anything, considering he's been gone since I first arrived, but the other doctors and nurses will if we don't keep up the façade.

"Dr. Bell, it's lovely to see you again." Dr. Umbridge greets me.

"Dr. Umbridge, it's been a few weeks. How was your vacation?" I offer him my hand, and when he takes it, then covers his other hand over it, sandwiching me in an affectionate greeting, I glance over at Evan whose jaw is ready to snap off. I laugh internally at the possessive look he's giving Dr. Umbridge behind his back, so just for fun, I see just how much I can get away with.

"Let's just say it was a much-needed vacation." He laughs. I lean into him and laugh, pressing my free hand against his chest.

"Well, good for you. Honestly. I'm sure your wife enjoyed having you all to herself for a bit."

"Nah, no wife. Most women don't understand the demands of the job and can't handle the long hours." He releases my hand, and I cross my arms over my chest.

"I totally get that," I say. "I've never had much luck in that department either."

Before he can respond, Dr. Umbridge's pager goes off, and when he glances down to read it, Evan shoots me death glares.

"I'll have to excuse myself…"

Evan cuts off his words and grabs my arm before he can finish. "No problem. We have a situation we need to deal with anyway."

I wave over my shoulder as Evan drags me down the hallway back to our lockers. Fortunately, it's empty, but as soon as he shuts the door, I burst out laughing.

"What the hell do you think you're doing?" His stance is hard as he places his hands on his hips. "You think that was funny?"

"Are you serious right now?" I take a step toward him. "I was testing you, and I'm sorry, but you failed miserably."

"Testing me for what? I'm not going to play these little games with you, Emily—"

"Okay, I'm sorry!" I hold my hand up to stop him. "I was just testing your reaction because when we're at work, you're supposed to act indifferent, not like you might murder the next guy who smiles at me."

"I would've been just fine had you not gone out of your way trying to seduce him," he badgers.

"Oh please…Dr. Umbridge is old enough to be my father, so now you're blowing things way out of proportion."

"So you weren't purposely trying to make me jealous?"

"Not jealous," I argue. "We agreed to keep things the same at work, so if we're going to do that, we have to bicker like we always have."

"Right so…" He stops when it finally clicks in his head. "So you gave me a reason to be pissed off. Is that what you're saying?"

"Do you really think you could've kept up the act otherwise? The second I walked over, you were undressing me with your eyes."

He brushes a hand through his hair, making it messier than before. "To be fair, I had just seen you naked, so it was still fresh in my mind."

I swat his chest, but he catches my hand and pulls me forward until our bodies come together. "I doubt we'd be the first office romance in this hospital, especially since it's a small town."

"Yes, but unless they're trying to prove themselves and gain respect based on their hard work ethic, they don't have much to worry about," I remind him. He knows how important it is for me to make a name for myself on my own merit. "I want to be labeled as a professional before being labeled as the new doctor who's sleeping with the hot doctor."

"You are a professional, and you have killer work ethic—no one doubts that." He presses a soft kiss to my nose. "But I understand. Though once my family all knows, it'll only be days before rumors start spreading around. Everyone knows everyone even if they're an hour away. Especially Mama. She's the gossip headquarter's queen."

I laugh, wrapping my arms around his neck and pulling his lips to mine. "Guess that means I still have a week to show everyone what I'm made of."

The morning goes by smoothly with only a few patients. Deciding to take my lunch early, I head to the cafeteria and grab some food. I call Kiera, but she doesn't answer. A few minutes later, she sends me a text.

Kiera: Sorry, Trent and I were…busy.

Emily: And now I've lost my appetite.

Kiera: What's up? Everything okay?

Emily: Yeah, everything's fine. Just eating lunch. Evan invited me to his sister's kids' birthday party next weekend. I'm excited to meet Courtney and her family, but I'm nervous too. He said I'd be

coming as his "girlfriend," and now I'm worried I'll make the worst first impression ever.

I hit send, and thirty seconds later, my phone rings and a picture of us pops on the screen.

"Crisis mode 101," I answer with a laugh.

"Tell me why you're freaking out."

"I'm not. I mean, not really. Just nervous, maybe anxious. I want them all to like me. He only has one sister, and it'd be nice if we got along, ya know?"

"Like I've told you before, Courtney is the most easygoing person you'll ever meet. She approved of River without question, and that woman basically showed up on Alex's doorstep telling him she was pregnant, so unless you're a pathological liar, she's going to love you."

"Even though I stole his clothes after our one-night stand because I thought Evan was Drew?"

"Oh, right. Okay, well maybe don't bring that up."

I chuckle, grabbing my food wrappers and tossing them before heading back to the elevator. "I'll make sure to steer clear of that topic."

"Plus, Trent and I will be there, so we can intervene if you need us to," she tells me matter-of-factly.

"Speaking of which, you and Trent having noon hookups, huh? Things must be getting serious."

She snorts. "I'm just gonna be blunt and say it. He's *really* good in bed."

"Oh my God," I respond, laughing as I step into the elevator. "You mean he knows how to work his gearshift."

I lean over to press the button to my floor, and when I look up, I gasp. The doors are sliding closed, but I see his face down the hallway. The phone slips out of my hand and falls to the floor. Once the doors close and the elevator starts moving, I suck in a long breath. I can hear Kiera talking, but I'm too stunned to move.

The moment I looked up and saw Richard's face, I completely panicked.

Finally reaching down for my phone, I pick it up and bring it to my ear, hoping Kiera's voice will soothe me enough so I don't have a panic attack.

"Sorry," I finally say.

"What the hell? Did you drop your phone?"

"Y-yeah. I-I…"

"What is it?" she asks rushed.

"I don't know. Maybe I'm seeing things, but I could've sworn I saw Richard."

"What? In the hospital?"

"Yeah, down the hallway just when the elevator doors were closing. He wasn't close, but I recognized his features."

The elevator stops on the ER floor, and when the doors open, I step out and walk right toward the lockers. I need to settle my nerves before I get back to work.

"This is starting to freak me out, Em. You better tell Evan and call that cop. What if he was following you this morning and disguised himself as a woman?"

I hadn't thought of that, and now that I am, I'm creeped the hell out. "Oh my God," I mutter, putting the pieces together. "The pictures on my mantle."

"What about them?"

"Last night before our date I was showing them to Evan, then when we got back, we basically ripped each other's clothes off and ended up in my bedroom all night, so I hadn't noticed anything. However, this morning when I walked into my living room, all the picture frames were facing down."

"Holy fuck, Em." She gasps. "That's freaky as hell. You think he was inside your place?"

"He's been following me, so I really wouldn't put it past him, but it didn't look like anyone had broken in. I figured the photos fell when we were stumbling down the hall last night. We tipped a plant over so—"

"Okay, but what if it's exactly what it sounds like, and the creeper is not only following you but also stalking you outside your house, probably with binoculars and night vision goggles, and saw you showing Evan those pictures? He would've seen you two leave together and could've easily gotten in through an open window or something. Then it's no coincidence you were followed to work the next day, and now he's at the hospital."

"I think I'm going to be sick." He's been in my home. He's watched me for who knows how long, and there's no telling what he's seen. It's been three weeks since he nearly chased me off the road and got away.

God, I feel so violated. Stalking me, watching me, obsessing about me. It sends shivers down my spine, and my skin breaks out in goose bumps. I'm so creeped out.

"Em, you need to tell Evan right away. Call that officer and don't go home by yourself."

"I don't understand what he wants!" I shout, feeling frustrated. "Does he really think hurting me will bring his wife back?"

"He's crazy, Em. Losing her made him lose it, and he needs help, but that isn't on you."

"But he thinks it is."

"Who cares what he thinks. He's psycho."

That's an understatement.

"Okay, I'm going to find Evan."

"Good idea. Please call me after, okay?"

"I will," I promise before we hang up.

I still have hours of my shift left, but I'm not sure how much I'll be able to focus after that. Constantly looking over my shoulder, worried he'll pop out of nowhere and show up. My foot taps nonstop as I dig around my locker for the rest of my licorice. The bag is almost empty, and I make a mental note to restock next time I'm at the store. I start making a list of other things I should probably get while I'm there to, and I let my mind wander for a few minutes when I feel someone behind me. My hands get clammy. My heart races with fear, paranoia sets over me, my chest tightens and it's like the car chase all over again.

Instinctively, I jerk my elbow back and hear an "umpf" when I nail him. Spinning around the bench I'm sitting on, my eyes widen when I see Evan hunched over in pain.

"Oh my God," I screech, rushing over to him when his body hits the floor. "Are you okay?" He's in the fetal position, and when I look down, I notice his hand cupping his groin. "Oh, shit. I nailed you in the balls, didn't I?"

He nods, and I feel even more awful when I see tears forming in his eyes. "Fuck. I'm so sorry. Do you want me to get you an ice pack or anything?"

"No…" he breathes out. "Just gimme a minute."

After he recoups, I help him stand and can't stop apologizing. I hadn't meant to junk punch him, and I feel even worse knowing what I need to tell him.

"Okay, I think they've fallen back down now," he says with a small grin.

"Why were you sneaking up on me?" I ask when we both take a seat at one of the round tables.

"I wasn't," he defends. "I called your name twice before, and you didn't even flinch."

"You did?" Fuck. "I'm sorry…I was two seconds away from having a panic attack, so it's probably good you came in when you did—"

"Why? What's wrong?" His panicked tone keeps my heart racing hard, and when I tell him the entire story, he looks like he's about to murder someone.

"I've fucking had it with that motherfucker," he spits out. "He wants to keep this shit up, I'm done letting the police handle it. He's had a warrant out for his arrest, and he's just been out there following and stalking you."

"I'll call the cop and let him know. Maybe they can bring an extra guard to the hospital until they catch him or something. Or they'll work a little harder to find him if I tell him all this new shit he's been doing," I say.

"I should've figured something was about to happen. It's been too quiet these past couple of weeks. Probably got a new car too."

Once Evan calms down, he stays with me as I call the officer who wrote up the police report and tell him everything. He reassures me his guys are on it and will be checking Richard's home again and any other properties he owns. They've been running his credit and debit cards, but no new charges have been placed. He's living off the grid just enough not to get caught.

The officer tells me to come in and file another report of him breaking the restraining order, stalking me, and for breaking and entering. Though I can't prove any of those events, keeping a paper trail is the only thing I can do right now. The more paperwork I have to show he's a threat to me, the better chances of him being charged once he's caught. They could easily bring him in for suspicious activity, and once they get the video footage from that floor, I'll be able to prove he was here.

We continue working our shift, but Evan could tell I was distracted. I didn't want to leave the ER short staffed, so he stayed by my side the entire time. So much for going under the radar as a couple. He was pissed I left the ER without telling him, but I was so hungry, and I didn't think going to the cafeteria would put me in danger. Now, I know Richard has no boundaries, and considering I have no idea what he's actually capable of, I'm freaked out even more.

"If we're going to make it to the station on time, we better get going," Evan reminds me as I shuffle through my locker again.

"Okay," I tell him, grabbing my duffel bag and throwing it over my shoulder. He's going to follow me to the station before following me home.

We walk out of the employees only door, and it's already dark out, but the parking lot lamps light our pathway. As soon as I see my car, I know something's wrong.

"Oh my God."

Evan rushes past me and kneels by my tires. "Fucking slashed." He runs a hand over the rubber, shaking his head and locking his jaw. "Motherfucker."

"I just got my damn car fixed!" I shout, my bag falling off my shoulder and landing on the pavement.

"Let's go." He stands up, grabbing my bag with one hand and taking my hand in the other. If I thought Evan was pissed before, he's boiling now. I've never seen his face so red and tense, and I'd be willing to bet he'd be releasing that anger if I wasn't here right now.

Evan drives us to the station, and we report everything, including the tire slashing. The officer tells us there's a guy staking out Richard's house right now and will keep someone there until he's caught. They're keeping an eye on as much as they possibly can.

"We can put an officer outside of your condo as well. Make sure he doesn't break in again and keep an eye on you when you're home."

"She won't be home," Evan interrupts. I turn to look at him and see his jaw clench. Squeezing his hand to get his attention, he doesn't budge. "She'll be staying with me until this asshole is behind bars. She's not safe there."

I wouldn't feel safe either, but I don't say that aloud.

"That's probably for the best," the officer says, honestly. "Write down the address and an alternate phone number, just in case."

Once we're done at the station, Evan drives me back to my house so I can pack a bag. I have no idea how long I'll be staying with him, so I pack a little of everything. The ride to his house is quiet and tense, neither of us knowing what to say. Things were going so great, and now I feel like I've brought him onto this crazy train ride with me.

By the time we get to his house and I unpack my things, I can't stand the silence between us anymore. I find him in the living room in one of the chairs that sits in the corner. The room is dark except for one small lamp that's lit nearby.

"I'm sorry," I say, kneeling between his legs. "This isn't what you signed up for, and I wouldn't blame you—"

He snaps his head toward me, then reaches down and grabs my arms before pulling me up onto his lap. My arms instinctively wrap around his neck as my legs straddle him. His hands cup the back of my neck as he brings my mouth down to his, kissing me so sweet and soft that I melt into his hard body.

"Evan…" I whisper his name—a quiet plead against his lips. I need to know what he's thinking, what this means for us, and how we're going to get through this.

"All in, baby. Remember?" It's as if he knows what I needed to hear, and my eyes swell with tears at the realization that this man isn't running away. He's going to fight this battle with me no matter what.

"All in," I confirm with a grateful smile.

"Never doubt that for a second. Got it?"

I nod as our mouths magnetize together in a heated kiss. His tongue slides between my lips, creating a hot desire low in my stomach as he arches his pelvis and urges me to reciprocate. I grind my hips against him, feeling the friction build between us, and when he releases a loud groan, I know he's seconds away from tearing off our clothes.

"Wait…" I say as he brings his hands to the hem of my shirt. "Aren't you going to give me a tour?" I grin as his erection pushes against my leg.

"Of course." He flashes a devious smirk before sliding his hands under my ass and lifting me up as he stands. "Let's start with the bedroom, shall we?" He smacks my ass, and I laugh all the way to his bed.

CHAPTER TWENTY-ONE

EVAN

SEVEN DAYS PASS by in a blink, and every morning, I've woken up with Emily in my arms. We've quickly fallen into a routine, and each morning, we have a cup of coffee before work, take turns making breakfast, and often shower together to save water, or at least that's the joke. Though the Richard thing pisses me the fuck off, he's only given us an unexpected opportunity to move our relationship to another level. Usually, I'd have taken things much slower, but now that she's practically living with me, I don't want her to leave. Today is our first day off since everything happened, and we're due to be at the ranch soon for that birthday party, though all I want to do is crawl back in bed and get naked.

"Are you almost ready?" I ask, leaning against the doorway as I watch Emily go back and forth between what to wear.

She turns from studying the sundresses lying across the bed and looks at me in complete frustration.

"Okay." I hold up my hands but keep the smile on my face. "You should just wear the dress you have on. You look great." I walk forward, pull her into my arms, and plant a kiss on her lips.

She sucks in a deep breath. "I texted Kiera some pictures, but she was zero help. If it were up to her, I'd be dressed like a go-go dancer twenty-four seven."

"For once, I don't disagree with her."

She releases a light laugh. "I know I'm probably overanalyzing it, but I want to look nice. It's only a birthday party with your entire family who probably already know everything about me." She shrugs her shoulders, looking defeated.

I give her a pointed look, then smirk.

"I just want to make a good impression since your sister will be there, and I haven't met her yet."

Running my fingers through her hair, I pull her face into my hands and force her to look into my eyes. "Courtney is the most laid-back of them all. Trust me when I say as soon as you two meet, you'll feel like you've known her for life. She has that kind of personality."

She slightly relaxes. "I'm taking your word for it."

"Also, Mama rented a bouncy house, and there's going to be lots of kids, food, and cake, and probably Kool-Aid. So if you know what's good for you, don't wear anything too nice." Finally, she lets out a laugh, and I grab her hand and lead her to where the gifts are in the living room.

One day after work last week, we went shopping for the triplets. Emily insisted on smart pads and stroller ride toys that we're going to have to ship to California for Courtney afterward.

"Don't forget the birthday cards," Emily says as she picks up one of the big boxes wrapped in pink paper. I grab them from the table and pick up the other two boxes. After I lock the door, we walk through the garage, and I can already tell it's going to be hot as hell today.

Glancing at Emily, she smiles at me, then climbs into the truck. As we drive to the ranch, we talk about a little of everything, and being around her feels natural and comfortable. It's then I realize how much I'm going to miss being with her every day like this. Though I've lived alone for years, I'm already used to having her around. Not to mention the morning sex. Getting up early is no longer an issue for either of us. Not many people around here fully understand this work lifestyle, so it's nice to have a companion who gets it. When Richard's finally caught, and she goes back to her condo, it'll be strange having an empty house again.

By the time we make it to my parents' house, I can tell Emily's nerves have gotten the best of her again. After I park, I grab her hand, kiss her knuckles, then look into her eyes. "Stop worrying. You'll get wrinkle lines," I tease. "Everyone already loves you."

She smiles. "We should've brought vodka."

Laughing, I shake my head. "No spiking the punch."

"Damn. You're no fun."

I wink back at her, hoping she'll finally relax and just be herself. There's no reason they won't like her, so I'm not the least bit worried.

After we grab the gifts from the back, I lead Emily to the backyard where everyone is huddled at picnic tables near a big bounce house with an inflatable slide. Dad is barbecuing, and I hear Courtney laughing with Jessica and Dylan. If my hands weren't full of gifts, I'd grab Emily's hand to give her an extra ounce of courage.

"That's Jessica, right? The girl who emceed the auction?" Emily asks.

I chuckle. "Yeah, that's Jessica, Dylan's lady. Mama adores her quirky personality."

"She could've written a book about all of you with how accurate her descriptions were." Emily gives me a smirk.

"Don't get cocky," I tell her, bumping her arm with mine.

As soon as I walk up and we set down the gifts, Courtney stands and basically jumps into my arms.

"My big brother! I missed you." She gives me a squeeze.

"Are you drunk?" I ask with a chuckle.

She gives me her signature shut-the-hell-up look. "No, I'm just happy to see you." Courtney glances over at Emily who's smiling sweetly.

"Court, this is my girlfriend, Emily." It seems like everyone stops talking and looks at us, but I try to ignore them because it feels so natural to call her that. Emily's smile grows, and I interlock my fingers with hers. The electricity that streams between us is so damn powerful that I can't help but smile too. Kiera is sitting by Benita and Aunt Charlotte, and she lets out a big aww. It's the first time I've admitted that publicly, but I want the whole world to know at this point. Emily is mine—exactly the way it should be.

Courtney immediately hugs Emily. "I'm so happy to meet you! I've heard so much about you."

Emily laughs. "I hope all good things. Nice to meet you too."

"Totally wonderful things. Oh, you gotta meet my husband, Drew."

Courtney waves him over from the guys. He's carrying one of the triplets in his arms, and I notice River and John are holding the other two.

"*This* is Drew." I look at Emily and see her cheeks redden. I hold back a laugh because she thought Drew was me the morning after the wedding. Though we're both built the same, we're opposites.

"Hi, there," he says.

"Oh my goodness. They're adorable," Emily says, glancing at the triplets. Courtney dressed them in matching "I'M ONE" birthday shirts, and admittedly, it's kinda cute.

On cue, Mama walks up. "I could always use some *more* grandkids." She winks at Emily and me.

"You're a greedy grandma," Alex says loud enough for everyone to hear, and River giggles, thankfully breaking Mama's attention away from us.

"And it's time for more. I want a minimum of twenty grandbabies to spoil, so y'all need to get to work." She points at all of her kids.

As soon as Mama walks away, Courtney speaks. "Hell to the no. I'm d-o-n-e, done."

"That's what I said too," Viola says, with Kayla next to her. Kayla is carrying her daughter in her arms and gives me a smile. Courtney met them in college, and the last time I saw either of them was at Courtney's wedding three years ago. There's a quick introduction, and I know Emily's head is spinning with all of the names. Luckily, she's sober this time so she can retain all the information.

I'm so happy to see everyone here. Considering Mama insisted the birthday party be held here for the kids since she barely gets to see them during the holidays, Courtney decided she wanted all the aunts and uncles in one place, which meant she dragged all her friends here—Travis, Viola, Kayla, and Logan—along with all the kids. I see Logan and Travis are chatting with John, and I give him a wave.

"Well, we know why you had tons of kids," Courtney tells Viola, glancing over at Viola's husband, Travis. He lifts his hands as if he's not guilty.

"Keep on talking, you're just jinxing yourself," Viola tells Courtney. "Once you open the flood gates..."

"Exactly," Kayla says. "I swear it's in the California water."

"Well, you're up next, Kay," Court tells her. "Seriously. We've got three. Viola has three. You need to push out two more."

Emily can't stop laughing as they go back and forth about getting pregnant and having more kids.

"Technically, we have two, so keep your mouth shut." Kayla points a finger at Courtney, but she doesn't even flinch. "Skylar is my stepdaughter, and our other daughter, Abigail, is only one, so trust me, we have our hands plenty full," Kayla tells Emily.

"See what you have to look forward to." Courtney looks at Emily and crosses her arms, then bursts into laughter.

Emily's mouth drops open. "Uh. Guess Evan wasn't joking when he said his mama would be asking about weddings and babies."

"Did someone say Courtney's pregnant?" Jackson stands up and yells across the way, causing everyone to look over at us again.

"Shut up, Jackson! No one's pregnant," Courtney narrows his eyes at him.

"Come on Court-Court, it's nothing to be embarrassed over."

Courtney flips him off where only he can see it, and as she opens her mouth to tell him off, one of the triplets starts crying, and Drew tries to calm him, but it's no use. Emily asks if she can hold him, and Drew hands him over. As soon as Emily has him in her arms, he stops crying.

"You're so cute with your big blue eyes," Emily tells him, and he just stares at her.

"Looks like you've got some competition." Courtney elbows me with a laugh.

"What's his name?" Emily asks.

"This one's Anderson. River is holding Creevey, and John has Delaney."

Emily's eyes light up when she puts the pieces together. "They all have last names as first names." She smiles when Courtney confirms with a nod.

"Drew and I couldn't agree on anything, which meant naming three babies became impossible. So instead of trying to decide on three random names, we decided to go with a theme. It was either names of presidents or last names, but ultimately the vote went to the latter."

"I love it. What a cute idea." Emily makes a silly face at Anderson, and he giggles.

All the Bishop kids have blue eyes and look exactly like we did when we were little. Anderson is an exact replica of Courtney as a baby. I glance around at them and see Alex holding Riley and can't help but think of how much of my heart my nieces and nephews already have. Being an uncle is one of the greatest things I've ever experienced.

Kiera and Benita walk up, and I leave the girls to chat, but before I walk away, I steal one more look of Emily holding the baby and take a mental snapshot.

I walk over to the picnic table where all the guys are sitting and take a seat. Drew, Travis, Logan, Benita's husband, Aaron, and John are talking about sports, so naturally, I change the subject.

"How was the flight?" I ask Drew. I think back to the first moment I met him and basically threatened to kill him if he hurt my sister. Glad he didn't. He actually turned out to be perfect for her. He's a police officer, and I know he's taken good care of my sister all these years. Watching her get married was hard because she's my only sister, but knowing she was marrying a guy like Drew made it a tad easier.

"Nothing like flying with three babies." He laughs. "If it weren't for having extra sets of arms, I'm not sure what we would've done. Luckily, Skylar is old enough to help out with Logan's baby girl, so Kayla and he also took turns holding the babies."

"I've heard it gets easier," Travis adds, glancing over at his daughter and two sons in the inflatable house. "Thank goodness they aren't babies anymore, though, or that flight would've been a fucking nightmare."

"Daddy! Watch me!" I hear Ginny, Travis' daughter, calling from the bounce house. She tries to jump and touch her toes at the same time. All the kids are laughing and yelling as they jump around. Benita's twin boys and Skylar are in there too.

"Yeah, baby. You're doing good." Travis walks over and watches her. "Go ahead, James. Good job, buddy," he praises when James does a somersault in the bounce house.

"Come on, Daddy. Get in with us," Ginny begs, and the other kids start begging too. He looks at Drew and me, and we wave him on. Kid peer pressure at its finest.

"Adults can get inside; just ask Jackson," I tell him. One time, Jackson rented one of them for his and John's birthday a few years ago as a joke.

Nothing like watching a handful of adults play inside of a big, pink, blow-up princess castle.

Travis takes off his shoes to join the kids, and soon, they're all screaming and laughing.

"So you and Emily are officially a thing, huh?" John asks, taking a sip of sweet tea just as Jackson walks up and plops next to me.

"What are y'all talkin' about? That fine ass you're officially datin' now?" Jackson turns to me with a shit-eating grin.

I grunt. "If you didn't look just like him, I'd swear you were adopted."

John laughs. "It's not easy havin' the same face. Trust me. The other day in the grocery store, this random woman walked up and grabbed my ass with both hands."

"Who was it?" Jackson asks. "Might need to give her a call."

"I have no idea. I got the hell out of there as quick as I could." John gives me a pointed look. I can't even imagine having to deal with anyone who's hooked up with Jackson. Most of them are full-blown psycho. Or he just turns them that way.

"Food's ready," Dad announces, carrying a couple of trays to the table where the rest of the food sits. On the other table are the three birthday cakes Mama made for the triplets and then another large cake for the rest of us to eat.

I stand and walk over to Emily, placing my arm around her as we walk to the line to make our plates.

"You were right," she whispers, looking over at Courtney.

"Aren't I always?"

"Look at these two lovebirds." Jackson whistles, patting me hard on the back. He's trying to embarrass me, but if he keeps it up, he's going to be the one put in an awkward situation. Just on cue, Kiera walks up, and Jackson stops talking. I smile at him, then turn to Kiera.

"So how're you and Trent?" I ask nice and loud. "Where is he today, by the way?"

Emily's eyes widen as she tries to stifle a laugh. Jackson groans behind me, and if I had to guess, his hands are probably balled into fists too.

Kiera is either completely oblivious or just ignores him. "Wonderful, actually. He got an emergency call out this morning and had to head to work."

"What a shame," Jackson comments quietly, but by the scowl Kiera makes, I'm positive she heard him.

"He's a great guy. Very kind and treats me right." There's a glow on her face that I don't miss. "And he isn't afraid to tell me how he feels, which is a nice change of pace," she adds. I'm pretty sure that was a direct burn meant only for Jackson.

"That's great to hear, Kiera." I pull her into a side hug. Even though I haven't been around a lot when she was younger, she's like another little sister. "Everyone deserves to have someone who makes them happy," I say, just as Mama walks up.

"Hey, honey." Mama hugs Emily, then looks between the two of us with a smile, but she doesn't say anything. By the look on her face, she doesn't need to. I know exactly what she's thinking. She's overjoyed that I brought her here today, and if I'm being honest, I am too.

Mama goes to Aunt Charlotte, and I hear them chatting about the weather. The sun beams down on us, and I'm happy there's a breeze at least. It's only May, and if this is any indication of how the summer will be, then the guys are going to sweat their asses off working in the pastures.

Just as we make our way to the table, I see Dad made enough hamburger patties and hot dogs to feed an army. Probably because Dad doesn't really care for crowds and prefers to occupy himself with the grilling. I grab a paper plate and hand one to Emily. After we prep our food, we find our place at the picnic table with Alex, River, and Riley.

"I'm so happy you're here," River tells Emily.

"Yeah, me too. What a great day for it, too." Emily looks at the inflatable house.

"We should go jump in it after we eat," I tell her.

"No way," she says before taking a bite of her hamburger.

"You should. It's actually a lot of fun," Alex encourages. "Riley giggles the whole time when I take him in there."

"Maybe." Emily smiles.

"You two are too cute." River looks at Emily, then back at me. Emily blushes but hides it behind her burger. "And good to have around. Someone needs to keep Evan on his toes," she teases.

John sits on the other side of Emily, and Kiera joins us too. Jackson is too busy giving Courtney a hard time, but she secretly likes it. Those two are always giving each other shit; they've picked on each other since we were kids.

I place my hand on Emily's back and listen to her and John talk about Houston and how she liked growing up there. It's the most words I've heard him say to someone he doesn't really know in a long time. Though I really shouldn't be that surprised. She has a way of breaking people out of their shell. It's part of what makes her a great doctor—people feel like they can easily trust her.

"I'm going to wash my hands real quick," I whisper to Emily.

"Okay." She gives me a smile, then pops a pickle into her mouth.

As I'm walking to the house, I look around at all the people who showed up for the birthday party and feel so damn blessed that this is my family. We give each other a hard time, but that's what I love most about them. All the different personalities mingle together to make for a damn good time.

I walk up the back steps of the porch, then walk inside. Once I'm in the kitchen, I turn on the water and pour soap into my hand. Benita comes around the corner and scares the shit out of me.

"Shit," I mutter.

She leans against the counter and lifts an eyebrow. "Don't be so damn jumpy." She chuckles. "So…" She lingers for way too long, and I can already guess what she's going to say.

She's just as bad as Mama when it comes to gossip, but I trust her. Basically, if I want to know anything about what's going on in the family, I know she's the cousin to call.

"Yes?" I ask with a smile.

"I can't believe you're actually dating someone. I'm really happy for you, Evan," she says.

"Thanks, B. It's been a while." I turn off the water and dry my hands and look at her. "I just had to find the right woman. That's all."

Benita smiles, and we head toward the door. "I think you did. You two seem perfect together."

I nod my head with a grin. "She makes me happier than I've been in a real long time."

We walk back to the party and sit down at the table. I watch Emily laugh and smile when she talks to River, and I wonder how I got so lucky.

Maybe taking a page from the "Bishop brothers dating book" wasn't such a bad idea after all.

"He's fussy," Alex says when Riley refuses to eat. He keeps pointing at the bounce house and mumbling something.

"He wants to go back in." I laugh. "I'll take him."

"Are you sure?" River asks.

"Yeah." I stand and lift Riley into my arms, and he gives me a smile, showing his one tooth. Emily watches me, and I shoot her a wink.

"Come on, buddy." I slip my shoes off and step inside. He instantly starts yelling and laughing with excitement as I barely bounce around.

"Y'all okay in there?" Alex peeks inside the door with a smile. He lowers his voice. "So when's the wedding?"

"What the hell are you talking about?" I ask.

"Between you and Emily," he jokes.

I narrow my eyes at him. "Don't you dare let Mama hear you say that, or I'll be kicking your ass."

Alex laughs, and so does Riley. Like father, like son.

CHAPTER TWENTY-TWO

EMILY

I WATCH as Evan carries Riley to the bounce house, and my ovaries nearly explode. The way he's so gentle and speaks softly to him makes my heart flutter. I wonder if this is what he wants someday—kids, a family, and the whole white picket fence. We're both addicted and passionate about our jobs, and I know what kind of responsibility having kids will be. Right now, my job is my life, but as I look around, I realize how I could easily accept this as a part of it too. People can have the best of both worlds, right? A career and a family?

As I'm lost in thought, Kiera gets a phone call and lets out a squeal. She's way too giddy, and I can hear the smile in her voice as she walks to a more private area, so I know it's Trent who called. John and Alex walk off next, leaving only River and me sitting at the table.

"I'm so happy you guys worked out." River smiles. "After I heard you stole his clothes, I really didn't know if he'd ever forgive you." She laughs.

I feel heat go straight to my cheeks. "That was a total mistake."

"It was good for him. Evan needs a little adventure in his life. Fair warning, though, these Bishop boys are relentless. When they know what they want, they won't ever let you go." She chuckles. "Well, at least that's how Alex was, and I have a feeling it runs in the family when the right one comes along." She glances over at him, and I can tell she loves him so damn much.

Her talking about this makes me want to know more about her and Alex's history. I've heard things in passing, but I haven't gotten the full story from the lion's mouth.

Just as I'm about to ask her, Courtney slides in next to me and places her arm around me and squeezes.

"I'm so freaking glad to see that Evan's finally found someone," she says with sincerity. Her words send butterflies to my stomach knowing that his family approves of me and our relationship.

"Thanks, Courtney. That means a lot coming from you."

After she lets go of me, she and River chat about the kids, and I can tell they're really close. A darker-haired girl walks up, and Courtney stands and gives her a big hug and introduces us.

"This is our cousin, Benita," Courtney says. "She's the other one with a set of multiples."

"Ah, yes." I grin. "Awesome to meet you."

"Nice to finally meet you," she says, smiling brightly. River tells her to join us.

"I've got to go help Aaron. The twins are going to drive him to drink." She points and her boys are trying to steal icing off the cakes. I can't help but laugh, and she waves bye to me.

All of Evan's family is close-knit, and this party is proof of that. I'm not sure he knows how lucky he really is to have them. I can't even remember the last time we had a family get-together. At that thought, I look over at the bounce house and watch Alex chat with Evan through the door. I catch peeks of him barely moving, holding Riley tight in his arms.

Courtney looks over at them too. Her voice drops low. "I haven't seen Evan smile like this in years. I didn't think he'd move on after Alicia. I wasn't sure he'd ever get over it."

I suck in a deep breath and force a smile, but considering this has been brought up more than once recently, I know I'm going to have to speak with Evan about it—sooner than later too. Thankfully, when Kiera returns, the subject is changed, and I'm so damn relieved about that.

"He wants to go on a date tonight." She's smiling so damn big that it's contagious.

"You and Jackson?" Courtney asks, not knowing any difference. It's obvious to everyone around them that they've had a crush on each other since the beginning of time, so it makes sense.

Kiera tenses then smiles. "Um, no. I'm actually dating Trent Laken."

Courtney gives her a big grin. "Trent Laken? The horse vet?"

Kiera nods. "He's been our equine vet for a while now. Your parents, too."

"Yeah, I remember him. He was a few grades above Evan, right?" Courtney isn't judging in her tone, but I think Kiera takes it that way.

Kiera nods again. "Yep."

"They're more mature when they're older." Courtney winks, and I suspect Drew must be older than her too. "Good for you, K."

After a moment, Kiera's shoulders relax. "Thanks, Court. I really like him."

I hear someone whistle, and I see it's Mrs. Bishop standing by the cake table waving everyone over. "Y'all come over. It's cake time."

"She really means 'mess time.'" Courtney stands and rounds up the babies from the different people who are holding them.

Evan carefully gets out of the bounce house still holding Riley, and when Alex tries to take him, Evan shifts his body and doesn't allow it. Alex grins and shrugs his shoulders, and by the look on his face, I can tell he doesn't mind giving Evan some nephew time.

I wait for him with a smile on my face before we walk over and join everyone near the cake table.

"That's a good look on you," I tell him when he's close enough to hear me. He lifts an eyebrow and smirks before he leans over and whispers in my ear.

"We can practice making one of these tonight."

I bite my lower lip and shake my head at him. "Somehow, I didn't expect you to say anything else."

Courtney and Drew place birthday hats on the triplets' heads while Mrs. Bishop sets a large number one candle in the middle of each cake but doesn't light them just yet. Kayla and Viola pass around pointy birthday hats for everyone, ordering us all to wear them.

It's such a sweet moment to see so many people here to celebrate the triplets' special day. I know Courtney and Drew struggled to get pregnant, so I can only imagine what a blessed day this is for them.

River takes Riley from Evan's arms, and he doesn't argue with her about it like he did with Alex. I glance over at him and smile.

"I'm surprised you let her take him from you."

"I think he needed a diaper change," he admits. "Or he has gas."

I shake my head. "You're terrible."

Once we all have the hats on our heads, Mrs. Bishop, Courtney, and Drew hold the cakes in front of the triplets. As soon as the candles are lit, we start singing "Happy Birthday" in a terrible off-key, but they love it regardless. Once the adults help them blow out their candles, the babies start destroying her masterpieces.

Within seconds, bright colored icing is all over their faces and in their hair. They look adorable all covered in cake. A handful of people start taking pictures and making funny faces to get them to laugh, which isn't hard considering we're all laughing along with them.

Mrs. Bishop breaks away and cuts the other cake and has Viola and Kayla pass out pieces to the bigger kids first, then to us.

I gladly take my plate and don't waste any time diving in. Before I even finish my piece, Jackson starts throwing cake at John, and that's when all hell breaks loose.

"You're gonna pay for that," I hear John shout.

Cake is flying everywhere, and I can't stop laughing when Jackson smashes Evan's cake in his face too. He was so quick, I didn't even see him coming.

"You're an asshole," Evan mutters, shaking cake out of his hair.

Dylan's carrying Jessica over his shoulder when she makes eye contact with me and laughs loudly. "Help me," she pleads with frosting all over her face. At this point, it's hard to see who's throwing cake at whom. I can't stop laughing, and Evan gives me a devious look before he quickly grabs my plate and smashes the rest of my cake directly onto my face.

"Ugh, you suck!" I wipe my face and know I'm going to be sticky the rest of the afternoon now.

"Payback for laughing at me."

"Seriously?" Mrs. Bishop says to the group of adults acting like kids. "Y'all are worse than these babies."

Evan leans over and licks icing off my face. "Can't waste it."

I tilt my face up toward him, and our lips connect. He kisses me, not caring who sees, and everything around us disappears when the kiss deepens. He tastes sweet and delicious.

"Mmm, buttercream," he says against our lips. "I forgot how much I love the taste of frosting on you." He smirks, reminding me of our first time together when I had wedding cake that night, and he could taste it off my lips.

"Should've figured you had some weird cake fetish," I tease.

With every tender moment we spend together like this, the more I find myself wanting to be around him. Being here with his family has allowed me to see a totally different side of him—one that's more vulnerable and unguarded. Though my past is full of terrible relationships and bad decisions, and I'm slightly jaded because of it, I know I'm already falling fast and hard for him. As cliché as that sounds, it's something I've never felt before. It's such a strong and intense feeling that I'm almost certain I was doomed since our first night together. Though I spend long hours with him at work and all of our free time is spent with each other, especially now that I'm staying with him, it still doesn't feel like enough.

When we release our kiss, he smiles. "Parties like this always end in a cake fight. Every. Single. Time."

I smile at the thought and how this family really knows how to enjoy life and have fun. The older kids walk past me, and they're all covered in cake too. I watch Travis give his kids high fives as Viola shakes her head in disapproval.

Mrs. Bishop passes out paper towels and wipes, and though we try our best to get it off our faces, the icing in my hair isn't coming out so easily.

After everyone is somewhat cleaned up, though we're all sticky as hell, Courtney and Drew begin helping the triplets open their gifts and reminding them to thank everyone for everything. It's a long process, considering they're still getting the hang of presents, but it's adorable to watch.

Once the party comes to an end, they make their rounds, exchanging hugs and thank yous with everyone. When Courtney gets to me, she hugs me so tight. "I really hope to see you again."

"You will," I promise.

"Good." She looks at Evan. "I like her. Put a ring on it."

He rolls his eyes at her before giving her a hug. "Y'all better stop with all that. You're going to scare her away," he teases.

Courtney is so sweet and funny, just like Kiera told me she would be. I love her, and I love how close they all are even though she no longer lives here. Actually, I love all of his family, and I'm so happy Evan invited me. I don't want this day to end, but I can tell the babies are getting cranky as they fuss and start getting into everything. Mrs. Bishop and Benita start cleaning up while Courtney and Drew start packing up all the gift bags.

Evan places his arm around me, and we make our rounds, telling everyone goodbye. After we tell his mother goodbye, we make our way back around the house to the truck.

"That wasn't so bad, was it?" He opens the passenger door for me.

I slightly shake my head. "It was perfect."

He grabs my hand and presses a soft kiss to my knuckles. "Good."

We drive back to the house with the windows down. My hair blows around as we listen to the radio. I look over at him, and he's smiling, and I don't ever want to forget the way he looks right now. So relaxed and happy.

We pull up to the house, and I'm so sticky that I can't wait to take a shower. We get out of the truck and race to the bathroom.

"I said I wanted a shower first," I pretend to pout.

"You snooze, you lose," he says, taking off his shirt. I can't get enough of his body and that sexy V that leads to the "holy lands."

"That's not fair. You know my weaknesses," I tell him, taking my shirt off too. That causes him to stop, but then he begins to unzip his pants. Soon we're standing in the bathroom in our underwear. Our lips magnetize toward one another, and nothing can stop us at this point. We're ravenous and greedy, and I hope this feeling never gets old. His fingertips brush across my skin as he removes my bra and panties. Taking my time, I slip his boxers below his hips until they hit the floor.

He smirks, leans over, and turns the water on in the shower, then we step in together. Warm water covers our bodies, and we can't keep our hands off each other.

"I need you so bad," I moan, running my fingers down his chest.

"We get clean first, then dirty," he murmurs, his lips kissing my neck as his soapy hands brush across my breasts.

"Tease. But ya know two can play that game," I say, allowing him to finish washing my body.

He adds shampoo to his hands and massages my scalp. I lean under the water and rinse before adding conditioner. Once I'm clean, I take the soap from his hand and return the favor. As I grab his shaft, his breathing increases. As he places his hand on the tile, enjoying it a little too much, I move to his chest. Stepping closer, his cock rubs against my bare stomach, so I make sure to shift my body just right to keep teasing him. I roam my hands around his lower back and dig my nails into his ass cheeks. He groans as his body tightens. The want and need is too strong, and I don't know how much longer I can wait to have him.

"Fuck this," he finally says, giving in. He steps out of the shower and wraps a towel around his waist before reaching for me. When I step out, I look at him and smirk. He's sex on legs in every way, and I can't believe he wants me the way I want him—considering he's Mr. Undateable.

Evan stands on the rug with a towel in his hand and softly dries every part of my body. Once I'm dry, I wrap the towel around my body and walk to the bedroom with Evan following behind.

"On the bed," he tells me as I turn to face him. His lips hover above mine until they finally touch. His kiss is heated and passionate, and by the time he pulls away, my lips are swollen, but my body is begging for more.

"Bossy." I lift an eyebrow and look into his blue eyes. "I like it."

"I know." He leans forward, wrapping his arms around my waist and sucks my earlobe into his mouth. His touch makes me feel weak in the knees, and it takes everything I have not to lose my balance.

"Well?" He smiles and waits for me to do exactly what he says.

Dropping the towel on the floor, I lie on the bed with my hair cascading around my head. Evan takes his time, studying my body, and when he looks at me, it feels different. It's more emotional as if he's trying to remember me exactly like this, and maybe he is. Stopping at the edge of the bed, Evan places his hands on my knees, opening my legs. He tucks his bottom lip into his mouth and falls to his knees in front of me. Placing his hands under my ass, he scoots me to the edge of the bed. Before he even touches me, my breathing and heart rate increases just from the anticipation of what's about to happen.

"I've been waiting all day for this," he says, taking his time kissing the inside of my thighs.

"Me too," I say my voice barely above a whisper. My eyes flutter closed when he hums against my clit before swirling his tongue against me. I quickly lose myself in him, not caring about anything, allowing him to take full control as he taunts and teases me with his tongue. Letting out a sigh, he slides his tongue down my slit and sinks deeper.

"You taste so fucking good," he says, becoming more greedy. I grab the comforter in my fists, trying to hold back the impending orgasm as he continues to drive me wild. Evan knows my body inside and out and knows exactly what I love. This gives him an advantage that I don't mind him having.

"Evan," I let out in a hushed whisper and can feel him smile against me.

"Yes?" He stops.

"No, no. Don't stop." I lift myself on my elbows at look at him.

"I couldn't deny you if I tried," he says, his lips curling up, but he doesn't immediately give me what I want, which only causes me to breathe heavier. I'm almost willing to beg when his mouth is on me. It doesn't take long before my body is buckling beneath him. With a quick movement, he hovers above me on the bed. He takes his time as I wait impatiently for his intrusion. He makes a small, breathless sound as he enters slowly—taking his time. I press against him, wanting our ends to meet, for us to be as close as possible. As I move my hips, I take him, all of him, and he inhales sharply.

"Emily." His voice trembles as he continues to increase his pace. I close my eyes, wanting him—all of him—more of him until I crumble beneath him again. He's everything I've been missing in life, everything I've wanted in a man. Gentle with enough roughness to keep me begging for more.

Evan looks directly into my eyes as he reenters. "I want to take my time, but fuck you feel so goddamn good."

"Mmm," I moan breathlessly as he moves slow and steady.

I'm falling head over heels, and there's nothing there to catch me—just

Evan. Our lips touch, and our tongues immediately swirl together. I can never get enough of him—his body or his lips against my skin. I try to imagine Evan Bishop not being in my life, and it's impossible, which is also frightening. They say only fools rush in, and if that's the case, I'll be the first to admit it—I'm a fool.

When his body tenses, I know he's close. I wrap my legs around his hips and open my eyes to watch him lose himself in me. The orgasm rocks through him, and he moans against my neck, which is music to my ears. After a minute, the only sound that fills the room is our unsteady breathing.

After we clean up, I'm wrapped up in Evan, and as I lie in his arms, I can't help but think about what Courtney had said at the party about Alicia. I figure now is as good as time as ever to bring it up because I think it's something we really need to discuss if we're going to continue moving forward in our relationship.

For minutes, I try to find the courage, try to figure out the words I need to say. After seeing his reaction to the coffee, hearing Veronica, then having Courtney drive it home, I know it has to be something significant enough that changed Evan's life. At this point, not knowing what happened in his past is more detrimental to our relationship than knowing.

"So I have to ask you something," I begin nervously.

"Okay, sure what is it?"

Inhaling, I continue. "Well, today at the party, Courtney said something that's been weighing on my mind."

He laughs. "I'm sure she said a lot of somethings."

I look at him, studying his face, knowing I can't go back on this conversation now.

"She said something to the point that she didn't think you'd move on after Alicia, which is why she's so happy to see we're together."

Evan sucks in a deep breath, and his eyes move to the ceiling instead of to me.

"It's not something I like talking about," he finally says.

"I'm sure it's not easy, but I want you to trust me. Everything I've shared with you is because I feel safe with you, and I want you to feel safe with me too. You have to allow me into your past, if we're going to move forward and have a future together."

"It's not that I don't trust you, baby. I do. It's just that it was a painful time in my past, and it really affected me. And not in the best way either," he admits, and my heart hurts seeing how hard this is for him.

"I wouldn't bring it up if I didn't think it was important for us. After having more than one person mention this to me, and Veronica giving me a little insight, I only want to hear it from you." My words are soft and to the point. The truth in them may sting, but I watch him slightly relax before he rolls over to face me.

"Take all the time you need," I whisper, seeing the emotion evident on his face.

He sucks in a deep breath and nods. "Alicia was a barista who worked at The Grind Café, and every morning before work, I'd go in and grab a cup of coffee. It became our ritual. I'd go in every day, and over time, we started chatting about little things. We formed a friendship, and it quickly became more than just getting coffee in the morning. I felt like my day wasn't complete if I didn't see Alicia. It became obvious to me that I liked her as more than just a friend, and I had a gut feeling she felt the same about me just by the little hints she gave. Even if I drank coffee at home, I'd stop in just to see her and hear her voice. However, I was working long hours, and I knew I'd never be able to have a real relationship due to the commitment of the hospital, but that didn't stop me from thinking about it. After a while, I decided I was going to go for it anyway, and I told myself as soon as the opportunity presented itself in our next conversation, I was going to ask her out."

Watching him, I can see the pain in his eyes when he glances back over at me and continues.

"I was running late for work one morning, and I didn't get a chance to stop by the coffee shop. A few hours later, there was a call that a woman was being rushed in from a car accident."

I close my eyes tight, remembering what little details Veronica had told me the morning I brought Evan coffee. His hoarse voice pulls me out of my thoughts.

"When the woman was rushed in, I immediately recognized her, and I was completely distraught. She was in bad shape, but I refused to let her die and did everything I could to save her life. The man who crashed into her was still drunk from the night before, and his truck destroyed her little car. When she arrived at the hospital, she was going in and out of consciousness, but her body was so broken, and blood was everywhere. I tried so fucking hard to resuscitate and did everything I possibly could. I went out of my way and was told to stop wasting my energy, but I couldn't let her die. However, her brain began to swell, and there was nothing anyone could do. The impact of the collision was too hard, and she never had a fighting chance. She was declared brain dead within twenty-four hours." His voice cracks. "That was one of the hardest fucking things I've ever experienced—to this day. I blamed myself for a long time even though logically I knew there was nothing I could've done differently; it still didn't help soothe the burn."

"Evan," I whisper. "I'm so sorry." I can't even imagine that kind of pain or seeing someone you care about lose their life. I've witnessed many tragedies and have experienced my mother's own pain, but to feel responsible for their life would affect me too.

He closes his eyes tight. "I've been having nightmares on and off about that day ever since it happened. For weeks after, I'd replayed every moment and all the things I could've done differently. It haunted me for years. So yeah, I don't go into that coffee shop anymore because it brings back too much pain and memories. I'd made plans and promised myself I'd find the courage to ask her out that week and never got the chance. I beat myself up for months over it, taunting myself about why I kept waiting and if I hadn't, maybe the circumstances of where she was that morning would've been different. The what-ifs were enough to drive me crazy. From that point on, I put all of my spare time into my work and had no desire to date anyone, hence how I got that stupid nickname."

"I can't even imagine." I lay my head on his chest, listening to the steadiness of his heartbeat as I wrap my arms around him. "I'm so sorry you went through that. Thank you for sharing it with me."

Leaning forward, he kisses my forehead, then holds me tight while brushing his fingers lightly through my wet hair. I'm not sure he'll ever let go, and truthfully, I don't want him to.

"I honestly didn't think I'd ever meet another woman who was right for me—or that I'd want to be in a relationship with—until you came along and barged into my life. Now I can't imagine it without you."

CHAPTER TWENTY-THREE

EVAN

ANOTHER DAY, another trauma.

Sometimes, I'm surprised how much happens in this town. It's not super small, but it's definitely not that big either. Yet it's never a boring day in the ER.

It's been two weeks since Emily's met my entire family at the birthday party, and I honestly haven't felt this content in a long time. I was worried how things would be at work between us, and if any of our co-workers would notice, but we're both smart and professional and have made sure to keep it that way during our shifts.

"Two adult females and an adult male are coming in with injuries sustained in the genitals and anal region," Veronica tells me in a serious tone. "ETA is four minutes."

"I'm sorry…what? Injuries are where?"

She clears her throat. "Genitals and anal region," she says louder to appease me.

"What kind of injuries?"

"Lodged sex toy in female's anal region and the male's penis is stuck in the other female's vagina. His piercing got hooked on something, and when he tries to pull it out, she says she feels tearing."

I keep waiting for her to break out in laughter, but she continues speaking in a flat tone like this is an everyday occurrence and not at all ridiculously odd.

"You're joking, right? That's not really the case." I cross my arms over my chest, waiting for her to confirm.

"Nope. Three minutes." She shifts around the ER, giving the update to the other doctor and nurses.

"Well, this is a new one," I mutter to no one. Looking around for Emily, I realize she's on her break still. "Veronica," I shout. "Please page Dr. Bell."

"Absolutely, Dr. Bishop."

Within minutes, the ER erupts in pure chaos. There's a stretcher with a female lying on it, and she looks moderately uncomfortable. The next stretcher to roll in has both the male and female lying on it. Correction: the female is lying on it, and the male is on top of her.

Jesus Christ.

Talk about a threesome gone wrong.

Dr. Umbridge tells the medics to take the female to trauma room one and the doting couple to trauma room two, then looks at me with a shit-eating grin and tells me to handle room two.

"Dr. Bell's with me," I tell him before realizing she's still not here yet. "Veronica, did you page her?"

"Yes, but I can page her again."

"Thank you. Then meet Fiona and me in there."

"Will do." She smiles.

Once my gloves are on, I enter the room and see Fiona doing her best to keep them calm while waiting for my instructions. She looks terrified, and when my eyes scan down the stretcher, I immediately regret it. Only a thin sheet covers them but when the guy shifts, it completely slides off.

"Stop moving, Justin!" the woman shouts, trying to cover her chest with both hands, but it's useless. "It hurts when you move," she shouts again. Fiona grabs the sheet and recovers them the best she can, giving me a puzzled look.

"Are you going to help us or keep staring?" Justin snaps at me. Considering he's hovering over a woman butt-ass naked in missionary, this guy has no room for an asshole attitude.

Instead of barking at him like I want to, I ignore him.

"What's your name, miss?"

"Debra Johnson," she answers, her cheeks reddening.

"Debra? You said your name was Kandi," Justin interrupts.

"It's my stage name, okay? We all use fake names."

"Okay, Debra," I speak up, ignoring Justin's outburst. "Can you tell me exactly what hurts?"

"His piercing is stuck on something inside me."

"And do you have something inside you it could be hooked on?" I ask.

"The only thing I can think of is my IUD."

"Okay, and what's it feel like when he tries to pull out?"

"Feels like a sharp pain or even tearing. Could his piercing really get stuck on it?"

"Well, an IUD is obviously very safe to use during intercourse, but if there is consistent penetration or perhaps rough intercourse, the threads of the IUD that extend into the vagina could've snagged the piercing, if that's what it's caught on. Or it could've even slipped. When did you get it inserted?"

"Why are you asking all these questions? Does it matter? Just help us detach, okay, doc?" he snaps again, his attitude really grating on my nerves.

"That's what I'm trying to do, but I need to know her medical history first before I try to dislodge your penis from her vagina, so if you could just hold tight, I'll do my best to release your penis in one piece."

He narrows his eyes at me, and I hear Veronica snicker next to me, though she covers it up with a fake cough and keeps her head down as she continues writing down notes.

"I got it about a year ago," she tells me.

"Okay, thank you."

"Now, mister…" I turn toward Justin, waiting.

"Hayes," he mutters.

"What gauge is your piercing?"

"Eight," he confirms.

"And is it a hoop?"

"Yes, it's a Prince Albert."

I clear my throat and look back at the couple. "Okay, anything else I need to know? Any allergies or things that would be critical to know before we try shifting you out?"

"Well..." Justin mutters. "No allergies, but I do have a butt plug in, and when I shift my weight, it hurts."

For fuck's sake.

"Okay, Fiona can you please assist me while I check him out." I pinch my lips together, hoping I'm concealing my smile, but I have a feeling I'm not the only one in the room who's trying to keep it together.

"I can help you, Dr. Bishop," Veronica jumps in.

"Where is Dr. Bell?" I snap. "Did you page her?"

"Yes, twice."

"Then page her again."

I walk to the end of the bed where Justin's ass is arched in the air. "Alright, Mr. Hayes, I'm going to bring the sheet up so I can take a look."

"Just do it," he sneers.

Once I see what I'm working with, I shake my head at the cucumber size butt plug shoved up this guy's ass like a turkey stuffed in a pineapple. "I'm going to need you to stick your hips out as far as you can without shifting your groin. I know that sounds complicated, but the wider, the better."

I hear some curse words, and when the girl shrieks, I order him to stop.

"Well, I can pull it out now, or after I get you two unhooked, but either way, it's going to hurt."

"Just do it now."

"Fiona, can you find me some lubricant please."

"Of course," she says sweetly.

Forty-five minutes later, I've added butt plug removal and Prince Albert piercing disengaging from a vagina to my resume.

"That was by far the weirdest thing I've seen in a long time," I say once the room is cleared. It's just Fiona and me when I realize Emily hasn't shown up yet. "She must've gotten called into Dr. Umbridge's trauma," Fiona suggests. "I saw Veronica page her several times."

"That's not like Emily to not at least check in. Even if she gets caught up with something else, she always makes sure to have someone report back to me."

I rip off my gloves and wash my hands. "I'm about to go find out."

Walking out of the trauma room, I search the ER and see it's fairly empty. Veronica's behind the nurses' station looking through files.

"Is Emily with Dr. Umbridge?" I ask.

Her eyes snap up to mine, and she shakes her head. "No, she didn't respond to any of my pages."

"That's unlike her. Did you check the break room by chance?"

"Uh, no. I actually misplaced my employee keycard and had planned on running up to HR on my break to get another one."

"Fuck." I brush a hand through my hair. "She never takes long breaks like this. She must've fallen asleep. I'm going to check the on-call rooms. Page me if she shows up while I'm gone," I tell her before walking out.

Reaching for my phone, I call Emily. Though during our shift it's usually off, I hope by chance she turned it on during her break to text Kiera or something. It rings a few times, then goes to voicemail, so I text her.

Evan: Where are you?

I walk down the hallway and check each of the on-call rooms, but they come up empty. The locker room is empty, too, but I notice her locker door is open. Peeking inside, I see a bag of black licorice open, which means she was definitely sitting here during her break. Glancing around, I look for another clue, and that's when I spot her cell phone.

Dammit.

It's on the floor and causes me to panic. It's not like her to leave her shit lying around, especially her phone. Tapping the screen, I see my message along with a few unread ones from Kiera. The first one from her was sent over an hour ago.

Where the hell has she been for the past hour?

Glancing down at the screen again, I read Kiera's messages.

Kiera: OMG! It is? Really?

Kiera: Have you told Evan yet?

Kiera: How are you gonna drop a major bomb on me like that and then not respond to any of my messages!

What the hell is she talking about?

Looking around the bare room, I notice a smell. It's a very distinct sweet scent, and once I recognize it, I barge out of the room and jog back to the ER. Once I spot Fiona and Claire at the nurses' station, I bark out orders. "Call the police immediately," I direct to Fiona. "Tell them we have a kidnapping."

"Wait, what?" Veronica screeches.

"A kidnapping? Who?" Claire asks.

"Emily," I respond, using her first name, which causes them all to flinch. "Dr. Bell. She's missing. I found her phone in the break room, and she's not responded to any of her pages."

"Okay, I'll call right now."

"Are you sure? Maybe she just fell asleep?" Veronica offers.

"I've checked all the on-call rooms, but regardless she wouldn't just leave her locker door open and her phone on the floor. This has Richard written all over it, and who the hell knows how long ago he took her."

The blood from Veronica's face drains, and it causes my adrenaline to spike. "I'm going to do a sweep throughout the hospital just in case. Call security and let them know what's going on, have them look through the exterior camera footage, and tell them to have a guard on every lower-level emergency exit," I direct to Claire. "If Richard took her, God only knows what he has planned."

Once everyone knows what to do, I fly into motion. My heart beats rapidly and finding Emily becomes my only mission. I can't believe this is happening, but I do know that if he hurts her, I will end him.

Starting my search, I run up the emergency staircase to the next floor and look through every supply and cleaning closet. I call her name, hoping wherever she is she'll hear me and respond. Racing to the next floor, I continue searching and repeat this until I've reached the final level. The hospital is a decent size, but this isn't the only building on the property, which causes my head to pound hard as I come to terms with the fact that she really is missing.

By the time I make it back to the ER, the police have arrived and have been briefed by Veronica and Fiona. Claire is speaking with security, and everything feels wrong.

"Her car is still in the parking lot," Dr. Umbridge adds. "So she didn't leave."

"At least not willingly," I mutter. Fuck.

"Hello, I'm Detective Willoughby. We're sweeping the area right now while we wait for security to check out the cameras," the officer reports. "Can you tell me more about the man you think took her?"

Though he's been given a summary of the circumstances, I go into more detail about the restraining order, car chase, and stalking. I explain that she's been staying with me since he broke into her house and followed her to work. My co-workers' heads turn, but I don't give a shit. Emily is mine, and I'm not going to hide it anymore.

"I smelled chloroform in the locker room," I tell him. "I'm pretty sure that's how he managed to grab her."

"Okay. Let's start there."

Leading him there, I get this unnerving feeling that guts me from the inside out. I should be doing something more, something besides standing in the break room, but right now, I feel so damn helpless. I want to protect Emily with every fiber of my being and not being able to makes me wants to go into a blind rage.

"So you have to scan your card to get in?" he asks as I open the door.

"Yes. All employees have a card and access to all rooms with an electronic card reader," I explain.

"So it's unlikely he got in by himself."

"Not unless he had a key card or someone left the door open," I add.

"Is there another way in or out?" he asks.

"Just the emergency exit in the back that leads to the Employee Only entrance." My heart hammers in my chest, anxiety and pressure weighing heavy on me. The anger burning inside me is almost too much, but I know in order to find her, I need to remain calm, but I'm moments away from losing my shit.

"Show me," the detective says.

I bring him to the back door and out to the hallway that leads to the employee parking lot, and that's when I see it.

"Is that…" he asks then stops.

"Blood," I confirm.

CHAPTER TWENTY-FOUR

EMILY

"WAKE UP, PRINCESS!"

I groan, my head hurting like a bitch. What the hell?

Better question: where am I?

The last thing I remember is sitting in the break room texting Kiera and eating. So how did I end up here?

"I said get up!" I hear the voice again, and this time, I open my eyes and see my worst nightmare.

Richard.

"Oh my God," I gasp, bringing my hand up to my mouth and feeling blood on my lips. "Where the hell am I?" My heart thumps so hard, I can feel it in my ears. Body shaking, lip trembling, eyes watering—on the brink of a panic attack, and there's nothing I can do to stop it.

"Doesn't really matter, because where you're headed is worse." The smile on his face is deadly.

"What do you want?" I wrap my arm around my stomach, my lunch threatening to make a reappearance.

"There's nothing you can give that'll be equivalent to what you took from me," he tells me in a too-calm voice. "So I'm going to take what I want instead."

I'm almost afraid to ask. "And what's that?" I spit out blood that's pooled in my mouth. My body aches from whatever he did to me while I was out. There must've been a struggle when he was trying to grab me or dragged me out of the locker room.

"You'll see soon enough, princess." He laughs manically. "Soon enough."

"Just let me go, and no one ever has to know." I try pleading with him.

"Oh, you have a sense of humor, funny girl." The way he speaks in a high-pitched tone sends shivers down my body, and not the good kind either.

"Please," I beg. "I swear I won't tell anyone if you just let me go right now."

He kneels and lowers his face to meet my eyes. "I said shut up, bitch. Otherwise, I'm going to have to cover your mouth with my good friend chloroform again." He begins reaching into his pocket, and my eyes go wide.

"No. Fine."

He pulls his hand away.

"Just tell me why you think killing me will bring Susan back?"

He backhands me before I can react. "Don't you fucking say her name. You killed her. You don't get to talk about her like that."

I've taken several psychology classes, and since bargaining isn't going to work on him, I have no option but to try using reverse psychology on him.

"You're right. I deserve it. Go ahead." I keep my voice flat and void of any emotion. He'll only feed off my fear, and if he really is going to kill me, I won't let him have the satisfaction that I'm scared out of my freaking mind right now.

"Glad we're on the same page then." He flashes a wicked grin and grabs me by the arm, jerking me to my feet. My head starts to spin the moment I'm standing. "Showtime."

It's not until I'm standing that I realize where we are. "The roof," I mutter. I notice the popped-up windows and heat vents as he drags me around. Even if I screamed for my life right now, it wouldn't matter. No one would hear me over the whistling sound of the blowing steam. Even if someone did by chance, they'd never get to me on time. This building is ten stories tall, and you can't even get on the roof without a key card.

I could run, but he'd easily be able to catch me by the time I made it to the door. The chloroform made me dizzy, which is what he was banking on, I'm sure.

"Who helped you?" I ask, knowing there's no way he could've done this on his own.

"What makes you think I had help?"

"The key card," I tell him. "It's how you got into the locker room, wasn't it?" It's the last place I remember, so it's the only logical place he could've grabbed me after putting chloroform over my mouth.

"I could've stolen it," he counters.

"You're going to kill me anyway so what does it matter if you tell me."

"Good point."

He walks us closer to the ledge, and that's when I notice we aren't even on the same building as the ER. We're on the adjacent one with the rehab center and where the long-term patients stay.

I have no idea how long it's been since I've gone missing, but I can only imagine how worried Evan must be. He's gotta be going out of his mind with worry, and I hate that this is happening when I've just learned so much about his past. I miss him so damn much and hate that I didn't get to sneak a kiss before I left for my break.

"Veronica Nans."

"Wait, Veronica?" The shock of hearing her name rolls through me.

"She's not so keen on you, princess." He releases a loud belly laugh as if that's the funniest thing in the world. All I can think about is the betrayal Evan will feel when he finds out, and I won't be there to console him. Or hell, warn him.

He pulls me closer to the edge, and I'm trying not to allow my panic to surface, so I try to keep his attention by talking. Maybe if he's distracted enough, I can get out of his grip, but he's holding my arm so tightly I know there's only a slim chance he'd let me go.

"So how'd you meet Veronica?" I ask, feeling the cool breeze hit my cheeks.

"She came to me," he admits. "Saw me outside the hospital one day and propositioned to help me."

I swallow hard. "And what does she get in return?"

He spins me around, so we're face-to-face, then cocks his head with a grin. "She gets Evan." My heart drops to my stomach, and I can't believe this.

"He'll never let you get away with it," I spit out.

"Step up," he orders, nodding his head toward a set of steps that lead to the top ledge of the roof.

"You better hope the cops find you before he does."

"It won't matter, Emily. Don't you get it?" All emotion is devoid from his voice, and that's when it hits me. He plans to die right along with me.

"Please, Richard." It's the first time I've said his name to him, and it makes the vein in his forehead twitch. "You don't have to do this," I whisper when he pushes me up the first step.

"Keep going," he demands harshly. "To the top so you can see exactly where your life is about to end."

God. Panic is setting in, and even though I'm reminding myself to stay calm, that maybe I can trick him into releasing me, it's the realization that everyone I love in my life is about to lose me. And I'm not ready to say goodbye.

Fight or flight, I remind myself.

I try wiggling my arm out of his grasp, shifting my body back and forth to loosen the weight of his hand, but when I feel a sharp object at the middle of my spine, I stop. He has a knife.

"Wouldn't do that if I were you," he threatens, speaking above my ear. "We can do this the easy way..." He presses the knife harder into my back. "Or the hard way."

Quick or painful.

Once I'm on the final step, I can see over the city. His chest is close to me as he taunts me with the knife, pushing it deeper against my skin.

"Stand on the ledge, princess." He looks down and sees what could be my saving grace. Police lights. "It's time."

With a shaky breath, I follow his orders. I go up to the final step that brings me to the ledge of the roof, afraid he'll puncture the blade through my flesh if I don't. I just need to stall him until the cops can see me.

"Turn around," Richard orders, releasing his hold on me. "I want to see your face when you realize your life is about to end."

It's not my life that flashes before my eyes but the past few weeks spent with Evan in his home. We've been playing house, waking up in each other's arms every morning and falling asleep side by side every night. He'd be up first to shower, then when I was getting ready, he'd bring me coffee just how I like it. We'd discuss the events of the day before and anticipate what was in store for us that shift. We could easily talk for hours about medicine, and it's brought us closer. Knowing I was only staying with him temporarily made it feel like a test run of what it'd be like to live with each other, and though his furniture and décor weren't my things, he still made me feel at home and comfortable. We'd wrap ourselves up in blankets and make love until the birds sang. It was bliss.

And it was about to all be over. Our future never to exist.

I didn't even get to tell him the news.

Swallowing, I wrap my arms around my stomach and finally allow the tears to fall. Keeping my head down, I slowly pivot my feet across the ledge until I'm facing back toward Richard.

"Look at me," he demands.

Blinking the tears away, I tilt my head up and see him smiling back at me. Fucking psycho.

Something behind him grabs my attention, and my breath hitches when I see Evan and a couple of police officers.

Oh my God. Evan. My shoulders relax in relief, knowing he's found me. I know Evan would be looking for me, but I didn't know if he'd find me in time. I've never seen him so distraught, but his expression is stone cold when he steps toward us on a mission.

The scene unravels so fast, I can barely comprehend what's happening. Richard notices me looking over his shoulder and quickly turns around just as Evan grabs him. An officer comes and helps me down and I'm finally able to breathe. He pulls me to the side as another officer is on Richard, trying to arrest him.

A split second later, I hear Evan release a heart-stopping roar. He falls to his back as he holds a hand up, and that's when I see the knife sticking out of his chest.

"Nooooo!" The high-pitched scream that erupts through the air comes from my throat as I run over and kneel beside him. The officers grab Richard and push him to the ground, but all I care about is Evan. An officer radios in for the paramedics, confirming the suspect's in custody. Glancing over, I see Richard in handcuffs.

"Baby, look at me." I hold his head, and when I feel his hand grab my thigh, I breathe a small sigh of relief. His eyes flutter close. "Keep them open, Evan. Help is on the way."

He tries opening them but isn't able to all the way, and that scares the shit out of me. He's losing consciousness, which means he's losing too much blood too fast.

"This might hurt, baby. I'm so sorry." I press my palms against his chest and add pressure to the surrounding area of the wound. If I pull the knife out, he'll definitely bleed out.

He groans as I press harder, and I wince knowing how much pain he must be in. "Hold on, okay? Take steady, even breaths."

I hear the stretcher's wheels scratch against the concrete as the paramedics rush over to us. They start asking me questions, and I quickly give them the details of what happened. I hadn't realized how big the knife was until I saw the end sticking out of his chest. "It's possible the blade nicked his lung," I explain as Evan's eyes close again. "His lung could collapse at any minute, and if it does, he'll need a chest tube put in right away."

I notice how much of Evan's blood has saturated his shirt as one of the medics take over, adding pressure to the wound as the other places an oxygen mask over his face. One of them lowers the stretcher to ground level as the other stabilizes the knife in place with tape and gauze. They won't take it out until they get him into the OR, but they have to get him off the roof and across the parking lot to the ER first.

"His heart rate is dropping. We need to put him on the gurney, miss," one of the medics tells me. Leaning over his body, I press a kiss to his forehead as tears run down my cheeks and land on his face. "I love you, Evan Bishop. Do you hear me? Don't you dare leave me!" More tears fall as I decide to tell him what I hadn't had the chance to earlier. "Don't leave our baby. I need you. *We* need you."

CHAPTER TWENTY-FIVE

EVAN

THE REPETITIOUS BEEPING is the first thing I hear and recognize. The sound of machines is something I've come to know for years, but I've never been the one attached to them. I can feel something on my face and know that it's the ventilator I'm hearing.

Whispers echo, and I know I'm not alone. A soft hand wraps around mine, and I squeeze it back.

"Evan." Emily's voice is gentle, sending warmth through my body. She's okay. "Can you hear me, baby?"

I squeeze her hand again. The medicine is wearing off enough to listen and respond to demands, but my eyes are too heavy to lift.

"Is he waking up?" I hear a man's voice I don't recognize, which makes me twitch with concern.

"Evan, sweetheart," my mom's soft voice whispers in my ear. "We all love you, okay?" Her cool fingers squeeze my hand, and I squeeze back. "I think he can hear me."

"It's not uncommon for people going in and out of consciousness to be able to hear their surroundings," Emily explains. "He just might not be able to respond until more of the medicine wears off."

I don't hear the rest of the conversation and slip back into sleep.

The beeping pulls me back to reality, but I have no idea how long it's been since the last time I woke up. I try opening my eyes, and this time, they crack open just enough to see the sunlight beaming through the window.

"Well hey there, stranger." I turn, and Fiona's standing next to me with a chart in her hands. "You're lookin' good."

Nodding, I give her the smallest of smiles. I'm still drowsy, but I don't want to close my eyes again until I know where Emily is and that she's safe.

The breathing tube is still in place. I look around the room, shifting my eyes from side to side.

"I sent her home to get some sleep," Fiona tells me, knowing that's who I'm looking for. "She'd been here for five days straight, and it wasn't healthy for her. She'll be back soon, I'm sure."

I furrow my brows, wanting to ask how Emily is and as if Fiona can read my mind, she answers.

"Her and the baby are fine." She smiles warmly.

The baby? My eyes widen in response, but I drift back to the darkness before she can explain.

When I feel someone's palm on my cheek, I reach up and place my hand over it, hoping it's Emily.

"Evan." Her small voice is music to my ears.

I peek up at her and smile. The tube has been removed but the oxygen line under my nose is still in place.

"Hi, baby." My voice is weak and gravelly, my throat dry and sore, but I'm just so relieved to see her that I don't care.

"Hi." She chuckles. "I was hoping you'd wake up today. They've been decreasing your medicine for the past eight hours and finally took you off the ventilator."

"Are you okay?" I ask, gripping her hand.

"I am now." She exhales, and I notice the dark circles under her eyes. "I've been anxiously waiting."

"I'm sorry, sweetheart." I bring her hand to my lips and press a soft kiss to her knuckles.

"You have nothing to be sorry for, babe. You saved my life."

"I'd do anything for you, Emily."

Her eyes tear up, and soon, they're falling down her cheeks.

"I know." She wipes her cheek and smiles. "Do you remember what happened?"

"Kinda. The last thing I remember is taking Richard to the ground, and then you leaning over me. I remember feeling a lot of pressure on my chest before things went black, and then I woke up in here."

"He stabbed you," she explains, the horror on her face telling me everything I need to know. "The cops arrested him, and the paramedics rushed you to the ER. You went right into surgery, and to prevent infection or complications, they kept you ventilated."

She saw everything and knew exactly what to do in order to contain the wound. Thank God she acted right away because we both know I could've easily bled out from a stab wound.

"You also hit your head pretty hard on the concrete when you fell backward, so they've been monitoring you closely for a week."

"A week?" I gasp.

"Yeah," she breathes out. "Longest week of my life."

"Come here."

She moves her body closer so I can kiss her lips. "You saved my life, too."

"I only wish I could've prevented it in the first place." Her pained expressed causes my heart to race. None of this is her fault, and I know she feels guilty, though she has no reason to. Richard deserves all the blame, and I won't let her think otherwise.

"Losing you would've destroyed me," I tell her sincerely. "I'd take a knife or bullet for you any day of the week if that meant keeping you safe."

She lowers her eyes and swallows as she continues to squeeze my hand. "I really thought I was going to die. In those moments, I could only think of you and what this would do to you and how I never told you how I really felt."

I smile up at her, remembering those three words she whispered to me. "So tell me again," I encourage, desperate to hear them.

"Again? You heard me?" Her eyes widen in surprise.

"I don't remember much after falling to the ground, but I remember your voice. It's what I held onto because I wasn't ready to leave you either."

She laughs between sobs, and I hadn't realized she was crying again. "Don't cry, sweetheart." I bring my thumb to her cheek.

"I love you so much, Evan. I've never been surer of anything in my life than those words, and I hated that I hadn't told you sooner."

Hearing her say that brings so much joy to my heart that if I weren't just recovering from surgery, I'd pull her into this bed with me and make love to her all night long.

"Good," I say. "Because I've been in love with your sassy mouth and red heels since the moment I laid eyes on you." I flash her a cocky grin. "I just didn't know it yet."

"Well, aren't you smooth?" she teases, leaning over and pressing her soft lips against mine.

"Don't need to be when you've already got the right girl." I wink.

"Glad to see nothing's changed," Emily mocks with a smirk.

"Just my dignity."

Emily snorts, shaking her head.

"Knowing someone's been changing out my piss bag for the past week really questions your manhood."

"Always the prideful poet." Emily snickers.

"Look who's up and talking," Fiona says, entering the room with my chart in her hand. "You're looking much better."

"Thanks," I respond. "How'd you get to be the lucky one to take care of me?"

"I fought off some of the ICU nurses," she teases. "But mostly, I've just been checking in on you so I could give updates to everyone in the ER. They all miss you."

"I miss you all too. I'm surprised Veronica didn't fight you for the position, though." I laugh, knowing how protective Veronica can be.

The room goes silent, and I notice Emily's eyes lower with sadness.

"What's wrong? Is she okay?" Veronica and I have worked together for years, and I'd be distraught if anything happened to her.

Emily shakes her head, and Fiona busies herself as Emily tries to explain. I hear her words, but they aren't making sense. Veronica would never betray me like that. Even though I kind of figured she wanted more than just a friendship, I never once implied that the feelings were mutual.

"I can't believe this," I say, completely stunned once Emily tells me everything.

She squeezes my hand, and I can tell she was just as shocked to find out as I am.

"So what's happened to her now?"

"They arrested her, and charges are pending for being an accomplice to my kidnapping, though according to Richard, she propositioned him to kidnap *and* kill me, so the prosecutor is pushing for an attempted homicide charge."

"Jesus," I mutter, shaking my head in disbelief. "And what's going to happen to Richard?'

Emily rolls her eyes, and I know she's been dealing with a lot more than just me this past week. "His attorney is pushing for an insanity plea."

"Bullshit."

"I know, but don't worry. The prosecutor will fight hard for all of us since we have documentation on everything he's done to me the past year, including the restraining order that he continuously broke even though he knew the restrictions."

"Justice will be served," I tell her. "That I believe."

"Can we come in?" I hear the same male's voice from before, and when Emily faces the door, she waves him in. "The Bishops are here, too," he adds.

"Yes, come in," Emily says. "He's awake now and talking."

My mother barrels in and immediately wraps her arms around my neck. My father comes to my side and cups his hand on my shoulder.

"Hi, Mama. Hey, Dad."

"Son." My dad nods. "Glad to see you're awake."

"Me too." I grin.

"I've been so worried about you. Thank God you're okay. I've had the entire church praying for your recovery."

I smile. "Thanks, Mama. I'll be fine."

"You scared the dickens out of me! Don't do that to me again," she scolds, patting my cheek.

"Evan, I want you to meet my father." Emily grabs my attention to the man standing next to her. "He came a few days ago."

"It's a pleasure to meet you, sir." I hold my hand out as far as I can, and he graciously takes it.

"The pleasure is all mine." His voice is deep and rough, but I hear the sincerity in his tone.

I'm surprised how much Emily looks like him. They share the same dark hair and facial features. From what she's told me, they're pretty close, and it's evident in the way he looks at her how much he loves and cares for her.

"I wanted to come here and personally thank you for saving my little girl's life. I know, given the circumstances, we both could've lost her that day, and I'll forever be grateful you came to her rescue."

Looking at Emily, my heart pounds harder hearing the truth in his words.

I love her so much, and if the opportunity to tell her would've been taken away from me, I would've been even more devastated. I'm not going to take being able to tell her how I truly feel for granted.

"I'd do it again in a heartbeat," I tell him truthfully.

Fiona enters the room and informs us I can probably go home in a couple of days, which is a goddamn relief. Any longer and I'll go stir-crazy in here, but I know it's all procedure.

My parents leave for the night, but I know they'll be back before I get discharged. I'm sure they've been giving updates to the rest of the family, and when Emily hands me my cell, I see dozens of messages and voicemails.

"Well, I'll let you get some rest and head back to my hotel," Dr. Bell says. "I'll stop in before I head back to Houston," he tells Emily. "I love you." She hugs him before he turns away. "Oh." He stops and spins back around. "Congrats. I'm happy for the both of you." He winks at us before walking out and closing the door behind him, so it's only Emily and me.

"Congrats?" I ask puzzled. "What's he talking about?"

"Well—" she begins, then stops when I interrupt her.

"Wait…" I rack my brain as the memories surfaces. "I remember." I look up at Emily, and a wide smile spreads across my face. "We're having a baby."

She nods and bursts into tears. She covers her mouth, trying to hold them back, but I don't want her to. Reaching for her hand, I pull her closer until her forehead is against mine.

"I didn't think I'd ever feel this kind of happiness in my lifetime, but you continue to surprise me, and every day, you make me happier and happier. I had no idea what true happiness felt like until you came into my life and showed me. Now that you're carrying my baby, I'm pretty sure my heart might burst." I cup her cheeks and press her mouth to mine, tasting her salty tears on my lips. "I love you and our baby so fucking much. Don't ever doubt that for a second."

"I'm so relieved to hear you say that because I'll be honest and say I was mildly freaking out at first. Then before I even had the chance to tell you, Richard grabbed me, and when he stabbed you, I thought for sure the opportunity for us to be a family had been taken away. I don't ever want to take that for granted again."

"I remember your words," I reassure her. "I just didn't grasp them until now."

"Are you sure you're ready for this? That we're ready?"

I smile and look into her gorgeous green eyes. "Never been surer of anything in my life as long as it's with you."

CHAPTER TWENTY-SIX

EMILY

THREE MONTHS LATER

Evan has been an absolute dream come true, and sometimes, I still pinch myself to make sure he's real. I love how excited he is for the baby even though the morning sickness all night long makes me miserable. He's always there to hold my hair back and get me anything I need—including the black licorice that makes him cringe. He definitely has a softer side that I love just as much as his hardass, brooding one.

Things definitely didn't start out easy for us, but it's all been worth it so far. I'm waiting for Evan to show me his third eye or tell me he has a love child or something, none of which he has. Though he's not perfect, I can't deny that he's perfect for *me*. Each day, my love for Evan grows, and I know he's going to make the best dad.

Together, we're going to give our little one a wonderful homelife on the ranch, and he or she will be surrounded by a family who loves wholeheartedly. I promised myself when I had kids, I'd make sure he or she was given everything I wished I had as a child—unconditional love, affection, and lots of adventures. Though having a baby wasn't something I'd planned on yet, considering I wanted to focus on my career, my plans have changed, and I'm okay with that.

It helps that Evan fully understands the lifestyle of being a doctor, and that'll always be something that bonds us together. It also doesn't hurt that he's sexy as sin, has a family that loves me, and continues to show me how loyal and protective he is. He's the full package, and I'm happy to say he's *mine.*

Kiera was more than ecstatic to hear I'm expecting. Of course, once the shock of everything that happened with Richard and Evan's injury wore off, she went into planner mode. She's already sent a list of her favorite baby names, links to cute nursery themes, and ideas for the baby shower she insists on hosting—she may have to fight Mrs. Bishop for that one though. She's gone completely nuts, but I wouldn't have it any other way.

"So I have a confession to make," I tell Evan as I continue getting ready.

"That you love me more than black licorice, I'm the best sex you've ever had, and that no other man has ever made you come as many times as I have," Evan spits out so effortlessly, I can't help but wonder if he's been thinking on that one for quite some time.

"Yeah, something like that." I snort, shaking my head at his arrogance. "Actually, I was snooping through some of the patient files from when I was off work that week and found a rather interesting one."

"Oh yeah?" he asks, reaching for his shirt and muttering curse words that my clothes have taken over half of his closet. Once Evan was discharged from the hospital, I stayed at his place and took care of him, and eventually, I sold my condo and moved in with him permanently. Then we decided to make plans to build a house closer to his family, which I'm the most excited for.

"Does the name Justin Hayes ring a bell?" I hold back a smile. I nearly choked laughing when I read over the chart yesterday.

His eyes widen as he pinches his lips together. "Yeah, you mean Mr. Butt Plug and his Prince Albert?"

I cluck my tongue and point my finger at him. "Bingo."

He chuckles. "What about him?"

"Well…" I hesitate but then go for it anyway. "It wasn't exactly the way I envisioned you meeting my ex-boyfriend, but I gotta say I'm quite glad I wasn't there." I burst out laughing, unable to contain it when the realization hits his face, and he scowls.

"You're joking."

"Wish I was because what the fuck was he thinking, but yeah, that was him." I cringe, thinking about his hands and mouth on me. Ugh. What a freak.

"Why the hell would he be all the way up here?" He asks the same question I had when I saw his name.

"I have no idea. He has friends all over the state from college and med school, but damn, that's a long drive for a booty call."

He snickers. "Literally."

"Oh God." A realization hits me. "Every few months, he'd take road trips to visit friends up here, and now I'm wondering if that's what he was doing the whole time." Considering I caught him cheating on me, it's not a farfetched idea. I never thought twice about it because I knew most of his guy friends, but now I'm wondering if it was all a cover-up to meet chicks and have weird, kinky sex with them.

"He's obviously an idiot," Evan says. "Didn't know a good thing when he had it. Should've shaken his hand and thanked him for giving you up." He chuckles, and I roll my eyes.

"Just so you know, I never did anything with a butt plug. In case you were wondering."

"Too bad." He stalks toward me, looking sexy as hell in his snug T-shirt. "I wouldn't mind playing with one in your tight little ass." He wraps his arms around me and leans over to whack me on the butt.

"You're awful," I tease, chuckling. "Is it weird that I'm wondering how far a person has to push a butt plug in for it to get stuck?"

He shakes his head at me then starts widening his fingers apart to show me how many inches the plug was. "Probably a good five or six inches."

I shudder at the thought of it.

"Well, if the baby didn't make me nauseous before, that just did."

He laughs, leaning down to press a soft kiss on my lips. "We should probably head out anyway."

"Okay, I think I'm ready."

Evan's wearing his cowboy boots and Levi's. Though he spends most of his days off helping on the ranch, I'm still not used to seeing him dressed like this and ready to work. Being a good sport and wanting to help out too, I put on my best impression of cowgirl clothes too—jeans, boots, and a snug T-shirt that hugs my growing baby bump.

"You know you're not working out in the pastures with us," he tells me as we walk to the truck with his arm around me. Since finding out I was pregnant, he's made sure I take it easy and don't overwork myself, though I'm perfectly capable.

"Why not? Your father already said it was fine."

Evan rolls his eyes but gives me a sideways smirk. "You know he was just trying to make you happy, but Mama isn't going to let you go out there carrying her grandbaby either."

"We'll see." I bite my bottom lip, and he pulls me into his arms and kisses me.

"You're so defiant, and you know what that does to me. We might need to be late," he says, arching his hips into my body, feeling his erection.

"No, sir." I chuckle, finding the strength to push him away. "You know punctuality is your middle name. Can't be late. Plus, your mama is making lunch and expects us to be there."

"Right." He grunts.

Mrs. Bishop insisted we come for lunch, and I couldn't deny the invitation. I've noticed she has a way of making people do exactly what she wants without the guilt trip; it's a part of her Southern charm. As we drive to the ranch, I can't stop laughing when Evan suggests we go home, take off our clothes, and lie around naked all day.

"We have plans, though," I remind him.

"It's hot as fuck outside," he snaps back with a smirk.

"And you're suggesting what again?"

He doesn't have to say another word. With a simple eyebrow raise, I know exactly what he wants to do instead. Being pregnant has made my sex drive increase to a crazy level, and I almost consider it, but skipping lunch isn't an option. I laugh again, but he gives me his infamous smoldering sexy look, and I'm tempted to tell him to turn the truck around to do exactly as he suggested.

As soon as I see the large farmhouse come into view, a big grin fills my face, and Evan notices. He gives me a side glance before parking.

"I love coming here with you," I tell him, and he grabs my hand and kisses my knuckles like he always does, which I love. The electricity that flows between us is hotter than the Texas heat. Evan notices me tense because there's nothing more that I want at this very moment than him.

Leaning over the console, he pulls my face to his, allowing our lips to dance in a slow, rhythmic movement. My breast is in his palm, and when he squeezes, the heat continues to flood through my body. He has control of me—every part of me—and with a single touch, he sets me ablaze. Slowly, his hand finds its way to the top button of my jeans, to my zipper, and before I can say his name, his hand slips inside my panties. As soon as he touches my clit, I feel as if I'm losing all my inhibitions. Knowing at any moment anyone could pull up next to us turns me on even more.

"Fuck, baby," he growls, slipping a finger inside. I sink into him, needing to feel him and wanting more. I moan against his mouth, my eyes fluttering closed as he slips another finger in and pushes deeper.

"Evan," I say, not wanting him to stop but knowing we have to go inside.

"You're so fucking wet, naughty girl." The low rumble of his voice and the way his lips slide over my neck combined with his hands in my panties practically blinds me. His thumb continues to tease my clit, and the orgasm starts to build so quickly that even I'm shocked by it.

"Can you come for me, sweetheart?" Evan asks between kisses, his hot breath against my mouth, my cheeks, my neck. Breathless moans fill the cab of the truck as he works me harder and deeper. Within minutes, I'm losing myself in him.

"Yes, yes, *more*." My body is greedy, wanting, begging—even demanding it. As my heart races, I tell him I'm close with staggered breaths. With a devilish grin, he slows his pace, allowing my cup to slowly fill until I completely spill over. He slides his fingers in and out one more time; the intensity of it all takes over, and I feel as if I've drifted into space as I sink into the euphoria of him. When I finally open my eyes, he's staring at me with a half-smile before placing his fingers in his mouth. God, that's so fucking hot when he does that.

"You taste so damn good, baby. I can never get enough of you."

I smile, searching his face, trying to memorize him, not ever wanting this time to end.

"We should really go in before someone comes out and smells your orgasm all over my truck," he tells me with a wicked grin.

"Do I look guilty?" I ask him, placing my hands on my cheeks, knowing my face is red and lips are swollen.

"Guilty as charged," he admits.

"I can't go in there now. Your mother's going to know we were just doing something," I say, paranoid.

"You'll be fine. Just pretend like nothing happened. Think of shoveling horse crap and how awful you're going to smell," he encourages with a shit-eating grin, knowing that's impossible.

I squeeze my knees together, feeling the throb between my legs, and let out a sigh before opening the door. Evan takes my hand, and we walk up the steps to the house together. Before turning the knob, he looks over at me. "So guilty."

"Ass," I whisper.

The house smells like fried food with a hint of sugar. As we walk down the hallway toward the kitchen, I slow at the pictures on the wall and wonder how I've not noticed them all this time. Of course Mrs. Bishop is proud of her kids and still has all their photos from kindergarten all the way up to high school hanging on the wall in picture frames. I find Evan's and can't help but laugh when I see he had a dorky haircut and braces. He's wearing a button-up western shirt.

"Sexy." I cross my arms and look over at him.

"All the ladies wanted me back then. I mean, come on, look at that hair."

"Yeah, the nineties were good to you." I snort, much preferring his longer hair. It suits his personality better.

I continue looking at the wall of photos and smile at how much everyone has changed over the years. There are pictures of Jackson at a rodeo, John wrestling a baby calf, and Courtney sitting on top of a horse. There's a photo collage of Mr. and Mrs. Bishop with all the kids at various ages.

"Your mom is like a TV mom," I say, noticing how prim and proper she looks in every photograph.

He chuckles. "Except she has a bark and backs it with a bite. Mama's pretty scary at times, especially when it comes to people messing with her kids." Evan grabs my hand and continues to lead me to the kitchen.

As soon as Mrs. Bishop sees me, she stops setting the table and comes and gives me a big hug. I squeeze her tightly, happy to feel her sincere affection.

"Oh honey, I'm so glad you guys came. How're you doin'? Feeling any better?" she asks, and it's confirmed that Evan's been keeping her updated on how crappy I've felt.

"I'm managing for now. Hoping the second trimester keeps the nausea away, and I can start keeping my food down." I sigh but give her a comforting smile, so she stops worrying about me so much.

"Well, I've been thinking about everything that happened lately and am just so happy you two are able to move forward after all of it." I know she's referring to Richard, but we don't talk about him much anymore.

It feels good to know she cares, but it's also a painful reminder that she's more concerned about me than my own mother. I keep a smile for her, staying strong, though the thought of Richard and what almost happened still scares the shit out of me.

"I heard he was transferred to a mental hospital for treatment. I'm just glad he's finally getting the help he needs," I tell her.

"As long as he stays there," she asserts with a firm head nod.

I smile in agreement.

"So," Mrs. Bishop starts, patting my stomach. "How's my little grandbaby doin'?"

"Great! He or she is the size of a lemon, sucking all the energy out of me, and everything was measuring just as expected during my last checkup," I say and glance over at Evan who's smiling big.

"Now it's time for a weddin'." Mrs. Bishop turns to Evan, and I see him shrug. Heat hits my cheeks, and I'm thankful the back door flies open and tears us from the moment. When I see John, I instantly smile. Out of all the brothers, I know he's the one who has some kept secrets. He's too quiet when it comes to anything personal, and I've learned that people are quiet for a reason. Though he's always nice to me, I often wonder what's hiding under that exterior of his.

"Hey Emily," he says, and I can tell he's tired by the dark circles under his eyes.

"Hey, how are things?" I ask, keeping my attention on him. Evan is staring as well, and I know I'm not the only one who notices something is up.

"Real good," John tells me. "I saw the foundation was laid for the house. Happy y'all will be moving closer. I'll get to see more of my big brother, hopefully." He grins and tilts his head at Evan.

"Yeah, I'm excited about building our dream home and making it exactly what we need for the baby," I tell him. "Plus, it will be nice living closer to family," I say, and Mama grins.

"And I hope you chose a floor plan with enough rooms so you can fill it with more babies."

I burst out laughing, knowing Evan hates it when his mama gets on him. Though he rolls his eyes, the smile on his face doesn't falter. "Mama, can you let us have one baby before you start signing us up to have ten?"

"I'm not getting any younger—and neither are you, by the way"—Mrs. Bishop points her finger at Evan—"and I want to be able to enjoy watching my little grandbabies grow up. So all y'all need to be having as many as you can." She gives John a stern look too. Leave it to a Southern mama to always be begging for more grandchildren.

Just as John opens his mouth to say something, Jackson comes barreling in explaining to Alex exactly how the horses got loose this morning.

"Damn," Jackson whistles, looking at John. "And I thought I got no sleep from you being so loud last night." Jackson swings his arms above his head like he's riding a bucking bull. John narrows his eyes, and I glance at Evan who has his arms crossed over his broad chest. He's holding back laughter.

"What're you boys talkin' about?" Mrs. Bishop asks, turning and looking back and forth between John and Jackson.

"Aw, shit," Jackson says under his breath. Mama's eyes widen when she hears him curse, and he swallows it down. She has a way of putting the fear of God into people. "Nuthin', Mama. Just givin' John sh—er, crap."

When she turns toward the sink, John flips him off behind her back. Considering the stories I've heard from Evan, Mrs. Bishop will probably bring it up later. Apparently, she's like an elephant and never forgets anything. Basically, she's a woman I'd never want to cross, that's for sure.

"Hi, Emily," Alex says as he sits down and places his hat on the table. He looks tired, too, but I'm sure it's from working the ranch or being up late with Riley, not from a late-night rendezvous. Knowing what little I do about John, I never would've pegged him for the type, but I'm beginning to realize I have a lot to learn about them all.

"Oh, Ma," Alex begins, "Dad said he wasn't gonna make it. Had some last minute things to do." She turns with her hands planted on her hips, looking unhappy about it.

"I'll just make him a plate and stick it in the oven to keep it warm then."

We sit at the table, and everyone removes covers from the food and passes it around, like a real family sit-down dinner.

"Emily, I heard you'll be helping me at the B&B this afternoon," John says between bites.

I turn and look at Evan, giving him shit. "I was going out to the pastures with Evan, I *thought*."

Evan stifles a laugh. Jerk. "I never said *wher*e you'd help."

Considering I'm pregnant, I really didn't expect to be out in the heat with them anyway; I just like to tease him about it because I know how worked up he gets about me doing anything laborious. Regardless, I shake my head at him with a side smile, but I'm sure with how tired John looks, he could use the extra hand.

"You can come help me clean the stables since you're dressed for it," Jackson adds, wiggling his eyebrows and looking between Evan and me with a smirk.

"Just being paired with you would be enough punishment. I wouldn't wish that on anyone," Evan blurts out. Jackson loves to push Evan's buttons when it comes to me, and I think it's hilarious because it's completely harmless. I've seen him do the same shit to Alex about River, and it's always funny when these Bishop men get riled up so easily.

John rolls his eyes and shakes his head. The conversation continues until we're all finished eating. Mama serves up ice cream and homemade apple pie, and though I'm full, I can't deny a sliver of heaven. As the cinnamon and fresh-baked apples hit my tongue, a small moan escapes from my lips. Evan lifts an eyebrow at me and smirks as he goes back to his pie. My breath quickens, and I'm happy when Mr. Bishop walks in and interrupts the tension. Sweat covers his face and neck, and when he takes off his hat, I see his hair and forehead are soaked, too. He sits at the table, and Mrs. Bishop serves him a plate.

"Thanks, darlin'," he says to her, looking up and giving her a wink and a sweet smile before digging in. There's so much adoration exchanged in a single look, and it makes me realize what's been missing with my parents—unconditional love. I think at one point, they cared deeply for each other, but it's nothing like what Mr. and Mrs. Bishop have. This is exactly why Evan is the way he is; he learned to treat women with respect from watching his father doing it all these years. As for Jackson's excuse, he remains a mystery to us all.

I listen to Alex chat with his dad about the tasks that need to be completed today, and Evan pipes in with what he plans to do as well. Evan volunteers to take on some of the duties, and when they talk about moving cattle and pulling weeds, I'm happy that I'll be helping John in the air conditioning wearing ridiculous boots and tight blue jeans instead.

After we help Mrs. Bishop clean up, Evan kisses me goodbye, then looks at John with a pointed stare. There's a silent agreement exchanged between them, and I'm willing to bet Evan gave him a list of things I can and can't do, but I don't ask. The two of them are so much alike, it's almost scary.

"So if you're coming with me, we best get movin'," John tells me, and I follow him out the back door. There's a utility vehicle waiting by a trail, and I almost laugh because these things don't really exist in Houston.

"Do you want to drive it?" he asks, grinning.

"Uh yeah," I say, and he throws me the keys. I catch them, and we walk to the side by side. "Is it just like riding a bike?" I stick the key in the ignition and start it.

"More like driving a car." He chuckles.

"So you're a smartass too?" I give him a sideways glance.

"If you only knew," he says, turning his head smiling.

"Must run in the family." I push down on the gas, and we jolt forward. John laughs under his breath, and I shake my head at him as we continue down the trail toward the B&B.

When the big house comes into view, John directs me where to park. I drive into the barn, and when we get out, I see a few people sitting out on the back porch playing board games and drinking sweet tea. Jackson walks up, and John immediately shakes his head when he sees him.

"Sure you don't want to help with the stables? Last chance," Jackson taunts, holding his arms out wide.

John places his hand on my shoulder and guides me forward, giving Jackson no attention. Before we walk inside, John turns and flips him off.

"I guess I deserve that," Jackson yells.

When we walk inside, I look at John. "What's that all about?" I know it's not any of my business, but I'm curious.

"You really wanna know?" he asks.

I nod.

"Aside from the fact that Jackson doesn't know how to keep his big mouth shut. You heard what he blurted out at lunch. Now Mama isn't gonna let that rest and will continue asking until I cave—or worse—she gets to Jackson, and he caves."

I smirk, knowing he's probably right about Mama being persistent. "Was he lying, though?"

He doesn't answer but instead leads me to an office that's right off the main area. He grabs a schedule book, then we return to the registration counter.

I guess he's pleading the fifth.

"Today we need to call and confirm reservations for next week," he explains, hoping to deter us from the subject, but when I give him a look, he knows it's not going to be that easy. He sighs and shrugs his shoulders. "Jackson may be a lot of things, but he's not a liar."

Damn, wasn't expecting that one.

"I didn't think he was, just curious is all," I offer, but he continues with the task at hand.

"So we'll start at the top of the list here. Just be real polite and confirm the dates of their stay. Should be fairly simple."

"Okay, sure," I say, clearing my throat and trying to get my best phone voice ready.

After I place a few calls, John brings me a bottle of water. "If you ever get tired of working at the hospital, I'd hire you on the spot."

That makes me chuckle. After about an hour, everyone on the list is officially confirmed, and I feel a small sense of accomplishment. Not wasting any time, John finds other tasks that need to get done since the person who usually helps him is on vacation this week. Now I understand why I was paired with John today; he really needs the extra help. He lists out laundry, changing sheets, and stocking towels in the rooms that don't have ***DO NOT DISTURB*** signs hanging. I've only been here for a short amount of time, but I'm starting to realize how much goes into running this place on a daily basis and all the behind-the-scenes work.

We head downstairs and go into a side room where John stuffs sheets and blankets into the washing machine. Once it's full and he adds the detergent, he turns and looks at me.

"So how are things really going since the incident? You and Evan doing okay with everything?"

"If I answer your questions, you'll have to answer mine." I smirk. John thinks about it for a moment. Narrowing his eyes, he finally nods. "Fine. But whatever I say doesn't leave us."

"Swear," I tell him, crossing my heart. "Doctor-patient confidentiality," I tease, but wholeheartedly mean it. I wouldn't tell his secrets.

"I just don't want my brothers in my personal business."

"I understand that more than you know." Considering my family was always knee-deep in my life and what I was doing and who I was dating—I get it.

"Okay, it's a deal." John holds out his hand, and I take it, and we shake on it.

"What was the question again?" I ask, pulling towels from the dryer.

"How're you and my brother doing after everything that's happened? It's been a few months since then, but we've only seen y'all a handful of times." The last time we saw the whole family was at Riley's first birthday party a couple of months ago. We come to the property to check on the progress on the house about once a week, but otherwise, we've been working, and when Evan comes out here on his days off, I spend time with Kiera.

"Ah yes," I tease, remembering the question. "Things were rough at first because I still didn't feel safe even though there weren't any threats, but it was just still so fresh that I couldn't shake the feeling I was being watched or that I could potentially lose Evan. We've both been trying not to take the little things for granted after it all. However, we're great now. We're having fun planning for the baby and thinking of decorating ideas for the house, so it keeps my mind busy. Evan's been my rock through this whole ordeal and is always checking on me and making sure I'm eating food other than licorice." I laugh, remembering the time I opened my locker to find a basket of fruit with a note he wrote. It said, 'Dear Mommy, I need to eat fruits and vegetables too. Daddy said so. Love, Baby P.S. Daddy thinks you're the most beautiful woman in the world.'

"I honestly didn't think a man like him really existed." I continue about the man I'm in love with.

John smiles. "You two are made for each other. He's needed someone like you for a long while. It's nice to see him like this, and I was happy to hear about the baby. Can't wait to spoil the shit out of it."

I hand him the folded towels, and he places them in the empty basket.

"Thanks. That really means a lot to me. I didn't have a close-knit family growing up, so I'm really looking forward to giving this baby a big family."

"Well, just a warnin', though. If you're not careful, Mama's gonna start planning the weddin' real soon. She adores you."

My eyes go wide. "I've already been warned about that and already experienced it actually."

"It's no joke. A few days ago, she told me I needed to find a nice girl like you."

"Seriously?" I ask.

"Yep. Courtney and Alex are both settled down with spouses and kids, and now that you and Evan are having a baby, she's taken it upon herself to try and find me someone too."

"But what about Jackson? He's single," I say, but then add, "Well, single in the sense that he doesn't do more than just hookups."

This question causes him to burst into laughter. "Mama thinks he's hopeless."

I tilt my head at him. "She doesn't really believe that."

He gives me a pointed look. "She knows he ain't ready to settle down anytime soon."

"And you are?"

"I want any relationship I'm in to happen naturally, not because my mother set me up. Also, just because I'm not braggin' about my lady friends like Jackson doesn't mean anything. I believe some things are better left private."

"Ha," I hear behind us and turn to see Jackson standing there smirking. "Didn't seem like you wanted it to be too private last night when the headboard was slamming against the wall and keeping everyone in town awake."

"And the evil twin strikes again." John grunts.

Jackson walks forward and leans against the counter. He pushes his cowboy hat up on his head and gives me a side smile. "John has more women in his bed than I do. Everyone thinks I'm the player, and I'll happily take the title, but John has me beat by a long shot. He's just too modest to admit it."

John reaches back and punches Jackson in his arm. "You really need to shut the hell up," he warns. "You're just tryin' to show off in front of Emily."

Jackson straightens his stance and folds his arms against his broad chest. "And now I'm gonna have to punch you back."

The only thing that stops them from continuing forward is my laughter. I try to hold it back, but by the way they're acting, I can't help it. Grown ass brothers acting like they're back at the playground. Their eyes widen, and they both turn and look at me.

"What's so funny?" Jackson asks, the smile returning to his face.

"It's almost like you're arguing with yourself in the mirror. You two are lucky to have each other. It's a blessing," I tell them.

"Or a curse," John adds.

Jackson gives him a big hug, squeezing him hard, and pretends to try to kiss him, but John just pushes him away and picks up a broom to sweep up the dirt that Jackson tracked in from outside. Eventually, Jackson gets bored with us and decides to return to the stables.

"Is he always like that?" I ask.

"If he wasn't, I'd think there was something wrong," John admits, looking back at his to-do list.

"You know I'm not going to say anything to anyone about your extracurriculars. Though I have a feeling Jackson's exaggerating just a little."

John lifts an eyebrow, and I hold back a scoff and make sure to keep my face straight. Though he wears the same face as Jackson, as I watch him, I see how similar his mannerisms are to Evan's. He's reserved and all business, but I have a feeling when he lets loose, he knows how to have a good time.

We spend the next few hours sweeping, mopping, organizing, and dusting. John takes full advantage of having the extra help, which I don't mind because I enjoy being productive. Though I'm sure he's giving me all the easy tasks because Evan probably told him to.

As I'm standing on my tiptoes trying to clean windows, arms wrap around my waist and rub my stomach. Instantly, I look over my shoulder only to see Evan. He kisses my neck and whispers in my ear. "You smell so damn good."

I chuckle. "Like bleach and window cleaner." I turn my body to fully face him. "And you smell like the outdoors and man."

"You mean sweat?" He chuckles against my mouth.

"Did you come to steal my help?" John asks, smiling at Evan and me.

"I sure did. I've got some more tasks for her to do," Evan tells him, picking me up in his arms.

John shakes his head. "Thanks for all your help today, Emily. You're more than welcome to be my helper when you're bored or just want to get out of Evan's hair."

"You're welcome. Anytime," I say as Evan continues to carry me through the common room and finally sets me down when we get to the door. "I kinda like it when you go all caveman on me."

"If I didn't capture you, I'm not sure John would ever let me take you away."

"So what are these tasks you need me to do?" I ask as we walk onto the front porch.

When Evan turns and lifts an eyebrow, then proceeds to suck on the corner of his bottom lip, I know exactly what tasks he's referring to.

CHAPTER TWENTY-SEVEN

EVAN

I WAKE up with Emily pressed against my body and smile against the softness of her neck. "Good morning," I whisper, trying to force myself up.

She rolls over and wraps her leg around mine. "Can we just call in sick today?"

I brush my thumb across her cheek. "You already know the answer to that."

"I know," she whispers and stretches.

Allowing her to sleep a little longer, I get up and jump in the shower. By the time I'm out, I find Emily in the kitchen all dressed and ready to go. "I wish I didn't give up coffee."

"The doctor said you could have one cup," I remind her, but she was persistent on completely giving it up for the baby.

"But we both know the risks. Plus, one cup is a tease when you're used to having three or four through the day." She pours coffee up to the top of the travel mug, takes a big sniff, then hands it over to me.

I lean over and place a kiss on her lips. "And this is why I love you."

"Because I know statistics?" She laughs.

"Exactly."

We head to the truck, and I look over at her and smile. I love our morning routine and spending as much time with her as possible. Being able to see Emily at the hospital and having lunch together is one of the highlights of my entire day.

By the time we make it to the hospital, the sun peeks over the horizon. After I park, we grab our bags with our scrubs from the back seat and head inside.

"What?" she asks, looking over at me as she changes clothes.

"Nothing, Dr. Bell. Nothing at all." I wink, and we make our way to the nurses' station, grab our pagers, and check in with the nurses.

Dr. Umbridge informs us an ambulance is in en route, and that Fiona will fill us in on the details. The rest of the staff already have patients so Emily or I will be on this one. "Twenty-eight-year-old female. Seven months pregnant. Experiencing migraines and nausea. Severely dehydrated. Passed out at work and her co-workers called it in. ETA is three minutes."

"Sounds good," Emily says. "I can take her."

I glance over at her, then to Fiona. "I'll be helping Dr. Bell on this one. Page me if I'm needed." She gives me a quick head nod before picking up the phone.

Emily and I walk away from the nurses' station, and she turns and speaks in a hushed voice. "You know I can handle this myself."

I place my hand on her shoulder and can feel the tension in her body. "I know you're more than capable. One of the best in the hospital." I wink to ease her of my overprotectiveness.

Before she can respond, the hustle and bustle of the paramedics wheeling in the patient interrupt us. Emily goes to the stretcher, and I follow behind her.

"Patient's name is Bailey Kensington. She's seven months pregnant. Fetal heart rate is strong," the medic informs us.

"Okay, take her to trauma room two please," Emily orders. I love watching her take charge, especially on days she wears her sexy, black-rimmed glasses. It's honestly the last thing I should be thinking about right now, but ever since her sex drive has tripled, it's always on my mind. I'm ready any time she decides to push me into one of the on-call rooms and demand I take off my pants. Working with my girlfriend definitely has its perks.

Once Bailey is transferred to a bed, we hook her up and check all her vitals. An electric fetal monitor is hooked up as well so we can keep an eye on the baby. Claire comes in to help since she just finished with a patient and sets her up with fluids right away.

Bailey looks up at the three of us, and the discomfort is written all over her face. Emily asks more questions about her medical history and the location of the pain. Not wanting to overstep my bounds with her patient, I stand and monitor the machines. Bailey winces when Emily asks her to lean forward so she can listen to her lungs. She tells her to take some deep breaths, but she can barely hold herself up before she gets a dizzy spell.

"How long have you experienced these headaches?" Emily asks.

"For a few months, but the vision issues started a few weeks ago," Bailey finally admits.

"Okay, I'm going to check your vision, since your pain is pinpoint," Emily explains before placing her finger behind her ear. "Tell me when you can first see my finger." Emily begins moving her fingers forward, and she doesn't speak until her finger is nearly in front of her face, which worries me, and when Emily glances back at me, I see the concern on her face too.

"And how long has the nausea lasted? Since the beginning of the pregnancy?" I ask, taking a step closer.

She shakes her head. "It started the past few weeks. I've noticed I've been slightly losing my balance as well, but I think it's because my headaches are so painful I can hardly bear it."

"We need to order an MRI immediately." I look at Emily, and she nods her head.

"What about the baby? Is that safe for the baby?"

Emily grabs Bailey's hand and squeezes it, giving her as much comfort as she can offer. "We're going to do everything we can. The MRI is perfectly safe for the baby since we're getting a scan of your head. This test will help us determine if there's something more serious going on. You're in the best hands in San Angelo, and as soon as we find out more information, you'll be the first to know."

Bailey releases a small smile, then leans back and closes her eyes. There's not much more we can do for her other than give her some Tylenol, but if it's more than just a headache, it won't help much until we can confirm her diagnosis.

As I walk out of the room, Emily continues giving orders, then follows me.

"It could be preeclampsia combined with dehydration, but her blood pressure is normal," Emily mutters, writing in her chart. I can tell her wheels are turning as she tries to pinpoint Bailey's diagnosis.

"Once we get the MRI scans back, we'll know more of what's going on. The way her vision is combined with her other symptoms, I'm worried it's something much worse than that," I tell her, but she already knows that.

When our eyes meet, she lets out a long breath. "I hope not, especially for the baby's sake."

I squeeze her shoulder. "I know."

"I told her we'd more than likely keep her overnight to watch her vitals. She's in line to get the testing done now."

"Good," I say just as Fiona pulls me away. "Dr. Umbridge needs your help in trauma room one."

I glance back at Emily, not really wanting to leave her, and she gives me a reassuring smile that she'll be fine, but I know her patient's symptoms are heavy on her mind. I smile back before jogging to the trauma room that's in complete chaos and see that blood is everywhere.

"Dr. Bishop. You're here. We need to do damage control and start surgery to stop the bleeding," he says, nonchalantly as if he's having a normal conversation over a cup of coffee as a man lies awake on his side with a knife protruding from his body. Dr. Vance, the trauma surgeon, is standing in the back of the room, scrubbing in.

One of the nurses who usually shadows Dr. Umbridge gives me the rundown as I scrub my hands and snap on my gloves. "Stab wound. The X-ray showed the blade barely missed his major organs."

The man screams out in pain. Flashes of my own stabbing incident surface, but I push the thoughts away. Thank God I barely remember any of it.

"Can we get him something?" I ask.

"Already been given a full dose of morphine and started antibiotics to kill any potential infection. Allergic to regular anesthesia and both ORs are full. He tried pulling the knife out himself and is now bleeding into his abdomen. So if we're going to stop the bleed, we need to get this knife out now," Dr. Umbridge explains, then looks at me.

"How the hell did this even happen?" I look at the man.

"My wife caught me cheatin'. Told me she'd make sure I'd never do it again." He groans behind the oxygen mask. Luckily, he's drugged, so he'll only feel mild pain, but it could've definitely been worse.

"She would've killed you if she stabbed closer to here," I tell him. "That's your abdominal aorta."

I put my hand around the hilt, making sure Dr. Vance and Dr. Umbridge are ready. "Be prepared to feel some pressure. As soon as the knife is out, the surgeon will locate the bleed and stitch you up," I explain, hoping to ease his nerves. We don't have much time, so it's now or never. "On the count of three."

I count down and pull the knife from his side. Blood surfaces and Dr. Umbridge rushes in to assist as Dr. Vance begins cleaning the wound. The nurse keeps an eye on his stats as she hands over the tools

Dr. Vance gives me a head nod and a small smile, then goes back to his patient. I remove my gloves, throw them in the medical waste bin, and move to the sink to wash any blood from my arms. I stand by as they continue working, fast and efficiently. The wound is cleaned, and they give the patient another dose of pain medication to help knock him out. Once the bleed is controlled and the wound is thoroughly cleaned, Dr. Vance stitches him up.

Another successful trauma on the books.

When I walk out of the room, I see Emily walking toward me with a file in her hand.

"The results are in," she says, pulling me back into the testing room where I can look at the computer generated images on a screen. "It doesn't look good," she mumbles when we walk in.

As soon as I see the results on the large screen, my mouth slightly falls open. "It looks like she might have a brain tumor. Look at the cloudiness in the image here. That's what's causing her vision loss, affecting her motor skills, and the migraines. We're going to have to call in a neurologist to confirm, but I'm quite certain that's what this is. Brain surgery might be an option, but considering the size and her being pregnant, I don't know. Do you know who's on duty today?"

"Dr. Patil. I already paged him, and he's on the way here now," Emily tells me.

I grab her hand and squeeze it, then place a kiss on her forehead. "We're going to do everything we possibly can."

Moments later, Dr. Patil enters and confirms what we thought.

"I'd like a CT Scan," he says. "Get a better look."

"She's pregnant. CT is out of the question," Emily tells him.

"Considering she's pregnant, that doesn't leave us many options until after she has the baby."

"That's if she makes it that long," I add. The tumor is large and could rupture at any moment.

Dr. Patil nods in agreement. "Surgery could be an option but would be too risky for the baby, and if I'm being honest, by the size and location of the mass, it seems too advanced at this point. The surgery would even be a success for only a small percentage," he states, and I know he means success as in she doesn't die during surgery. "She'd need to do chemo if we can't remove the mass completely, which comes with its own risks."

"So what are her options right now?" Emily asks.

"Well, if she doesn't want surgery, she can try chemo and see if that shrinks the tumor first. However, it'll affect the pregnancy more than likely, and considering she's already in her third trimester, it wouldn't be a good outcome. If she chooses to move forward with surgery right away, it would need to happen immediately before the tumor gets any bigger," he continues.

"What if she wants to wait to have the surgery until after the baby is born?" Emily asks.

"How long have her symptoms been prevalent?" he asks.

"She said the past few months it's gotten worse."

"Considering the severity of her symptoms, the tumor is aggressive in its growth. I'm not sure she could wait another two or three months honestly. The tumor could double in size, could burst, could make her completely blind." He stares at the scans, frowning. "Either way, this isn't going to be an easy decision for the mother-to-be."

I thank him for his consultation, and he tells us to let him know what she decides. Surgery could save her life but kill her baby. Even then, there'd be no guarantee the surgery would be a success. She'd have to do chemo on top of all that and still… there's no guarantee any of that would work.

Emily is emotionless as she looks at Dr. Patil. He gives a soft smile before exiting the room.

"This is one part of my job that I hate," she mumbles.

"I can deliver the news, if you want," I tell her.

"I need to do this," Emily says, taking a deep breath, grabbing the X-rays from the screen, then exiting the room. I follow behind her. For a minute, Emily stands outside of the door, knowing the news she's about to give is life changing.

Emily knocks, then opens the door and sees Bailey sleeping. She steps in quietly, hoping not to startle her.

"Hey, Dr. Bell," Bailey says with a faint smile. We gave her some medicine to keep her comfortable while we waited for the results.

Emily plasters on a smile, pulls up a chair, and sits next to Bailey. I stand back as she delivers the news, and it guts me.

"But my baby girl is okay right now?" she asks.

"Yes, all her stats are within normal ranges. Her heart rate is strong and healthy, and the ultrasound showed no issues," Emily confirms.

"So what if I wait until after she's born?"

Emily lowers her head before looking her in the eyes. "It might be inoperable at that point. Your only option would be chemo or radiation, but it wouldn't be a guarantee. It might shrink the tumor enough for you to get surgery then, but at this rate, it's very aggressive and unpredictable."

"And what if I get chemo or radiation now instead of the surgery?"

"It would most likely abort the baby," Emily explains, and I can tell it takes a toll on both of them when the room grows eerily silent. "Surgery would be a risk for both of you, but the chemo would definitely put the baby at risk."

"Your best option right now is surgery and depending on the results, chemo or radiation after that. That would give you the best options for long-term survival." Emily lays it all out there for her, though I know it's hard for her to even say.

Bailey shakes her head. "Surgery and chemo are *not* an option for me then. Even if I did go through with it, I'd lose my baby and then could still end up dying, so I'd lose either way."

"I understand, Bailey, I do. Is there any family you want to discuss this with first?"

Her eyes widen as the blood drains from her face. "No. I don't get along with my parents, and I'm an only child. It's just me."

"Okay, and what about the baby's father?"

She looks down and folds her hands over her belly. "He doesn't know." She shrugs. "I planned on raising her by myself."

Emily's breathing picks up, and I can tell she's struggling to come to terms with what her patient is deciding.

"I want to have this baby and enjoy her for the few months I have left," Bailey says, choking up and trying to be strong.

Emily stays quiet.

I want to ask questions—ones I can't ask as a doctor—but questions that concern me for her baby. If she has no family and the father doesn't even know, where will the baby go when she inevitably dies?

"Her life is more important than mine at this point," Bailey says, holding her stomach, tears flooding down her face. "She deserves a chance to have a life. It's the least I can give her."

"Bailey, we can find you a top-rated specialist in Houston who can give you the best outcome possible. You don't have to make a final decision today," Emily reminds her, and I know whatever option Bailey chooses will be heartbreaking either way.

Bailey shakes her head. "How long do I have if I don't do anything?"

Emily swallows hard, and the air in the room stills. "Four months. Maybe six at the most." Bailey's tears fall down her cheeks harder. "But your symptoms will get worse. Your migraines and vision will worsen by the day. You need to be extremely careful."

Covering her face with her hands, Bailey lets out a sob. "Enough time to deliver my baby, then plan my own funeral."

"We have great social workers who can help if you need it," Emily tells her.

Bailey looks up, her eyes red and blotchy. "No, thank you. I'll figure it out."

"I'm so sorry." Emily stands and places her hand on her shoulder. "I want you to come back if the pain becomes unbearable, okay?" Bailey nods. "I'll send the nurse in to give you the final discharge papers."

We walk out of the room, and a few tears well in her eyes before dropping. I take her hand and lead her to the locker room. Once inside, I pull her into my arms and hold her.

"She's giving her life to save her child," Emily says against my chest. "It's not fair. She shouldn't be doing this alone. She shouldn't have to choose. She's too young."

"I know, baby. It's the epitome of a mother's love." I place a kiss on her forehead, then on her lips. "Why don't you take a short break, and I'll go handle the ER."

She nods as my pager goes off, and I leave her to her thoughts. The rest of the day is busy between patients coming in and checking on those who are currently admitted, and I barely see Emily in passing. We have a quick lunch together in the cafeteria, and I can tell she's exhausted, which is what I've been worrying about now that she's getting further along in her pregnancy.

"My dad called," she says between bites.

"Yeah?" She doesn't bring up her parents often but has been more lately since the news of the baby and after the incident with Richard. They've always had a close relationship, but he's mentioned to her several times that they're all excited for their first grandchild.

"He wants me to come visit and have a family dinner. He told my mother he'd actually take a few days off and asked if I'd come down. He's trying to get my brother and sister to come too."

"You should go then. Be with your family. Pretty soon, you won't be able to fly and riding in a car for five to six hours won't be that comfortable."

Emily looks at me and smiles. "Will you come with me?"

I look up at her and grin. "Of course, sweetheart. If you want me to. It's been a while since I've been to Houston, and the last time was for nothing but business. I'll check the schedule and request time off." I wink at her.

"Have I told you that I love you today?" she asks, smiling.

"Hmm." I rub the short stubble on my chin and playfully shake my head.

"I love you," she tells me without missing a beat. "I love you so much."

"I love you, too, baby."

CHAPTER TWENTY-EIGHT

EMILY

After an hour flight, we land in Houston at Hobby Airport. It's been three weeks since we planned this trip and even though I'm excited to see my family again, I'm also very anxious to see my mom again.

As we wait to deplane, Evan grabs my hand and kisses my knuckles, which still gives me butterflies. Raindrops stream down the window, and I hate that it's raining, but at least we aren't in the air anymore.

Once we exit the plane and grab our luggage, Evan and I pick up the rental car and head to my parents' house.

"I'm a little nervous," he admits, pulling onto the highway.

"But you've already met my dad," I say because my father is the one who usually freaks people out, especially those in the medical profession.

"Well, yeah, I've met your dad, but not the rest of your family. It's a big deal. Bringing me home for the first time. What if they don't like me?"

I burst out into laughter. "Trust me, they're going to love you! Either way, they all know they don't have a choice, considering we're having a baby. But honestly, you have nothing to worry about. Meeting my dad was the hard part, and you've already passed that barrier with flying colors. Plus, it can't be as bad as meeting your family after a one-night stand where I stole your clothes and left you high and dry. Let's also mention the majority of them knew about what happened. So yeah, you'll be fine." I pat his cheek playfully.

We pull up to the gate that secures my parents' property, and after inputting the code, it opens immediately.

"Fancy," he jokes. "Might need to get one of these for our house on the ranch. It'll keep Jackson out at least. But then again, he's not afraid to hop fences, so probably not."

His words cause me to chuckle, and my stomach bobs up and down.

Evan places the car in park and just stares at the house.

"Welcome to River Oaks." I introduce him to the luxurious neighborhood I grew up in. "My parents have expensive taste but just try to ignore it, please. That's what I do."

We both get out of the car and walk up the grand staircase. Glancing over at Evan, I smile before opening the front door and walking in. His eyes nearly bulge out of his head when he sees the marble flooring and Tiffany glass chandeliers, not to mention everything is stark white just like the hospital. "It's a lot. I know."

There were many times I'd screamed through the hallways only to hear my voice echo off the walls. As a kid, I felt so insignificant here, which makes me even happier when I think about the house we're building on the ranch. It's perfect and not so big it will swallow a kid whole.

"Just wait until I show you the opulent formal room, flower garden, and terraces." I roll my eyes, repeating the amenities that were repeated during the extravagant parties my father would host for his elite friends.

"Hello?" I call out, leading us farther down the hallway, the aromas of the food the chefs are busy preparing fill the house. My mom stopped cooking after the accident, and my dad was always too busy working. So on top of growing up with nannies, I grew up with chefs who taught me how to cook instead of my own mother.

"In here," my father hollers from his office at the end of the hallway. Our shoes click against the floor, and I squeeze Evan's hand, offering him a tad bit of courage, but the closer we get, the more nervous I become. I don't know if it's because I haven't been home in a while or if it's pregnancy hormones, but either way, my heart rate increases.

As soon as we step into his office, my father takes off his glasses and walks toward me with open arms. "There you are," he says, pulling me into a hug. He turns to Evan and shakes his hand. "Good to see you again and doing well I hear," he says to Evan.

"Yes, sir. Much better," Evan replies.

"How was the flight?" my father asks. "Good, I hope."

Evan nods with a grin.

"You know first class is always good," I tell him. He insisted on purchasing the tickets and upgraded our seats.

Evan glances at the desk, and so do I, and we both see he was reading current medical journals. Even when he's supposed to be taking a vacation, he's still researching and working. I hope after years of practicing, I'm still as passionate and interested in my work as he is, but I also hope I can turn it off at times, too.

"Your brother and sister are on their way. Your mother is in the den watching TV," he tells me. "I'm sure she'll be happy to see you. And to finally meet your boyfriend." The smile hits his eyes, but I'm not sure I believe his words. My mother hasn't shown an interest in my life in years.

Dad places his hand on my shoulder and asks me about the pregnancy on the way to see my mother.

"It's going as planned. No complications. No issues," I tell him. "Going great."

"And you've found a highly qualified doctor to see you?"

"Yes, Dad. The very best." I have to hold back an eye roll because considering he specializes in infertility, I'm not sure any doctor that's not in Houston would be good enough for me in his eyes.

We walk into the den, and my nerves take over when I see the back of my mother's head.

"Sally," my father says. "Emily's arrived." She turns down the TV and looks over at me with a smile.

"Hi, Mom." I grab Evan's hand and walk toward her. She seems as if she's in good spirits today, which helps calm my nerves. It would've made things real awkward otherwise. Though Evan knows our history, I was hoping the first time they met would be a positive experience.

"This must be Evan Bishop," she says. "The man who's stolen my little girl's heart."

"Yes, ma'am," Evan confirms, smiling.

"And he's polite too." She glances over at me. "Come here." She pats the seat next to her on the couch.

I go to her and sit. Looking at my stomach, she smiles. "How far along are you now?"

"Almost eighteen weeks," I say.

"When are you due?" she asks.

"End of March."

This all feels really awkward until she pulls me into a hug. "I've missed you, Emily," she whispers, and I feel my emotions begin to take over.

"I've missed you too, Mom."

Just as we're releasing our embrace, Annie and Daniel come barreling in, laughing. When they see me, they rush through the den and almost tackle me, but I stop them before they can.

"Whoa, whoa baby on board." I point down at my stomach.

"Oh yeah," Daniel says, chuckling.

I stand and give them each a big hug. "Meet my boyfriend." Turning to Evan, I give the formal introductions, and my brother and sister exchange hugs with him, though he's as stiff as a board. I laugh to myself because Evan should be used to a family of huggers, considering his own family.

"I'm starving," Annie finally says. "Food almost ready? I've been waiting for this Tetrazzini casserole all day."

"It's ready whenever we are," Dad says.

"Then let's eat," Mom adds, patting my hand before I stand. I reach for her wheelchair and bring it to the edge of the couch so she can pivot her body into the seat. Dad then takes over and pushes her through the den and hallway.

Annie leans over and whispers, "Your boyfriend is really hot." She snickers.

"I know, right?" I whisper back like we're teenagers again. "Seriously, the hottest."

"The doctors don't look like that down here," she complains.

"That's because they never had to do manual labor on a ranch," I remind her, and she nods with a smile in agreement.

Once we're in the dining room, we sit around the table, and moments later, our plates are served. Evan sits next to me, and I grab his hand and hold it. He's smiling, continuing his conversation with Daniel.

"So you really grew up riding horses?" Daniel asks, breaking a piece of bread in two.

"Sure did." Evan grins. "Horses, roping cattle, cleaning barns. My childhood was a real-life Texas cliché." Evan makes jokes, and the room bursts out into laughter, and they keep the questions coming. I feel bad that he's talking instead of eating, but I love listening to him chat about the ranch with that hint of Southern twang he has. Most people can barely tell I'm from Texas when I travel, but with Evan, there's no doubt about it.

As we continue eating, I think about all the little things I love about him. How the corner of his eyes crinkle when he laughs, the way he looks at me like I'm his whole world, and how he manages to put everyone around him at ease. He loves fully, with everything that he is, and there is not a doubtful bone in my body that what we have is special. Though everyone is chatting, I don't pay attention to the conversation; I just watch as Evan entertains and fits right in with my family. Not that I was worried, but I can tell they genuinely adore him already, which has me smiling from ear to ear with pride.

"So Emily, what's the plan after the baby?" Annie asks, changing the conversation.

"I plan to take leave for a while, then eventually return back to work," I tell her. It's a discussion Evan and I have had several times. "My career is important to me, but so is this baby. I'm hoping I can have the best of both worlds of being a mom and a doctor. I don't want to have to choose between the two because I'm not sure my career would win."

"I wouldn't expect anything less," Daniel pipes in like a proud little brother. He'll be graduating med school soon and understands the passion.

"Evan's mother volunteered to babysit, too, so I know the baby will be in good hands," I explain. "I was concerned about daycare and dealing with all of that, so I'm relieved we'll have help."

"Did you find out what you're having yet?" Annie asks, between bites.

"Not yet," Evan chimes in. "Hopefully during our next ultrasound appointment." Evan gives me a wink. He's so damn excited to find out the gender, but I don't have a preference as long as he or she is healthy.

"You do plan to bring the baby to visit us, don't you?" my mother asks with concern, looking directly at me.

"Of course. It's a priority. And I'm hoping you all can come and visit me too. The plan is to move into the new house before the baby arrives, and we'll have plenty of room. Plus, the Bishops' bed and breakfast is on the property, too, if you prefer to stay there. It's a beautiful drive, Mom. You'd love it in the fall." I smile, hoping she really does consider traveling to visit us. I know how hard long distances can be on her.

"We'll have to do that." Mom looks at Dad who nods with a grin.

"We plan to visit after the baby is born, so you'll have to keep us up-to-date with how things are going," Dad says.

"You'll be the first to know," I say, finishing my food.

"I can't wait to be an aunt," Annie says. "I'm going to spoil that little booger."

I laugh. "I'm sure you will. Might need an extra room in our house for all the spoiling of this kid." Between my family and the Bishops, I have no doubt this baby will be extra loved and cared for, which is just the way it should be.

The conversation continues, and I make myself promise that I'll keep them in the loop during the rest of my pregnancy. It's my parents' first grandbaby, and I know it's a big deal for all of them.

After dinner, we make our way to the living room to finish our conversation. Annie gets paged and groans.

"I've got to go." She sighs. "I'm on call this weekend and have a delivery." She stands and walks over to me, giving me a big hug. "Please call me more. I miss you."

"The phone works both ways," I remind her.

"Doctor life," we say at the same time with a laugh.

She walks over to Evan and gives him a big hug. "If you break my sister's heart, I'll kill you."

Annie lets out a chuckle, but I don't doubt her promise, and I don't think Evan does either. Before she leaves, she hugs Mom, then rushes out.

Dad, Evan, and Daniel continue their detailed discussion about the new research he's doing, and they decide to make their way to his office to check it out. I wave him on and shake my head smiling.

"Emily," my mother says, pulling me away from my thoughts.

"Yes, Mom?"

"I can see how happy you are. You're glowing. Makes me so pleased to see."

I swallow down my emotions. "Thanks, Mom." I smile. "I'm the happiest I've ever been."

"I'm also very proud of you. Even if I don't say it enough, I really am. I've also had a lot of time to think about things, especially since you moved away. I finally agreed to go to therapy after all these years, and it's really helped me to see how self-destructive I became after the accident and the way I took it out on you. It wasn't fair to you or anyone, and I knew that, but at the time, I was so emotionally numb that I didn't care about anything. I don't expect you to forgive me or forget, but I'm hoping you'll accept my apology at least. I'm truly sorry, Emily. For everything."

I hug her, trying to push my emotions to the side, but it's been so long since we've been able to talk like this. "Thank you for saying that, Mom. I'm so happy to hear you're getting some help. I love you, and I always have." A few tears stream down my face, and I try to wipe them away.

She tilts her head at me. "Don't cry, sweetie."

"It's the hormones, Mom. I'm an emotional mess lately."

She lets out a chuckle. "You know, when I was pregnant with you, all I wanted to do was eat pickles dipped in mustard. It was the grossest thing I've ever eaten, but I wasn't satisfied until I had them."

"Oh my God. Yes, pickles for me too, but not mustard. What kind of monster was I in the womb?" We both laugh, and the only thing that pulls my attention away is Evan. He's smiling from ear to ear when they enter the room.

"What?" I ask, wanting to know.

"Your dad is a genius," he says, my father smiling and patting him on the back.

"Don't give him too many compliments. He'll start believing them, and his ego is big enough," I tease, glancing over at my dad with a smirk.

An hour later, the yawns start, and I feel the exhaustion from traveling begin to take over.

"You should get some rest," Mom says, patting my leg. "I'm sure you're tired."

I nod and glance over at Evan, and he's yawning too. "Ready?"

Evan looks over at my dad and my brother and grins. "Yeah, we'll have to do this again sometime."

"Definitely," Daniel says, walking over to me and pulling me into a hug. "Don't be a stranger, okay? I'll drive to the middle of nowhere Texas to kick your ass after the baby is born if you ghost us."

When he lets me go, I look straight into his eyes. Time has been good to him, but I can see the years of overworking himself on his face. He could use a good vacation in West Texas. "I won't ever plan on ghosting you mainly because I know you'll come knocking on my door, which you should. I want to show you around. Take you horseback riding or something."

"You haven't even been horseback riding yet," Evan blurts out.

"So! If Jackson can teach a child, I'm sure he can teach the Bells."

Evan lifts his hands. "Okay, okay. You're the boss. But really, you should come and visit."

"I might take you up on that offer." Daniel nods.

I watch as Evan gives my mother a hug and tells her how happy he is to finally meet her.

"I like him, Emily," she shouts, loud enough for Evan to hear.

Dad gives me a big hug bye and squeezes me tightly. "I love you, Emily."

"Love you, too, Dad."

By the time Evan and I finish saying our goodbyes and walk outside, I'm smiling ear to ear.

"Your family is awesome," he declares, opening the door for me and kissing me before I climb in. He jogs to the other side and gets in.

"I'm so happy we came," I say once we hit the main road. "I was worried about seeing my mom again, knowing it could've ended in a disaster, but it all went really well." I'm shocked at the way my mother opened up but also really glad we can start working on our relationship again.

"They love you, Emily. I can tell they'd do anything for you. I know how your childhood was. I know what you went through, but tonight, I saw a family that really cares about you." Evan glances over at me as we head back to the hotel.

"I think it's the baby that's softened them up."

He shakes his head. "Maybe, but I'm willing to bet it's their love for you. It was obvious to me how proud of you they are and happy to see you happy. They're really trying to make an effort." He squeezes my hand, reaffirming how much I love him.

The next day we decided to fly back to San Angelo so we could spend a day recovering from traveling. It was easy to exchange the tickets last minute, but that meant flying out at six in the morning. I was okay with it because I knew once we were home, I'd sleep for a few hours, then have the day to be with Evan.

After we make it home, we have nothing but a lazy day, which is exactly what we both needed.

The following morning comes early, though, especially considering our internal clock is still on our work schedule.

"Good morning, beautiful." Evan nuzzles my neck.

"I want to go look at the house today," I whisper.

"They started framing. I've been having Jackson send me pictures every few days." Evan sits up. "I'm going to make you breakfast, then we can head over just as the roosters start crowing."

I let out a small chuckle. "You're not joking about the roosters, are you?"

"Not. At. All."

After I eat the most delicious bacon and fresh farm eggs, Evan and I head over to the ranch. The sun is rising, and the sky is full of bright purples and pinks. Seeing the morning like this never gets old.

We turn down the old gravel road, pass Evan's parents' house, and tucked away at the end of the road is the dirt driveway that leads to our new house. My blood is pumping as I see the wooden skeleton standing tall. Once he parks, I can barely contain my excitement.

I lean over, and he plants a soft, sweet kiss on my lips. "Let's go see our house," I say, ready to bolt out of the vehicle.

We get out of the truck, and as I walk through what will soon be our front door, a warmth of happiness overwhelms me.

"I'll give you the grand tour, my lady," Evan says, holding out his arm. I lock my arm through his, and he leads us inside. Of course, I know the floor plan by heart, but it's different now that the studs are placed.

"This is where the fireplace will be. Over here is the kitchen. This big window overlooks all of that." He points out to the rolling hills, then pulls me around to another part of the house.

"Here's where the magic will happen." He wiggles his eyebrows, and I let out a big laugh.

"Your giant closet, our master bathroom. Over here is the baby's room." We stop at the door and look inside. I close my eyes, trying to imagine what it'll be like once the sheetrock is placed and it's painted. Soon, we'll be living here together and starting over in a brand new house with a baby.

When my eyes flutter open, I see Evan staring at me. "You're so damn beautiful," he says, tucking loose strands of hair behind my ear. I shiver at the softness of his touch, and so much love streams between us when our lips collide. I lose myself in him, in us, and our little family, and that thought alone brings me so much joy.

"I love you, Evan Bishop. I love you with all my heart."

"I love you too, Emily. More than you'll ever know."

Evan kisses me, and when we finally pull away, I search his face and look into his baby blue eyes. When our eyes lock, I know deep down that I've truly found my other half—the missing key to my heart. It took years to find him, and there's no way in hell I'll ever let him go.

EPILOGUE

EMILY

FOUR MONTHS LATER

I've never really cared to celebrate my birthdays. Growing up, my mother planned these extravagant parties, and they were always so over-the-top that when I got older, I begged her to stop. After the accident, she had no desire to celebrate my birthday at all.

In college, I studied more than I partied, and after I graduated from medical school, I worked twelve-hour shifts through my birthday. But this year is different.

This is the first year I'm genuinely excited to celebrate it. Evan made sure we both have off work, and the anticipation of what he has planned is killing me. At almost eight months pregnant, I'm only hoping whatever surprise he has in store doesn't put me into early labor.

"Happy Birthday, baby." Evan nuzzles his lips against my neck, waking me with his erection grinding against my ass. "How are my girls this morning?"

"Mmm… is that my first gift I feel?" I tease, wiggling my hips to torture him. I've felt less than sexy over the last couple of months as my stomach grew along with everything else—my boobs, legs, ass. This giant Bishop baby is turning my body into her own personal food buffet.

"Yes, so take off your panties," he demands, sliding his hand between my legs.

"I feel like a giant house," I groan.

"But you look sexy as hell," he mutters, feathering kisses along my neck and shoulder. His words still make me shiver after all these months.

"But I can get sex out of you anytime I want," I quip, turning around to face him. "Today I want more than sex, so you better have something good planned." I lean in and kiss him softly on the lips. Those days worrying about morning breath, messy hair, and leftover makeup are long gone.

"I love it when you're demanding," he growls. "Panties. Off. Now." He nips the bottom of my earlobe.

I smack his chest and laugh. "We'll save that for the evening celebrations." I wink, rolling over to get out of bed, but realize I'm stuck. "Crap. My belly is too big." I groan, ready to cry at how pathetic I feel. "I need help."

Evan walks around to my side and starts laughing the second he sees my helpless face.

"I hate you right now," I mutter, holding my arms out. "Help me up!"

"You love me." He pulls me up and presses me against his chest, kissing the top of my nose.

"River warned me about carrying a Bishop baby. I should've taken her more seriously."

"How do you think Mama felt?" He chuckles. "Get in the shower, and I'll make breakfast." He smacks my ass, making me yelp. "Gotta feed that baby girl."

"Trust me. She's well fed." I roll my eyes, stepping around him to head toward the bathroom.

Half an hour later, I'm showered and half-dressed. Wearing scrubs is much more comfortable with my belly, so I haven't stocked up on a lot of maternity clothes. Mostly dresses and maxi skirts are all I can wear now.

"Babe?" I call out, walking to the kitchen where an array of smells hit my nose. "Oh God, that smells amazing!" Rounding the corner, I spot a shirtless Evan at the stove.

"It's almost ready," he calls over his shoulder, and when our eyes meet, he flashes me a wink.

"I know what you're doing, mister. It's not going to work."

"I'm just cooking breakfast," he denies, smirking.

"Uh-huh." I smile as he moves effortlessly around the kitchen. God. How does he manage to get sexier every single day? He's tempting me with his tan skin, chiseled muscles, and broad shoulders—knowing I can't deny his delicious six-pack and that sinful V that points to the greatest place on earth.

Evan tells me to sit and serves me a large glass of juice with my plate. He's made me a ham and cheese omelet, toast, and hash browns. I love his omelets, which is clearly evident when the baby starts dancing in my belly.

"Quick, come here!" I wave him over and grab his hand. "She's kicking up a storm." I place his hand on the side where she's moving.

"Must be the juice," Evan says with a smile.

"Probably." I chuckle. "That's one way to wake her up in the morning."

Evan kneels and places both palms on my stomach before lifting my shirt and pressing a soft kiss to my belly. I adore the way he already loves his baby girl. I can't even imagine what it'll be like to see him holding her for the first time.

"Okay, Elizabeth Rose." He starts talking to my stomach, which I love. "Today is your mommy's special day, and I'm going to need you to cooperate with me here. That means no making your mama sick, so I can get to home base later."

I laugh, my belly shaking up and down at the smooth way he talks to her. Once we found out we were having a girl, we brainstormed names for a few weeks before landing on Elizabeth—after the first female doctor in US history, Elizabeth Blackwell—and Rose, after Mama Rose Bishop. It just sounded like the perfect name for her, and I couldn't be more excited about it.

After breakfast, Evan gets ready and makes me wear a blindfold as he drives us. I have no idea where he's taking me, but I have a feeling he's going to want me to wear this blindfold later tonight, too.

"You ready?" he asks, helping me out of the truck.

"Yes!" I squeal with a smile.

He takes my hand and leads me forward. I walk with him, hoping I don't trip and fall on my face. Evan's a closet romantic, which is another thing I love about him. He pretends not to make a big deal out of special occasions, but deep inside, he plans for weeks.

"Are you ready to see our house?" He holds me to his chest and whispers in my ear.

"What? I thought it wasn't going to be ready for another month?" Construction got behind due to the weather a few weeks ago and put the schedule back.

"No, that was just a little white lie so I could surprise you." I feel his lips curl up into a devilish smile. He pulls the blindfold off, and that's when I realize we're standing on the front steps of our house—completely finished and perfect.

"Oh my God," I squeal, wrapping a hand over my mouth. There's a couple of wooden rocking chairs on the porch and planters hanging from the ceiling. "It's really finished?"

"Yep." He kisses my cheek. "But that's not your birthday surprise."

He walks in front of me and opens the door. "This is."

I step inside and see the house is completely furnished. We'd been looking at magazines and pictures for months, trying to decide what kind of theme we wanted. For months, I dreaded decorating with how pregnant I'd be by the time the house was finished, but now I don't have to. He studied my Pinterest boards and mimicked the things I loved the most.

"I can't believe you did this." I gasp, walking deeper into the foyer that leads into the kitchen and dining room. "It's gorgeous." Spinning around to look at everything, I'm in complete awe at all the details he included down to the wall décor, the large sectional couch I wanted, and even the light fixtures. It's everything I dreamed of and more. "It's absolutely perfect." Tears fall down my cheeks out of nowhere, but I don't care. My emotions are boiling over, and they're uncontrollable at this point.

"Good," Evan says, bringing his arms around my belly and holding me close. "I wanted to take away the work and stress I knew you'd feel the moment it was move-in ready."

"How'd you even manage to do all of this without me knowing?" I turn around and wrap my arms around his neck.

"I recruited some help." He smirks. "And lots of favors."

Shaking my head, my mind is still reeling at all of this. "I'm shocked. I really can't believe it."

"Believe it, baby. Home sweet home." He cups my face and brings our mouths together in a heated kiss. "Let me give you the grand tour now that it's officially ours."

Evan shows me the rest of the rooms before bringing us to the master bedroom and nursery.

"Her room is beautiful." I beam, reaching for the pink baby blanket off the crib. I bring it to my face and feel the softness against my cheek. "I can't believe she'll be here in about six weeks." Evan even hung picture frames around the room, ready to be filled with her baby photos, and I can't wait.

"She'll be here before we know it." He palms my belly, kneels, and places a sweet kiss on my stomach. "I have one more surprise for you."

"I can't imagine anything better than what you've already given me," I tell him honestly, cupping his face and bringing his mouth to mine. "Seriously, the best birthday by far."

"Well, I've been planning this last one for a while, so c'mon." He flashes me a wink, grabbing my hand and leading me to the kitchen. "I know we didn't talk about this addition, but I knew you'd want it."

He opens up a cupboard door that isn't actually a cupboard and then I realize what it is. "No way!" I laugh, stepping closer to look inside. "You got me a built-in ice chip maker?"

"I know how much you love your ice, and now you can have ice anytime you want."

"It's perfect." I shake my head in disbelief at how amazing everything is. "You're perfect."

"*You* are." He kisses my lips. "I even made sure to stock up on your disgusting black licorice."

"You did?" I exclaim. "Where?"

"In that drawer over there by the pantry." He points, and I'm quick to go check it out.

"You seriously thought of everything, didn't you?" I open the drawer but only see one piece of licorice in the middle. I pick up the black strip, and that's when I notice the large diamond ring around it. "What is this?"

When I turn around, my eyes widen, and I release a gasp when I see Evan down on one knee. "What are you doing?" I blurt out, shocked as I take in his gorgeous face looking up at me with his infamous shit-eating grin.

"Emily, sweetheart." He reaches for my free hand and holds it between his palms. "I love you more than words can say, and I can't even begin to explain how much you've changed my life. Before you, the world brought pain and disappointment, and now that I get to wake up with you by my side every morning makes living this life worth it. I want you in my world every day for the rest of my life—as my wife." He grabs the piece of licorice out of my hand and slides the ring off before holding it up between us. "Will you marry me?"

"Are you serious right now? Really?" I cover my mouth with both hands in complete disbelief. Smiling up at me, he nods his head and waits. "Yes! Yes, of course!" The emotions are so strong, I feel like I may burst. My eyes water as he stands up and cups my face, pressing a hot kiss on my lips. Once we part, he grabs my hand and slides the ring on. "I can't believe you," I say, staring at the ring. "I had no idea."

"I'm a pretty good secret keeper." He winks.

"You are! I didn't suspect a damn thing. You're sneaky!" I chuckle as he wraps his arms around me.

"I might've had a motive, though," he admits, pushing his face into my hair. "Since I know we have to wait once the baby's born, I figured getting us in the house early meant we could christen it now."

"Is sex never not on your mind?" I tease, pulling back to look into his guilty eyes.

"I knocked you up in a matter of months. What do you think?"

"Always the romantic." I laugh.

"C'mon, wife to be. Time to break in our new bed." He leans down to pick me up, and I yelp as he carries me to our new bedroom.

Once the master bedroom is thoroughly christened, we decide to drive over to his parents' house to officially announce the happy news. Mrs. Bishop is in the kitchen as usual, and Mr. Bishop is sitting at the table reading a newspaper.

"Oh, happy birthday! I didn't know you two were stoppin' in today!" She wraps her arms around my bump before rubbing her palms on my stomach. "And how's the little sweet pea?"

"She's perfect."

Evan's arm is around me, and I'm bursting with so much happiness, she notices instantly.

"Well?" Her eyes nearly bug out of her head as if she's anticipating the good news.

"Go ahead. Show her," Evan encourages with a smile on his face.

I hold up my left hand and nearly blind her with the ring. "Oh my goodness!" she squeals, grabbing my hand and gasping. "It's gorgeous." She flashes an approving smile.

"You did good." She pats Evan on the cheek like the proud mama she is.

Mr. Bishop takes notice and finally stands to shake Evan's hand and give me a hug. "Happy you're officially joining the family."

"Thank you. Me too." I smile wide then turn to Evan. "Since we're here, let's go find your brothers and tell them."

"Okay, but then I'm taking you back to the house to christen another room," he whispers in my hair, making my cheeks heat right in front of his parents.

Once we find Jackson and Alex and tell them the exciting news, they both give me a hug and can't stop saying how excited they are to be adding another sister to their family. River is working at the hospital today and Kiera had to pick up a horse out of town, but I plan to text them both a picture later. Evan pinky promises we'll FaceTime Courtney later and explains how my parents already know. Apparently, the cheeky bastard asked my dad when we visited Houston. Always the proper Southern gentleman.

"Can we go to the B&B before we leave?" I ask, and Jackson and Alex invite themselves to tag along, so the four of us jump back into Evan's truck and drive over to tell John the news.

"What the hell is this?" John asks the second he sees the four of us barrel in through the side door. "This can't be good." He crosses his arms, looking concerned.

"It's not bad news," I reassure him, holding out my hand so he can see the ring.

"Well damn." He relaxes and smiles. "Looks like we have another weddin' to plan. Congrats, you two." John pats Evan on the shoulder with an approving nod.

"Baby first, then wedding," I confirm. "I'm not walking down the aisle ten months pregnant."

Jackson snorts. "Another party! Yeehaw!" He hip thrusts the air, and Evan punches him in the shoulder.

"I'm shooting you with a tranquilizer," Evan deadpans.

"I'll help you," Alex adds.

"Can't stop, won't stop," Jackson taunts, spinning around and shaking his butt. He looks over his shoulder, then slaps his ass just to get a rise out of his brothers.

"Oh my God." John groans. "Stop it. You're giving my face a bad name."

"I'm the only reason you're getting laid, and you know it."

"Speaking of laid, Emily and I have plans that don't include any of you." Evan grabs my hand and starts dragging me toward the front door as I burst out laughing.

"Don't be rude." I smack his shoulder, laughing.

"Trust me, John wants us out as much as we do." Evan jerks his head toward John who confirms with a nod.

"Yes and take the evil twin with you."

"Love you, bro!" Jackson wraps his arm around John's shoulders and makes a big show out of kissing him on the cheek.

Alex shakes his head, grabbing Jackson by the arm. "C'mon. The horses won't feed themselves."

John continues following us as we walk through the main room. He tells us congrats one more time and then wishes me a happy birthday. I give him a side hug to avoid squishing my belly, then laugh at the realization of how something as simple as hugging has become a difficult task.

"My niece will be here soon enough." John winks.

Evan places his hand on the small of my back as he opens the door, but we both immediately come to a halt at the sight in front of us.

"What the…?" Alex is the first to break the silence.

"Jesus," Evan mutters.

"Is that a baby?" Jackson gasps.

"A what?" John steps between us and stops when he sees the sleeping baby in a car seat on the porch.

"A baby," I confirm, stunned.

"Whose baby?" Evan asks what we're all thinking.

Alex, John, Evan, and I all look at Jackson.

"You think this is *my* baby?" he bellows. "I double wrap my shit, thank you very much." He crosses his arms over his chest, and I snort.

"There's a note!" I spot the envelope taped to the car seat handle. "Oh no."

"What?" Evan asks, leaning over to see the name written on the front. "Oh shit."

"It's for you," I say, handing the envelope to John.

"What?" All the blood drains from his face when he realizes what I just said.

The air is thick with tension as John reluctantly takes it from me.

"Shit, I didn't see that coming," Jackson howls.

Alex nudges him in the arm to shut him up. John opens the envelope and unfolds the piece of paper. We all watch as his eyes scan the letter, which feels like an eternity, but then he drops his arm and stares into space.

"She's *mine*."

Stay tuned for more Bishops in the next installment featuring John Bishop in *Chasing Him*. Available now!

Chasing Him

Stay tuned for more Bishops in the next installment featuring John Bishop in *Chasing Him*. Available now!

John Bishop isn't your typical single dad.
Reserved, impatient, and utterly clueless.

Running the family's bed and breakfast has many perks. Working long hours, picking up after the guests, and hearing couples going at it all night long aren't any of them. Hooking up with girls who come to the ranch for horseback riding lessons? Best perk of them all.

That is until a baby shows up at his doorstep with a note claiming it's his. Growing up on a ranch was anything but easy, but raising a newborn is proving to be the hardest task he'll ever tackle. Leaving the bachelor life behind, his only priority is to hire a nanny who can teach him a thing or two about parenting—except he doesn't anticipate her being gorgeous and quirky with an unhealthy football obsession.

Mila Carmichael has many talents—making balloon animals, creating origami art, and remaining in the friend zone. Often seen as one of the guys, she's struck out more times than a rookie baseball player.

Seeking a new adventure, she flies to Texas to visit family and is offered a position she can't refuse. Helping out a new dad should come easy to her, considering her past experience, but what she doesn't anticipate is him being an attractive Southern temptation.

But that's only the beginning.

While growing close to his family and falling madly in love with the baby girl who's stealing their hearts, things are bound to get complicated. Everyone knows not to mix business with pleasure. That means no late movie nights, no stolen glances, and definitely no kissing behind closed doors. Too bad the universe has other plans—one that'll threaten taking away the main thing that binds them together.

Available now!

CIRCLE B RANCH SERIES

Stay tuned for more Bishops in the second generation series featuring the Bishop kids!

Hitching the Cowboy
Catching the Cowboy
Wrangling the Cowboy
Bossing the Cowboy
...and more

ABOUT THE AUTHOR

Brooke Cumberland and Lyra Parish are a duo of romance authors who teamed up under the *USA Today* pseudonym, Kennedy Fox. They share a love of Hallmark movies & overpriced coffee. When they aren't bonding over romantic comedies, they like to brainstorm new book ideas. One day, they decided to collaborate under a pseudonym and have some fun creating new characters that'll make you blush and your heart melt. If you enjoy romance stories with sexy, tattooed alpha males and smart, quirky, independent women, then a Kennedy Fox book is for you! They're looking forward to bringing you many more stories to fall in love with!

CONNECT WITH US

Find us on our website:
www.kennedyfoxbooks.com

facebook.com/kennedyfoxbooks
twitter.com/kennedyfoxbooks
instagram.com/kennedyfoxbooks
amazon.com/author/kennedyfoxbooks
goodreads.com/kennedyfox
bookbub.com/authors/kennedy-fox

BOOKS BY KENNEDY FOX

CHECKMATE DUET SERIES

BISHOP BROTHERS SERIES

BEDTIME READS SERIES

ROOMMATE DUET SERIES

CIRCLE B RANCH SERIES

EX-CON DUET SERIES

LOVE IN ISOLATION SERIES

Find the entire Kennedy Fox reading order at
Kennedyfoxbooks.com/reading-order

Find all of our current freebies at **Kennedyfoxbooks.com/freeromance**

CPSIA information can be obtained
at www.ICGtesting.com
Printed in the USA
LVHW090902280720
661291LV00009BA/171

9 781946 087492